MISS SMILLA'S FEELING FOR SNOW

PETER HØEG was born in 1957 and followed various callings – dancer, actor, fencer, sailor, mountaineer – before he turned seriously to writing. He published his first novel in 1988, a book which was acclaimed in Denmark by *Information* as evidence enough that Høeg was "the foremost writer of his generation". It is now published in English as *The History of Danish Dreams*. With the publication of his crime novel *Miss Smilla's Feeling for Snow* he achieved an international reputation and found a settled place on the bestseller lists.

Peter Høeg

MISS SMILLA'S
FEELING FOR SNOW

*Translated from the Danish
by F. David*

THE HARVILL PRESS
LONDON

First published in Denmark with the title *Frøken Smillas Fornemmelse for Sne* by Munksgaard/Rosinante, Copenhagen 1992

First published in Great Britain in 1993 by Harvill, an imprint of HarperCollins*Publishers*, in 1993

This paperback edition first published in 1997 by The Harvill Press, 84 Thornhill Road, London N1 1RD

5 7 9 8 6 4

Copyright © Peter Høeg and Munksgaard/Rosinante, Copenhagen 1992
English translation © Farrar, Straus & Giroux Inc. and The Harvill Press 1993

Maps by Reginald Piggott

Peter Høeg asserts the moral right to be identified as the author of this work.

A CIP catalogue record for this book is available from the British Library.

ISBN 1 86046 331 2

Printed and bound in Great Britain by Mackays of Chatham

Half title illustration: snow crystals, design by Newell and Sorrell

THE CITY

1

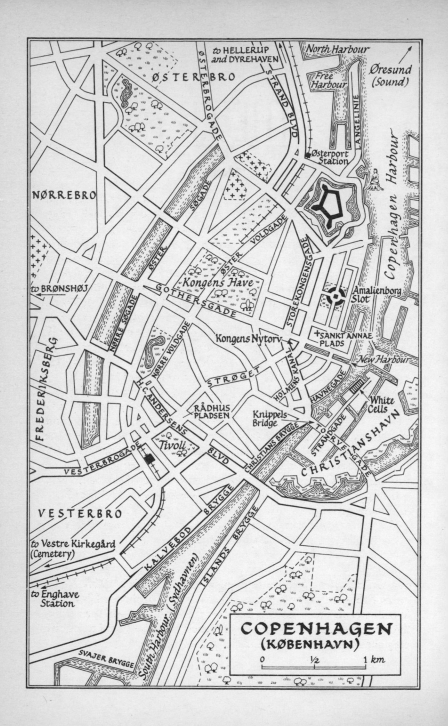

COPENHAGEN
(KØBENHAVN)

0   ½   1 km

IT IS FREEZING, an extraordinary −18 °C, and it's snowing, and in the language which is no longer mine, the snow is *qanik* − big, almost weightless crystals falling in stacks and covering the ground with a layer of pulverized white frost.

December darkness rises up from the grave, seeming as limitless as the sky above us. In this darkness our faces are merely pale, shining discs, but even so I can sense the disapproval of the pastor and the verger directed at my black net stockings and at Juliane's whimpering, made worse by the fact that she took disulfiram this morning and is now confronting her grief almost sober. They think that she and I have no respect for either the weather or the tragic circumstances. The truth is that both the stockings and the pills, each in their own way, are a tribute to the cold and to Isaiah.

The women surrounding Juliane and the pastor and the verger all are Greenlanders, and when we sing "Guutiga, illimi", "Thou, My Lord", and as Juliane's legs buckle under her and she begins weeping, the volume slowly increasing, and when the pastor speaks in West Greenlandic, taking his point of departure in the Moravians' favourite passage from St Paul about redemption through the blood, then with only a tiny lapse of concentration one might feel oneself transported to Upernavik or Holsteinsborg or Qaanaaq.

But out in the darkness, like the bow of a ship, loom the walls of Vestre Prison; we are in Copenhagen.

The Greenlanders' cemetery is part of Vestre Cemetery. With Isaiah in his coffin has come a procession consisting of those of Juliane's friends who are now holding her upright, the pastor and the verger, the mechanic, and a small group of Danes, among whom I recognize only the probation officer and the guardian.

The pastor is now saying something that makes me think he must have actually met Isaiah, even though, as far as I know, Juliane has never gone to church.

Later his voice disappears, because now the other women are weeping along with Juliane.

Many have come, perhaps twenty, and now they let their sorrow wash through them like a black flood, into which they dive and let themselves be carried along in a way that no outsider could understand, no one who has not grown up in Greenland. And even that might not be enough. Because I can't follow them, either.

For the first time I look closely at the coffin. It's hexagonal. At a certain point ice crystals take the same form.

Now they are lowering him into the ground. The coffin is made of dark wood, it looks so small, and there is already a layer of snow on it. The flakes are no bigger than tiny feathers, and that's the way snow is, it's not necessarily cold. What is happening at this moment is that the heavens are weeping for Isaiah, and the tears are turning into down of frost that is covering him up. In this way the universe is pulling an eiderdown over him, so that he will never again feel the cold.

The moment the pastor throws earth on the coffin and we are supposed to turn around and leave, a silence falls which seems to last for a long time. In this silence the women are quiet, no one moves, it's like a silence which is waiting for something to break. From where I'm standing, two things happen.

First, Juliane falls to her knees and puts her face to the ground, and the women leave her alone.

The second event is internal, inside me, and what breaks is an insight.

All along I must have had an extensive pact with Isaiah about not leaving him in the lurch, never, not now either.

4

(2)

WE LIVE IN THE WHITE CELLS.

On a building site donated to them, the Housing Association has put up a number of prefabricated boxes of white concrete, for which it had been awarded a prize by the Association for the Beautification of the Capital.

The whole thing, including the prize, makes a cheap and scant impression, but there's nothing mean about the rent, which is so high that the only people who can afford to live here are those like Juliane, whom the state is supporting; the mechanic, who had to take what he could get; and those living a more marginal existence, like myself.

So the nickname, the White Cells, is something of a sick joke to those of us who live here, but still in its way appropriate.

There are reasons for moving in and reasons for staying on. With time, the water has become important to me. The White Cells are located right on the Harbour. This winter I have been able to watch the ice forming.

The frost set in in November. I have respect for the Danish winter. The cold – not what is measured on a thermometer, but what you can actually feel – depends more on the force of the wind and the relative humidity in the air than on the actual temperature. I have been colder in Denmark than I ever was in Thule. When the first clammy rain showers begin slapping me and November in the face with a wet towel, I meet them with fur-lined *capucines*, black alpaca leggings, a long Scottish skirt, a sweater, and a black waterproof cape.

The temperature then starts to drop. At a certain point the surface of the sea reaches -1.8 °C, and the first ice crystals form, a temporary membrane that the wind and waves break up into frazil ice. This is kneaded together into the soapy mash called porridge ice which gradually forms free-floating plates, pancake ice, which, one cold noonday hour, on a Sunday, freezes into a single solid sheet.

And it gets colder, and I'm happy because I know that now the frost has gained momentum; now the ice will stay, now the crystals have formed bridges and enclosed the salt water in pockets that have a structure like the veins of a tree through which the liquid slowly seeps; which not many of those who look across towards Holmen think about, but which is one reason for believing that ice and life are related in several ways.

The ice is normally what I look for first when I come up on to Knippels Bridge. But on this day in December I see something else. I see light.

It's yellow, the way light mostly is in a city in winter; and it has been snowing, so even though it's a faint light, it produces a strong reflection. It's shining at the base of one of the warehouses, which in a moment of weakness they decided to leave standing when they built our housing blocks. At the gable-end of the building, towards Strandgade and Christianshavn, the blue light of a patrol car is revolving. I can see a police officer. The temporary roping off with red-and-white tape. Up against the building I can make out what has been blocked off: a small, dark shadow in the snow.

Because I'm running and because it's just barely five o'clock and the evening traffic hasn't thinned out, I get there some minutes ahead of the ambulance.

Isaiah is lying with his legs tucked up under him, with his face in the snow and his hands round his head, as if he were shielding himself from the little spotlight shining on him, as if the snow were a window through which he has caught sight of something deep inside the earth.

Surely the police officer ought to ask me who I am and take down my name and address, and in general prepare the ground for those of his colleagues who will shortly have to start ringing door-bells. But he's a young man with a queasy expression on his face. He avoids looking directly at Isaiah. After assuring himself that I won't step inside his tape, he lets me stand there.

He could have roped off a larger area. But it wouldn't have made any difference. The warehouses are in the process of being partially modernized. People and machines have compacted the snow as hard as a terrazzo floor.

6

Even in death Isaiah seems to have turned his face away, as if he wants no part of anyone's sympathy.

High overhead, outside the spotlight, a rooftop is barely discernible. The warehouse is high, probably as tall as a seven- or eight-storey housing block. The adjoining building is under construction. It has scaffolding along the gable-end facing Strandgade. That's where I make for as the ambulance works its way across the bridge and then moves in among the buildings.

The scaffolding covers the gable all the way up to the roof. The last ladder is down. The structure seems shakier the higher I go.

They're putting on a new roof. Above me loom the triangular rafters, covered with tarpaulins. They stretch half the length of the building. The other half of the roof, facing the harbour, is a snow-covered surface. On it are Isaiah's tracks.

At the edge of the snow a man is huddled with his arms around his knees, rocking back and forth.

Even hunched up, the mechanic gives the impression of being big. And even in this position of total surrender he seems reticent.

It's so bright. Some years ago they measured the light at Siora-paluk. From December to February, three months during which the sun is gone. People imagine one eternal night. But there are stars and the moon, and now and then the northern lights. And the snow. They registered the same luminescence as outside a medium-sized provincial town in Denmark. That's how I remember my own child-hood. That we always played outside, and that it was always light. In those days we took the light for granted. A child takes so many things for granted. With time, you begin to ask questions.

In any case, it strikes me how bright the roof is in front of me. As if it was the snow, in a layer maybe ten centimetres thick, which has all along created the light on this winter day, and which still shines with a sporadic glitter like brilliant little grey beads.

At ground level the snow melts slightly, even in hard frost, because of the heat of the city. But up here it lies loosely, the way it fell. Only Isaiah has walked on it.

Even when there's no heat, no new snow, no wind, even then the snow changes. As if it were breathing, as if it condenses and rises and sinks and disintegrates.

He wore sneakers, even in winter, and those are his footprints, the worn-down sole of his basketball boots with the barely visible outline of concentric circles in front of the arch on which the player is supposed to pirouette.

7

He stepped out into the snow from where we're standing. The footprints head diagonally towards the edge and continue along the roof for maybe ten metres. There they stop. And then continue towards the corner and end of the building. Then they follow the edge at a distance of about half a metre, up to the corner facing the other warehouse. From there he has turned approximately three metres in towards the centre to get a running start. Then the tracks go straight for the edge where he jumped off.

The other roof consists of glazed black tiles that come to such a steep angle at the gutter that the snow has slid off. There wasn't anything to hold on to. He might just as well have jumped straight out into thin air.

There are no other footprints besides Isaiah's. No one has been across the surface of the snow except him.

"I found him," says the mechanic.

It will never be easy for me to watch men cry. Perhaps because I know how fatal crying is to their self-respect. Perhaps because they are so unaccustomed to it that it always carries them back to their childhood. The mechanic has reached the stage where he has given up wiping his eyes; his face is a mask of blubbering.

"Strangers are coming," I say.

The two men who arrive on the roof are not happy to see us.

One is lugging photographic equipment and is out of breath. The other reminds me a little of an ingrown nail. Flat and hard and full of impatient irritation.

"Who are you?"

"The lady upstairs," I say. "And this gentleman is the man downstairs."

"Would you please leave."

Then he notices the footprints and forgets about us.

The photographer takes the first pictures with a big Polaroid camera and a flash.

"Only the footprints of the deceased," says the Nail. He talks as if he is filling out his report in his mind. "The mother is a drunk. So he was playing up here."

He catches sight of us again.

"They must go down."

At that moment I am clear about nothing, only confused. So confused that I could share it out. So I don't budge.

"Strange way to play, don't you think?"

Some people might say that I'm vain. And I wouldn't exactly

8

contradict them. I may have my own reasons for this. At any rate, my clothes are what makes him listen to me now. The cashmere, the fur hat, the gloves. He certainly would like to send me down. But he can see that I look like an elegant lady. So he hesitates for a moment. And he doesn't meet that many elegant ladies on the various rooftops of Copenhagen.

"What do you mean?"

"When you were that age," I say, "and your father and mother hadn't come home from the salt mines yet, and you were alone playing on the roof of the barracks for the homeless, did you run in a straight line along the edge?"

He chews on that.

"I grew up in Jutland," he says. But he doesn't take his eyes off me as he speaks.

Then he turns to his colleague. "Let's get some lights up here. And would you mind accompanying the lady and the gentleman downstairs."

I feel the same way about solitude as some people feel about the blessing of the church. It's the light of grace for me. Never do I close my door behind me without being conscious that I am carrying out an act of charity towards myself. Cantor illustrated the concept of infinity for his students by telling them that there was once a man who had a hotel with an infinite number of rooms, and the hotel was fully occupied. Then one more guest arrived. So the owner moved the guest in room number one into room number two; the guest in room number two into number three; the guest in three into room four, and so on. In that way room number one became vacant for the new guest.

What delights me about this story is that everyone involved, the guests and the owner, accept it as perfectly in order to carry out an infinite number of operations so that one guest can have peace and quiet in a room of his own. That is a great tribute to solitude.

I realize, as well, that I have arranged my apartment like a hotel room – without getting rid of the impression that the person living here is in transit. Whenever I feel a need to explain it to myself, I think about the fact that my mother's family, and she herself, were to some extent nomads. In terms of an excuse it's a feeble explanation.

But I have two big windows facing the water. I can see Holmens

Church and the Marine Insurance Company's building and the National Bank, whose marble façade is the same colour tonight as the ice in the harbour.

I thought that I must grieve. I spoke to the police officers and offered Juliane a shoulder to lean on and took her over to a friend's place and came back, and the whole time I held the grief at bay with my left hand. Now it should be my turn to give in to sorrow.

But it's not yet time. Grief is a gift, something you have to earn. I have made myself a cup of peppermint tea and gone over to stand by the window. But nothing happens. Maybe because there's still one little thing I have to do, a single thing unfinished, the kind that can block a flow of emotions.

So I drink my tea while the traffic on Knippels Bridge thins out, becoming separate red stripes of light in the night. Gradually a kind of peace comes over me. Finally it's enough that I can fall asleep.

$$3$$

IT IS A DAY IN AUGUST a year and a half earlier that I meet Isaiah for the first time. A humid, leaden heat has transformed Copenhagen into an incubator for imminent madness. I have been sitting in a bus with that special pressure-cooker atmosphere, wearing a new dress of white linen, cut low in the back, trimmed with Valenciennes ruffles which took me a long time to steam-press so they'd stand up properly, and they have now wilted in the general depression.

There are those who head south this time of year. South to the heat. Personally, I've never been further than Køge, fifty kilometres south of Copenhagen. And don't plan to go either, until the nuclear winter has cooled down the whole continent.

It's the kind of day that might make you wonder about the meaning of life, and discover that there is none. And something is rooting around on the stairway, on the landing below my apartment.

When the first large shipments of Greenlanders began arriving in Denmark in the 1930s, one of the first things they wrote home was that Danes are such pigs: they keep dogs in their houses. For a moment I think it's a dog lying on the stairs. Then I see that it's a child, and this particular day that is not much better.

"Beat it, you little shit," I say.

Isaiah looks up.

"*Peerit*," he says. Beat it yourself.

There aren't many Danes who can tell by looking at me. They think there's a trace of something Asian, especially when I put a shadow under my cheekbones. But the boy on the stairs looks right at me with a gaze that cuts straight through to what he and I have in common. It's the kind of look you see in newborns. Later it vanishes, sometimes reappearing in extremely old people. This could be one reason I've never burdened my life with children —

I've thought too much about why people lose the courage to look each other in the eye.

"Will you read me a story?"

I have a book in my hand. That's what prompted his question.

One might say that he looks like a forest elf. But since he is filthy, dressed only in underpants, and glistening with sweat, one might also say he looks like a seal pup.

"Piss off," I say.

"Don't you like kids?"

"I eat kids."

He steps aside.

"*Salluvutit*, you're lying," he says as I go past.

At that moment I see two things in him that somehow link us together. I see that he is alone. The way someone in exile will always be. And I see that he is not afraid of solitude.

"What's the book?" he shouts after me.

"Euclid's *Elements*," I say, slamming the door.

It turned out to be Euclid's *Elements*, after all.

That's the one I take out that very evening when the doorbell rings and he's standing outside, still in his underpants, staring straight at me; and I step aside and he walks into my apartment and into my life, never really to leave it again; then it is Euclid's *Elements* I take down from the bookshelf. As if to chase him away. As if to establish from the start that I have no books that can interest a child, that he and I cannot meet over a book, or in any other way. As if to avoid something.

We sit down on the sofa. He sits on the very edge, with his legs crossed, the way kids from Thule used to sit at Inglefield in the summertime, on the edge of the dog sleigh used as a bed inside the tent.

"'A point is that which cannot be divided. A line is a length without breadth.'"

This book turns out to be the one he never comments on, and the one we keep returning to. Occasionally I try others. On one occasion I borrow the children's book *Rasmus Klump on the Ice Cap*. In all serenity he listens to the description of the first pictures. Then he points a finger at the drawing of the bear Rasmus Klump.

"What does that one taste like?" he asks.

"'A semicircle is a figure contained within a diameter . . . and the circumference intersected by the diameter.'"

For me, the reading goes through three phases on that first evening in August.

First there is simply irritation at the whole impractical situation. Then there is the state of mind that always comes over me at the mere thought of that book: veneration. The knowledge that it is the foundation, the boundary. That if you work your way backwards, past Lobachevsky and Newton and as far back as you can go, you end up with Euclid.

"'On the greater of two given unequal straight lines . . .'"

Then at some point I no longer see what I'm reading. At some point there is only my voice in the living room and the light of the sunset from Sydhavnen. And then my voice isn't even there; it's just me and the boy. At some point I stop. And we simply sit there, gazing straight ahead, as if I were fifteen and he were sixteen, and we have reached "the point of no return". Some time later he gets up very quietly and leaves. I watch the sunset, which lasts three hours at this time of year. As if the sun, on the verge of leaving, had discovered qualities in the world that are now causing it to have second thoughts about departing.

Of course Euclid didn't scare him off. Of course it made no difference what I read. For that matter, I could have read aloud from the telephone directory. Or from Lewis and Carrisa's *Detection and Classification of Ice*. He would have come anyway, just to sit with me on the sofa.

During some periods he would come every day. And then a couple of weeks might pass when I would see him only once, and from a distance. But when he did come, it was usually just starting to get dark, when the day was over and Juliane was out cold.

Once in a while I would give him a bath. He didn't like hot water, but it was impossible to get him clean in cold. I would put him in the bathtub and turn on the hand-held shower. He wouldn't complain. Long ago he had learned to put up with adversity. But not for one moment did he take his reproachful eyes off my face.

4

THERE HAVE BEEN quite a few boarding schools in my life. I regularly work at suppressing the memory of them, and for long periods of time I succeed. It's only in glimpses that a single memory sometimes manages to work its way into the light. The way the particular feeling of a dormitory does now. At Stenhøj Boarding School, near Humlebæk, we slept in dorms. One for girls and one for boys. They opened all the windows at night. And our blankets were too thin.

In the Copenhagen county morgue in the basement of the Institute of Forensic Medicine at the University Hospital, the dead sleep their last, cold sleep in dormitories cooled to just above freezing.

Everything is clean, modern, and final. Even in the examination room, which is painted like a living room, they've brought in a couple of floor lamps, and a green plant is trying to hold its own.

A white sheet covers Isaiah. On it someone has placed a little bunch of flowers, as if in an attempt to give the potted plant support. He is completely covered, but from the small body and large head, you can tell it's him. The French cranium measurers ran into serious problems in Greenland. They were working from the theory that there was a linear relation between a person's intelligence and the size of his skull. They discovered that the Greenlanders, whom they regarded as a transitional form of ape, had the largest skulls in the world.

A man in a white lab coat lifts the sheet away from Isaiah's face. He looks so intact, as if he had been carefully drained of all blood and colour and then put to sleep.

Juliane is standing next to me. She's dressed in black, and she is sober for the second day in a row.

As we walk down the hallway, the white coat goes with us.

"You're a relative?" he suggests. "Her sister?"

14

He's no taller than me, but broad and with a stance like a ram about to butt someone.

"Doctor," he says. He points to the breast pocket of his lab coat and discovers that there is no name tag to identify him. "Damn it to hell," he says.

I continue down the hallway. He's right behind me.

"I have children myself," he says. "Do you know whether it was a doctor who found him?"

"A mechanic," I say.

He takes the lift up with us. I am overcome by a need to know who has touched Isaiah.

"Did you examine him?"

He doesn't answer. Maybe he didn't hear me. He strides on ahead of us. At the glass door he whips out a card, the way a flasher tears aside his coat.

"My card. Jean Pierre, like the flute player. Lagermann, like the liquorice."

Juliane and I haven't said a word to each other. But as she gets into the taxi and I'm just about to close the door, she grabs hold of my hand.

"That Smilla is a damn great lady," she says, as if she were talking about someone who's not there. "One hundred per cent."

The taxi drives off, and I straighten up. It's almost noon. I have an appointment.

It says STATE AUTOPSY CENTRE FOR GREENLAND on the glass door I come to after I walk back along Frederik V Street, past the Teilum building and the Institute of Forensic Medicine over to the new annex of the University Hospital; I have taken the lift up past floors marked on the button panel as the Greenland Medical Association, the Arctic Centre, and the Institute for Arctic Medicine, on up to the sixth floor, which is a penthouse suite.

This morning I have called police headquarters and they transferred me to A Division, who put the Nail on the line.

"You can see him in the morgue," he says.

"I also want to talk to the doctor."

"Loyen," he says. "You can talk to Loyen."

Beyond the glass door there is a short passageway leading to a sign on which it says PROFESSOR and, in smaller letters, J. LOYEN. Below the sign there is a doorway, and beyond the door a cloakroom, and beyond that a chilly office with two secretaries sitting under photostats of icebergs on blue water in brilliant sunlight, and beyond that the real office begins.

Here they haven't put in a tennis court. But not for lack of space. It's probably because Loyen has a couple of them in his back garden in Hellerup, and two more at his summer home on Klitvej in Skagen. And because tennis courts would have ruined the weighty solemnity of the room.

There's a thick carpet on the floor, two walls covered with books, picture windows looking out over the city and Fælled Park, a safe built into the wall, paintings in gold frames, a microscope over a light table, a glass case with a gilded mask which appears to be from an Egyptian sarcophagus, two sofa groups, two monitors on pedestals that have been turned off, and there's still enough floor space to go for a jog should you get tired of sitting behind a desk.

The desk is a vast mahogany ellipse from which he rises and comes forward to greet me. He is two metres tall and about seventy years old, straight-backed, and tanned as a desert sheik in his white lab coat. He has a tolerant expression on his face, as of someone sitting up on a camel, benevolently gazing down on the rest of the world crawling past in the sand.

"Loyen."

Even though he omits his title, it's still understood. Along with the fact that we must not forget that the rest of the world's population is at least a head shorter than him, and here, under his feet, he has legions of other doctors who have not succeeded in becoming professors, and above him is only the white ceiling, the blue sky, and Our Lord – and maybe not even that.

"Please sit down, madam."

He radiates courtesy and dominance, and I ought to be happy. Other women before me have been happy, and there will be many more. For what could be better at life's difficult moments than having two metres of polished medical self-confidence to lean on? And in such reassuring surroundings as these?

On his desk are framed photographs of the doctor's wife and the Airedale and Daddy's three big boys, who are bound to study medicine and get top grades in all their exams, including clinical sexology.

I've never claimed that I was perfect. Confronted with people who have power, and who enjoy using it, I turn into a different person, a baser and meaner one.

But I don't show it. I sit down on the very edge of the chair, and I place my dark gloves and the hat with the dark veil on the very edge of the mahogany surface. Facing Professor Loyen, like so many times before, there is a black-clad, grieving, enquiring, uncertain woman.

"You're a Greenlander?"

It's because of his professional experience that he can see it.

"My mother was from Thule. You were the one who . . . examined Isaiah?"

He gestures yes.

"What I'd like to know is: what did he die of?"

The question catches him a little off guard.

"From the fall."

"But what does that mean, physiologically?"

He thinks it over for a moment, not used to having to explain the obvious.

"He fell from a height of seven storeys. The organism as a whole quite simply collapses."

"But somehow he looked so unscathed."

"That's normal with accidental falls, madam. But . . ."

I know what he's going to say: Until we open them up, that is. Then it's nothing but splinters of bone and internal bleeding.

"But he wasn't," he finishes his sentence.

He straightens up. He has other things to do. The conversation is drawing to a close without ever getting started. Like so many conversations before and after this one.

"Was there any trace of violence?"

This doesn't surprise him. At his age and in his business he is not easily surprised.

"None at all," he says.

I sit there in total silence. It's always interesting to leave Europeans in silence. For them it's a vacuum in which the tension grows and converges towards the intolerable.

"What gave you that idea?"

He has now dropped the "madam". I ignore his question.

"Why is it that this office and this department are not located in Greenland?" I ask.

"The institute is only three years old. Previously there was no autopsy centre for Greenland. The district attorney in Godthåb would send word to the Institute of Forensic Medicine in Copenhagen whenever it was necessary. This department is new and temporary. The whole thing is going to be moved to Godthåb sometime next year."

"And you?" I ask.

He's not used to being interrogated, and any moment now he's going to stop answering. "I'm head of the Institute for Arctic Medicine. But originally I was a forensic pathologist. During this initial phase I am the acting director of the autopsy centre."

"Do you perform all of the forensic autopsies on Greenlanders?"

It's a shot in the dark. But it must have been a hard, flat shot all the same, because it makes him blink.

"No," he says, speaking slowly now, "but I sometimes assist the Danish autopsy centre. They have thousands of cases every year, from all over the country."

I think about Jean Pierre Lagermann.

"Did you perform the autopsy alone?"

"We have a set routine that is followed except in extraordinary cases. There is one doctor, with a lab technician or sometimes a nurse to assist him."

"Is it possible to see the autopsy report?"

"You wouldn't be able to understand it, anyway. And you wouldn't like what you did understand!"

For a brief moment he has lost his self-control. But it's instantly restored. "These reports are the property of the police, who formally request the autopsies. And who decide, by the way, when the burial can take place after they sign the death certificate. Public access to administrative details applies to civil matters, not criminal ones."

He's into the game and approaching the net. His voice takes on a soothing tone. "You must understand, in a case like this, if there is even the slightest doubt about the circumstances of the accident, both we and the police are interested in the most thorough investigation possible. We look for everything. And we find everything. In a case of molestation it's virtually impossible to avoid leaving marks. There are fingerprints, torn clothing; the child defends himself and gets skin cells under his fingernails. There was nothing like that. Nothing."

So that was the set and match. I get up and put on my gloves. He leans back.

"We looked at the police report, of course," he says. "It was

18

quite clear from the footprints that he was alone on the roof when it happened."

I start the long walk to the middle of the room, and from there I look back at him. I was on to something, but I didn't know what it was. But now he's back up on his camel.

"You're welcome to phone again, my dear lady."

It takes a moment before the dizziness subsides.

"We all have our phobias," I say. "Something that we're truly terrified of. I have mine. You probably have yours, when you take off that bulletproof white coat. Do you know what Isaiah's was? It was heights. He would race up to the second floor. But from there he crawled, with his eyes closed and both hands on the banister. Picture that – every day, on the stairway, inside the building, with sweat on his forehead and his knees buckling, five minutes to get from the second to the fourth floor. His mother had tried to get a ground-floor apartment before they moved in. But you know how it is – when you're a Greenlander and on welfare . . ."

There's a good long pause before he replies. "Nevertheless, he *was* up there."

"Yes," I say, "he was. But you could have tried a hydraulic lift. You could have tried a Hercules crane and you still wouldn't have shifted him so much as a step up that scaffolding. What puzzles me, what keeps me awake at night, is wondering what made him go up there at all."

I can still see Isaiah's tiny figure before me, lying down there in the basement morgue. I don't even look at Loyen. I simply walk out of the door.

5

JULIANE CHRISTIANSEN, Isaiah's mother, is a strong endorsement for the curative powers of alcohol. When she's sober, she is stiff, mute, and inhibited. When she's drunk, she is lively and happy as a sandboy.

Because she took the disulfiram this morning and has been drinking on top of the pills, so to speak, since she returned from the hospital this beautiful transformation naturally appears through a veil of the overall poisoning of the organism. And yet she is feeling markedly better.

"Smilla," she says, "I love you."

They say that people drink a lot in Greenland. That is a totally absurd understatement. People drink a colossal amount. That's why my relationship to alcohol is the way it is. Whenever I feel the urge for something stronger than herbal tea, I always remember what went on before the voluntary liquor rationing in Thule.

I've been in Juliane's apartment before, but we have always sat in her kitchen drinking coffee. You have to respect people's privacy. Especially when their lives are otherwise exposed like an open wound. But now I feel driven by an urgent sense of responsibility; someone has overlooked something.

So I rummage around, and Juliane lets me do as I please. Partly because she bought some apple wine at the supermarket, partly because she's been on social security and under the electron microscope of the authorities for so long that she has stopped imagining that anything can be kept private.

The apartment is full of that domestic cosiness that comes from walking too often across polished hardwood floors with wooden-soled boots, and from forgetting burning cigarettes on the tabletop, and from sleeping off plenty of hangovers on the sofa; and when the only thing that's new and works properly is the TV, which is big and black, like a grand piano.

There is one more room than in my apartment: Isaiah's room.

A bed, a low table, and a wardrobe. On the floor a cardboard box. On the table two sticks, a hopscotch marker, a kind of suction cup, a model car. Colourless as beach pebbles in a drawer.

In the wardrobe a raincoat, rubber boots, clogs, sweaters, vests, socks, all stuffed in every which way. I run my fingers through the piles of clothes and over the top of the wardrobe. There is nothing but the dust that fell last year.

On the bed are his things from the hospital in a clear plastic bag. Waterproof dungarees, sneakers, sweatshirt, underwear, and socks. From his pocket a soft white stone that he used for chalk.

Juliane is standing in the doorway, crying. "The nappies were the only thing I threw out."

Once a month, when his fear of heights grew worse, Isaiah would wear nappies for a couple of days. Once I bought them for him myself.

"Where's his knife?"

She doesn't know.

On the windowsill there is a model ship, like an expensive shout into the soft-spokenness of the room. On the pedestal it says: "SS *Johannes Thomsen* of the Cryolite Corporation Danmark."

I have never before attempted to pry into how she keeps her head above water.

I put my arm around her shoulders.

"Juliane," I say, "would you please show me your papers?"

The rest of us have a drawer, a notebook, a file folder. Juliane has seven grubby envelopes for the safekeeping of the printed testimony of her existence. For many Greenlanders, the most difficult thing about Denmark is the paperwork. The state bureaucracy's front line of paper: application forms, documents, and official correspondence with the proper public authorities. There is a certain elegant and delicate irony in the fact that even a practically illiterate life like Juliane's has sloughed off this mountain of paper.

The little appointment slips from the alcoholism clinic on Sundholm, her birth certificate, fifty coupons from the bakery on Christianshavns Torv (when they add up to 500 kroner you get a free pastry). An appointment card from the Rudolph Bergh VD clinic, old tax deduction cards, statements from Bikuben Savings & Loan. A photograph of Juliane in Kongens Have in the sunshine. Public Health insurance certificates, a passport, final demands from the Electricity Board. Letters from the Riber Credit Information Bureau. A bundle of thin slips of papers, like pay slips, from which it's apparent that Juliane receives a pension of 9,400 kroner a month. At the bottom of the stack there is a bunch of letters. I have never been able to read people's letters, so I skip the private ones. The ones at the bottom are official, typewritten. I'm about to put them all away when I see it.

A peculiar letter. "We hereby wish to inform you that the directors of the Cryolite Corporation Danmark, at their most recent meeting, have decided to grant you a widow's pension following the death of Norsaq Christiansen. The monthly pension awarded to you is in the amount of 9,000 kroner, to be adjusted according to the current cost-of-living index." The letter is signed, on behalf of the board of directors, by "E. Lübing, Chief Accountant".

There's nothing very odd about that. But after the letter was typed up, someone turned it ninety degrees. And with a fountain pen that person wrote diagonally in the margin: "I am so sorry. Elsa Lübing."

You can learn something about your fellow human beings from what they write in the margin. People have speculated a great deal about Fermat's vanished proof. In a book concerning the never-proven postulate that whereas it is frequently possible to divide the square of a number into the sum of two other squares, this is not possible with powers higher than two, Fermat wrote in the margin: "I've discovered a truly wonderful proof for this argument. Unfortunately, this margin is too narrow to contain it."

Two years ago some woman sat in the office of the Cryolite Corporation Danmark and dictated this extremely proper letter. It adheres to all formalities, it has no typing mistakes, it is as it should be. Then she received it for approval and read it over and signed it. She sat there for a moment. And then she turned the paper around and wrote, "I am so sorry."

"What did he die of?"

"Norsaq? He was on an expedition to the west coast of Greenland. There was an accident."

"What kind of accident?"

"He ate something that made him sick. I think."

She gazes at me helplessly. People die. You won't get anywhere by wondering how or why.

* * *

22

"We consider the case closed."

I have the Nail on the phone. I've left Juliane to her own thoughts, which are now moving like plankton in a sea of sweet wine. Maybe I should have stayed with her. But I'm no angel of mercy. I can hardly take care of my *own* soul. And besides, I have my own hang-ups. That's what made me call police headquarters. They connect me with A Division, and they tell me that the inspector is still in his office. Judging by his voice, he's been there far too long.

"The death certificate was signed today at four o'clock."

"What about the footprints?" I ask.

"If you'd seen what I've seen, or if you had children of your own, you'd know how completely irresponsible and unpredictable they are."

His voice shifts into a growl at the thought of all the grief his own brats have caused him.

"Of course, this is only a matter of a shitty Greenlander," I say.

There's silence in the receiver. He is a man who, even after a long workday, has reserves for adjusting his thermostat to quick frost.

"Now I'm damned well going to tell you one thing. We do not discriminate. Whether it's a pygmy that fell, or a serial killer and sex offender, we go all the way. All the way. Do you understand? I picked up the forensics report myself. There is no indication that this was anything but an accident. It's tragic, but we have 175 of them a year."

"I'm thinking of filing a complaint."

"By all means, file a complaint."

Then we hang up. In reality, I hadn't thought about complaining. But I've had a hard day, too.

I realize the police have masses to do. I understand him quite well. I understood everything he said.

Except for one thing. When I gave my statement the day before yesterday, I answered a lot of questions. But some of them I didn't answer. One of them had to do with "marital status".

"That's none of your business," I told the officer. "Unless you're interested in a date."

So why would the police know anything about my private life? I ask myself: how did the Nail know that I don't have any children? I can't answer that question.

It's just a little question. But the world is always so busy wondering why a single, defenceless woman, if she's in my age group, doesn't have a husband and a couple of charming little toddlers. Over time you develop an allergic reaction to the question.

I get out a few sheets of unlined paper and an envelope and sit down at the kitchen table. At the top I write: "Copenhagen, 19 December 1993. To the Attorney General. My name is Smilla Jaspersen, and with this letter I would like to file a complaint."

6

HE LOOKS AS IF he's in his late forties, but he's twenty years older. He's wearing a black thermal jogging suit, cleated shoes, an American baseball cap, and fingerless leather gloves. He takes a little brown medicine bottle out of his breast pocket and empties it into his mouth with a practised, almost secretive movement. It's propranolol, a beta-blocker that slows his heartbeat. He opens one of his hands and looks at it. It's big and white and manicured and quite steady. He selects a number one club, a driver, Taylormade, with a polished bell-shaped head of Brazilian rosewood. He places it beside the ball, then takes his backswing. When he strikes, he has all of his strength, all of his ninety kilos, focused on a point as big as a postage stamp, and the little yellow ball seems to dissolve and vanish. It comes into view again only when it lands on the green, right at the edge of the garden, where it obediently drops close to the flag.

"Cayman balls," he says. "From McGregor. I always had trouble with the neighbours before. These only go half as far."

He is my father. This show has been for my benefit, and I see right through it to what it really is. A little boy's plea for love. Which I have absolutely no intention of giving him.

Seen from my perspective, Denmark's entire population is middle-class. The truly poor and the truly rich are so few as to be almost exotic.

I have been fortunate enough to know quite a few of the poor, since many of them are Greenlanders.

My father belongs to the truly wealthy.

He has a 67-foot Swan at Rungsted Marina with a full-time three-man crew. He has his own little island at the mouth of Ise Fjord where he can retreat to his Norwegian log cabin, and he can tell any uninvited tourists to beat it, fuck off. He is one of the few people in Denmark to own a Bugatti and have a man employed to polish it and warm up the grease in the axle box with a Bunsen burner on the two occasions a year when he puts in an appearance at the Bugatti Club vintage-car race. The rest of the time he makes do with playing the gramophone record sent out by the club, on which you can hear someone cranking up one of these wonderful vehicles, fine-tuning the choke, and revving the engine.

He owns this house, white as snow and decorated with white-washed cement seashells, with a roof of natural shale and with a winding stairway up to the entrance. With rosebeds in a front garden that drops steeply down to Strandvejen, and a back garden that's big enough for a nine-hole practice course, which is just right, now that he's acquired the new balls.

He earned his money giving injections.

He has never been one to leak information about himself, but whoever is interested can look him up in *Who's Who* and discover that he became a chief of staff when he was thirty, that he held Denmark's first chair in anaesthetics when it was established, and that five years later he left the hospital system to devote himself – as it's so nicely put – to private practice. Later his fame took him out travelling. Not as a vagabond, but in private jets. He has given injections to the famous. He was in charge of the anaesthesia at the first pioneering heart transplants in South Africa. He was with the American delegation of doctors in the Soviet Union when Brezhnev died. I've heard it said that my father was the one who delayed death during the last weeks of Brezhnev's life, wielding his long syringes.

He resembles a docker and discreetly cultivates this look by letting his beard grow out now and then. A beard that is now grey but which was once blue-black and still requires two shaves a day with a straight razor for him to look presentable.

His hands are unfailingly steady. With those hands he can push a 150-mm syringe through the flank, retroperitoneally, through the deep back muscles, into the aorta. Then he taps the tip of the needle lightly against the large artery, to be sure that he has gone far enough, and then goes behind it to leave a deposit of lidocaine up at the large nerve plexus. The central nervous system controls the tone of the arteries. He has a theory that by using this blockade, he can help the poor circulation in the legs of overweight wealthy people.

While he's giving an injection he is as focused as any human being could be. He thinks of nothing else, not even the bill for tens of thousands of kroner that his secretary is typing up, and which will fall due before the first of January. Merry Christmas and Happy New Year – next, please.

During the past twenty-five years he has been among the two hundred golf players fighting for the last fifty Eurocards. He lives with a ballet dancer who is thirteen years younger than me and who walks around looking at him as if the only thing she lives for is the hope that he will strip the tulle tutu and silk slippers off her.

So my father is a man who possesses everything he can get his hands on. And that's what he thinks he's showing me here on the golf course. That he has everything his heart could desire. Even the beta-blockers, which he's been taking for the past ten years to steady his hands, are largely without side effects.

We walk around the house, along the raked gravel paths; in the summer Sørensen, the gardener, takes a pair of shears to the edges, so you could cut your feet on them if you don't watch out. I'm wearing a sealskin coat over a tracksuit of embroidered wool with a zipper. Seen from a distance, we are a father and daughter with a plethora of wealth and vitality. On closer examination, we are simply a banal tragedy spread over two generations.

The living room has a floor of bog oak and borders of stainless steel around a wall of glass facing the birdbath and rose bushes and the drop in social status towards Strandvejen. Benja is standing at the fireplace wearing a leotard and woollen socks, stretching the muscles in her feet and ignoring me. She looks pale and lovely and naughty, like an elf maiden turned stripper.

"Brentan," I say.

"I beg your pardon?"

She enunciates every syllable, the way she learned at the Royal Theatre school.

"For bad feet, dear. Brentan for fungus between your toes. You can get it without a prescription nowadays."

"It's not fungus," she says coldly. "I don't think people get that until they reach your age."

"Juveniles do too, dear. Especially people who work out a lot. And it spreads to the crotch quite easily."

Snarling, Benja retreats backwards into the adjoining room. She has an abundance of raw energy, but she had a protected childhood and a skyrocketing career. She hasn't yet experienced the adversity

27

necessary to develop a psyche that can keep fighting back.

Señora Gonzales arranges the tea things on the coffee table, which is a seventy-millimetre-thick glass plate on top of a polished marble block.

"It's been a long time, Smilla."

He talks about his new paintings for a while, about the memoirs he's writing, and about what he's practising on the piano. He's stalling. Preparing himself for the impact from the blow that will come when I state my business, which has nothing to do with him. He's grateful that I let him talk. But we are realists, neither of us has any illusions.

"Tell me about Johannes Loyen," I say.

My father was in his early thirties when he came to Greenland and met my mother.

The polar Eskimo Aisivak told Knud Rasmussen that in the beginning the world was inhabited only by two men, who were both great sorcerers. Since they wanted to multiply, one of them transformed his body in such a way that he could give birth; and then the two of them created many children.

In the 1860s the Greenland catechist Hanseeraq recorded in the diary of the Brethren Congregation, *Diarium Friedrichstal*, many examples of women who hunted as men did. There are examples in Rink's collection of legends, and in *Reports from Greenland*. It has certainly never been commonplace, but it *has* happened. Because of the numerousness of women, by dint of death and need, and because of the natural acceptance in Greenland that each of the sexes contains the potential to become its opposite.

As a rule, however, women then have had to dress like men, and they have had to renounce any sort of family life. The collective could tolerate a change in sex, but not a constant transition to and fro.

It was different with my mother. She laughed and gave birth to her children and gossiped about her friends and cleaned skins like a woman. But she shot and paddled a kayak and dragged meat home like a man.

When she was about twelve years old, she went out on the ice with her father in April, and there he shot at an *uuttoq*, a seal sunning itself on the ice. He missed. For other men there might be various reasons why they would miss. For my grandfather there

28

was only one. Something irreversible was about to happen. Calcification of the optic nerve. A year later he was totally blind.

On that day in April my mother stayed behind while her father walked on to check a long line. There she had time to ponder the various possibilities for her future. Such as the welfare assistance which even today is below subsistence level in Greenland and at that time was a kind of unintentional joke. Or death by starvation, which was not uncommon, or a life of depending on kinfolk who didn't have enough even for themselves.

When the seal popped up again, she shot it.

Before, she had jigged for sea scorpions and Greenland halibut, and hunted for grouse. With this seal she became a hunter.

I think it was rare for her to step outside herself and take an objective look at her role. But it happened once when we were living in tents at the summer encampment near Atikerluk, a mountain which is invaded by auks in the summertime, by so many black white-breasted birds that only someone who has seen it can fully grasp the vast quantity of them. It transcends what can be measured.

We had come from the north, where we were fishing for narwhals from small, diesel-powered cutters. One day we caught eight animals. Partly because the ice had trapped them in a restricted area, partly because the three boats lost contact with each other. Eight narwhals are far too much meat, even for dog food. Far too much meat.

One of them was a pregnant female. The nipple is located right above the genital opening. When my mother opened the abdominal cavity with a single cut to remove the intestines, an angel-white, perfectly formed calf half a metre long slid out onto the ice.

For close to four hours the hunters stood around in virtual silence, gazing out at the midnight sun, which at that time of year brings perpetual light, and ate *mattak*, narwhal skin. I couldn't eat a single bite.

One week later we are camping out near the bird mountain, and we haven't eaten for twenty-four hours. The technique is to melt into the landscape, waiting, and take the bird with a large net. On the second try I get three.

They were females, on their way to their young. They nest on ledges on the steep slopes, where the young make an infernal racket. The mothers hide the worms they find in a kind of pouch in their beaks. You kill them by pressing on their heart. I had three birds.

There had been so many before these. So many birds killed,

29

cooked in clay, and eaten; so many that I couldn't remember them all. And yet I suddenly see their eyes as tunnels, at the end of which their young are waiting, and the chicks' eyes are again new tunnels, at the end of which is the narwhal calf, whose gaze leads inward and away. Ever so slowly I tilt the net, and with a great explosion of sound, the birds rise into the air.

My mother is sitting next to me, quite still. And she looks at me as if seeing something for the first time.

I don't know what it was that stopped me. Compassion is not a virtue in the Arctic. Rather it is a kind of insensitivity: a lack of feeling for the animals, the environment, and the nature of necessity.

"Smilla," she says, "I have carried you in *amaat*."

It's the month of May, and her skin has a deep brown sheen, like a dozen layers of varnish. She is wearing gold earrings and a chain with two crosses and an anchor around her neck. Her hair is pulled into a bun at the nape of her neck, and she is big and beautiful. Even now, when I think of her, she is the most beautiful woman I ever saw.

I must have been around five years old. I don't know exactly what she means, but this is the first time I understand that we are of the same sex.

"And yet," she says, "I am strong like a man."

She has on a red-and-black checked cotton shirt. Now she rolls up one sleeve and shows me her lower arm, which is as broad and hard as a paddle. Then she slowly unbuttons her shirt. "Come, Smilla," she says quietly. She never kisses me, and she seldom touches me. But at moments of great intimacy, she lets me drink from the milk that is always there, beneath her skin, just as her blood is. She spreads her legs so I can walk in between them. Like the other hunters, she wears trousers made of bearskin given only a rudimentary tanning. She loves ashes, sometimes eating them straight from the fire, and she has smeared some underneath her eyes. In this aroma of burned coal and bearskin, I go to her breast, which is brilliantly white, with a big, delicate rose areola. There I drink *immuk*, my mother's milk.

Later she once tried to explain to me why one month there are three thousand narwhals gathered in a single fjord seething with life. The following month the ice traps them and they freeze to death. Why in May and June there are so many auks that they colour the cliffs black. The next month half a million birds have died of starvation. In her own way she wants to point out that behind the life of the Arctic animals there has always been this extreme fluctuation in the populations. And that in the context of these variations, the number we take means less than nothing.

I understood her, understood every word. Then and later on. But that didn't change a thing. The year after – that was the year before she disappeared – I began to feel nausea when I went fishing. I was then about six years old. Not old enough to speculate about the cause, but old enough to understand that it was a feeling of alienation towards nature. That some part of it was no longer accessible to me in the obvious way that it had been before. Perhaps I had already begun to want to understand the ice. To want to understand is an attempt to recapture something we have lost.

"Professor Loyen . . ."

He pronounces the name with the interest and armed respect with which one brontosaurus has always regarded another.

"A very talented man."

He lets a white palm glide over his cheek and chin. It's a carefully studied gesture which makes a sound like the rasp of a coarse file on a piece of driftwood.

"The Institute for Arctic Medicine – he created it."

"What's his interest in forensic medicine? He's let himself be appointed provisional pathologist for Greenland."

"He was originally a forensic pathologist. But he accepts anything that brings merit. He must think it's a good career move."

"What drives him?"

There is a pause. My father has gone through most of his life with his head under his arm. In old age he has begun to take intense interest in people's motives.

"In my generation there are three kinds of doctors. There are those who get stuck as hospital physicians or end up in private practice. There are many fine people among them. Then there are those who manage to get a doctorate, which is – as you know, Smilla – the arbitrary and ludicrous and inadequate prerequisite for upward mobility in the system. They end up as chiefs of staff. They are minor monarchs in the local society of medicine. Then there are the third kind. Those of us who have risen above that level and have come out on top."

This is said without any hint of self-mockery. One would be able to get my father to state, in all seriousness, that one of his problems

31

is that he isn't half as pleased with himself as he has every reason to be.

"To take those last swimming strokes demands a particular strength. A strong desire or ambition. For money. Or power. Or perhaps insight. In the history of medicine this struggle has always been symbolized by fire. The eternal flame of the alchemist beneath the retort."

He gazes straight ahead, as if he had a syringe in his hand, as if the needle were about to reach its goal.

"Loyen," he says, "from the time of his school days, has wanted only one thing, next to which everything else is trivial. He has wanted to be recognized as the best in his field. Not the best in Denmark, among all the peasants. The best in the universe. His professional ambition is the perpetual flame inside him. And it is no gas jet, mind you. It's a Midsummer bonfire."

I don't know how my mother and father met. I do know that he came to Greenland because this hospitable land has always been a field for scientific experiments. He was in the process of developing a new technique for the treatment of trigeminal neuralgia, an inflammation of the facial sensory nerve. Previously, this condition was assuaged by killing the nerve with injections of alcohol, which led to partial facial paralysis and loss of sensation on one side of the musculature of the mouth, the so-called drooping lip. This can afflict even the best and richest of families, which is why my father had become interested in it. There were many incidences of that illness in North Greenland. In order to treat them with his new technique – a partial heat-denaturing of the affected nerve – he had come.

Photographs of him exist. Wearing his Kastinger boots and his down clothing, with ice axe and glacier goggles, in front of the house they put at his disposal on the American base. With his hands on the shoulders of the two short, dark men who are to interpret for him.

For him, North Greenland was truly the outermost Thule. Not for a minute did he imagine that he would stay more than the one required month in a windblown ice desert, where not even a golf course was to be procured.

You might get a vague notion of the white-hot energy between him and my mother if you consider the fact that he stayed there three years. He tried to get her to move on to the base, but she refused. As for anyone born in North Greenland, the suggestion of being cooped up was intolerable for my mother. Instead, he followed her out to one of the barracks made of plywood and corrugated iron put up when the Americans drove the Inuit out of the area in which the base was built. Even today I still ask myself how he managed it. The answer, of course, is that as long as she was alive, he would have left his golf bag and clubs behind at any time to follow her, even straight into searing black downtown hell.

"*They* had children," people say. In this case that wouldn't be correct. I would say that *my mother* had my little brother and me. Outside this scenario was my father, present without being able to take any real part, dangerous as a male polar bear, imprisoned in a land which he hated by a love which he did not understand and which held him captive, over which he seemed to have not even the slightest influence. The man with the syringes and the steady hands, the golf player Moritz Jaspersen.

When I was three years old, he left. Or rather, his own character drove him away. Deep within every blind, absolute love grows the hatred towards the beloved, who now holds the only existing key to one's happiness. I was, as I said, only three years old, but I remember how he left. He left in a state of bubbling, pent-up, livid, profane rage. As a form of energy this was surpassed only by the longing that flung him back again. He was fixed to my mother with a tether which was invisible to the rest of the world but which had the effect and physical reality of a fan belt.

He didn't have much to do with us children when he was there. From my first six years I remember the traces of him. The perfume of the Latakia tobacco he smoked. The autoclave in which he sterilized his instruments. The interest he aroused whenever he would occasionally put on his spikes, take up a stance, and drive a bucket's worth of balls across the new ice. And the mood he brought with him, which was the sum of the feelings he held for my mother. The same kind of soothing warmth that you might expect to find in a nuclear reactor.

What was my mother's role in this? I don't know, and I shall never find out. Those who understand such things say that the two partners must always assist each other if a relationship is truly to founder and turn into flotsam. That's possible. Like everybody else, from the age of seven I have painted my childhood with lots of false gilding, and some may have rubbed off on my mother as well.

But in any case, she was the one who stayed where she was, and set out her seal nets and braided my hair. She was there, a huge presence, while Moritz with his golf clubs and his unshaven stubble and syringes oscillated between the two extremes of his love: either a total merging or putting the entire North Atlantic between him and his beloved.

Whoever falls into the water in Greenland does not come up again. The sea is less than 4 °C, and at that temperature all processes of decomposition have ceased. That's why the fermentation of the stomach contents does not occur here; in Denmark it gives suicides renewed buoyancy and brings them to the surface, to be washed ashore.

But they found the remains of her kayak, which led them to conclude that it must have been a walrus. Walruses are unpredictable. They can be hypersensitive and shy. But if they come a little further south, and if it's autumn, and the fish are few, they can be transformed into some of the swiftest and most meticulous killers in the great ocean. With their two tusks they can stave in the side of a ship made of ferrocement. I once saw hunters holding up a cod to a walrus that they had captured alive. The walrus puckered up his lips as for a kiss and then sucked the meat right off the bones of the fish.

"It would be nice if you came out here for Christmas, Smilla."

"Christmas doesn't mean anything to me."

"Have you thought about the fact that your father will be sitting here all alone?"

This is one of the more tiresome tendencies which Moritz has developed with age – this mixture of nastiness and sentimentality.

"Couldn't you try the Old Men's Home?"

I have stood up, and now he comes over to me. "You're bloody heartless, Smilla. And that's why you've never been able to hold on to a man."

He's as close to tears as he can get.

"Father," I say, "write me a prescription."

He switches immediately, fast as lightning, from complaint to concern, just as he did with my mother.

"Are you ill, Smilla?"

"Very. But with this piece of paper you can save my life and keep your Hippocratic oath. It has to be five figures."

He winces; it's a matter of his life's blood. We're talking about his vital organs: his wallet and his chequebook.

I put on my fur coat. Benja does not come out to say goodbye. At the door he hands me the cheque. He knows that this pipeline is his only connection to my life. Even this he is afraid of losing.

"Don't you want Fernando to drive you home?"

Then something dawns on him. "Smilla," he shouts, "you're not going away, are you?"

There is a snow-covered lawn between us. It might just as well have been the ice cap.

"There's something weighing on my conscience," I say. "It'll take money to do something about it."

"In that case," he says, half to himself, "I'm afraid that cheque isn't nearly enough."

In this way he gets the last word. You can't win them all.

7

MAYBE IT'S A COINCIDENCE, maybe it's not a coincidence, that he arrives while the workers are at lunch, so that the roof is deserted.

It is bright sunshine with a hint of warmth, blue sky, white seagulls, a view of the shipyard at Limhamn in Sweden across the Sound, and not a trace of the snow that was the reason for us standing here: me and Mr Ravn, the investigator for the district attorney.

He's short, no taller than I am, but he's wearing a very large grey coat with so much padding in the shoulders that he looks like a ten-year-old boy acting in a musical about the time of Prohibition. His face is dark and burned-out like lava, and so gaunt that his skin is stretched across his skull like a mummy. But his eyes are alert and observant.

"I thought I'd just drop by," he says.

"You're much too kind. Do you always drop by when someone makes a complaint?"

"Only rarely. Normally the case goes to the local board. Let's just say it's because of the nature of this case and because of your suggestive letter of complaint."

I say nothing. I let the silence work on the investigator a little. It has no visible effect. His sand-coloured eyes rest on me without flinching and without embarrassment. He will stand here as long as it takes. This alone makes him an unusual man.

"I spoke to Professor Loyen. He told me that you'd been to see him. That you think the boy suffered from a fear of heights."

His position in the world makes it impossible for me to have any real trust in him. But I feel an urge to reveal part of what is bothering me.

"There were the tracks in the snow."

Very few people know how to listen. Their haste pulls them out of the conversation, or they try internally to improve the situation,

36

or they're preparing what their next speech will be when you shut up and it's their turn to take the stage.

With the man standing in front of me it's different. When I talk, he listens without distraction to what I say, and only to what I say.

"I read the report and looked at the pictures . . ."

"Something else, something more."

Now we're on our way into something which has to be said but can't be explained.

"They were acceleration tracks. When you jump from snow or ice, there is a pronation in the ankle joint. As there is when you walk barefoot in the sand."

I try to demonstrate the slight outward rotation with my wrist.

"If the movement is too fast, not firm enough, there will be a little slip backwards."

"As with every child who is playing . . ."

"When you're used to playing in snow, you don't leave that kind of track, because that movement is not efficient, like faulty distribution of your weight going uphill cross-country skiing."

Even I can hear how unconvincing it must sound. I wait for a scornful remark. But it doesn't come.

He looks out across the roof. He hasn't any nervous tics, no habit of touching his hat or lighting his pipe or shifting his weight from one foot to another. He has no notebook which he pulls out. He is simply a very small man who listens and thinks things over carefully.

"Interesting," he says at last. "But also rather . . . insubstantial. It would be difficult to present this to a layman. Difficult to *base* anything on it."

He is right. Reading snow is like listening to music. To describe what you've read is to try to explain music in writing.

When it happens for the first time, it's like discovering that you're awake while everyone else is sleeping. Equal parts loneliness and omnipotence. We're on our way from Qinnissut to the Inglefield estuary. It's winter, the wind is blowing, and it's terrifyingly cold. When the women need to pee, they have to light a Primus under a blanket to be able to pull down their trousers without getting frost-bite instantly.

For some time we've noticed that fog is on the way, but when it comes, it comes suddenly, like a collective blindness. Even the dogs

37

huddle together. But for me there really isn't any fog. There is a wild, bright feeling of elation, because I know with absolute certainty which way we should go.

My mother listens to me, and the others listen to her. I am placed on the front sleigh, and I can remember feeling that we were driving along a string of silver, stretched between me and the house in Qaanaaq. The instant before the gable appears out of the night, I know that it's there.

Perhaps it wasn't the first time. But that's how I remember it. Perhaps it's wrong when we remember breakthroughs which have affected our own being as things that occur in discrete, extraordinary moments. Perhaps falling in love, the piercing knowledge that we ourselves will some day die, and the love of snow are in reality not sudden events; perhaps they are always present. Perhaps they never completely vanish, either.

There is another image of fog, possibly from that same summer. I have never sailed much. I'm not familiar with the underwater landscape. It's unclear why they've taken me along. But I always know where we are in relation to landmarks on shore.

From then on they start taking me along almost every time.

At the American military Coldwater Laboratory on Pylot Island they had people on the staff to research the "sense of orientation" phenomenon. There I saw thick books and long lists of articles about the fact that directionally constant winds blow along the ground, giving ice crystals a particular angle, so that even in bad visibility you should be able to determine the points of the compass. That another barely noticeable breeze a little higher up causes a definite cooling of one side of the face in fog. That the subconscious registers subliminally the light not normally noticed. There is a theory that in the Arctic regions the human brain is able to register the powerful electromagnetic turbulence from the magnetic North Pole in the vicinity of Bucha Felix.

Verbal lectures on the experience of music.

My only spiritual brother is Newton. I was moved when, at the university, they introduced us to the passage in *Principia Mathematica*, Book One, where he tips a bucket full of water and uses the tilted surface of the water to argue that within and surrounding the rotating earth and the turning sun and the tumbling stars, which make it impossible to find any constant starting point and initial system and fixed point in life, there is Absolute Space – that which stands still, that which we can cling to.

I could have kissed Newton. Later I despaired over Ernst Mach's criticism of the bucket experiment, the criticism which formed the basis for Einstein's work. I was younger then and more easily moved. Today I know that all we did was prove that Newton's argumentation was inadequate. Every theoretical explanation is a reduction of intuition. No one has budged my or Newton's certainty about Absolute Space. No one is going to find his way home to Qaanaaq with his nose stuck in Einstein's writings.

"So what do *you* think happened?"

There is nothing as disarming as a sympathetic response.

"I don't know," I say.

That's very close to being the truth.

"What do you want us to do?"

Here in the daylight, where the snow has melted, and across Knippels Bridge life is going on, and someone is speaking to me courteously. My objections suddenly seem so transparent I find no reply.

"I'll review the case again," he says, "from beginning to end, and look at it in the light of what you have told me."

We climb down, and it's also a descent into the depression waiting for me down there.

"I'm parked at the corner," he says.

And then he makes his big mistake.

"I would suggest that while we review the case, you withdraw your complaint. So that we can work undisturbed. And for the same reason, if the newspapers should contact you, I think you ought to refuse to comment on the case. And don't mention what you've told me, either. Refer them to the police; tell them we're still working on the case."

I can feel myself blushing. But it's not from embarrassment. It's from anger.

I'm not perfect. I think more highly of snow and ice than of love. It's easier for me to be interested in mathematics than to have affection for my fellow human beings. But I am anchored to something in life that is constant. You can call it a sense of orientation; you can call it woman's intuition; you can call it whatever you like. I'm standing on rock bottom and further than that I cannot fall. It could be that I haven't managed to organize my life very well. But

I always have a grip – with at least one finger at a time – on Absolute Space.

That's why there's a limit to how far the world can twist out of joint, and to how wrong, off course, things can go before I notice. I now know, without a shadow of a doubt, that something is wrong.

I don't have a driver's licence. If one is wearing decent clothes, there are too many parameters to keep in check if one has to steer a bicycle, keep an eye on the traffic, maintain one's dignity, and hold on to a chic little hunter's hat I bought at Vagn's on Østergade. So I usually end up either walking or taking a bus.

Today I walk. It's Tuesday, 21 December, and it's cold and clear. First I stroll to the library of the Geological Institute on Øster Voldgade.

One sentence that I'm quite fond of is Dedekind's postulate about linear compression. It says – more or less – that anywhere in a series of numbers, within an infinitesimally small interval, you can find infinity. When I look for the Cryolite Corporation Danmark in the library's computer, I find enough material for a year's worth of reading.

I select *White Gold*. It turns out to be a book full of sparkles. The workers at the cryolite quarry have a sparkle in their eyes, the industrial tycoons who earn the lucre have a sparkle in their eyes, the Greenlandic clean-up staff have a sparkle in their eyes, and the blue fjords of Greenland are full of reflections and flashes of sunshine.

Then I stroll past Østerport station and down along Strand Boulevard. To number 72B, where the Cryolite Corporation Danmark – next to its competitor, the Øresund Cryolite Corporation – used to have five hundred employees and two laboratory buildings and a raw cryolite hall and a sorting hall and a canteen and workshops. Now all that's left are railway tracks, the demolished plant, some sheds and shacks, and a single red brick villa. From my reading I know that the two big cryolite deposits at Saqqaq in Greenland were finally depleted in the sixties and that during the seventies the company switched over to other activities.

Now there is only a fenced-in area, a driveway, and a group of workmen wearing white overalls enjoying a quiet Christmas beer, getting ready for the approaching holiday.

A bold and enterprising girl guide would go right up to them and salute like a girl scout and talk their lingo and pump them for information about who Mrs Lübing was and what happened to her.

I don't have that kind of directness. I don't like talking to strangers. I don't like Danish workmen in groups. Actually, I don't like any men at all in groups.

While I've been thinking, I've walked all the way round the block, and the workmen have caught sight of me and wave me closer. They turn out to be affable gentlemen who have been employed here for thirty years, and now have the melancholy task of closing down the place, and who know that Mrs Lübing is still alive and that she lives in the Frederiksberg district and is listed in the phone book, and why do I want to know?

"She did me a favour once," I tell them. "Now I want to ask her about something."

They nod and say that Mrs Lübing did a lot of favours for people, and they have daughters of their own my age, and do stop by some other time.

On my way back towards the city along Strand Boulevard I think that inside even the most paranoid suspicion the sense of humanity and the desire for contact are waiting to emerge.

No one who has lived side by side with animals which have plenty of room can ever visit the zoo. But once I take Isaiah along to the Natural History Museum to show him the room with the seals.

He thinks they look sickly. But he's fascinated with the model of the aurochs. On the way home we walk through Fælled Park.

"How old was it again?" he asks.

"Forty thousand years old."

"Then it's going to die soon."

"You're probably right."

"When you die, Smilla, can I have your hide?"

"All right," I say.

We walk across the Triangle. It's a warm autumn day, the air is misty.

"Smilla, can we go to Greenland?"

I see no reason to spare children from unavoidable truths. They have to grow up to bear the same burdens as the rest of us.

"No," I say.

"All right."

I've never promised him anything. I can't promise him anything. Nobody can promise anyone anything.

"But we can read about Greenland."

He says "we" about our reading aloud, aware that by his presence he contributes just as much as I do.

"In what book?"

"In Euclid's *Elements*. . . ."

By the time I get home it's dark. The mechanic is pushing his bicycle down into the basement.

He is very broad, like a bear, and if he straightened up his head he would be quite imposing. But he keeps his head down, perhaps to apologize for his height, perhaps to avoid the doorframes of this world.

I like him. I have a weakness for losers. Invalids, foreigners, the fat boy of the class, the ones nobody ever wants to dance with. My heart beats for them. Maybe because I've always known that in some way I will forever be one of them.

Isaiah and the mechanic had a friendship. From the time before Isaiah learned to speak Danish. They probably didn't need many words. One craftsman recognizing another. Two males who were alone in the world, each in his own way.

I follow along as he pushes the bike downstairs. I have an idea about the basement.

He has got a double room for a workshop. It has a cement floor, warm, dry air, and a bright yellow electric light. The limited space is packed full. There's a workbench running along two walls. Bicycle wheels and inner tubes on hooks. A milk crate full of defective potentiometers. A plastic panel with nails and screws on it. A board with small insulated pliers for working with electronics. A board full of hooks. Nine square metres of plywood with what looks like all the tools in the world. A row of soldering irons. Four shelves of plumbing supplies, paint cans, dismantled stereos, sets of socket wrenches, welding electrodes, and an entire set of Metabo electrical tools. Against the wall two large canisters for a CO_2 welder, and two small ones for a blowtorch. There is also a washing machine in pieces. Buckets full of a solution to preserve wood against dry rot. A bicycle stand. A foot pump.

There are so many objects gathered here that they seem to be waiting for the slightest excuse to turn into chaos. On a purely personal level, I think all you'd have to do is send me in here alone to turn on the light, and that would trigger such a state of confusion that you wouldn't even be able to find the light switch afterwards. But as it is now, everything is kept in its place by the thoroughly functional sense of order of a person who wants to make sure he will always be able to find whatever he needs.

The place is a double world. Above is the workbench, the tools, the tall office chair. Below, under the table, the universe is duplicated half-size. A little masonite table with a coping saw, screwdriver, chisel. A little stool. A workbench. A little vice. A beer crate. A cigar box with about thirty cans of Humbrol. Isaiah's things. I've been in here once before when they were sitting and working. The mechanic on the chair, bent over a magnifying glass on a stand; Isaiah on the floor, in his underpants, lost to the world. There was the smell of burning solder and epoxy resin in the air. And something else, something stronger: total, all-consuming concentration. I stood there for almost ten minutes. They didn't look up once.

Isaiah wasn't equipped for the Danish winter. Only occasionally would Juliane manage to dress him adequately. When I had known him for six months, he contracted his fourth severe middle ear infection in eight weeks. When he came out of the penicillin daze, he was hard-of-hearing. After that I would sit in front of him when I read so that he could follow the movement of my lips. In the mechanic he found someone with whom he could communicate in other ways than through language.

For several days I've been walking around with something in my pocket because I've been expecting this meeting. I show it to him now.

"What's this?"

It's the suction device that I took from Isaiah's room.

"A 'cup'. Glaziers use them to carry large pieces of glass."

I take the things out of the beer crate. There are several pieces of carved wood. A harpoon, an axe. A boat carved from a dense, rather speckled kind of wood, maybe pear. An *umiak*. It's rubbed smooth on the outside and hollowed out with a gouge. A slow, meticulous, carefully executed job. There is also a car made of bent and glued aluminium strips cut from an almost paper-thin sheet. Pieces of rough coloured glass that have been melted and stretched over a Bunsen burner. Several pairs of glasses. A Walkman. The cover is gone but it has been ingeniously repaired with a Plexiglas plate and tiny hinges screwed on. It's lying in a hand-sewn vinyl

43

case. The whole thing bears the mark of a project shared between a child and an adult. There is also a stack of cassette tapes.

"Where's his knife?"

The mechanic shrugs. After a moment he plods off. He's the whole world's hundred-kilo friend, and buddies with the boilerman, too. He has keys to all the basement rooms and can come and go as he pleases.

I pick up the little stool and sit down on it by the door, so I can see the whole room.

At boarding school we each had a thirty-by-fifty-centimetre cupboard. It had a lock. The owner had a key for it. Everyone else could open it with a steel comb.

There's a widespread notion that children are open, that the truth about their inner selves just seeps out of them. That's all wrong. No one is more covert than a child, and no one has greater cause to be that way. It's a response to a world that's always using a tin-opener on them to see what they have inside, just in case it ought to be replaced with a more useful type of tinned foodstuff.

The first need that developed at boarding school — aside from the perpetual, never truly satisfied hunger — was the need for peace. There is no peace in a dormitory. So the desire is suppressed. It turns into a need for a hiding place, for a secret room.

I try to imagine Isaiah's situation, the places he went. The apartment, the housing block, the kindergarten, the embankment. Places that can never be thoroughly searched. So I stick to the place at hand.

I look around the room. Very carefully. Without finding anything. Other than the memory of Isaiah. Then I call up the image of the way it looked the two times I was here before, a long time ago.

I must have been sitting there half an hour when it came to me. Six months ago the building was inspected for dry rot. The insurance company brought over a dog that was trained to sniff it out. It found two small patches. They knocked them down and then swabbed the area. One of the places where they worked was in this room. They opened the wall a metre off the floor. They bricked it up again, but it still hasn't been covered with plaster like the rest of the wall. Underneath the workbench, in the shadows, there is still a rectangle of ten-by-ten-centimetre bricks.

Even so I almost don't find it. He must have stood by as the workers were finishing up. Then he has gone in while the mortar was still damp and pushed one brick slightly inwards. And then he has waited for a moment and then pulled it back into place. He has kept at it until the mortar was dry. Quietly and patiently, the whole evening, at fifteen-minute intervals, he has drifted down to the basement to move the brick one centimetre. That's what I imagine. You couldn't fit the blade of a knife in between the brick and the mortar. But when I press on it, it slides right in. At first I can't understand how he got it out, because there's nothing to grab hold of. Then I pick up the suction cup and stare at it. I can't shove the brick inwards because it would simply fall into the wall cavity. But when I put the black rubber disc against the brick and use the little handle to create suction, the brick comes out towards me with a great deal of resistance. When I have it out, I understand why. A little blue nail has been hammered into the back. Twisted around it is a thin nylon cord. A big drop of epoxy, now hard as stone, has been applied to the nail and cord. The cord runs down into the wall cavity. On the end hangs a flat cigar box with two thick rubber bands around it. The whole thing is like a poem of technical ingenuity.

I put the box in my coat pocket. Then I tuck the brick back into place.

Chivalry is an archetype. When I came to Denmark, Copenhagen County gathered a class of children who had to learn Danish at Rugmarken's School, near the welfare barracks for immigrants in Sundby on Amager. I sat next to a boy named Baral. I was seven and had short hair. During playtime I played ball with the boys. After about three months there was a class in which we were supposed to recite each other's names.

"And next to you, Baral, what is her name?"

"His name is Smilla."

"*Her* name is Smilla. Smilla is a girl."

He looked at me in mute astonishment. After the first shock had receded, and for the rest of the school year, there was only one real difference in his behaviour towards me. It had now been reinforced by an amiable, gentle attentiveness.

I found the same thing in Isaiah. He might suddenly switch over to Danish in order to use *De*, the polite form of address, with me after he came to understand the inherent respect contained in that expression. Over the last three months, when Juliane's self-destruction was greater and more directed than ever, he some-times didn't want to go home at night.

"Do you," he said, addressing me formally in Danish, "think that I could sleep here?"

After I had given him a bath I would stand him up on the lavatory seat while I rubbed him with lotion. From there he could see his own face in the mirror, sniffing suspiciously at the rose scent of Elizabeth Arden's night cream.

He has never, while awake, touched me. He never took my hand, he never caressed me, nor sought to be caressed himself. But during the night, he would sometimes roll over towards me, sound asleep, and lie there for several minutes. Against my skin he would get a diminutive erection that came and went, came and went, like Punch in a puppet show.

On those nights I wouldn't sleep much. At the slightest change in his rapid breathing, I woke up. Often I would simply lie awake, thinking that the air I was breathing was the air he had just exhaled.

8

BERTRAND RUSSELL WROTE that pure mathematics is the field in which we don't know what we're talking about or to what extent what we say is true or false.

That's the way I feel about cooking.

I eat mostly meat. Fatty meat. I can't keep warm on vegetables and bread. I've never managed to acquire an understanding of my kitchen, of raw ingredients, or of the basic chemistry of cooking. I have only one simple work principle: I always make hot food. That's important when you live alone. It serves a mental hygienic purpose. It keeps you going.

Today it serves another purpose as well. It puts off two telephone calls. I don't like talking on the phone. I need to see whom I'm talking to.

I put Isaiah's cigar box on the table. Then I make the first call.

I'm rather hoping that it's too late; it'll be Christmas soon, and people should be leaving work early.

I call the Cryolite Corporation. The director is still in his office. He doesn't introduce himself; he is merely a voice, dry, implacable, and unsympathetic, like sand running through an hourglass. He informs me that as the government was represented on the board, and since the company is now in the process of closing down, and the foundation is being reorganized, it has been decided to transfer all papers to the national archives, which houses documents dealing with decisions made by public authorities. Some of the papers – he was not able to tell me which ones – would fall into the category of "general resolutions", which remain confidential for fifty years, while others – again he could not, as I must understand, tell me which ones – would be regarded as personal files, which enjoy eighty years of protection.

I try asking him where the papers are, the papers as such.

All information is still physically in the safekeeping of the corporation, but formally they have already been included in the National Archives, which is where I would have to enquire, and is there anything else he could do for me?

"Yes," I say, "drop dead."

I take the rubber bands off Isaiah's box.

The knives I keep in my apartment are just sharp enough to open envelopes with. Cutting a slice of coarse bread is on the borderline of their capacity. I don't need anything sharper. Otherwise, on bad days, it might easily occur to me that I could always go and stand in the bathroom in front of the mirror and slit my throat. Against such a contingency it's nice to have the added security of needing to go downstairs and borrow a decent knife from a neighbour.

But I understand the love for a shiny blade. One day I bought a Puma skinner for Isaiah. He didn't thank me. His face showed no surprise. He lifted the short, wide-bladed knife out of the green felt box, carefully, and five minutes later he left. He knew, and I knew, and he knew that I knew, that he had left to go down to the basement to curl up under the mechanic's workbench with his new possession, and that it would take months for him to comprehend that it was actually his.

Now it's lying in front of me, in its sheath, in his cigar box. With a wide, meticulously polished hilt of antler. There are four other things in the box. A harpoon point of the type children in Greenland find at abandoned encampments and which they know they're supposed to leave for the archaeologists but which they pick up and lug around anyway. A bear claw, and as usual I'm amazed at the hardness, weight, and sharpness of this one nail. A cassette tape, without a box but wrapped in a sheet of faded green graph paper covered with numbers. At the top it says in capital letters: NIFLHEIM.

And there is a plastic bus pass holder. The pass itself has been removed, so the holder now serves as a sleeve for a photograph. A colour photo, probably taken with an Instamatic. In the summer, and it must be in North Greenland, because the man has his jeans stuffed into a pair of *kamiks*. He's sitting on a rock in the sunshine. He's bare-chested and has a big black diver's watch on his left wrist. He's laughing at the photographer, and at that moment, with every tooth and every wrinkle enhanced by his laughter, he is Isaiah's father.

*   *   *

48

It's late. But it seems to be a time when those of us who keep the machinery of society going give it one last kick before Christmas in order to earn our bonuses – this year it's a frozen duck and a little kiss behind the ear from the director.

So I open the phone book. The Copenhagen district attorney has offices on Jens Kofods Gade.

I don't know exactly what I'm going to say to Ravn. Perhaps I just need to tell him that I haven't been duped, that I haven't given up. I need to tell him, "You know what, you little twit? I just want you to know I'm keeping an eye on you."

I'm prepared for any sort of reply.

Except for the one I get.

"There is no one by that name working here," says a cold female voice.

I sit down. There's nothing to do but breathe gently into the receiver to stall for time.

"To whom am I speaking?" she asks.

I almost hang up the phone. But there's something in her voice that makes me stay on the line. There's something parochial about her. Narrow-minded and nosy. I'm suddenly inspired by that nosiness.

"This is Smilla," I whisper, trying to put cotton candy between me and the mouthpiece. "From Smilla's Sauna Parlour. Mr Ravn had an appointment for a massage that he wanted to change . . ."

"This Ravn, is he short and thin?"

"Like a toothpick, honey."

"Wears big coats?"

"Like marquees."

I can hear her breathing harder. I'm positive her eyes are shining.

"It's the guy in the fraud division."

Now she's happy. In her own way. I've given her the fairy tale of the year to tell her bosom friends over coffee and Danish the next morning.

"You have simply saved my day," I say. "If you ever need a massage . . ."

She hangs up.

I take my tea over to the window. Denmark is a lovely country. And the police are particularly lovely. And surprising. They accompany the Royal Guard to Amalienborg Palace. They help lost ducklings cross the street. And when a little boy falls off a rooftop, first the uniformed police show up. And then the detectives. And finally the assistant district attorney for special economic crime sends his representative. How reassuring.

I pull out the jack. I've talked enough on the phone today. I've had the mechanic rig up something so I can turn off the doorbell, too.

I sit down on the sofa. First come the images from the day. I let them pass. Then come memories from when I was a child, vacillating between slight depression and mild elation; I let them go, too. Then comes peace. That's when I put on a record. Then I sit down and cry. I'm not crying about anything or anyone in particular. The life I live I created for myself, and I wouldn't want it any different. I cry because in the universe there is something as beautiful as Kremer playing the Brahms violin concerto.

9

ACCORDING TO A CERTAIN scientific theory, you can only be sure of the existence of what you yourself have experienced. So there can be very few people who are completely convinced that Godthåbsvej exists at five o'clock in the morning. At any rate, the windows are dark and empty, the streets are bare, and the number two bus is empty except for the driver and me.

There's something special about five o'clock in the morning. It's as if sleep touches bottom. The curve of the REM cycle shifts direction and begins to lift the sleeper up towards the recognition that it cannot go on like this much longer. Human beings are as vulnerable as tiny new-born infants at that hour. That's when the big wild animals hunt, and when the police show up to demand payment of overdue parking fines.

And that's when I take the number two bus to Brønshøj, where Kabbelejevej runs along the edge of Utterslev Marsh, to visit forensic medicine expert Lagermann. "Like the liquorice."

He recognized my voice on the phone before I had time to say my name and rattled off a time. "Six-thirty," he said. "Can you make it?"

So I arrive a little before six. People hold their lives together by means of the clock. If you make a slight change, something interesting nearly always happens.

Kabbelejevej is dark. The houses are dark. The marsh at the end of the street is dark. It's freezing cold, the pavement is light grey with frost, the parked cars are covered with a glittering white fur coat. I'll be curious to see the sleepy face of the forensic medicine expert.

There is one house with lights on. Not merely with lights on but illuminated, and with figures moving behind the windows, as if a grand gala ball has been going on since last night and it's not over yet. I ring the bell. Smilla, the good fairy, the last guest before dawn.

Five people open the door, all at once, and then wedge themselves tightly into the doorway. Five children, from very small to medium-sized. And inside there are more. They're dressed for a raid, with ski boots and backpacks, leaving their hands free to punch somebody. They have milky-white skin, freckles, and copper-red hair under hats with earflaps, and they exude an air of hyperactive vandalism.

Right in the middle stands a woman who has the children's skin and hair colour, with the height, shoulders, and back of an American football player. Behind her the forensic medicine expert comes into view.

He's half a metre shorter than his wife. He is fully dressed and immutably red-eyed and chirpy.

He doesn't raise an eyebrow at the sight of me. He lowers his head, and we plough our way through the shouts and through some rooms that show signs of barbarian migration, as if the wild hordes had passed this way and back again on their way home; then through a kitchen where sandwiches have been prepared for an entire battalion, and out through a door. He closes the door; it's suddenly quiet, dry, very hot, and there's a purple glow.

We're standing in a greenhouse built on to the house as a kind of winter garden. Except for a couple of narrow pathways, a little terrace with white wrought-iron furniture, and a table, the floor is covered with cacti in beds and pots. Cacti of all sizes, from one millimetre up to two metres high. In all stages of prickliness. Lit by ultraviolet grow lights.

"Dallas," he says. "Marvellous place for putting together a collection. Other than that I don't know whether I'd recommend going there; damned if I know. On a Saturday night we could have up to fifty murders. We often had to work downstairs next to the emergency room. It was set up so we could do the autopsies there. It was practical. I learned a lot about gunshot wounds and stab wounds. My wife said I never saw the children. She was right, too."

As he talks, he stares unremittingly at me.

"You're early, all right. Not that it matters to us; we're up, anyway. My wife got the kids into a kindergarten in Allerød. So that they can get out into the country a bit. Did you know the little boy?"

"I was a friend of the family. Especially him."

We sit down across from each other.

"What do you want?"

"You gave me your card."

He simply ignores this. I sense that he's a man who has seen too much to waste time beating about the bush. If he's going to reveal anything, he expects honesty.

So I tell him about Isaiah's fear of heights. About the tracks on the roof. About my visit to Professor Loyen. About Investigator Ravn.

He lights a cigar and looks at his cacti. Maybe he hasn't understood what I've been telling him. I'm not sure I understand it myself.

"We have the only real institute," he says. "The others have four people fumbling around and they can't even get money for pipettes or for the white mice they need to graft their cell tests on. We have an entire building. We have pathologists and chemists and forensic geneticists. And the whole warehouse in the basement. Teach students, too. And we've got two hundred fucking employees. We get three thousand cases a year. If you're sitting in Odense you might see forty murders. I've had fifteen hundred here in Copenhagen. And just as many in Germany and the United States. There are only about three people, at the most, in Denmark who can call themselves experts in forensic medicine. Loyen and I are two of them."

Next to his chair there is a cactus that looks like a tree stump in bloom. An explosion of purple and orange has risen out of the languid green, thorny, tree-like growth.

"The morning after the boy was brought in, we were busy. Drunk drivers and pre-Christmas parties. Every afternoon at four o'clock the damn police are standing there waiting for a report. So at eight o'clock I start on the boy. You're not squeamish, are you? We have a certain routine. First an external examination. We look for cell tissue under the fingernails, for sperm in the rectum, and then we open them up and look at the internal organs."

"Are the police present?"

"Only under unusual circumstances, for instance if there is a strong suspicion of murder. Not on this occasion. This was routine. He was wearing waterproof dungarees. I hold them up, thinking to myself that they're not what you would wear for doing the long jump. I have a little trick. The kind of thing you invent in any profession. I hold a light bulb inside the trouser legs. Helly Hansen. Sturdy stuff. I wear them myself when I work in the garden. But near the thigh there's a perforation. I examine the boy. Purely routine. There I find a hole. I should have noticed it when I was doing the surface examination, I tell you that quite frankly, but what the hell, we're all human. Then I start to frown. Because there wasn't any bleeding, and the tissue hasn't contracted. Do you know what that means?"

"No," I say.

"It means that whatever happened at that spot occurred after his heart stopped beating. Now I take a closer look at his rain gear. There's a little indentation around the hole, and the whole thing rings a bell. So I get out a biopsy needle. A kind of syringe, quite big, attached to a handle. You plunge it into the tissue to get a sample. The way geologists take core samples. Used a lot by sports physiologists over at the August Krogh Institute. And damn if it doesn't fit! The circle on the rain gear could have been caused by someone who was in a hurry, who shoved it in with a good whack."

He leans towards me. "I'll eat my old hat if someone hasn't taken a muscle biopsy from him."

"The ambulance medic?"

"I thought of that, too. It doesn't make any sense, but who the hell else could it be? So I call them up and ask them. I talk to the driver. And the medic. And to our orderlies who received the body. They all swear on a stack of Bibles that they did nothing of the kind."

"Why didn't Loyen tell me this?"

For a moment he seems about to explain. Then the intimacy between us is broken.

"Must be a goddamn coincidence," he mutters to himself.

He turns off the grow lights. We have been sitting surrounded by night on all sides. Now it's becoming noticeable that, in spite of everything, there will be some sort of daylight, after all. The house is quiet. It's sitting there gasping soundlessly, trying to catch its breath before the next Armageddon.

I take a short walk along the narrow pathways. There's something obstinate about cacti. The sun tries to hold them down, the desert wind wants to hold them down, and the drought, and the night frost. Yet they thrive. They bristle, they retreat behind a thick shell. And they don't budge a millimetre. I feel sympathetic towards them.

Lagermann reminds me of his plants. Perhaps that's why he collects cacti. Without knowing his background, I can tell that he must have had to break through several cubic metres of concrete to reach the light.

We are standing next to a bed with green sea urchins that look as if they've been out in a storm of cotton.

"*Pilocereus senilis,*" he says.

Nearby there is a row of pots with smaller green and violet plants. "Mescaline. Even the big places – the Botanical Gardens in Mexico City, say, or Cesar Mandriques's cactus museum on Lanzarote – have no more than I do. One little sliver of this stuff and you're out of it. Or so I've heard. I'm a sensible man. A rationalist. We examine the brain. Slice off a piece. Afterwards the assistant puts the skull back in place and pulls up the scalp. Can't tell the difference. I've seen thousands of brains. There's nothing mysterious about it. It's chemistry – the whole works. As long as you have enough information. Why do you think he ran up on to that roof?"

For the first time I feel like giving an honest answer. "I think someone was after him."

He shakes his head. "It's not like kids to run that far. Mine sit down and start howling. Or freeze."

The mechanic once rebuilt a bicycle for Isaiah. He hadn't learned to ride a bike in Greenland. When it was ready he took off. The mechanic found him ten kilometres away on the Old Køge Highway, on training wheels with a lunchbox on the carrier. On his way to Greenland. He was heading in that direction because Juliane had been in Hvidovre Hospital once with the DTs.

From the age of seven, when I came to Denmark for the first time, until I was thirteen and gave up, I ran away more times than I can remember. Twice I made it to Greenland, and one of those times as far as Thule. It's just a matter of attaching yourself to a family and pretending your mother is sitting five seats ahead in the plane or standing a little further back in the queue. The world is full of adventure stories about lost parrots and Persian cats and French bulldogs that miraculously find their way home to Mother and Father on Frydenholms Allé. That's nothing compared to the countless kilometres children have put behind them in search of a decent life.

This is all something I might try to explain to Lagermann. But I don't.

We're standing in the front hallway, among the boots, the rollerblade protectors, remains of provisions, and miscellaneous items left behind by the armed forces.

"What now?"

"I'm looking for the logical explanation," I say, "that you were talking about before. Until I find it, I'm not going to feel much in the Christmas spirit."

"Don't you have a job you have to go to?"

I don't answer. Suddenly he lays down all his thorns. When he speaks, he has stopped swearing.

"I've seen hundreds of relatives who have been overwhelmed by grief. Hundreds of talented private citizens who thought they could do it better than us and the police. I've looked at their ideas and their tenacity, and said to myself, I give them five minutes. But with you I'm not so sure . . ."

I attempt a smile that's supposed to reciprocate his optimism. But it's too early in the morning even for me.

Instead, I suddenly discover that I've turned towards him and blown him a kiss. From one desert plant to another.

I'm no expert on types of cars. As far as I'm concerned, you could send all the cars in the world through a compacter and shoot them out into the stratosphere and put them in orbit around Mars. Except, of course, the taxis that have to be at my disposal when I need them.

But I do have some idea what a Volvo 840 looks like. For the past few years Volvo has sponsored the Europe Tour golf tournament, and they used my father in a series of ads about men and women who had made it on the international scene. In one photo he was teeing off in front of the terrace at Søllerød Golf Club, and in another he was wearing a white lab coat, sitting in front of a tray of instruments with an expression in his eyes as if to say, If you need a block inserted, bam, into the pituitary, I'm the one to do it. In both ads he had persuaded them to take the photo from the angle that makes him look like Picasso with a toupee, and the caption was something about "those who never fail". For three months, in buses and underground stations, that ad made me think of what *I* might have added to the caption. And it stamped in my mind forever the angular, somewhat shrunken shape of a Volvo 840.

If the temperature goes up right before sunrise, the way it did today, the frost will retreat last from a car's roof and above the windscreen wipers. A banal fact that only a few people are aware of. The car on Kabbelejevej that has no frost on it, either because it was wiped off or because it has been recently driven, is a blue Volvo 840.

There are probably any number of reasons why someone might have parked here at twenty past seven in the morning. But just at the moment I can't think of any. So I walk to the car, bend over the bonnet, and peer in through the tinted front window. At first I can hardly reach it. But when I step up on the front bumper I can see the driver's seat. There sits a man, sleeping. I stand there for a few moments, but he doesn't move. Finally I step down and saunter off towards Brønshøj Torv.

It's important to sleep. I would have liked a couple more hours myself that morning. But I wouldn't have chosen to sit in a Volvo on Kabbelejevej.

"My name is Smilla Jaspersen."

"Groceries from the store?"

"No, *Smilla Jaspersen*."

It's not entirely true that phone conversations are the worst communication imaginable. Security intercoms, after all, are closer to the bottom. To fit in with the rest of the building, which is tall, silvery grey, and imposing, the intercom is made of anodized aluminium and shaped like a conch shell. Unfortunately, it has also absorbed the roar of the great oceans, which now drown out the conversation.

"The cleaning lady?"

"No," I say, "and not the pedicurist, either. I have some questions about the Cryolite Corporation."

Elsa Lübing takes a break. You have that prerogative when you're standing at the proper end of the intercom. Where it's warm, and where the buzzer to open the door is.

"This is really most inconvenient. You will have to write or come back some other time."

She hangs up.

I take a step back and look up. The building stands alone, in the Frederiksberg district, at the end of Hejrevej. It's unusually tall for Copenhagen. Elsa Lübing lives on the seventh floor. On the balcony beneath hers the ornate wrought iron is studded with flower boxes. From the directory it's apparent that these flower lovers are Mr and Mrs Schou. I give the doorbell a short and authoritative ring.

"Yes?" The voice is at least eighty years old.

"Delivery from the florist shop. I have a bouquet for Elsa Lübing upstairs, but she's not at home. Would you please let me in?"

"I'm sorry, we have strict instructions not to open the door for the other apartments."

I am enchanted by people in their eighties who still obey strict instructions.

"Mrs Schou," I say, "they are orchids. Straight off the plane from Madeira. They're suffering down here in the cold."

"That's terrible!"

"Awful," I say. "But a tiny push on that little buzzer will bring them into the warmth where they belong."

She buzzes me in.

The lift is the kind that makes you want to ride up and down seven or eight times just to enjoy the little built-in plush sofa, the polished Brazilian rosewood, the gold grating, and the sand-blasted cupids on the panes of glass, through which you can see the cable and the counterbalance sink into the depths you've left behind.

Lübing's door is shut. Downstairs Mrs Schou has opened hers to hear whether the orchid story is a cover for a quick Christmas rape.

I have a piece of paper in my pocket, among the loose money and reminders from the science department of the university library. I drop the paper through the letter box. Then Mrs Schou and I wait.

The door has a brass letter box, hand-painted nameplate, and panels of grey and white.

It swings inwards. In the doorway stands Elsa Lübing.

She takes her time looking me over.

"Well," she says finally, "you are certainly persistent."

She steps aside. I walk past her into the apartment.

She and the building share the same colouring: polished silver and fresh cream. She is quite tall, a good one metre eighty, and she is wearing a long, simple, off-white dress. She has put up her hair, but several loose strands fall like a cascade of shiny metal over her cheeks. No makeup, no perfume, and no jewellery apart from a silver cross at her throat. An angel. The kind you can trust to guard something with a flaming sword.

She looks at the letter I stuck through the door. It's the letter to Juliane about her being awarded a pension.

"I remember this letter quite well," she says.

There's a painting on the wall. From the heavens, down towards the earth, flows a stream of long-bearded patriarchs, fat little children, fruit, cornucopias, hearts, anchors, royal crowns, cannons, and a text you can read if you know Latin. This picture is the only sign of luxury. Other than that, the room has bare white walls, a parquet floor with wool carpets, an oak desk, a low, round table, a pair of high-backed chairs, a sofa, a tall bookcase, and a crucifix.

Nothing else is needed. Because there is something else here. A view that only a pilot would normally see, tolerable provided you don't suffer from vertigo. The apartment seems to consist mainly of one very large, bright room. Over by the balcony, along the entire width of the room, there is a wall of glass. From there you can see all of Frederiksberg, Bellahøj, and, in the distance, Høje Gladsaxe. The light of the winter morning comes in through the window, as white as if we were outside. On the other side there is another large window. From there you can see the spires of Copenhagen, across an endless expanse of rooftops. High above the city, Elsa Lübing and I stand as if in a bell jar, trying to size each other up.

She offers me a hanger for my coat. Spontaneously I slip off my shoes. Something about the room demands it. We sit down in two high-backed chairs.

"This time of day," she says, "I am normally at prayer."

She says this as naturally as if she were usually in the middle of the heart association's exercise programme at this time of day.

"So – unwittingly – you have chosen an inconvenient time," she says.

"I saw your name on the letter and looked you up in the phone book."

She looks at the paper again. Then she takes off her thick-lensed reading glasses.

"A tragic accident. Especially for the child. A child needs both parents. That is one of the practical reasons why marriage is sacred."

"Mr Lübing would be pleased to hear that."

If her husband is dead, I'm not insulting anyone. If he's alive, it's a tasteful compliment.

"There is no Mr Lübing," she says. "I am the bride of Jesus."

She says this in a manner both serious and coquettish, as if they had been married a few years ago and the relationship is still happy and seems to be going to last.

"But that does not mean that I do not regard love between man and woman as holy. It is, however, only one stage along the way. A stage that I have permitted myself to skip, so to speak."

She gazes at me with something that looks like subtle humour. "Like skipping a year in school."

"Or," I say, "like going directly from bookkeeper to chief accountant at the Cryolite Corporation Danmark."

When she laughs, her laughter is as resonant as a man's.

"My dear," she says, "are you married?"

"No. Never have been."

We move our chairs closer together. Two mature women who both know what it's like to live without men. She seems to be managing better than I am.

"The boy is dead," I say. "Four days ago he fell off a roof."

She gets up and goes over to the glass wall. If one could look that dignified and that good it would be a pleasure getting old. I drop the idea at the mere thought of having to grow another thirty centimetres.

"I met him once," she says. "Having met him, one understood why it is written that unless you become as little children, you will not enter into the Kingdom of Heaven. I hope his poor mother will find her way to Jesus."

"That will only happen if you can find Him right at the bottom of the bottle."

She looks at me without smiling. "He is everywhere. Even there."

In the early sixties the Christian mission in Greenland still had some of the quivering vigour of imperialism. More recent times — especially at Thule Air Base — with their containers full of porno magazines and whisky and the demand for semi-prostitution, have left us on the outskirts of religion in a vacuum of wonder. I have lost the sense of how to tackle a believing European.

"How did you meet Isaiah?"

"I used my modest influence within the corporation to increase the contact with Greenlanders. Our quarry in Saqqaq was a restricted area, just as the Øresund Cryolite Corporation's quarry in Ivittuut was. The workers were Danish. The only Greenlanders we employed were on the cleaning staff, the *kivfaks*. From the day the mine opened, a strict separation had been maintained between

Danes and Eskimos. In this situation I tried to draw attention to the commandment 'Love thy neighbour'. Every few years we would hire Eskimos in connection with geological expeditions. It was on one of these that Isaiah's father died. Even though his wife had left him and their child, he had continued to contribute to her support. When the board of directors awarded the pension, I invited her and the child to my office. That's where I saw him."

Something about the word "award" gives me an idea.

"Why was the pension granted? Was there a legal obligation?"

She hesitates for a moment. "There was probably no obligation. I cannot rule out that my advice may have had some influence."

I see yet another side of Miss Lübing. Power. Maybe that's the way it is with angels. Perhaps a certain pressure was put on Our Lord in Paradise, too.

I go over to join her at the window. Frederiksberg, the area around Genforeningspladsen, Brønshøj – the snow makes it all look like a village. Hejrevej is short and narrow. It runs into Duevej. On Duevej there are many parked cars. One of them is a blue Volvo 840. The products of the Volvo factories do get around. They would have to, in order for the company to afford sponsoring the Europe Tour. And to pay the fee my father boasts that he demanded for his photograph.

"What did Isaiah's father die of?"

"Food poisoning. You are interested in the past, Miss Jaspersen?"

At this point I have to decide whether I'm going to feed her some phoney story or take the more difficult route with the truth. On the low table is the Bible. One of the Greenlandic catechists at the Moravian mission's Sunday school was obsessed with the Dead Sea Scrolls. I remember his voice as he said, "And Jesus said: 'Thou shalt not lie.'" I let that thought be a warning.

"I think something scared him, that someone was chasing him on that roof he fell from."

Her equanimity does not waver even for a second. The last few days I've been meeting people who view with the greatest calm the things that surprise me the most.

"The Devil assumes manifold forms."

"It's one of those forms that I'm searching for."

"Vengeance is mine, saith the Lord."

"That kind of justice is too long-term for me."

"It was my understanding that for the short term we have the police."

"They've closed the case."

She stares at me.

"Tea," she says. "I haven't even offered you anything to drink."

On her way out to the kitchen she turns round in the doorway. "Do you know the parable of the talents? It's about loyalty. There is a loyalty towards the worldly as well as the heavenly. I was an official of the Cryolite Corporation for forty-five years. Do you understand?"

"Every second or third year the corporation fitted out a geological expedition to Greenland."

We're drinking tea. Out of Trankebar Royal Porcelain, from a Georg Jensen silver teapot. Elsa Lübing's taste is, upon closer observation, more elegant than it is modest.

"The expedition in the summer of '91 to Gela Alta on the west coast cost 1,870,747 kroner and 50 øre, half of which was paid in Danish kroner, half in 'Cape York dollars', the corporation's own monetary unit, named after Knud Rasmussen's trading post in Thule in 1910. That's all I can tell you."

I am sitting there rather gingerly. I have had Rohrmann on Ordrupvej sew a silk lining into my kidskin trousers. She didn't want to do it. She says that it makes the seams give. But I insisted. My life depends on small pleasures. I wanted the combination of coolness and warmth from the silk against my thighs. But the price I pay is having to sit down cautiously. It's the back-and-forth movement against the chair that strains the seams. That's my minor problem during this conversation. Miss Lübing has a bigger problem. It is written, I think, that you should not make your heart a den of thieves, and she knows that there is some pressure on her right now.

"I joined the Cryolite Corporation in '47. When manufacturer Virl said to me on 17 August, 'You will receive 240 kroner per month, free lunch, and three weeks' vacation,' I didn't say a word. But inside I was thinking that it's true, after all. Look at the birds of the air – they neither sow nor reap. So will He not watch over you? At Grøn & Witzke on Kongens Nytorv, where I came from, I had been getting 187 kroner a month."

The telephone is next to the front door. There are two things worth noting about it. The jack is pulled out, and there is no notepad, address book, or pencil. I noticed that when I came in. Now

I begin to understand what she does with the stray telephone numbers that the rest of us write on the wall, on the back of our hands, or drop into oblivion. She deposits them in her prodigious memory for numbers.

"Since then, as far as I know, no one has ever had reason to complain about the corporation's generosity or openness. And whatever complaints there were have been rectified. When I started, there were six canteens. A canteen for the workers, a canteen for office personnel, one for the skilled technicians, one for office supervisors and the chief accountant and the bookkeepers, one for the scientific staff over in the laboratory buildings, and one for the director and the board. But that was changed."

"Perhaps you made your influence felt?" I suggest.

"We had several politicians on the board. At that time Steincke, the minister for social welfare, was one of them. Since what I saw went against my conscience, I went to see him – on 17 May 1957, at four o'clock in the afternoon, on the very day I was named Chief Accountant. I said, 'I don't know anything about socialism, Mr Steincke, but I am given to understand that it has certain things in common with the conduct of the first Christian congregation. They gave what they had to the poor and lived together as brothers and sisters. How can these ideas be reconciled with six canteens, Mr Steincke?' He replied with a quote from the Bible. He said that you should render unto God what is God's, but also render unto Caesar what is Caesar's. But after a few years, there was only one canteen left."

When she pours the tea, she uses a strainer to prevent any leaves from getting into the cup. There is a piece of cotton under the teapot spout so it won't drip on the table. Something similar is taking place inside her. What's bothering her is the unaccustomed effort of filtering out what I must not glean.

"We are – were – partially state-supported. Not fifty per cent like Øresund Cryolite Corporation. But the government was represented on the board and owned one third of the shares. There was also great openness about the accounts. Copies were made of everything on old-fashioned photostats. Portions of the accounts were examined by the Audit Department, the institution which, as of 1 January 1976, became the National Bureau of Auditing. The problem was cooperation with the private sector. With the Swedish Diamond Drilling Corporation, Greenex, and, later, with Greenland's Geological Survey. The half-time and quarter-time employees. This created complex situations. There was also the hierarchy. Every company has one. There were sections of the account books that even I didn't have access to. I had my account ledgers bound in grey moleskin stamped in red. We keep them in a safe in the archives. But there was also a smaller, confidential ledger. There must have been. It had to be that way in a large corporation."

"'Keep them in the archives'. That's present tense."

"I retired two years ago. Since then I've been associated with the corporation as an accounting consultant."

I try one last time. "The accounts for the expedition in the summer of '91 – was there anything special about them?"

For a moment I imagine that I'm on the verge of getting through to her. Then the filter slides back into place.

"I'm not certain I remember."

I try one last time. Which is tactless and doomed to failure. "May I see the archive?"

She merely shakes her head.

My mother smoked a pipe made of an old shell casing. She never told a lie. But if there was some truth she wanted to conceal, she would scrape out the pipe, put the scrapings in her mouth, say *mamartoq*, "lovely", and then pretend to be unable to speak. Keeping silent is also an art.

"Wasn't it difficult", I say as I put on my shoes, "for a woman to be financially responsible for a large corporation in the fifties?"

"The Lord has been merciful."

I think to myself that in Elsa Lübing the Lord has had an effective instrument for manifesting His mercy.

"What makes you think the boy was being chased?"

"There was snow on the roof that he fell from. I saw his footprints. I have a feeling for snow."

She gazes wearily straight ahead. Suddenly her frailty is apparent.

"Snow is the symbol of inconstancy," she says. "As in the Book of Job."

I have put on my cape. I'm not very familiar with the Bible. But odd fragments from my childhood lessons occasionally get stuck on the flypaper of my brain.

"Yes," I say. "And a symbol of the light of truth. As in Revelation. 'His raiment was white as snow.'"

She looks at me anxiously as she closes the door behind me. Smilla Jaspersen. The dear guest. Spreader of light. When she leaves there is a blue sky and good spirits.

The moment I step out on to Hejrevej, the building intercom buzzes.

"Would you please come back up for a moment?"

Her voice is hoarse. But that might be due to the underwater intercom.

So I ride up in the lift again. And she receives me again in the doorway.

But nothing is as before, as Jesus says somewhere.

"I have a ritual," she says. "I open the Bible at random when I am in doubt. To get a sign. A little game between God and me, if you like."

With someone else this ritual might have seemed like one of the little functional tics that Europeans develop when they're alone too much. But not with her. She is never alone. She is married to Jesus.

"A moment ago, when you closed the door, I opened the Bible. It was the first page of Revelation. Which you mentioned. 'I come with the keys of Heaven.'"

We stand there looking at each other.

"The keys of heaven," she says. "How far will you go?"

"Try me."

For a moment something still struggles inside her.

"There's a double archive, in the basement, in the building on Strand Boulevard. In the first one are the accounts and correspondence. The principals, the bookkeepers, I myself, and sometimes the department heads all have access. The other archive is behind the first one. That's where the expedition reports are kept. Certain mineral samples. There is a whole wall full of topographical maps. A case of drilling cores, geological core samples about the size of a narwhal tusk. Technically, access is granted only with the permission of the board or the president."

She turns her back to me.

I sense the appropriate solemnity. She is about to commit one of her life's (without doubt very few) breaches of the regulations.

"Naturally I cannot mention that there is a passkey system. Or that the Abloy key over there on the board is for the main entrance."

I slowly turn my head. Behind me there are three brass hooks, three keys. One of them is an Abloy.

"The villa itself does not have a security system. The key to the

65

archives in the basement is hanging in the safe in the office. An electronic safe with a six-digit code, the date on which I became the Chief Accountant: 17–05–57. The key fits both the first and second basement rooms."

She turns around and comes over to me. It's my guess that this proximity is the closest she ever comes to touching another human being.

"Do you believe?" she asks.

"I don't know whether I believe in your God."

"That doesn't matter. You believe in a Supreme Being?"

"There are mornings when I don't even believe in myself."

She laughs for the second time that day. Then she turns round and walks over towards her panoramic view.

When she's halfway across the room, I put the key in my pocket. With the tips of my fingers I make sure that Rohrmann's silk lining hasn't given, at least in that pocket.

Then I leave. I take the stairs. If there is divine providence, one of the great questions is how directly it intervenes. Whether it is the Lord Himself for instance who saw me at 6 Hejrevej and said, "Let there be a hole," and there was a hole. In one of his own angels.

When I turn the corner on to Duevej I have a ballpoint pen in my hand. There is a licence plate I feel like jotting down on my hand. There is no need. When I reach the corner, there is no Volvo 840.

10

"WE BROUGHT NOTHING INTO THIS WORLD."

Occasionally gyrfalcons would appear when we were hunting for auks. At first they would be nothing but two tiny dots on the horizon. Then the mountain seemed to dissolve and rise up into the sky. When a million auks take off, space turns black for a moment, as if winter had returned in a flash.

My mother would shoot at the falcons. A gyrfalcon dives at a speed of two hundred kilometres per hour. She usually hit them. She shot them with a nickel-plated, small-calibre bullet. We would pick them up for her. On one occasion the bullet entered one eye and lodged in the other, as if the dead falcon were staring at us with a shiny, shrewd gaze.

A taxidermist on the base stuffed them for her. Gyrfalcons are a protected species. On the black market in Germany or the United States you can sell a baby falcon for $50,000 to be bred for hunting. No one dared to believe that my mother had violated the ban on hunting them.

She didn't sell them. She gave them away. To my father, to one of the ethnographers who sought her out because she was a female hunter, to one of the officers from the base.

The stuffed falcons were both a gruesome and a dazzling gift. She would ceremoniously present them with an apparent display of absolute generosity. Then she would drop a remark about needing a pair of tailor's shears. She hinted that she was in need of seventy-five metres of nylon rope. Or she let it be known that we children could certainly use two pairs of thermal underwear.

She got whatever she asked for. By wrapping her guest in a web of fierce, mutually obliging kindness.

This made me ashamed of her, and it made me love her. It was her response to European culture. She opened herself to it with a courtesy full of pallid premeditation. And she closed around it, encapsulating what she could use. A pair of scissors, a coil of rope, the spermatozoa that brought Moritz Jaspersen into her womb.

That's why Thule will never become a museum. The ethnographers have cast a dream of innocence over North Greenland. A dream that the Inuit will continue to be the bowlegged, drum-dancing, legend-telling, widely smiling exhibition images that the first explorers thought they were meeting south of Qaanaaq at the turn of the century. My mother gave them a dead bird. And made them buy half the store for her. She paddled a kayak that was made in the same way they were made in the seventeenth century, before the art of kayak building disappeared from North Greenland. But she used a sealed plastic container for her hunting float.

". . . and it is certain we can carry nothing out."

I can see how others are successful. But I can't find success myself.

Isaiah was on the verge of success. He could have made it. He would have been able to absorb Denmark and transform it and become both.

I had an anorak made for him out of white silk. Even the pattern had been passed down by Europeans. The painter Gitz-Johansen once gave it to my father. He had come across it in North Greenland when he was illustrating his great reference work on the birds of Greenland. I put the anorak on Isaiah, combed his hair, and then I lifted him up on to the lavatory seat. When he saw himself in the mirror, that's when it happened. The tropical fabric, the Greenlandic respect for fine clothes, the Danish joy in luxury all merged together. Maybe it also meant something that I had given it to him.

A second later he had to sneeze.

"Hold my nose!"

I held his nose.

"Why?" I asked. He usually blew his nose into the sink.

As soon as I opened my mouth, his eyes found my lips in the mirror. I often realized that he understood things even before they were expressed.

"When I'm wearing *annoraaq qaqortoq*, this fine anorak, I don't want snot on my fingers."

"The Lord gave, and the Lord hath taken away."

I try scanning the women standing around Juliane to see if any of them might be pregnant. With a boy who could be given Isaiah's name. The dead live on in their names. There were four girls who were named Ane after my mother. I've visited them many times

68

and sat and talked with them, in order to find, through the woman in front of me, a glimpse of the one who left me.

They're pulling the ropes out of the eyelets on the side of the coffin. For a brief instant my yearning comes on like madness. If only they would open the coffin for a moment and let me lie down beside his cold little body which someone has stuck a needle into, that they have opened up and photographed and cut slices out of and closed up again; if only I could just once feel his erection against my thigh, a gesture of intimated, boundless eroticism, the beating of a moth's wing against my skin, the dark insects of happiness.

It's so cold that they will have to wait to fill the grave, so when we leave, it lies open behind us. The mechanic and I walk side by side.

His name is Peter. It's less than thirteen hours since I said his name for the first time.

Sixteen hours ago it was midnight. On Kalkbrænderivej. I've bought twelve big black plastic bags, four rolls of duct tape, four tubes of superglue, and a Maglite torch. I have slit open the bags, doubled them up, and glued them together. Then stuffed them into my Louis Vuitton handbag.

I'm wearing a pair of high boots, a red turtleneck sweater, a sealskin coat from Groenlandia, and a skirt from Scottish Corner. I've learned that it's always easier to explain away things if you're nicely dressed.

What happens next to a certain degree lacks elegance.

The entire factory area is surrounded by a fence three and a half metres high, which has a single strand of barbed wire along the top. In my mind I imagine a door at the back, facing Kalkbrænderivej and the railway tracks. I've seen it before.

What I didn't see was the sign saying that Danish Watchdogs are on guard here. It might not mean much. So many signs are put up for no other reason than to maintain the proper atmosphere. So I give a trial kick at the door. Within five seconds a dog is standing at the gate. He might be a German shepherd. He looks like something that was lying in front of the door for people to wipe their feet on. That might well be the reason for the foul mood that he's in.

There are people in Greenland who have a way with dogs. My mother did. Before nylon ropes became common in the seventies, we used harnesses made of sealskin as towlines. The other dog teams chewed through their harnesses. Our dogs didn't touch theirs. My mother had forbidden it.

Then there are those born with a fear of dogs who never overcome it. I'm one of those people. So I walk back along Strand Boulevard and take a taxi home.

I don't go up to my apartment. I go to Juliane's. I take half a kilo of cod liver out of her refrigerator. Her friend at the fish market gives her free liver if it's split. In her bathroom I pour half a bottle of Rohybnol pills into my pocket. Her doctor prescribed them for her recently. She sells them. Rohybnol is marketable among junkies. She uses the money to buy her own medicine, the kind that customs officers charge duty on.

In Rink's collection there is a story from West Greenland about a bogeyman who can't fall asleep but must keep watch for all eternity. But that's because he hasn't tried Rohybnol. When you take it for the first time, half a tablet can put you into a deep coma.

Juliane lets me forage. She has given up on almost everything, including asking me questions.

"You've forgotten me!" she shouts after me.

I take a taxi back to Kalkbrænderivej. The cab starts to smell of fish.

Standing beneath the streetlamp under the viaduct facing Frihavnen, I crush the pills into the liver. Now I smell of fish, too.

This time I don't have to call the dog. He's standing there waiting, hoping that I would come back. I toss the liver over the fence. You hear so much about dogs' keen sense of smell, I'm afraid he might smell the pills. My worries are for naught. The dog sucks up the liver like a vacuum cleaner.

Then we wait, the dog and I. The dog is waiting for more liver. I am waiting to see what the pharmaceutical industry can do for sleepless animals.

A car pulls up. An estate car from Danish Watchdogs. There's no place to make yourself invisible or even discreet on Kalkbrænderivej. So I just stand there. A man wearing a uniform gets out of the car. He looks me over but can't come up with a satisfactory explanation. Solitary woman wearing a fur coat at one in the morning on the outskirts of the Østerbro district? He unlocks the gate and puts the dog on a leash. He brings him out to the pavement. The dog growls nastily at me. Suddenly his legs turn to rubber and he's about to fall over. The man stares at the dog, worried. The dog looks at him mournfully. The man opens the back of the car. The dog manages to get his front paws in, but the man has to shove him the rest of the way. He's mystified. Then he drives off. Leaving me to my own thoughts about the way Danish Watchdogs works. I come to the conclusion that they put the dogs out as a kind of random sampling, every once in a while, and for only a short time at each place. Now the dog's on his way to the next place. I hope there's something soft for him to sleep on.

Then I stick the key in the lock. But it doesn't open the gate. I can just picture it. Elsa Lübing has always arrived at work at a time when a guard opened the gate. That's why she didn't know that the entrances on the outer periphery are on a different key system.

I'll have to go over the fence. It takes a long time. I end up throwing my boots over first. A piece of sealskin gets caught in the process.

I only have to look at a map once and the landscape rises up from the paper. It's not something that I learned. Although, of course, I had to acquire a nomenclature, a system of symbols. The ridged elevation peaks on the topographical maps of the Geodesic Institute. The red and green parabolas on the military maps of the ice pack. The discus-shaped, greyish-white photographs of X-band radar. The multi-spectrum scans of LANDSAT 3. The candy-coloured sediment maps of the geologists. The red-and-blue thermal photographs. But in the truest sense it has been like learning a new alphabet. Which you then forget about as soon as you start reading. The text about ice.

There was a map of the Cryolite Corporation Danmark in the book at the Geological Institute. A cadastral map, an aerial photograph, and a floor plan. Now, standing in the grounds, I know how it all once looked.

It's a demolition site now. Dark as a cave, with white spots where the snow has been blown into drifts.

I've entered the grounds at what was once the rear of the raw cryolite hall. The foundation is still there. An abandoned football field of frozen concrete. I look for the railway tracks, and at that very moment stumble over the sleepers. The tracks of the train that brought the ore in from the company's dock. Silhouetted in the darkness is the workers' shed where the smithy, the machine shop, and the carpentry shop once were housed. A cellar full of bricks was once the basement under the canteen. The factory grounds

71

are bisected by Svanekegade. On the other side of the road is the residential district with lots of electric Christmas stars, lots of candles, and lots of daddies, mummies and little ones. And outside their windows: the two rectangular laboratory buildings which haven't been torn down yet. Is this a portrait of Denmark's relationship to its former colony? Disillusionment, resignation, and retreat? While retaining the last administrative grip: control over foreign policy, mineral rights, and military interests?

In front of me, against the light from Strand Boulevard, the building looks like a small castle.

It's an L-shaped building. The entrance is at the top of a fan-shaped, granite staircase, in the wing facing Strand Boulevard. This time the key works.

The door opens on to a small square foyer with black and white marble tiles and acoustics that reverberate, no matter how quietly you move. From here one stairway leads down to the darkness and the archives below, and another goes five steps up to the floor where Elsa Lübing, for forty-five years, has exerted her influence.

The stairs lead up to some French windows. Beyond them is one large room, which must run the full length of the wing. There are eight desks, six bay windows facing the street, filing cabinets, telephones, word processors, two photocopiers, metal shelves with red and blue plastic file folders. On one wall a map of Greenland. On a long table a coffee machine and several mugs. In the corner a big electronic safe with a little window glowing with the word CLOSED.

One desk is set apart from the others and slightly larger. It has plate glass on top. On the glass stands a little crucifix. No private office for the Chief Accountant. Merely a desk in the regular pool. Just as in the first Christian congregation.

I sit down in her high-backed chair. Trying to understand what it was like sitting here for forty-five years among the bank stationery and rubbers, with part of her consciousness elevated to a spiritual dimension, where a light burns with a strength that makes her shrug cheerfully at earthly love – which for the rest of us is a mixture of the cathedral in Nuuk and the potential for a third world war.

After a moment I get up, none the wiser.

There are Venetian blinds on the windows. The yellow light of Strand Boulevard is zebra-striped in the room. I tap in the date when she became Chief Accountant: 17–05–57.

The safe hums, and the door opens outward. There is no handle, only a wide ridge to take hold of and use your own weight on.

On the narrow metal shelves are the account books of the Cryo-lite Corporation since 1885, when it was separated from the Øresund Corporation by government charter. An average of six ledgers for each year. Hundreds of volumes in grey moleskin with red stamping. A piece of history. About the politically and economically most profitable and most important investments in Greenland.

I take out a book marked 1991 and page through it at random. It says: *salary, pension, harbour fees, labour costs, room and board, tonnage charges, laundry and dry cleaning, travel expenses, share-holders' dividends, paid to Struer Chemical Laboratory.*

Rows of keys are hanging to the right, on the wall of the safe. I find the one marked ARCHIVES.

When I push the door of the safe closed, the numbers disappear one by one, and when I leave the room and go downstairs in the dark, it once again says CLOSED.

The first room in the archives is the entire basement under one wing of the building. A low-ceilinged room with countless wooden shelves, countless quantities of ledger paper wrapped in brown paper, and filled with the air that always hovers over vast paper deserts, enervating and drained of all moisture.

The second room is at right angles to the first. It has the same kind of shelving. But it also contains archive cabinets with shallow drawers for topographical maps. A hanging file with hundreds of maps, some of them clamped on to brass rods. A locked wooden cabinet, like a coffin ten metres long. That must be where the drilling cores sleep.

The room has two windows high on the wall facing Strand Boulevard, and four towards the factory grounds. This is where my preparations with the plastic bags come in. I intend to cover the windows so I can turn on a light.

There are girls who paint their own attractive attic apartments themselves. Re-upholster the furniture. Sandblast the façade. I have always called the professionals in. Or left it until next year.

These windows are large, with iron bars on the inside. It takes me forty-five minutes to drape all six.

When I'm finished I don't dare turn on the overhead lights, after all, but make do with my torch.

Merciless order ought to prevail in archives. They are quite simply the crystallization of a wish to put the past in order. So that busy, energetic young people can come waltzing in, select a specific

73

case, a specific core sample, and waltz out again with precisely that segment of the past.

These archives, however, leave something to be desired. There are no labels on the shelves. There are no numbers, dates, or letters on the spines of the filed material. And when I select a couple at random, I get: *Coal petrographic analyses on seams from Atâ (low group profiles), Nûgssuaq, West Greenland*, and *On the use of processed raw cryolite in the production of electric light bulbs*, and *Demarcation of borders at the land parcelling of 1862*.

I go upstairs and make a phone call. It always feels wrong to call someone on the phone. It feels especially wrong to call from the scene of the crime. As if I had obtained a direct line to police headquarters to turn myself in.

"This is Elsa Lübing."

"I'm standing here amid mountains of papers trying to remember where it says something about the fact that even the chosen ones risk being led astray."

First she hesitates, then she laughs.

"In St Matthew. But perhaps more appropriate on this occasion would be in Mark, where Jesus says: 'Ye do err, not knowing the scriptures, nor the power of God.'"

We giggle together on the phone.

"I disavow any responsibility," she says. "I've asked for a clean up and cataloguing for forty-five years."

"I'm so glad there's something you didn't manage to get done."

She's silent on the phone.

"Where?" I ask.

"There are two shelves above the bench – the long wooden case. That's where the expedition reports are. Arranged alphabetically according to the minerals they were looking for. The volumes closest to the window are the trips that had both a geological and a historical purpose. The one you're looking for should be one of the last ones."

She's about to hang up.

"Miss Lübing," I say.

"Yes?"

"Were you ever off sick?"

"The Lord has watched over me."

"I thought so," I say. "I could tell."

Then we hang up.

It takes me less than two minutes to find the report. It's in a black ring binder. There are forty pages, numbered in the lower right-hand corner.

It's just the right size to stuff into my handbag. Afterwards I have to remove the plastic blackout curtains, and I'll disappear down Kalkbrænderivej without a trace, the same way I came.

I can't restrain my curiosity. I take the report over to the far corner of the room and sit down on the floor, leaning against a bookcase. It gives under my weight. It's a flimsy, wooden bookcase. They never thought that the archives would get so big. That Greenland would be so surprisingly inexhaustible. They've simply filled up the shelves. The traces of time on a flimsy wooden skeleton.

"The geologic expedition of the Cryolite Corporation Danmark to Gela Alta, July through August 1991", it says on the title page. Then follow twenty closely typed pages of expedition report. I skim the first pages, which start off by describing the objective of the expedition: "To investigate the deposits of granular ruby crystals on the Barren Glacier on Gela Alta". The text also lists the five European members of the expedition. Among others, a professor of Arctic ethnology, Dr Andreas Fine Licht, Ph.D. The name rings a bell somewhere deep inside me. But when I try to listen, it stops. I assume that his presence explains why it says at the bottom that the expedition is supported by the Institute for Arctic Ethnology.

Next comes a report with both an English and a Danish section. I page through this part, too. It concerns a rescue operation from Holsteinsborg to Barren Glacier by helicopter. The helicopter wasn't able to land very close because of the risk of avalanche due to the noise from the engine. That's why it turned round and they sent a Cherokee Six–3000 instead, whatever that is, but it says that it landed on the water, with a pilot, navigator, doctor, and nurse on board. There's a brief report from the rescue team and a doctor's certificate from the hospital. There were five fatalities. One Finn and four Eskimos. One of the Eskimos was named Norsaq Christiansen.

There is a twenty-page appendix. A summary of the mineralogical samples brought back. The logs. A series of black-and-white aerial photos of a glacier, splitting and floating around a bright, fractured conical cliff.

A plastic folder contains copies of about twenty letters, all concerning transport of the bodies.

The whole thing looks clean and above board. It's tragic, and yet no more than an accident. Nothing to explain why a little boy, two years later, falls off a rooftop in Copenhagen. It occurs to me that I've been seeing ghosts. That I've gone astray. That it's all a figment of my imagination.

For the first time I notice how burdened the room is with the past. With hundreds of days, hundreds of numbers, hundreds of people, who every day, year in and year out, have eaten their two sandwiches in the canteen and shared a beer with Amanda, but never more than one except at Christmas, when the laboratory spikes a twenty-five-litre carboy of 96-proof disinfecting alcohol with cumin for the Christmas party. The archives are shouting at me that they have been content. And that's also what it said in the book at the library, and what Elsa Lübing said: "We were content. It was a good place to work."

As so often before, I feel a yearning to participate, to take part. In Thule and Siorapaluk no one ever asked people what they did, because everybody was a hunter, everybody had work to do. In Denmark, if you are a wage earner, it lends meaning and fulfilment to your life to know that now we're rolling up our sleeves and putting pens behind our ears and pulling up our bootstraps and going to work. And when you're off, you watch TV or visit friends or play badminton or take an evening class in computers. You don't live out your life in a basement beneath Strand Boulevard in the middle of the night at Christmastime.

This is not the first or the last time that I have had these thoughts. What is it that makes us seek out the plunge into depression?

As I close the report, I have an idea. I open it again and flick through to the medical report. There I see something. And then I know that it's been worth all the trouble.

I've seen girlfriends in Greenland who, discovering that they're pregnant, suddenly take better care of themselves than ever before. That's the feeling that passes over me now. From now on I have to watch out for myself.

The traffic has stopped. I don't wear a watch, but it must be about three a.m. I switch off my torch.

The building is quiet. In the silence there is suddenly a sound that is wrong. It's too close to be coming from the street. But faint, like a whisper. From where I'm sitting, the doorway into the first small room is a faintly lit grey rectangle. One moment it's visible, the next it's not. Someone has stepped into the room, someone who is blocking the light with his body.

By moving my head slightly I can follow his movement along the shelves. I take off my boots. They're no good for running. I stand up. By moving my head slightly I can place the figure inside the faintly lit frame of the doorway.

We think there are limits to the dimensions of fear. Until we encounter the unknown. Terror we can all feel in boundless amounts.

I take hold of one of the bookcases and topple it towards him. Just as it picks up speed, the first volumes fall out. That warns him, and he puts up his hands and tries to stop the bookcase. First it sounds like the bones of his forearms are snapping. Then what sounds like fifteen tons of books fall on to the floor. He can't let go of the bookcase. But it's resting very heavily on him. And slowly his legs begin to buckle.

The misconception that violence always favours the physically strong has spread to a large segment of the population. It's not correct. The results of a fight are a matter of speed in the first few metres. When I moved out to Skovgårds School after six months at Rugmarkens School, I encountered for the first time the classic Danish persecution of those who are different. In the school we came from, we were all foreigners and in the same boat. In my new class I was the only one with black hair and broken Danish. There was one boy in particular, from one of the older classes, who was really quite brutal. I found out where he lived. Then I got up early and waited for him where he crossed Skovshovedvej. He was fifteen kilos heavier than I was. He didn't have a chance. He never got the couple of minutes that he needed to work himself into a trance. I hit him right in the face and broke his nose. I kicked him on one kneecap and then on the other, to bring him down to a more operational height. It took twelve stitches to put his nasal septum back in place. No one ever really believed that it could have been me.

This time I don't stand there picking my nose either, waiting for Christmas to arrive. From the wall I grab one of the brass rods with fifty topographical maps attached and hit him as hard as I can on the back of the neck.

He drops at once. The bookcase comes down on top of him. I wait for a moment. To see whether he has brought any friends with him. Or a little dog. But there is no sound except his breathing from under thirty metres of bookcase.

I shine my torch on his face. A great deal of dust has settled on him. The blow has split the edge of one ear.

He's wearing black tracksuit bottoms, a dark blue sweater, a black wool cap, dark blue plimsolls, and a guilty conscience. It's the mechanic.

"Clumsy Peter," I say. "What's the matter, did you trip?"

He can't answer because of the bookcase. I try to push it aside, but it won't budge.

I have to give up on professional precautions and turn on the light. I start shovelling papers, books, folders, reports, and book-ends made of solid steel away from the bookcase. I have to clear away three metres. It takes fifteen minutes. Then I can lift it two centimetres, and he crawls out on his own. Over to the wall, where he sits down, feeling his skull.

Not until then do my legs start to shake.

"My vision is blurry," he says. "I think I have a c-concussion."

"We can always hope so," I say.

It is fifteen minutes more before he can stand. And even then he's like Bambi on the ice. It takes another half-hour to get the bookcase upright. We have to take off all the papers first before we can lift it and then put them all back. It gets so hot that I have to take off my skirt and work in my tights. He walks around bare-foot and bare-chested and gets frequent hot flashes and dizzy spells and has to rest. Shock and unanswered questions hang in the air along with enough dust to fill a sandbox.

"It smells like fish in here, Smilla."

"Cod liver," I say. "It's supposed to be so healthy."

He watches in silence as I open the electronic safe and hang the key in its place. Then we lock up after us. He leads me over to a gate in the fence facing Svanekegade. It's open. After we go through, he bends over the lock and it clicks shut.

His car is parked on the next street. I have to support him with one hand. In the other I'm carrying a dustbin bag full of other dustbin bags. A police car passes us slowly, but without stopping. They see so much going on in the streets at this time of year. People should be allowed to amuse themselves in whatever manner they choose.

He tells me that he's trying to get his car accepted by a classic car museum. It's a '61 Morris 1000, he says. With red leather seats and wooden top and instrument panel.

"I can't drive," he says.

"I don't have a licence."

"Have you ever driven before?"

"Snow-cats on the ice cap."

But he isn't going to subject his Morris to that. So he drives. There's barely room for his large body behind the wheel. The top is full of holes and we're freezing. I wish that he had succeeded in getting it into a museum a long time ago.

The temperature has fallen from just below freezing to hard frost, and on our way home it starts to snow. With *qanik*, fine-grained powder snow.

The most dangerous kind of avalanches are powder snow avalanches. They're set off by extremely small energy disturbances, such as a loud noise. They have a very small mass, but they move at two hundred kilometres per hour, and they leave behind them a deadly vacuum. There are people who have had their lungs sucked out of their bodies by powder snow avalanches.

In miniature form, these are the kind of avalanche that started on the steep, slippery roof that Isaiah fell from and which I now force myself to look up at. One of the things you can learn from snow is the way great forces and catastrophes can always be found in miniature form in daily life. Not one day of my adult life has passed that I haven't been amazed at how poorly Danes and Greenlanders understand each other. It's worse for Greenlanders, of course. It's not healthy for the tightrope walker to be misunderstood by the person who's holding the rope. And in this century the Inuit's life has been a tightrope dance on a cord fastened at one end to the world's least hospitable land with the world's most severe and fluctuating climate, and fastened at the other end to the Danish colonial administration.

That's the big picture. The little everyday picture is that I have lived on the floor above the mechanic for a year and a half, have spoken to him countless times, and he has fixed my doorbell and repaired my bicycle, and I have helped him check a letter to the housing authorities for spelling mistakes. There were about twenty misspelled words out of a total of twenty-eight. He's dyslexic.

We ought to take a shower and rinse off the dust and the blood and the cod liver. But we are bound together by what has happened. So we both go up to his apartment. Where I've never been before.

Order reigns in the living room. The furniture is made of sanded, lye-treated blond wood, with cushions and upholstery of woollen horse blankets. There are candlesticks with candles, a bookcase with books, a bulletin board with photographs and drawings by the children of friends. "To Big Peter from Mara, five years old". There are rose bushes in large porcelain pots, and they have red blossoms, and it looks as if someone waters them and talks to them and promises them that they will never be sent on holiday to my place, where, for some strange reason, the climate is bad for green plants.

"C-coffee?"

Coffee is poison. And yet I suddenly have the urge to roll in the mud and I say, "Yes, please."

I stand in the doorway and watch while he makes it. The kitchen is completely white. He takes up his position in the middle, the way a badminton player does on the court, so he has to move as little as possible. He has a small electric grinder. First he grinds a lot of light-coloured beans and then some which are tiny, almost black, and shiny as glass. He mixes them in a little metal funnel which he attaches to an espresso machine, which he places on a gas hob.

People acquire bad coffee habits in Greenland. I pour hot milk right on to the Nescafé. I'm not above dissolving the powder in water straight from the hot-water tap.

He pours one-part whipping cream and two-parts whole milk into two tall glasses with handles.

When he draws out the coffee from the machine, it's thick and black like crude oil. Then he froths the milk with the steam nozzle and divides the coffee between the two glasses.

We take it to the sofa. I do appreciate it when someone serves me something good. In the tall glasses the drink is dark as an old oak tree and has an overwhelming, almost perfumed tropical scent.

"I was following you," he says.

The glass is scorching hot. The coffee is scalding. Normally hot drinks lose heat when they're poured. But in this case the steam nozzle has heated up the glass to 100 °C along with the milk.

"The door's open. So I go in. I had no idea that you'd be s-sitting in the d-dark waiting."

I cautiously sip at the rim. The drink is so strong that it makes my eyes water and I can suddenly feel my heart.

"I'd been thinking about what you said on the roof. About the footprints."

His stammer is barely noticeable now. Sometimes it vanishes altogether.

"We were friends, you know. He was so young. But we were still friends . . . We don't talk much. But we have fun. Damn, we really have fun. He m-makes faces. He puts his head in his hands. And he raises it, and he looks like a sick old monkey. He hides it again. He raises it. He looks like a rabbit. Again and he looks like Frankenstein's monster. I'm on the floor and finally I have to tell him to stop it. I give him a block of wood and a chisel. A knife and a piece of soapstone. He sits there swaying and rumbling like a little bear. Every so often he says something. But it's in Greenlandic. Talking to himself. So we sit and work. Independently but together. I think it's fine he can be such a good person, with a mother like that."

He pauses for a long time, hoping I'll take over. But I don't come to his rescue. We both know that I'm the one who deserves an explanation.

"So one night we're sitting there as usual. Then Petersen the caretaker comes in. He keeps his wine carboys under the stairs next to the furnace. Comes in to get his apricot wine. He's not usually there that time of day. So there he is with his deep voice and his wooden clogs. And then I happen to look down at the boy. And he's sitting all huddled up. Like an animal. With the knife you gave him in his hand. Shaking all over. Looking ferocious. Even after he realized it was only Petersen, he still kept shaking. I take him on my lap. For the first time. I talk to him. He doesn't want to go home. I b-bring him up here. Put him on the sofa. I think about calling you up, but what would I say? We don't know each other very well. He sleeps here. I stay up, sitting next to the sofa. Every fifteen minutes he bolts up like a spring, shaking and crying."

He's not a talker. In the last five minutes he has said more to me than in the past year and a half. He has so far relaxed his guard that I can't look him in the eye; I stare down at my coffee. A film of tiny, clear bubbles has formed on it, catching the light and breaking it up into red and purple.

"From that day on, I have the feeling that he's afraid of something. What you said about the footprints keeps on going through my mind. So I sort of keep my eye on you. You and the Baron understand . . . understood each other."

Isaiah arrived in Denmark a month before I moved in. Juliane had given him a pair of patent-leather shoes. Patent-leather shoes are considered stylish in Greenland. They couldn't get a pair wide enough for his fan-shaped feet. But Juliane managed to find a pair with square enough toes. After that, the mechanic called Isaiah "the Baron". When a petname sticks, it's because it captures some deeper truth. In this case, it was Isaiah's dignity. Which had something to do with the fact that he was so self-sufficient. That there was so little he needed from the world to be happy.

"By chance I see you go up to Juliane's apartment and leave again. I sneak after you in the Morris. Watch you feed the dog. See you climb over. I open the other gate."

That's how it all fits together. He hears something, he catches a little glimpse, he follows somebody, he opens a gate, gets bashed in the head, and we sit here. No mysteries, nothing new or disturbing under the sun.

He gives me a crooked smile. I smile back. We sit there drinking coffee and smiling at each other. We know that I know he's lying.

I tell him about Elsa Lübing. About the Cryolite Corporation Danmark. About the report lying in front of us on the table in a plastic bag.

I tell him about Ravn. Who doesn't exactly work where he works, but somewhere else instead.

He sits there looking down as I talk. His head bent, motionless.

It's hidden, lying out there on the edge of consciousness. But we both sense that we are participating in a barter. That, with profound, mutual suspicion, we are trading information that we have to reveal in order to get some in return.

"Then there's the l-lawyer."

Outside, above the harbour, a light appears, as if it had been sleeping in the canals, under the bridges, and is now hesitantly rising up on to the ice, which grows brighter. In Thule the light returned in February. For weeks ahead of time we could see the sun while it was still far beneath the mountains and we were living in darkness; its rays fell on Pearl Island, hundreds of miles out to sea, making it glow like a shard of rose mother-of-pearl. I was positive, no matter what the adults said, that the sun had been hibernating in the sea and was now waking up.

"It all started when I noticed the car, a red BMW, on Strand Boulevard," he says.

"Yes?" I say. It seems to me that the cars on Strand Boulevard change every day.

"Once a month. He picks up the Baron. When he got home, the Baron was impossible to talk to."

"I see." You have to give slow people all the time in the world.

"Then one day I open the car – I have a tool with me – and look in the glove compartment. Belongs to a lawyer. Name of Ving."

"You might have been looking in the wrong car."

"Flowers. It's like flowers. When you're a g-gardener. I see a car once or twice and I remember it. The way you do with snow. The way you were on the roof."

"Maybe I was mistaken."

He shakes his head. "I watched you and the Baron play that jumping game."

A large part of my childhood was spent playing that game. I often still play it in my sleep. You jump across an untouched expanse of snow. The others wait with their backs turned. Afterwards – on the basis of the footprints – you have to reconstruct the way the first person jumped. Isaiah and I played that game. I often went with him to the kindergarten. Sometimes we arrived an hour and a half late. I got into trouble. They warned me that a kindergarten couldn't function if the children came drifting in late in the day. But we were happy.

"He could leap like a flea," says the mechanic, daydreaming. "He was sly, you see. He turns halfway around in the air and lands on one foot. He walks back in his own footprints."

He looks at me, shaking his head. "But you guessed right every time."

"How long were they gone?"

The jackhammers on Knippels Bridge. The traffic starting up. The seagulls. The distant bass sound, actually more like a deep vibration, of the first hydrofoil to Sweden. The short toots on the horn of the Bornholm ferry as it turns in front of Amalienborg Palace. It's almost morning.

"Maybe several hours. But a different car brought him home. A taxi. He always came back alone in a taxi."

He makes us an omelette while I stand in the doorway telling him about the Institute of Forensic Medicine. About Professor Loyen. About Lagermann. About the trace of something that might be a muscle biopsy, taken from a child. After he fell.

He slices onions and tomatoes, sautés them in butter, whips the egg whites until they're stiff, blends in the yolks, and fries the whole thing on both sides. He takes the pan over to the table. We drink milk and eat slices of a moist black rye bread which smells of tar.

We eat in silence. Whenever I eat with strangers – like now – or if I'm very hungry – like now – I am reminded of the ritual significance of meals. That I remember associating the unity of the solemnity of companionship with great taste experiences in my childhood. The pink, slightly frothy whale blubber eaten from a communal platter. The feeling that practically everything in life is meant to be shared.

I get up.

He's standing in the door as if to block my way.

I think about the inadequacies of what he has told me today.

He steps aside. I walk past. With my boots and my fur coat in my hand.

"I'll leave part of the report. It'll be good practice for your dyslexia."

There's a look of mischief in his eyes. "Smilla. Why is it that an elegant and petite girl like you has such a rough voice?"

"I'm sorry," I say, "if I give the impression that it's only my mouth that's rough. I do my best to be rough all over."

Then I close the door.

11

I SLEPT ALL MORNING and got up a little late, so I only have an hour and a half to take a shower, get dressed, and put on my funeral makeup, which is far too little time, as anyone who has tried to make the best of herself will confirm. That's why I'm feeling flustered when we arrive at the chapel, and after the service I haven't improved. As I'm walking along beside the mechanic, I feel as if someone had unscrewed my lid and plunged a big bottle brush up and down inside.

Something warm falls over my shoulders. He has taken off his coat and put it around me. It reaches all the way down to my feet.

We stop and look back towards the grave and our own footprints. His are big, run over at the heels. Apparently he's slightly bowlegged, though it's hardly visible. Tiny perforations from my high heels. They look rather like deer tracks. A slanted, downward-sloping movement, and in the bottom of the track black marks where the hooves have pierced through the layer of snow to the ground.

The women walk past us. I see only their boots and shoes. Three of them are holding Juliane up; the tips of her shoes drag across the snow. Next to the pastor's robes there is a pair of black boots made of embroidered leather. Above the gate out to the driveway with high trees on both sides there is a streetlamp. When I look up, the woman lifts her head and tosses it so that her long hair flies to one side in the darkness and her face catches the light, a white face with big eyes, like dark water amid the pallor. She's holding the pastor by the arm and talking to him earnestly. Something about those two figures next to each other freezes the image and makes it stick in my mind.

"Miss Jaspersen."

It's Ravn. With friends. Two men. Wearing coats as big as his, but who can fill them out. Underneath they're wearing blue suits and white shirts and ties, and sunglasses so that the winter dusk at four o'clock in the afternoon won't hurt their eyes.

"I'd like to have a word with you."

"At the office of the fraud division? About my investments?"

He listens without reacting. He has a face which, over the years, has seen so much that nothing really leaves a mark on it any more. He motions towards his car.

"I'm not sure I feel like it right now."

He doesn't budge an inch. But his two lodge brothers ooze imperceptibly closer.

"Smilla, if you don't f-feel like it, I don't think you should go."

It's the mechanic. He's blocking the men's path.

When animals – and almost all normal people – face a physical threat, their bodies assume a certain rigidity. Physiologically it's not efficient, but it's the general rule. Polar bears are the exception. They can lie in wait, perfectly relaxed, for two hours without once relaxing the maximum readiness of their muscles. Now I realize that the mechanic is also an exception. His posture is almost loose. But there is a latent menace in his focus on the men in front of him which reminds me once again how little I know about him.

It has no detectable effect on Ravn. But it makes the two men in blue suits take a step back, as they unbutton their jackets. It could be that they're too hot. It could be that they share a nervous tic. It could also be that they each have a truncheon with a lead core.

"Will I be driven home?"

"Right to your door."

In the car I sit in the back with Ravn. At one point I lean forward and take off the driver's sunglasses.

"I'm silent as the grave, my little tit," I say. "My lips are sealed with seven seals. Ravn won't hear from me that you were sleeping on the job. At seven-thirty in the morning on Kabbelejevej."

At the Police Headquarters we drive in between the red brick buildings where the Division of Motor Vehicles has its offices. We're heading for a low red barracks facing the harbour.

There's no sign on the building. We meet no one. There's no tapping of typewriters. There are no nameplates on the doors. There is simply peace and quiet. Like in a reading room. Or in the morgue beneath the Institute of Forensic Medicine.

The two blue choirboys have vanished. We enter a dark office. There are Venetian blinds on the windows. Through the blinds you can see the electric lights, the docks, the water, the Islands Brygge.

It's a room that must get a lot of light in the daytime. There's nothing much else in it. Nothing on the walls. Nothing on the tables. Nothing on the windowsills.

Ravn turns on the light. In the corner a man is sitting on a chair. He has been sitting and waiting in the dark. Sinewy, with close-cropped hair, almost plush black, distant blue eyes, and a harsh mouth. He is meticulously dressed.

Ravn sits down behind the desk.

"Smilla Jaspersen," he introduces me. "Captain Telling."

With my back to the windows I am facing the two men.

There are no cigarettes, no coffee in plastic cups, no tape recorder, and no bare light bulb, no mood of interrogation. There is only an atmosphere of waiting.

In this atmosphere I withdraw into myself.

Into the silence steps a woman carrying a tray with tea, sugar, milk, and lemon slices, all on white porcelain. Afterwards the abandoned building swallows her up and she is gone. Ravn pours the tea.

He takes a folder out of a drawer. It's pink. He reads it slowly. As if he wants to try – again – to experience it for the first time.

"Smilla Qaavigaaq Jaspersen. Born 16 June 1956, in Qaanaaq. Parents: Ane Qaavigaaq, hunter, and Dr Jørgen Moritz Jaspersen, physician. Attended primary school in Greenland and Copenhagen. Graduated from Birkerød High School, 1976. Courses at the H. C. Ørsted Institute and the Geographical Institute in Copenhagen. Glacial morphology, statistics, and fundamental problems of mathematics. Travels in West Greenland and Thule in '75, '76, and '77. Putting out supplies in advance of Danish and French expeditions to North Greenland in '78, '79, and '80. In 1982 employed by the Geodetic Institute. From '82 to '85 scientific participant in expeditions to the ice cap, the Arctic Ocean, and Arctic North America. Various references are attached. One from Major Guldbrandsen, who led the Sirius Patrol. It dates back to '79. He complains that you won't drive a dog team. Are you afraid of dogs?"

"Just cautious."

"But he adds that he would recommend any civilian expedition to take you along as navigator, even if they have to carry you on their backs. Then there are your scientific articles. A dozen or so, several published abroad. With titles that go over the heads of Captain Telling and me. 'Statistics on Glacial Graphology'. 'Mathematical Models for Brine Drainage from Sea Water Ice'. And a compendium for students that you once wrote: *Main Characteristics of the Glacial Morphology of North Greenland*."

He closes the report.

"There are various other references. From teachers. From colleagues at the US Army's Coldwater Laboratory in some place called Pylot Island. All of them state unanimously that anybody needing to know anything about ice will benefit by consulting Smilla Jaspersen."

Ravn takes off his coat. Beneath it he's as thin as a pipe cleaner. I take off my shoes and pull up my legs to sit cross-legged on the chair so I can massage my toes. They're numb from the cold, and there are still clumps of ice in my stockings.

"This information is largely identical with the *curriculum vitae* you submitted when you applied for a visa to North Greenland in connection with the Norwegian Arctic Institute's expedition to tag polar bears. We've sniffed around a little. The information is absolutely correct. On this basis, I think we have to assume that we are dealing with a very independent young woman who has unusual resources which she has administered with ambition and talent. Don't you agree that's the conclusion one ought to arrive at?"

"You can arrive at any conclusion you like," I say.

"I've also obtained several other pieces of information, however."

This folder is quite thin, and dark green.

"This is largely identical with the report that Captain Telling and his office had at their disposal when they stamped DENIED on your last application for a visa to North Greenland. It starts off by summarizing several private matters. Your mother reported missing on 12 June 1963, while hunting. Presumed dead. Your brother commits suicide in September of '81 in Upernavik. Parents married 1956, divorced 1958. Custody transferred to the father after the mother's death. Complaint by the mother's brother denied by the Ministry of Justice in May 1964. To Denmark in September 1963. Reported missing, searched for, and found by the police six times between '63 and '71, twice in Greenland.

"Danish grade school for immigrants, 1963. Skovgårds School in Charlottenlund, '64–'65. Expelled. Stenhøj Boarding School in Humlebæk '65–'67. Expelled. Then come brief terms at smaller private schools. Graduated from junior school after private instruction at home. Then high school. Re-sat the senior year. High-school diploma 1976 after private tuition. Admitted to Copenhagen University. Signed out in 1984 without a degree. And then there's the political activity. Arrested several times during the occupation of the Ministry of the Environment by the Council of Young Greenlanders. Active in the founding of IA after the CYG split."

He gives Captain Telling an inquisitive look.

"*Inuit Ataqatigiit.* 'Those who will succeed.' Aggressive Marxism." This is the first time the captain has spoken.

"Leaves the party the same year because of numerous disagreements. Since then unaffiliated. Then there are some minor infractions. Three unresolved cases dealing with breaches of Canadian territorial law on Peary Sound. Why?"

"I was tagging polar bears. Bears can't read maps, so they don't respect national boundaries."

"Several pedestrian/bicycle offences. A verdict of defamation of character in connection with an article entitled 'Ice Research and the Profit Motive in Denmark in Connection with the Exploitation of Oil Resources in the Arctic Ocean'. As a result excluded from the Danish Glaciology Society."

He looks up.

"Is there any institution you *haven't* been thrown out of, Miss Jaspersen?"

"As far as I know," I say, "I'm still listed in the national registry of citizens."

"In addition, we have also had a look over the shoulders of the tax authorities and public administration. A little comes in from your articles, sporadic jobs, and social security. But it doesn't seem to match your expenses. We wonder if you have a sponsor. How's your relationship with your father?"

"Warm and respectful."

"That might explain a lot. Captain Telling has had a look at his tax returns, you see."

For me, it's no news that they know all this. Ever since the establishment of Thule Air Base, there has been a limit to how many civilian passengers each aircraft could take to Greenland. To give the intelligence service time to investigate whether everybody had been confirmed in the Lutheran Church, came of good family, and had been ideologically immunized against the red fever from the East. What's astonishing is that they're telling me what they know.

"This information presents a more complicated picture. It paints a portrait of a woman who has never finished a course of study. Who is unemployed. Who has no family. Who has stirred up conflict wherever she has been. Who has never been able to fit in. Who is aggressive. And who vacillates around political extremes. And yet you have managed to take part in nine expeditions in twelve years. I don't know Greenland, but I imagine that if you're frustrated with your life, it would be easier to hide this fact on the ice cap."

I make no comment. But I file it in the black book under his name.

"On these expeditions you have served as navigator. Each time they have made use of confidential map material, satellite and radar photos, and meteorological observations supplied by the military. Nine times in the course of the last twelve years you have signed a declaration of secrecy and confidentiality. All of which we have copies of."

I'm beginning to have an idea where he's heading, what the main point is.

"In a little country like ours, you are a sensitive issue, Miss Jaspersen. You have seen and heard a lot. Which automatically happens when you're allowed into North Greenland. But you have a past and a character which would have ensured that you would not have been permitted to see or hear anything if you had found yourself in any other place inside Danish territory."

The circulation is returning to my feet.

"Anyone with even an ounce of common sense would keep a very low profile in your position."

"Is it my clothes you don't like?"

"What we don't like is your fruitless or outright damaging attempts to meddle in the investigation of the case, which I already promised you I would look into."

Of course this is the direction we've been heading, all along.

"Yes," I say, "I remember what you promised me. That was when you were working for the district attorney of Copenhagen."

"Miss Smilla," he says quite gently, "we can throw you in the clink at any time. Do you understand me? We can give you solitary confinement, an isolation cell whenever we feel like it. No judge would hesitate, after he saw your dossier."

From the start, this meeting has been about credibility. He wanted to show me what he's capable of. That he can obtain information that I sent to Greenland's government and to the military. That he has been able to follow my movements. That he has access to any archives. And that at any time he can summon an intelligence officer at six o'clock in the evening at Christmastime. And he has done all this so I won't have a shadow of a doubt that he can lock me up at any moment.

He has succeeded. Now I know what he can do. That he will have his way. Because underneath his threat lies a deeper layer of knowledge. Which he now drags into the light.

"Imprisonment", he says slowly, "in a little soundproof room with no windows is, I've been told, particularly uncomfortable for somebody who grew up in Greenland."

There is no sadism in him. Merely a precise and perhaps faintly melancholy appreciation of the instruments at his disposal.

There are no prisons in Greenland. The greatest difference in the administration of the law in Copenhagen and in Nuuk is that in Greenland the punishment is more often a fine for offences which in Denmark would have resulted in imprisonment. The Greenlandic hell is not the European rocky landscape with pools of sulphur. The Greenlandic hell is the locked room. As I remember my childhood it seemed as though we were never indoors. Living in the same place for a long time was unthinkable for my mother. I feel the same way about my spatial freedom as I've noticed men feel about their testicles. I cradle it like a baby, and worship it as a goddess.

In my investigation of Isaiah's death, I have reached the end of the road.

We stand up. We haven't touched our cups. The tea has grown cold.

THE CITY

2

YOU CAN TRY TO COVER UP depression in various ways. You can listen to Bach's compositions for the organ in Our Saviour's Church. You can arrange a line of good cheer in powder form on a pocket mirror with a razor blade and ingest it with a straw. You can call for help. For instance, by telephone, so that you know who's listening.

That's the European method. Hoping to work your way out of problems through action.

I take the Greenlandic way. It consists of walking into yourself in the dark mood. Putting your defeat under a microscope and dwelling on the sight.

When things are really bad – like now – I picture a black tunnel in front of me. I go up to it. I strip off my nice clothes, my under-wear, my hard hat, my Danish passport, and then I walk into the dark.

I *know* that a train is coming. A lead-lined diesel transporting strontium-90. I go to meet it.

This I can do because I'm thirty-seven years old. I *know* that inside the tunnel, underneath the wheels, down between the sleep-ers, there is a little spot of light.

It's the morning of Christmas Eve. For several days I've been gradually withdrawing from the world. Now I'm preparing for the final descent. Which has to come. Because I have allowed myself to be cowed by Ravn. Because I am failing Isaiah. Because I can't get my father out of my thoughts. Because I don't know what to say to the mechanic. Because it feels as if I'm never going to get any smarter.

I've prepared myself by not eating breakfast. That expedites the confrontation. I've locked the door. I sit down in the big chair. And invoke the bad mood: Here sits Smilla. Starving. In debt. The morning of Christmas Eve. While other people have their families, their sweethearts, their blue-eared starlings. While other people have each other.

It proves effective. I'm already standing in front of the tunnel. Ageing. A failure. Abandoned.

The doorbell rings. It's the mechanic. I can tell by the way he rings the bell. Cautiously, tentatively, as if the bell were screwed right into the skull of an old woman he doesn't want to disturb. I haven't seen him since the funeral. Haven't wanted to think about him.

I go out and disconnect the mechanism. I sit down again.

Internally I begin to evoke the images from the second time I ran away and Moritz came to get me in Thule. We were standing on the uncovered cement apron that you walk on for the last twenty metres out to the plane. My aunt was whimpering. I took as many deep breaths as I could. I thought this might be a way to take the clear, dry, somehow sweet air back to Denmark with me.

Someone is knocking on my door. It's Juliane. She gets down on her knees and calls through the letter box. "Smilla, I'm making fish ball batter!"

"Leave me alone."

She's offended. "I'll tip it in through your letter box."

Right before we climbed the stairs into the plane, my aunt gave me a pair of *kamiks* to wear indoors. The beadwork alone had taken her a month.

The phone rings.

"There's something I would like to talk to you about." It's Elsa Lübing's voice.

"I'm sorry," I say. "Tell it to somebody else. Cast not thy pearls before swine."

I pull out the phone jack. I'm starting to feel rather attracted to the thought of Ravn's isolation cell. This is the kind of day when you can't rule out the possibility of someone knocking on your windows. On the fifth floor.

Someone knocks on my window. Outside stands a green man. I open the window.

"I'm the window cleaner. I just wanted to warn you, so you don't go and take off your clothes."

He gives me a big smile. As if he were cleaning the windows by putting one pane at a time into his mouth.

"What the hell do you mean? Are you implying that you don't want to see me nude?"

His smile fades. He pushes a button, and the platform he's standing on takes him out of reach.

"I don't want my windows cleaned," I shout after him. "At my age I can barely see out of them, anyway."

During my first years in Denmark I didn't speak to Moritz. We ate dinner together. He had demanded that. Without uttering a word we would sit there flint-like, while successive housekeepers served successive dishes. Mrs Mikkelsen, Dagny, Miss Holm, Boline Hsu. Rissole, hare in cream sauce, Japanese vegetables, Hungarian spaghetti. Without exchanging a single word.

When people talk about how fast children forget, how fast they forgive, how sensitive they are, I let it go in one ear and out the other. Children can remember and forget and totally freeze to death the people they don't like.

I must have been about twelve before I understood even part of the reason why he had brought me to Denmark.

I had run away from the school in Charlottenlund. I was hitchhiking west. I had heard that if you headed west you would come to Jutland. In Jutland was Frederikshavn. From there you could go to Oslo. From Oslo freighters regularly departed for Nuuk.

Near Sorø, late in the afternoon, I got a lift from a forest ranger. He drove me to his home, gave me milk and sandwiches, and told me to wait a minute. While he was calling the police, I stood with my ear to the door.

Outside the garage I found his son's motorbike. I set out across the ploughed fields. The ranger chased after me, but his slippers got stuck in the mud.

It was wintertime. On a curve near a lake, I skidded and crashed and tore my jacket and grazed my hand. From there I walked for a large part of the night. I sat down to sleep in a shelter near a bus stop. When I woke up, I was sitting on a kitchen table, and a woman was disinfecting the scrapes on my ribs with pine spirit. It felt as if I'd been knocked down by a pile-driver.

At the hospital they picked the asphalt out of the wound and put a cast on my broken wrist bones. Then Moritz arrived to pick me up.

He was very angry. He was shaking as we walked side by side down the hospital corridor.

He was holding on to my arm. When he let go to take out his car keys, I took off. I was on my way to Oslo. But I wasn't in the best shape in my life, and he has always been quick. Golf players

97

jog in order to last the course, which is often two times twenty-five kilometres if they play seventy-two holes in two days. He caught up with me in a flash.

I had a surprise for him. A surgical scalpel from the emergency room that I had hidden in my hood. They slice through flesh like butter that's been sitting in the sun. But because my right hand was in a cast, I only managed to give him a gash across the palm of one hand.

He looked at his hand, and then he raised it to hit me. But I had slipped back a bit, so we circled around each other there in the car park. If physical violence has stalked underneath a human relationship for a long time, it's sometimes a relief to get it out in the open.

Suddenly he straightened up.

"You are just like your mother," he said. And then he started to cry.

In that moment I caught a glimpse of his soul. When my mother disappeared, she must have taken part of Moritz with her. Or even worse: part of his physical world must have drowned along with her. There in the car park, early on that winter morning, as we stood and stared at each other, while his blood dripped and burned a little red tunnel through the snow, I remembered something about him. I remembered him in Greenland before my mother's death. I remembered that in the midst of his lurking, unpredictable mood swings there had been a gaiety expressing a joy in life, maybe even a kind of warmth. My mother had taken that part of his world with her. She had vanished with all the colours. Since then he had been imprisoned in a world that was only black and white.

He had brought me to Denmark because I was the only thing that could remind him of what he had lost. People in love, they worship a photograph. They fall on their knees before a scarf. They make a journey to look at the wall of a building. Whatever can ignite the coals that both warm and sear them.

With Moritz it was much worse. He was hopelessly in love with someone whose molecules had been sucked out into the vast emptiness. His love had given up hope. But it had latched on to memory. I was that memory. With great difficulty he had brought me here, and over the years he had withstood an endless number of rejections in a desert of hostility so that he could look at me and find some momentary respite observing the traits I had in common with the woman who was my mother.

We both straightened up. I threw the scalpel into the bushes. We

98

walked back to the emergency room and got his wound bandaged.

That was the last time I tried to run away. I won't say that I forgave him. I will always disapprove when adults, who are unable to deal with the pressure of love they could never express, take it out on small children. But I *will* say that, in some sense, I understood him.

From the chair where I'm sitting I can see the letter box. It's the last entrance that the world hasn't tried to force its way through. Now a long strip of grey cardboard is pushed through it. There's writing on it. I let it lie there for a while. But it's hard to ignore a message that's almost a metre long.

"Anything is better than suicide," it says. That's what it's supposed to say, anyway. He has managed to include two or three spelling mistakes in the brief text.

His door is open. I know that he never locks it. I knock and go in.

I've thrown a little cold water on my face. The possibility of my having brushed my hair can not be ruled out.

He's sitting in the living room reading. It's the first time I've seen him wearing glasses.

The window cleaner is busy outside. When he catches sight of me, he decides to move on to the floor below.

The mechanic still has a clip on his ear. But it looks as if it's healing. He has dark circles under his eyes, but he is freshly shaven.

"There was another expedition." He taps the papers in front of him. "Here's the map."

I sit down next to him. He smells of shampoo and garlic. "Somebody wrote on the map."

For the first time I take a closer look at the large-scale map of the glacier. It's a photocopy. Someone has written in the margin in pencil. The copying has made the note clearer. It's a mixture of English and Danish. "Revised according to the Carlsberg Foundation Expedition, 1966."

He looks at me expectantly. "So I think to m-myself that there must have been a second expedition. And for a moment I consider going back to the archives."

"Without a key?"

"I've got some tools."

No reason to doubt that. He has tools that could open the basement of the National Bank.

"Then I get the idea of calling the brewery. It turns out to be d-difficult. They transfer me. I end up having to talk to the Carlsberg Foundation. They inform me that they funded an expedition in 1966. But nobody from those days is still there. And they didn't have the report. But they did have something else."

It's his trump card.

"They had the account books and the list of expedition participants and colleagues to whom they paid a salary. Do you know where I said I was c-calling from? The inland revenue. They gave me the names at once. And you know what? There was an old friend."

He puts a piece of paper in front of me. There is a list of printed names, two of which I recognize. He points at one of them.

"Odd name, isn't it? After you've heard it once, you remember it. He was on both expeditions."

Andreas Fine Licht, it says. Six hundred CYD 9/12.

"What's CYD?"

"Cape York dollars. The Cryolite Corporation's own currency in Greenland."

"I called the office of the National Registry. They want the names and National Insurance numbers and the last known addresses of everybody. I had to call the foundation back. But then I found them. There are ten names, right? Three of them were Greenlanders. Of the seven others, only two are still alive. N-nineteen sixty-six is starting to seem like a long time ago. One of them is Licht. The other one is a woman. Carlsberg said they had paid her for translating something. They didn't know what. Her name is Benedicte Clahn."

"There's one more," I say.

He looks at me, puzzled.

I put the medical report in front of him and point to the signature. He slowly spells it out. "Loyen." Then he nods. "He was there in '66, too."

He makes us dinner.

On principle, when people feel comfortable in a home, they end up in the kitchen. In Qaanaaq that's where we lived. Here I settle for standing in the doorway. The kitchen is spacious enough, but he fills it up all by himself.

There are women who can make soufflés. Who just happen to have a recipe for Mocha parfait stuffed into their sports bra. Who can stack up their own wedding cakes with one hand and produce pepper steak Nossi Bé with the other.

That ought to make all of us happy. As long as it doesn't mean that the rest of us have to have a guilty conscience because we're still not on a first-name basis with our toasters.

He has a mountain of fish and a mountain of vegetables. Salmon, mackerel, cod, various types of flounder. Tails, heads, fins. Two big crabs. And carrots, onions, leeks, parsnips, fennel, and Jerusalem artichokes.

He peels and boils the vegetables.

I tell him about Ravn and Captain Telling.

He puts on some rice. With cardamom and star aniseed.

I tell him about the confidentiality clauses I've signed. About the reports Ravn had.

He strains off the vegetable water and gets ready to cook the fish.

I tell him about the threats. That they can arrest me whenever they like.

He takes out the pieces of fish one by one. I remember this from Greenland. From the days when we took time to cook our food. Different kinds of fish have different cooking times. Cod are done right away. Mackerel a little later, and salmon even later.

"I'm afraid of being locked up," I say.

He puts the crabs in last. He lets them boil for no more than five minutes.

In a way, I'm relieved that he doesn't say anything, doesn't yell at me. He's the only other person who knows how much we know. How much we will now have to forget.

It seems necessary to explain my claustrophobia to him.

"Do you know what the foundation of mathematics is?" I ask. "The foundation of mathematics is numbers. If anyone asked me what makes me truly happy, I would say: numbers. Snow and ice and numbers. And do you know why?"

He splits the claws with a nutcracker and pulls out the meat with curved tweezers.

"Because the number system is like human life. First you have the natural numbers. The ones that are whole and positive. The numbers of the small child. But human consciousness expands. The child discovers longing, and do you know what the mathematical expression is for longing?"

He adds cream and some drops of orange juice to the soup.

"The negative numbers. The formalization of the feeling that you are missing something. And human consciousness expands and grows even more, and the child discovers the in-between spaces. Between stones, between pieces of moss on the stones, between people. And between numbers. And do you know what that leads to? It leads to fractions. Whole numbers plus fractions produce the rational numbers. And human consciousness doesn't stop there. It wants to go beyond reason. It adds an operation as absurd as the extraction of roots. And produces irrational numbers."

He warms French bread in the oven and fills the pepper mill.

"It's a form of madness. Because the irrational numbers are infinite. They can't be written down. They force human consciousness out beyond the limits. And by adding irrational numbers to rational numbers, you get real numbers."

I've stepped into the middle of the room to have more space. It's rare that you have a chance to explain yourself to a fellow human being. Usually you have to fight for the floor. And this is important to me.

"It doesn't stop. It never stops. Because now, on the spot, we expand the real numbers with the imaginary ones, square roots of negative numbers. These are numbers we can't picture, numbers that normal human consciousness cannot comprehend. And when we add the imaginary numbers to the real numbers, we have the complex number system. The first number system in which it's possible to explain satisfactorily the crystal formation of ice. It's like a vast, open landscape. The horizons. You head towards them and they keep receding. That is Greenland, and that's what I can't be without! That's why I don't want to be locked up."

I wind up standing in front of him.

"Smilla," he says, "can I kiss you?"

We probably all have an image of ourselves. I've always thought of myself as Ms Fierce with the big mouth. Now I don't know what to say. I feel as if he has betrayed me. Not listened the way he should have. That he has deceived me. On the other hand, he's not doing anything. He's not bothering me. He's standing in front of the steaming pots and looking at me.

I can't think of anything to say. I just stand there, not knowing what to do with myself, and the moment is there and then, fortunately, it has passed.

"M-merry Christmas."

We have eaten without exchanging a word. Partly, of course, because what was not said before is still hovering in the room. But mostly because the soup demands it. You can't talk over this soup. It's shouting from the bowl, demanding your undivided attention.

Isaiah was the same way. Sometimes when I read aloud to him or when we listened to *Peter and the Wolf*, my attention would be distracted by something else and my thoughts would run away with me. After a while he would clear his throat. A friendly, remonstrating, telling sound. It meant something like: Smilla – you're daydreaming.

It is the same with the soup. I'm eating it from a deep soup plate. The mechanic is drinking it from a big cup. It tastes of fish. Of the deep Atlantic Ocean, of icebergs, of seaweed. The rice has traces of the tropics, of the folded leaves of the banana palm. Of the floating spice markets in Burma. My imagination is running away with me.

We're drinking mineral water. He knows that I don't touch alcohol. He hasn't asked me why. In fact, he has never really asked me anything. Except for that request a few minutes ago.

He puts down his spoon.

"That ship," he says. "The model ship in the Baron's room. It looked so expensive."

He places a printed brochure in front of me.

"That b-box he had in his room. The one he made into a cave. That was the box the ship was delivered in. That's where I found this."

Why hadn't I seen it myself?

On the front it says: "Arctic Museum. The SS *Johannes Thomsen* of the Cryolite Corporation Danmark. Scale: 1:50."

"What's the Arctic Museum?" I ask.

He doesn't know.

"But there's an address on the box."

He has something up his sleeve. He has cut the address out of the cardboard box with a knife. Probably to avoid spelling mistakes. Now he puts it down in front of me.

"The law office of Hammer & Ving." And an address on Østergade, the end near Kongens Nytorv.

"He was the one who picked up the Baron in his car."

"What does Juliane say?"

"She's so scared that she's shaking."

He makes coffee. With two kinds of beans, and the grinder and the funnel and the machine, and that same unhurried meticulousness. We drink it in silence. It's Christmas Eve. For me, silence is usually an ally. Today it's pressing lightly on my ears.

"Did you have a Christmas tree when you were a child?" I ask.

A question with a trustworthy surface. But I ask it to find out who he is.

"Every year. Until I turned f-fifteen. Then the cat jumped up on it. And her fur caught fire from the candles."

"What did you do?"

Not until I ask the question do I realize that I took it for granted that he would have done something.

"Took off my shirt and wrapped it around the cat. That put out the fire."

I imagine him without a shirt. In the glow of the lamps. In the glow of the Christmas candles. In the glow of the cat on fire. I push the thought aside. It comes back. Some thoughts have glue on them.

"Good night," I say, getting up.

He goes with me to the door. "I'm p-positive that I'm going to dream tonight."

There's something sly about that remark. I scan his face, looking for a hint that he's making fun of me, but his expression is serious.

"Thanks for the nice evening," I say.

One of the signs that your life needs tidying up is when your possessions gradually have come to consist mainly of things that you borrowed a long time ago but which it's now too late to give back because you'd rather shave your head than confront the bogeyman who is the rightful owner.

My cassette player is stamped: GEODETIC INSTITUTE. It has built-in speakers, built-in seventy per cent distortion, built-in indestructibility, so I can't even find an excuse to buy a new one.

In front of me on the table I have Isaiah's cigar box. I've weighed the things in my hand, one at a time. I've looked up the harpoon tip in Birket-Smith's *The Eskimos*. It's a head from the Dorset culture, AD 700–900. The book says that at least five thousand of them have been found. Spread over three thousand kilometres of coastline.

I take the tape out of its box. It's a Maxell XLI–S. A high-quality tape. A tape for people who want to record music.

There's no music on the tape. It's a man talking. A Greenlander.

On Disko Island in 1981 I helped test the corrosion effects of sea fog on the snaplinks used for safety lines on glacier crossings. We simply hung them up on a cord and came back three months later. They still looked reliable. A little tarnished, but reliable. The manufacturer claimed the breaking strength would be four thousand kilogrammes. It turned out that we could pull them apart with a fingernail. Exposed to a hostile environment, they had disintegrated.

It is through a similar process of deterioration that you lose your language.

When we moved from the village school to Qaanaaq, we had teachers who didn't know one word of Greenlandic, nor did they have any plans to learn it. They told us that, for those who excelled, there would be an admission ticket to Denmark and a degree and a way out of the Arctic misery. This golden ascent would take place in Danish. This was when the foundation was being laid for the politics of the sixties. Which led to Greenland officially becoming "Denmark's northernmost county", and the Inuit were officially supposed to be called "Northern Danes" and "be educated to the same rights as all other Danes", as the prime minister put it.

That's how the foundation is laid. Then you arrive in Denmark and six months pass and it feels as if you will never forget your mother tongue. It's the language you think in, the way you remember your past. Then you meet a Greenlander on the street. You exchange a few words. And suddenly you have to search for a completely ordinary word. Another six months pass. A girlfriend takes you along to the Greenlanders' House on Løv Lane. That's where you discover that your own Greenlandic can be picked apart with a fingernail.

Later, when I've gone back, I've tried to learn it again. As with so many other things, I haven't exactly succeeded, or failed either. That's about where I stand with my mother tongue – as if I were sixteen or seventeen years old.

And besides, there isn't one language in Greenland. There are three. The man on Isaiah's tape is speaking East Greenlandic. A southern dialect. It's incomprehensible to me.

From his tone of voice, I imagine that he's talking to someone else. But no one interrupts him. It sounds as if he's talking in a kitchen or a dining room, because every once in a while there's noise like cutlery. Every once in a while there's the sound of an engine. Maybe it's a generator. Or electronic noise from the cassette recorder.

He's explaining something that's important to him. The explanation is lengthy, urgent, complicated, but there are also long pauses. In the pauses I can hear that behind his speech there is a faint noise of something like music, maybe the sound of a wind instrument. The remnants of a previous recording that has not been completely erased.

I give up trying to understand what he's saying and let my thoughts wander. The speaker can't be Isaiah's father; the dialect isn't right.

The voice finishes a sentence and stops. The pause button must have been pushed, because there's no crackling. One minute the voice is there, the next it's white noise. And far away, deep down, the remains of some distant music.

I let it hiss and put my feet up on the table.

Every so often I would play music for Isaiah. I would move the speakers over to the sofa, close to his damaged ears, and turn up the volume. He would lean back against the sofa and close his eyes. Often he would fall asleep. Very quietly he would slump over on one side without waking up. Then I would gather him up and carry him downstairs. If it was too noisy down there, I would carry him back up and put him on the bed. The instant I put him down, he would always wake up. And in that half-sleep state, hoarsely humming, he seemed to be trying to sing some bars of what he had heard.

I've closed my eyes. It's night. The last Christmas guests have taken their trailers full of presents home. Now they're lying in bed looking forward to the day after tomorrow, when they can go out and exchange them or get cash instead.

It's time for peppermint tea. Time to look out over the city. I turn towards the window. There's always the hope that it may have started to snow while my back was turned.

At that moment someone laughs.

106

I'm on my feet with my hands out in front of me. It's not a delicate, little-girl laugh. It's the phantom of the opera. I'll sell my life as dearly as possible.

There are four light taps and then the music starts. It's jazz. In the foreground there's the sound of a trumpet. It's coming from Isaiah's tape.

I push the stop button. It takes me a long time to come back down to earth. To build up a solid panic takes a fraction of a second. Getting rid of it can take half an evening.

I rewind and play the last part of the tape again. Again, the pause button has been used. There's no warning, suddenly the laughter is there. Deep, triumphant, sonorous. Then the taps. Then the music. It's jazz and yet not jazz. There's something euphoric, disconnected about it. Like four instruments that have run amok. But it fools you. Because there is also a strange precision to it. Like a clown act in a circus ring. What takes the greatest precision is that it's supposed to sound like total chaos.

The tune goes on for about seven minutes. Then the tape runs out, and the notes are abruptly cut off.

There has been energy in the music. A strange lift, here, on top of the anxiety, at three o'clock on Christmas morning.

I sang in the church choir in Qaanaaq. I pictured the Three Wise Men wearing snowshoes, on dog sleighs across the ice. With their gaze fixed on the star. I knew how they felt inside. They had grasped hold of Absolute Space. They knew they were on the right track. Moving towards an energy phenomenon. That's what the Infant Jesus was for me, as I stood there pretending to read the notes, while in reality I had never understood them but always learned by ear.

It's the same way now, with more than half my life behind me, in the White Cells. So never mind the fact that I've never had a child of my own. I enjoy the sea and the ice without continually feeling cheated out of Creation. A child who is born is something to seek out, something to search for, a star, a northern light, a column of energy in the universe. And a child who dies – that's an abomination.

I get up and go downstairs and ring the doorbell.

He comes out in his pyjamas. Groggy with sleep.

"Peter," I say. "I'm scared. But I'll do it, anyway."

He smiles, half awake, half asleep.

"I knew it," he says. "I knew it."

$$\textbf{2}$$

"THIRTY IS A BIBLICAL NUMBER," says Elsa Lübing. "Judas received thirty silver coins. Jesus was thirty years old when he was baptized. With the new year it will be thirty years ago that the Cryolite Corporation switched over to automated bookkeeping."

It's 27 December. We're sitting in the same chairs. The same teapot is on the table, the same coasters under the teacups. The same dizzying view, the same white winter light. It might seem as if time had stood still. As if we've been sitting here for the past week without moving, and now a button is pushed and we take up where we left off. Except for one thing. She seems to have made a decision. There is something determined about her.

Her eyes are deep-set, and she's paler than last time, as if it has cost her sleepless nights to get this far.

Or perhaps it's all in my imagination. Perhaps she looks the way she does because she has celebrated Christmas by fasting and keeping vigil and rhythmically intoning her devotions seven hundred times twice a day.

"In some ways those thirty years changed everything. In other ways everything has stayed the same. The director at that time – in the fifties and early sixties – was Alderman Ebel. He and his wife each had their own custom-made Rolls Royce. Every so often one of the cars would be parked outside, with the uniformed chauffeur waiting behind the wheel. Then we would know that he or his wife was visiting the factory. We never saw them in person. She had a private railway carriage that was kept in Hamburg, and several times a year it was hooked up to the train and they travelled to the Riviera. The daily administration was handled by the finance director, the sales director, and chief engineer Ottesen. Ottesen was always in the laboratory or at the quarry in Saqqaq. We never saw him. The sales director was always travelling. Occasionally he came home, scattering smiles, gifts, and frivolous anecdotes to all sides.

I remember that the first time he came back from Paris, after the war, he brought silk stockings."

She laughs at the thought that silk stockings had once made her happy. "I've noticed that you're interested in clothes, too. That disappears with age. For the last thirty years I've worn only white. If you restrict earthly things, you set your thoughts free for the spiritual."

I don't say a word, but I make a mental note of the remark – for the next time I have trousers made by tailor Tvilling on Heinesgade. He collects sparkling gems like that.

"It was an apparatus 165 by 100 by 120 centimetres. It operated with two different levers. One for Continental types of decimal coinage and one for British currency. The relevant information was punched in a form of hole code on data entry cards that were fed into the machine. This meant that the information was less accessible. When numbers are compressed on to punch cards and transformed into code, it's more difficult to understand them. That's centralization. That's what the director said. Centralization always has certain associated costs."

In some ways it has become easier to orient oneself in the modern world. Every phenomenon has become international. The Greenland Trade Company – as part of centralization – closed its business on Maxwell Island in 1979. My brother had been a hunter there for ten years, the king of the island, as unassailable as a male baboon. The closing of the store drove him south to Upernavik. When I was posted at the meteorological station, he was sweeping the docks in the harbour. The following year he hanged himself. That was the year when the suicide rate in Greenland became the highest in the world. The Greenland Ministry wrote in *Atuagagdliutit* that it looked as if it was going to be difficult to combine the necessary centralization with the hunting trade. They didn't write that there were bound to be quite a few more suicides along the way. But that was understood.

"Try the biscuits," she says. "*Spekulaas*. I baked them myself. It has taken me an entire lifetime to find a way to take them out of the mould without ruining the pattern."

The biscuits are flat, dark brown, with slivers of burnt almonds pressed into the bottom. She looks at them intently. People who have lived alone all their lives can allow themselves to refine highly specialized interests. Such as how to take the biscuits out of the mould.

"I cheat a little," she says. "For example, this one here. The mould is a married couple. It's quite difficult to get the eyes right. That's the trouble with very dry pastry dough. So I use a knitting needle once they're out of the mould and lying on the table. So it's not the original design, but close to it. Something similar takes place in a company. Then it's called 'good accounting practice'. It's a flexible term that covers what the auditors will accept. Do you know how responsibility is shared in companies listed on the stock exchange?"

I shake my head. The biscuits combine butter and spices in such a way that you could eat a hundred of them and only realize how sick you are after it's too late.

"The management, of course, is fiscally accountable to the board of directors, and ultimately to the shareholders. The finance director was the 'executive chairman of the board'. That may seem a very practical division of power. But it demands the utmost trust. Ottesen was always at the quarry. The sales director was always away. I don't think it's an exaggeration to say that for many years the finance director made all decisions of importance for the corporation. Naturally, there was no reason to doubt his integrity. An absolutely trustworthy decision-maker. Both a lawyer and an accountant. Former city council member. Representing the Social Democratic Party. He has been and still is on several boards of directors. Housing associations and savings banks."

She hands me the bowl. Danes express their strongest feelings in conjunction with food. That became clear to me the first time I was out visiting friends with Moritz. When I took a third helping of biscuits, he looked straight at me.

"Help yourself until you're ashamed of yourself," he said.

I wasn't confident about my Danish, but I understood what he meant. I helped myself three more times. Without taking my eyes off him. The room disappeared, the people we were visiting disappeared, I didn't taste the biscuits. Only Moritz existed.

"I'm still not ashamed," I said.

I helped myself three more times. Then he grabbed the plate and put it out of my reach. I had won. The first of a long series of small, important victories over him and Danish manners.

Elsa Lübing's biscuits are of a different kind. They are supposed to make me both her confidante and her accomplice.

"The auditors are chosen at the shareholders' meeting. But the corporation's shares – aside from those owned by the finance director himself and the government – are divided among many hands. They are held by all the heirs of the eight partners who acquired the first mineral rights in the last century. It has never been possible to gather them all for a general shareholders' meeting. That means that the director has had an inappropriately decisive influence. It's worth noting that all decisions dealing with the most economically significant part of Greenland's mineral rights have been made by one individual, don't you think?"

"How uplifting."

"There is also a business aspect. The corporation was a major customer. Any auditor who took a stand against the director had to be prepared to lose this client. Finally, there was the fact that the same people played various roles in the corporation. The corporation's auditor through the sixties later became one of the director's colleagues when he started his law practice. On 7 January 1967, I balanced the semiannual accounts. There was one entry that was not itemized. For 115,000 kroner. A large amount in those days. Perhaps it wouldn't have surprised an outsider. The board probably wouldn't have caught it. Not in a sales volume of fifty million kroner. But for me, who dealt with the daily accounts, it was unacceptable. So I looked for the pertinent file card. It wasn't there. They were all numbered. It should have been there. But it was missing. Then I went up to the director's office. I had worked under his leadership for twenty years. He listened to me, looked down at his papers, and then said, 'Miss Lübing, I authorized that entry. For technical bookkeeping reasons, it was too difficult to itemize. Our auditor feels that the present listing is acceptable accounting practice. Anything beyond that lies outside your sphere of expertise.'"

"What did you do?" I asked.

"I went back and entered the figures. As I had been instructed to do. And with that I made myself an accomplice. To something which I didn't understand, which I have never understood. I did not administer the 'talents' entrusted to my care. I showed myself to be unworthy of trust."

I empathize with her. The problem was not that they called her competence into question by withholding information from her. Or that they gave her an impudent answer. The problem was that they had tampered with her ideals of honesty.

"I will tell you where this amount appears in the books."

"Let me guess," I say. "It appears in the accounts for the

corporation's geological expedition to the Barren Glacier on Gela Alta off the west coast of Greenland in the summer of '66."

She looks at me with narrowed eyes.

"In the report from '91 there were references to an earlier expedition," I explain. "It's as simple as that."

"There was an accident that time, too," she says. "An accident with explosives. Two of the eight participants died."

I have an idea why she has summoned me. She sees me as a kind of auditor. Someone who might be able to help her and Our Lord by auditing an unsettled account from 7 January 1967.

"What are you thinking?" she asks.

What should I tell her? My thoughts are chaotic.

"I'm thinking that the Barren Glacier seems to be an unhealthy place to visit," I say.

We've been sitting in silence for a while; we've finished our tea and eaten our biscuits and looked at the world lying at our feet, snow-covered and mundane.

And there's even a swath of sunshine cutting across Solsortevej and the football field at the school on Duevej. But the whole time I am positive that she has more to tell.

"Alderman Ebel died in 1964," she says. "Everyone says that an epoch in Danish commercial life died with him. In his will he demanded that his Rolls Royce be sunk in the North Atlantic, while the Swedish actor Gösta Ekman recited Hamlet's soliloquy on the deck of the ship."

I can just picture the scene. This funeral could be considered a symbol of a political death and resurrection. The old, blatantly colonial policy in Greenland was abandoned at this time. Making room for the policies of the sixties – the educating of Northern Danes to equal rights.

"The corporation was reorganized. We noticed it because there was a new office manager and two new women in bookkeeping. But otherwise the greatest changes were in the research department. That's because the cryolite was almost exhausted. They were constantly having to develop new methods of sorting and extraction because the quality of the ore was getting poorer and poorer. But we all knew what was going on. Occasionally, during lunch in the canteen, rumours would circulate about a new find. It was like a passing fever. After a few days the rumours were always disavowed.

Originally there were only five people on the laboratory staff. It was expanded. At one time there were twenty. Earlier, additional geologists had been hired for brief periods. They often came from Finland. But now a permanent research group was created. Then, in 1967, they formed the Advisory Scientific Commission. This made the daily work more secretive. We were told very little. But it was created to find new deposits. It was made up of representatives from some of the big companies and institutions that the corporation worked with. The Swedish Diamond Drilling Company, Denmark's Underground Ltd, the Geologic Institute, Greenland's Geologic Survey. That complicated the bookkeeping. Things were more difficult because of the many new fees, the numerous expedition expenses. And all along I thought about the unresolved matter of the 115,000 kroner."

I ponder what it must have been like to be her, with her inordinate sense for numbers and her belief in honesty, having to work on a daily basis with someone she suspected of covering up an irregularity.

She gives me her own answer. "'For there is nothing hid, which shall not be manifested; neither was any thing kept secret, but that it should come abroad.' Mark 4:22."

Faith in divine justice has given her patience.

"In 1977 we were computerized. I never managed to understand it. At my request we continued to keep manual accounts. In 1992 I retired. Three weeks before my last workday we balanced the books. The finance director suggested that I leave this balance sheet to the office manager. I insisted on doing it myself. On 7 January – exactly twenty-five years after the event I mentioned – I sat there with the books for the expedition to Gela Alta from the previous summer. It was like an omen. I took out the old accounts. I compared the two, item by item. This was difficult, of course. The expedition of '91 was financed through the Scientific Commission, which had become common practice. And yet it *was* possible to compare them. The biggest entry in '91 was for 450,000 kroner. I called the commission and requested an itemization."

She pauses, mastering her indignation.

"Later I received a letter which stated, briefly summarized, that I should not have gone over the heads of my immediate superiors with that type of request. But by then it was too late. Because on the telephone that day they had given me the answer. The 450,000 kroner had been used to charter a ship."

She sees that I don't understand a thing.

"A ship," she says, "a coaster, to transport eight men to the west coast of Greenland to pick up a few kilos of sample gemstones. It doesn't make sense. We often chartered the *Disko* from the Greenland Trading Company. To transport the cryolite. But a ship for a small expedition, that was unthinkable. Do you ever remember your dreams, Miss Smilla?"

"Sometimes."

"Recently I've dreamed several times that you were sent by Providence."

"You should hear what the police say about me."

Like many elderly people, she has developed a selective sense of hearing. She ignores me and continues on her own track. "Perhaps you think I'm old. Perhaps you're wondering whether I'm senile. But remember, Joel: 'Your old men shall dream dreams.'"

She looks straight through me, straight through the wall. Straight into the past.

"I think that the 115,000 kroner in 1966 must have been used to charter a ship. I think that someone, under the guise of the Cryolite Corporation, has sent two expeditions to the west coast."

I hold my breath. With her honesty and her breach of a lifelong loyalty, this is a delicate moment.

"There can only be one explanation for this. At any rate, after forty-five years with the corporation, I cannot think of any other reason. They wanted to transport something back to Denmark, something so heavy that it required a ship."

I put on my cape. The black one with the hood that makes me look like a nun and that I thought would be suitable for the occasion.

"The Carlsberg Foundation financed part of the expedition in '91. In their accounts there is a fee for one Benedicte Clahn," I say.

She gazes, dreamy-eyed, straight ahead, as she pages through her complete, error-free internal account books.

"In 1966, too," she says slowly. "A translator's fee of 267 kroner. That was another of the entries I did not find an explanation for. But I remember her. She was one of the director's acquaintances. She had been living in Germany. I had the impression that they knew each other from Berlin in 1946. Immediately after the end of the war the Allies negotiated in Berlin regarding the division of aluminium supplies. A number of people from the corporation were often down there during those years."

"Such as?"

"Ottesen was there. The director of sales. And Alderman Ebel."

"Any others?"

She's groggy from talking so much and from pouring out her heart into what might turn out to be the gutter. She wearily considers my question.

"I can't remember hearing about any others. Is it important?"

I shrug my shoulders. She takes hold of me. She can practically lift me off the floor. "The little boy's death. What are you planning to do?"

Denmark is a hierarchical society. She finds a mistake, and she complains to her boss. She is rejected. She complains to the board. She is rejected. But above the board sits Our Lord. She has turned to Him in prayer. Now she wants me to show that I am one of His assistants dispatched to help.

"That coaster. Did it sail off with what it came to get?"

She shakes her head. "That's hard to say. After the accident the survivors and their equipment were flown to Godthåb and then home. I am positive about that because the accounting department paid for the freight and their plane tickets."

She follows me all the way out to the lift. I feel a sudden tenderness for her. A motherly feeling, even though she is twice my age and three times as strong.

The lift arrives.

"Now don't let your honesty give you bad dreams," I say.

"I'm too old to regret anything."

Then I ride down. On my way out of the front door, I suddenly think of something. When I call her up on the silver-plated conch shell, she answers as if she had been standing there waiting for my call.

"Miss Lübing."

One would never dream of using her first name.

"The director of finance. Who is he?"

"He's going to retire next year. He runs his own law office. His name is David Ving. The firm is Hammer & Ving. It's located somewhere on Østergade."

I thank her.

"God be with you," she says.

No one has ever said that to me before, outside of church. Maybe I've never had such a need for it before, either.

"I had a c-colleague who worked on the cleaning staff at the phone company's switching station on Nørregade."

We're sitting in the mechanic's living room.

"He told me that they just call in and say that now they have a court order. Then some clips are put on a relay and via the telephone network they can sit at police headquarters and tap all incoming and outgoing calls on a certain number."

"I've never liked telephones."

He has a big roll of wide red insulation tape and a little pair of scissors on the table. He cuts a long strip and attaches it to the telephone receiver.

"Do the same thing in your apartment. From now on, every time you make a call and every time someone calls you, you'll have to remove the t-tape first. That will make you remember that there may be an audience listening somewhere in the city. People always forget that telephones might not be private. The tape will remind you to be careful. If, for instance, you happen to make a declaration of love."

If I were going to declare my love to someone, I certainly wouldn't do it over the phone. But I don't say anything.

I know nothing about him. Over the last ten days I've seen little drops of his past. They don't tally. Like now, this knowledge of the procedure for tapping phones.

The tea he makes for us is another one of those little drops that surprise me but that I don't want to ask about.

He boils milk with fresh ginger, a quarter of a vanilla pod, and tea that is so dark and fine-leaved that it looks like black dust. He strains it and puts cane sugar in both of our cups. There's something euphorically invigorating and yet filling about it. It tastes the way I imagine the Far East must taste.

I tell him about my visit to Elsa Lübing. He now knows everything that I know. Except for a few details, such as Isaiah's cigar box and its contents, including a tape on which a man is laughing.

"Who, other than the Carlsberg Foundation, financed the expedition in '91? Did she know? Who arranged for the ship?"

I kick myself for not asking that precise question. I reach for the telephone. The receiver is taped on.

"That's why the t-tape is there," he says. "Without the tape always on you'd forget all about it in five minutes."

Together we walk over to the phone booth on the square. His stride is one and a half times as long as mine. And yet it still feels comfortable walking next to each other. He walks just as slowly as I do.

When my mother didn't come back I realized that any moment could be the last. Nothing in life should simply be a passage from one place to another. Each walk should be taken as if it is the only thing you have left.

You can demand something like this of yourself as an unattainable ideal. After that, you have to remind yourself about it every time you're sloppy about something. For me that means two hundred and fifty times a day.

She picks up the phone at once. It strikes me how self-confident her voice is.

"Yes?"

I don't give my name. "The 450,000 kroner. Who paid it?"

She doesn't ask me about anything. Maybe it has been revealed to her too, that the telephone line might be crowded. She thinks for a moment in silence.

"Geoinform," she says then. "That was the name of the company. They had two representatives on the Scientific Commission. They own a block of shares. Five per cent, as far as I can recall. Enough so that it had to be registered with the Trade Commission. The company is owned by a woman."

The mechanic has stepped into the booth with me. It makes me think of three things. The first is that he fills it up. If he stood up straight he could push the bottom out of it, and walk away with me and the booth.

The second thing is that his hands against the glass in front of me are smooth and clean. Used to hard work but smooth and clean. Occasionally he gets a job at a garage on Toftegårds Plads. How, I ask myself, can he mess around all day long with cutting oil and socket wrenches and keep his fingers so smooth?

The third thing is that I'm honest enough to admit that there's a certain pleasure in standing next to him this way. I have to stop myself from prolonging the conversation solely for that reason.

"I've been thinking about something you asked me. About Berlin after the war. There was one other colleague. At that time he was not employed by us. But he was later on. Not at the quarry, but here in Copenhagen. As a medical consultant. Dr Loyen. Johannes Loyen. He did some work for the Americans. I think he was a forensics expert."

"How does someone become a fully-fledged professor, Smilla?"

On a piece of paper we've made a list of names. There is High Court barrister and chartered accountant David Ving. Someone who knows something about ships. How to cover up the expenses of chartering one, for example, and send them as a Christmas present to young children in Greenland.

There is Benedicte Clahn. The mechanic found her in the phone book. If it's the same one, that is. It turns out that she lives two hundred metres from where we are now sitting. In one of the renovated warehouses on Strand Boulevard. Which contain Denmark's most expensive apartments. Three million kroner for eighty-four square metres. But then there's also a brick wall one and a half metres thick to beat your head against when you have calculated the price per square metre. And beams of Pomeranian pine to hang yourself from if the wall doesn't do the trick. He has written down her phone number next to her name.

And there are the two professors, Johannes Loyen and Andreas Fine Licht. Two men about whom we know very little, except that their names are associated with both expeditions to Gela Alta. Two expeditions, about which we really don't know anything either.

"My father," I say, "was once a professor. Now that he isn't one any more, he says that in most cases the people who become professors are clever without being too clever."

"So what happens to the ones who *are* too clever?"

I hate quoting Moritz. What can you do about people you don't want to quote but who are still the ones who have said it most succinctly?

"He says that they either rise up to the stars or they go to the dogs."

"Which of the two happened to your father?"

I have to think about that for a moment before I come up with an answer. "I think he's really coming apart in the middle," I say.

Silently we listen to the sounds of the city. The cars on the bridge. The sound of pneumatic drills from the night shift at one of Holmen's dry docks. The chimes of Our Saviour's Church. They say that anyone can get permission to play the bells in the tower.

That's certainly the impression you get. Sometimes it sounds like Horowitz, sometimes as if they opted, sight unseen, for some drunk at the Monkey Wrench Café.

"The Trade Commission," I say. "Lübing said that if you want to find out who controls a company or who sits on a board, you can look it up at the Trade Commission. Supposedly they have the balance sheets for all companies in Denmark listed on the stock exchange."

"It's on K-Kampmannsgade."

"How do you know that?" I ask.

He gazes out the window. "I paid attention in school."

THERE ARE MORNINGS when it feels as if you rise up to the surface through a mud bath. With both feet bolted to a ship's anchor. When you know that you've expired in the night and have nothing to be happy about except the fact that at least you're well and truly dead, so they can't transplant your lifeless organs.

Six out of seven mornings are like that.

The seventh is like today. I wake up feeling crystal clear. I climb out of bed as if I had some reason to get up.

I do the four yoga exercises I managed to learn before I received the eightieth reminder from the library, and they sent a messenger, and I had to pay such a big fine that I might just as well have bought the book.

I take a shower in ice-cold water. Put on leggings, a big sweater, grey boots, and a fur hat from Jane Eberlein. It's made in sort of a Greenland style.

I've lost my cultural identity for good, I usually tell myself. And after I've said this enough times, I wake up one morning, like today, with a solid sense of identity. Smilla Jaspersen – Greenlander *de luxe*.

It's seven o'clock in the morning. I walk down to the harbour and out on to the ice.

The ice in Copenhagen Harbour is not a place where you'd recommend parents to send their children out to play, even in a hard frost such as this one. Even I have to be careful when I go out there.

About forty metres out I stop. Here the surface is slightly darker. One more step and I would fall through. I stand there, rocking up and down. Sea ice is porous and elastic, the water seeps up through it, forming around my boots two mirror surfaces that reflect the scattered lights in the darkness.

A man is standing on the wharf. A black silhouette against the white walls of the buildings. Fear spreads out like a vibrating tone.

The mortal danger of the seal when it's lying on the ice. So sensitive, so visible, so immobile. Then the tone dies out. It's the mechanic, stooped, rectangular, like a big rock. I have not seen him for two days. Maybe I have avoided him.

You get so used to looking at the city from certain angles that from here it seems like some foreign capital never before seen. Like Venice. Or Atlantis. A city which, wrapped in snow and the night, could be made of marble. I walk back towards the dock.

He could be someone else. I could be someone else. We could be young lovers. Instead of a dyslexic stutterer and a bitter shrew who tell each other half-truths and are walking together along some dubious path.

When I'm standing in front of him, he takes me by the shoulders. "That's dangerous!"

If I didn't know better, I could have sworn there was something almost pleading in his voice.

I slip out of his hold.

"I have a good relationship with ice."

When we disbanded the Young Greenlanders' Council to form IA, and had to position ourselves in relation to the social democrats in the Siumut Party and the reactionary Greenlandic upper class in Atassut, we read Karl Marx's *Das Kapital*. It was a book I grew quite fond of. For its trembling, feminine empathy and its potent indignation. I know of no other book with such a strong belief in how much you can accomplish if you just have the will to change.

Unfortunately, I'm not that confident myself. I've been given a great deal, and I've wanted a lot. And I've ended up not really having anything and not really knowing what I want. I've acquired the basics of an education. I've travelled. Occasionally I've felt that I've done what I wanted to do. And yet I've been directed. Some invisible hand has had me by the scruff of the neck, and every time I thought that now I was taking an important step up towards the light, it has pushed me further along a network of sewer pipes running beneath a landscape that I do not know and cannot tell what it looks like. As if it had been determined that I would have to swallow a specific amount of sewage before I would be allowed a breathing hole.

As a rule I swim against the current. But on certain mornings, such as today, I have enough surplus energy to surrender. Now, as

I'm walking along beside the mechanic, I am strangely, inexplicably happy.

It dawns on me that we could eat breakfast together. I can't remember how long it's been since I ate breakfast with someone. It has been my own choice. I'm sensitive in the morning. I need time to throw cold water on my face and put on my eyeliner and drink a glass of juice before I'm feeling sociable. But this morning has taken care of itself. We met, and now we're walking along side by side. I'm just about to suggest it.

Suddenly I'm floating.

He has picked me up and carried me over to the scaffolding. I think it's a joke and am about to say something. Then I see what his sixth sense had anticipated and keep quiet. The stairwell is dark on all floors. But a door is opening. It floods yellow light out into the darkness. And two figures – Juliane and a man. He's talking to her. She staggers. Whatever he's saying, his words fall like blows. She drops to her knees. Then the door shuts. The man takes the outdoor stairway.

Juliane's friends don't leave at seven in the morning. At that hour they haven't even come home yet. And if they do leave, they don't walk with the nimble ease of this man. They crawl.

We're standing in the shadow of the scaffolding. He can't see us. He's wearing a long Burberry raincoat and a hat.

At the end of the building facing Christianshavn the mechanic gives my arm a squeeze, and I continue on alone. The hat in front of me gets into a car. When he pulls away from the kerb, the little Morris stops right next to me. The seats are cold and so low that I have to stretch to see out the windscreen. It's iced over, so we drive peeking through a strip, barely able to see from the bonnet ornament to the red rear lights in front of us.

We drive across the bridge. Turn right before Holmens Church, past the National Bank, across Kongens Nytorv. There may be other traffic, we may be the only ones. It's impossible to tell through the windscreen.

He parks the car at Krinsen Park. We drive past and stop across from the French Embassy. He doesn't look back.

He walks past the Hotel d'Angleterre and turns down Strøget, the pedestrian street. We're twenty-five metres behind him. Now there are other people around us. He walks up to a doorway and lets himself in with a key.

If I had been alone, I would have stopped here. I don't need to go over to the door to know what it says on the nameplate. I know who the man is that we've been following, as surely as if he had shown me his practising certificate. If I had been alone, I would have walked home and thought things over along the way.

But today there are two of us. For the first time in a long time we are two.

One moment he's standing at my side, and the next he's over by the door, sticking his hand in before it closes.

I follow him. When you're playing ball or some other game, sometimes there is a moment like this of spontaneous, wordless, mutual understanding.

We enter an archway with a vaulted ceiling of white and gold bronze, marble panels, soft yellow light, and a door with glass panes and a brass handle. The archway leads into a garden courtyard with evergreen shrubbery, little Japanese ginkgo trees, and a fountain. Everything is covered with the snow of the last two weeks, which once started to melt but now has a thin, frozen crust on the surface. From somewhere up above, the first light of day drifts downward, like dust.

An electric lead is lying inside the stairwell. It goes around a corner. From there comes the sound of a vacuum cleaner. In front of us is a cleaner's trolley, with two buckets, mops, scrubbing brushes, and a couple of roller contraptions for wringing out wet rags. The mechanic grabs the trolley.

There are footsteps above us. Light steps, muted by the blue runner held down by brass rods the width of the stairs. There's a pleasant scent surrounding us. A scent I recognize but can't identify.

We reach the third floor the moment the door shuts behind him. The mechanic carries the trolley under his arm as if it were nothing.

The gilding and the cream-coloured inlay from the doorway are repeated in the stairwell and on the doors. There are engraved brass nameplates. The plate in front of us is placed above an extra-wide letter box. So that even the largest cheques can get through. LAW OFFICE, it says. Of course. Law Office of Hammer & Ving. The door isn't locked, so we go in. All three. We and the trolley.

We enter a large foyer. One door is open, leading to a series of offices that are extensions of one another, like the reception rooms in the photographs of Amalienborg Palace. And here are photographs of the Queen and the Prince, and shiny parquet floors, and paintings in gilt frames, and the most elegant office furniture I've ever seen. There is the same scent as in the stairwell, and now I recognize it. It's the scent of money.

Not a soul is around. I pick up a rag and wring it out, and the mechanic picks up a big mop.

At the end of the offices there is a closed double door. I knock on it. He must have a control panel near him, because when the door opens, he's sitting at the opposite end of the room, in an office with a window facing the courtyard.

He's sitting behind a black mahogany desk which stands on four lion's feet and is so big that you can't help wondering how they managed to get it up here. On the wall behind him hang three gloomy paintings of the Marble Bridge in heavy frames.

It's difficult to judge his age. From Elsa Lübing I know that he must be more than seventy. But he looks healthy and athletic, as if every morning he walks barefoot across his beachfront and down to the Sound, where he saws a hole in the ice and takes a refreshing dip, then runs back and eats a little bowl of gladiator muesli with skimmed milk.

It has kept his skin smooth and ruddy. But it hasn't been beneficial for hair growth. He's as bald as a hard-boiled egg.

He's wearing glasses with gold frames that give off so many reflections that you never really get to see his eyes.

"Good morning," I say. "Quality control. We're checking on the morning cleaning."

He doesn't say anything, merely looks at us. As clearly as if he had spoken, I remember his voice – dry and proper – from a telephone conversation a long time ago.

The mechanic withdraws to a corner and starts mopping. I take the windowsill closest to the desk.

He looks down at his papers. I wipe the sill with the rag. It leaves striped tracks of dirty water.

Soon he'll start to wonder.

"There's nothing like having your place properly cleaned, is there?" I say.

He frowns, now mildly annoyed.

Next to the window hangs a picture of a sailing ship. I take it down and wipe the back of it with the rag.

"What a nice picture this is," I say. "I'm rather interested in ships myself. When I get home after a long work day among rubber gloves and disinfectants, I put my feet up and leaf through a good book about ships."

Now he's wondering whether I'm deranged.

"We all have our favourites, of course. Mine are the ships which

124

sailed to Greenland. And, as chance will have it, when I saw your name on the fancy nameplate, I said to myself, My God, Smilla, I said. Ving! That nice man who once gave one of your friends a model ship for Christmas. The good ship *Johannes Thomsen*. To a young Greenlandic boy."

I hang the picture up again. The water wasn't good for it. All cleaning has its price. I think about Juliane, on her knees before him, in the doorway.

"The other thing I never get tired of reading about is ships chartered for expeditions to Greenland."

He's sitting perfectly still now. Only in the reflections of his glasses is there a faint movement.

"For example, the two ships that were chartered in '66 and '91. For the expeditions to Gela Alta."

I go over to the trolley and wring out the rag.

"I hope you'll be satisfied now," I say. "We have to move on. Duty calls."

On our way out we can look back through the long series of rooms all the way into his office. He's sitting behind the desk. He hasn't moved.

At the bottom of the stairs a middle-aged woman in a white smock is standing. She's patting her vacuum cleaner, her expression sorrowful. As if she's been discussing how the two of them are going to manage in the big world without that trolley.

The mechanic puts it down in front of her. He's not very happy about having taken someone else's equipment. He wants to say a few words. From one craftsperson to another. But he can't think of anything to say.

"We're from the firm," I say. "We've been checking your work. We are very, very satisfied."

I find one of Moritz's spanking new 100-kroner notes in my pocket and balance it on the edge of the bucket.

"Please accept this bonus. On such a fine morning. To buy a piece of pastry for your coffee."

She looks at me with melancholy eyes.

"I own the firm," she says. "There's only me and four employees."

We stand there a moment, staring at each other, all three of us.

"So what?" I say. "Even bosses eat pastry with their coffee."

*   *   *

We get into the car and sit there for a while, gazing out across Kongens Nytorv. It's too late for us to eat breakfast together. We agree to meet later. Now that the tension is past, we talk to each other like strangers. After I get out, he rolls down the window.

"Smilla, was that wise?"

"It was an impulse," I say. "And besides, have you ever done any hunting?"

"A little."

"If you're hunting timid animals, like reindeer, you let them catch sight of you a few times on purpose. You stand up and wave the butt of your rifle. In all living creatures, fear and curiosity are neighbouring brain cells. The deer comes closer. It knows that it's dangerous. But it has to come and see what's moving like that."

"What did you do when it came close?"

"Nothing," I said. "I've never been able to make myself shoot. But maybe you're lucky enough to have someone nearby who *knows* what has to be done."

I walk home across Knippels Bridge. It's eight o'clock, the day has hardly begun. I feel as if I've accomplished as much as if I had done a paper round.

A letter is waiting for me, a rectangular envelope of deckle-edged, hand-made stationery. It's from my father. It's a lined envelope from the United Paper Companies with his initials embossed on it. His handwriting looks as if he has taken a course in bragging about himself calligraphically. Which he has. That was while I was living with him. After two evening classes he had forgotten his old handwriting. And still hadn't learned a new one. After three months he wrote like a child. I had to forge his signature on the invoices he sent out. He was afraid his patients would have a relapse when they saw the great medicine man's wobbly signature.

Later it became more controlled. The world admires it. To me it simply seems toffee-nosed.

But the letter is friendly enough. It consists of one line on a piece of paper with a watermark, which I know costs five kroner per sheet. And a bunch of photocopies of newspaper clippings, held together with a paper clip.

"Dear Smilla," it says. "Here's what *Berlingske Tidende*'s archives had on Loyen and Greenland."

There is one more sheet.

"A complete list of his scientific publications," it says in Moritz's handwriting. The list is typed.

Underneath it says that the information is from something called *Index Medicus*, acquired from a database in Stockholm. There are articles in four languages, including Russian. Most of them are in English. I can't even understand the titles of half of them. But Moritz has added a brief explanation in the margin. There are articles on crash injuries. On toxicology. A co-authored article on the difficulties in assimilation of vitamin B_{12} by the stomach as a complication of gunshot wounds. They're from the forties and fifties. In the sixties the articles start dealing with Arctic medicine. Trichinosis, frostbite. A book about influenza epidemics around the Barents Sea. There is a long list of shorter articles on parasites. Many on the use of X-rays. His work has been in a great many fields.

It looks as if he has done historical research on several occasions. There's an article on the examination of the Iron Age bog people. And there are three articles I put a tick next to. They deal with the examination of mummies by X-ray. One of them was carried out in Berlin in the seventies, at the Pergamon Museum, on mummies from Tutankhamen's tomb. The second one deals with pre-Buddhist embalming methods in Malaysia and Thailand, published by a museum in Singapore. The third is a treatise on the Greenlandic Qilakitsoq mummies.

At the bottom of the list I write: "With thanks – Smilla", put it in an envelope, and address it to my father. Then I go through the clippings.

There are eighteen of them, and they're in chronological order. I start with the most recent. There's an article from October, announcing that preparations are now almost complete for the establishment of a forensic medical office for Greenland under the leadership of Professor Johannes Loyen, MD. The next one is from a year earlier. There's a photo with a brief caption: "The ethics council at the conference in Godthåb". Wearing *kamiks* and fur hats. Loyen is second from the left. He towers as high as those standing behind him a couple of steps up. The next one is from his seventieth birthday the year before. The text says that due to his work with an autopsy centre for Greenland, they have made an exception and extended his tenure. The articles continue this way, backwards in time. "Congratulations on your sixtieth, Professor Loyen". "Professor Loyen lectures at Greenland's newly opened university". "Representatives from the board of health in Greenland, Copenhagen's chief medical officer to the left, and chief of staff J. Loyen, head of the newly established Institute for Arctic Medicine". And so on, backwards through the seventies and sixties. The expeditions of '91 and '66 are not mentioned.

The next-to-last clipping is from 1949. It's a little piece of verbal prostitution. An enthusiastic description of the Cryolite Corporation Danmark's new dumpsters, which have eased the transport of ore from the deeper sections of the quarry up to the earth's surface. A heartfelt tribute to Alderman Ebel and his wife, who are pictured in front. Behind stand chief engineer Dr Wilhelm Ottesen and the corporation's medical consultant, Dr Johannes Loyen. The photo was taken at the quarry in Saqqaq, at the moment when the new machines brought the first load to the surface.

After this picture there's a gap of ten years. The last clipping is from May 1939.

It's a photo with a caption. The picture was taken in a harbour. A dark ship is in the background. About a dozen people are standing in the foreground. Gentlemen in lightweight suits, women in long skirts and thin wraps. The setting makes it seem staged. The caption is quite brief: "The courageous and enthusiastic company from Freia Film upon departure for Greenland". Then follows a list of the courageous and enthusiastic company. It consists of actors and a director, the film company's doctor and his assistant. The doctor's name is Rovsing. The assistant is unnamed. Assistants didn't have names in the conservative press in the thirties. But his later career has preserved also this photo in an archive, and prompted someone to add his name with a ballpoint pen. He's visible in the photograph. Taller than everyone else. And in spite of his youth, his subordinate position, and his standing behind eccentrics pandering to the camera, his arrogance shines through even then. It's Loyen. I fold up the clipping.

After breakfast I put on a long suede coat and the Jane Eberlein fur hat. The coat has deep inside pockets. Into them I put the last, folded clipping, a bundle of folding money, Isaiah's tape, and the letter to my father. Then I leave. The day has begun.

At Pronto Print on Torvegade I have a copy of the tape made. I also borrow their phone book. The Institute for Eskimology is located on Fiolstræde. I call them from the phone booth on the square. I'm transferred to a teacher who sounds as if he is of Greenlandic extraction. I explain that I have a tape in East Greenlandic that I can't understand. He asks me why I don't go over to the Greenlanders' House.

"I want an expert. It's not just a matter of understanding what is said. I want to try to identify who is speaking. I'm looking for someone who can listen to the voice and tell me that the speaker has henna-dyed hair and was spanked as a five-year-old when he was sitting on the potty, and from his vowels it sounds as if this happened in Akunnaaq in 1947."

He starts chuckling to himself.

"Do you have money, madam?"

"Do you? And it's not madam. It's miss."

"Svajerbryggen. It's on Sydhavnen. Berth number 126. Ask for the curator."

He's still chuckling as he hangs up.

I take the train to Enghave Station. From there I walk. I've had a look at Krak's Map of Copenhagen at the library on Torvegade. In my mind I have an image of a labyrinth of winding streets.

The station is cold. A man is standing on the opposite platform. He's staring longingly towards the train that will take him away, into the city, into the crowds. He's the last person I see.

Right now the inner city is like an anthill. People are crowding into the department stores. They're getting ready for theatre premières. They're standing in line in front of Hviid's Wine Cellar.

Sydhavnen is a ghost town. The sky is low and grey. The inhaled air tastes of coal smoke and chemicals.

Anyone who is afraid that machines will soon take over should not take a stroll in Sydhavnen. The snow hasn't been cleared away. The pavements are impassable. Along the narrow, ploughed tracks now and then enormous articulated lorries with dark windows devoid of any humans move. A blanket of green smoke hovers over a soap factory. A cafeteria advertises potato fry-up and sausages. Behind the windows red and yellow lights shine on lonely deep-fat fryers in an empty kitchen. Above a pile of coal and slush a crane moves aimlessly and restlessly back and forth on its rails. From the cracks in closed garage doors there are some bluish glimmers and the crackling of arc welders, and the jingling of the illegal money being earned, but no human voices.

Then the road opens on to a picture postcard: a large harbour basin surrounded by low yellow warehouses. The water is iced over, and while I'm still taking stock of the view, the sun appears, low, white-gold, surprising, and lights up the ice like an underground electric bulb behind frosted glass. There are small fishing boats at the wharf with blue hulls the colour of the sea where it meets the horizon. On the outer edge of the basin, out in the harbour itself, there is a big three-masted sailing ship. That's Svajerbryggen.

Berth 126 is the sailing ship. I don't meet a soul on the way. All the machine sounds have disappeared behind me. Everything is quiet.

A post is sticking up from the wharf with a white letterbox on it. Above is a large sign, still wrapped in white plastic.

On the stern it says in gilded letters that the ship's name is *Northern Light*. It has a figurehead carved like a man holding a torch; it has a shiny black hull at least thirty metres long, masts that tower up to the sky and give the impression that you're standing in front of a church, and a smell of tar and sawdust. Someone has recently spent a fortune renovating it.

I go on board via a gangway with a thick coir mat and railings with polished bronze knobs. The entire deck is filled with big wooden crates marked FRAGILE and stacks of planks and tins of paint. All the ropes are meticulously coiled, all the woodwork has the deep, dark brown sheen of a dozen layers of expensive ship's lacquer. The enamel paint shines like glass. The air shimmers with polish, two-component epoxy, and joint paste. Aside from this shimmering, the ship is apparently deserted.

A narrow ladder between the crates leads to a lacquered double door that isn't locked. Beyond the door a companionway descends into the darkness.

At the bottom of the steps a man stands. He's leaning on a spear, and he doesn't move. Not even when I'm quite close to him.

The room must have several skylights that are still covered. But along the edges of the covers, thin stripes of white light filter in. Enough so that I can see it's a big saloon. All the dividing walls have been torn out to create an area that is about twenty-five metres long and the width of the ship.

Now there is enough light for me to see that the man in front of me is an Eskimo. What he's leaning on is a long harpoon. In his left hand he's holding a dart thrower. He is not in full dress, in high *kamiks* and a suit of bird skin and feathers. He isn't much taller than me. I pat him on the cheek. He is cast from hollow fibreglass and then cleverly painted. His face is attentive.

"Lifelike, isn't it?"

The voice comes from somewhere behind a screen. On my way over to it I have to go around a kayak that is still partially wrapped and a glass counter lying there on its side like an empty 3,000-litre aquarium. The screen is a hide stretched between two whalebones. Behind it is a desk. Behind the desk sits a man. He stands up and I shake his proffered hand. He looks exactly like the manikin. But he's thirty years older. His hair is thick and cut pageboy-style, but grey. His background is like mine. Greenlandic in some way.

"You're the curator?"

"Yes, I am."

His Danish is without accent. He gestures with his hand.

"We're in the process of setting up the collection. It costs a fortune."

I place the tape in front of him. He touches it cautiously.

"I'm trying to identify the man speaking. I found my way over here by calling the Institute for Eskimology."

He smiles with satisfaction. "Word of mouth is the best advertisement. And by far the cheapest. Do you know what it costs to advertise?"

"Only personal ads."

"Is that expensive?"

He is sincerely interested. Humour is wasted on him.

"Very."

He nods. "It's terrible. They clean you out. The newspapers. The inland revenue, the customs office . . ."

It appears to me that I've seen him before. It's a feeling that I get from faces and places more and more often. I don't know whether it's because I've seen so much that the world is starting to repeat itself, or whether it's due to premature wear and tear on the mental apparatus.

He has a square, flat, matte-black cassette tape recorder on the table in front of him. He puts in the tape. The sound comes from distant speakers on the perimeter of the room. Now that my eyes are becoming adjusted to the darkness, I can intuit the way the walls curve where they follow the sides of the ship.

He listens for half a minute with his head in his hands. Then he stops the tape.

"Mid-forties. Grew up near Ammassalik. Very little formal

education. On top of the East Greenlandic there are traces of more northern dialects. But up there they move around too much to say which exactly. He has probably never been away from Greenland for any significant period of time."

He looks at me with light-grey, almost milky eyes, with an expression as if he's waiting for something. Suddenly I know what it is. It's the applause after the first act.

"Impressive," I say. "Can you tell me more?"

"He's describing a journey. Across ice. With sleighs pulled by rope. Well, yes – and dogs. He's probably a hunter, because he uses a series of technical terms, such as *anut* for the dog harnesses. He's probably talking to a European. He uses English names for locations. And he seems to think he has to repeat many things."

He listened to the tape for a very short time. I wonder whether he's pulling my leg.

"You don't believe me," he says coldly.

"I just wonder how you can conclude so much from so little."

"Language is a hologram."

He says this slowly and firmly.

"In every human utterance lies the sum total of that person's linguistic past. Now, you yourself . . . You're in your mid-thirties. Grew up in Thule or north of there. One or both parents Inuit. You came to Denmark after assimilating the entire linguistic foundation of Greenlandic, but before you lost the child's instinctive talent for learning a foreign language perfectly. Let's say you were between seven and eleven years old. After that it gets more difficult. There are traces of several sociolects. Perhaps you lived or went to school in the northern suburbs, Gentofte or Charlottenlund. There is also a trace of a North Sealand accent. And strangely enough, even a later hint of West Greenlandic."

I make no attempt to hide my astonishment.

"That's true," I say. "It's all basically accurate."

He smacks his lips in satisfaction.

"Is there any possibility of determining where the conversation took place?"

"You really can't tell?"

I notice it again. His bold self-confidence and his sense of triumph at his knowledge.

He rewinds. He doesn't look at the tape recorder while he's handling it. He plays about ten seconds for me.

"What do you hear?"

I hear only the incomprehensible voice.

"Behind the voice. Another sound."

He plays it again. Then I hear it. The faint, escalating sound of a motor, like a generator starting up and then shut off.

"A prop plane," he says. "A big prop plane."

He fast-forwards. Turns it on again. A segment with the faint clatter of dishes.

"A large room. Low-ceilinged. Tables being set. Some kind of restaurant."

I can see that he knows the answer. But he's enjoying pulling it very slowly out of his top hat.

"A voice in the background."

He plays the same segment several times. Now I can just make it out.

"A woman," I say.

"A man talking like a woman. He's yelling. In Danish and American English. Danish is his mother tongue. Presumably he's yelling at the person setting the table. He's probably the restaurant manager."

One last time I wonder whether he's just guessing. But I know he's right. He must have an abnormally precise and skilled sense of hearing and a gift for languages.

The tape is playing again.

"Another prop plane," I suggest.

He shakes his head. "A jet. A smaller jet. Quite soon after the previous plane. An airport with heavy traffic."

He leans back.

"Where in the world can an East Greenlandic hunter sit and talk in a restaurant where the tables are being set, where a Dane is yelling in American English, and where you can hear an airport in the background?"

Now I know, too, but I let him tell me. Let little kids have their fun. Even grown-up kids.

"Only one place. At Thule Air Base."

On the base the club is called the Northern Star. A restaurant in two sections, with a concert hall.

He starts the tape again. "It's strange."

I don't say a word.

"The music . . . behind the voice . . . remnants from the previous recording. It's pop, of course. 'There Must Be an Angel' by the Eurythmics. But the trumpet . . ."

He looks up.

"The piano, of course you can hear that, is a Yamaha Grand."
I can't hear any piano at all.

"A loud, heavy, flashy tone. A rather clumsy bass. Often a little off-key. Certainly no Bösendorfer . . . But it's the trumpet that surprises me."

"There's some of the music left at the end of the tape," I say.

He fast-forwards. When he presses the play button, we're at a spot right after the music starts.

"Mr PC!" he says. Then his face goes blank, self-absorbed.

He lets it play to the end. When he stops the tape, he seems very far away. I give him time to come back. He wipes his eyes.

"Jazz," he says quietly. "My passion . . ."

It was a brief moment of letting down his guard. When he comes back, he's as cocky as ever. Three-quarters of the politicians and bureaucrats who are part of the Home Rule belong to his generation. They were the first Greenlanders to get a university education. Some of them have survived and held on to their identities. Others – like the curator – with their fragile but abnormally overblown self-confidence, have become genuine, intellectual Northern Danes.

"It's actually quite difficult to recognize a musician from the tone. Who can you identify this way? Stan Getz when he plays Latin-American style. Miles Davis from his naked, precise, vibrato-less sound. Armstrong by his meticulous crystallization of New Orleans jazz. And this musician."

He looks at me, full of anticipation and reproach.

"Great jazz is synonymous with the John Coltrane quartet. McCoy Tyner on the piano, Jimmy Garrison on bass, Elvin Jones on drums. And in the periods when Jones was in prison: Roy Hanes. Just those four. Except on four occasions. The four concerts at the New York Independent Club. That's when Roy Louber joined them on trumpet. He learned his sense for European harmonizing and his incantatory African nerve from Coltrane himself."

We sit there for a moment thinking about this.

"Alcohol", he says suddenly, "has never been good for music. Cannabis is supposed to be great. But alcohol is a ticking bomb under jazz."

We sit there listening to the bomb ticking.

"Since that time in '64, Louber has been studying to drink himself to death. On his way down, in both human and musical terms, he happened to come through Scandinavia. And he stayed here."

Now I remember his name from concert posters. From certain

scandalous newspaper headlines. One of them said: FAMOUS DRUNK JAZZ MUSICIAN TRIES TO TIP OVER CITY BUS.

"He must have been playing in the restaurant. It's the same acoustics. The people eating in the background. Someone has seized the opportunity to make a pirate recording."

He smiles, full of sympathy for such a project.

"They've managed to get themselves a free live recording. You can save a lot of money with a little Walkman. If you dare take the risk."

"Why would he go to Thule?"

"Money, of course. Jazz musicians live on so-called bare-ass jobs. Imagine what it costs . . ."

"What costs?"

"To drink yourself to death. Have you ever thought about how much money you save by not being an alcoholic?"

"No," I say.

"Five thousand kroner," he says.

"I beg your pardon?"

"That will be five thousand kroner for the session. Ten thousand if you want a notarized transcription of the contents."

There's not a trace of a smile on his face. He's deadly serious.

"Can I get a receipt?"

"Then I'll have to add sales tax."

"Go ahead," I say. "Go right ahead."

I really can't use the receipt for anything. But I'm going to hang it up on the wall at home. As a reminder of what can happen to the famous Greenlandic generosity and indifference to money.

He types it up, on a sheet of A4 paper.

"I'll need at least a week. Do you want to call me five or six days after New Year's?"

I take five crisp new thousand-kroner notes from the bundle. He closes his eyes and listens as I count them out. He has at least one passion more burning than modal jazz. It's the sensual crackle of money changing hands, with him on the receiving end.

After I stand up I think of one other thing I have to ask him.

"How did you learn to pick up so much from listening?"

He beams like a sun. "I was originally a theologian. An occupation that presents excellent opportunities for listening to people."

It's because the pastoral robes are such a total mask that it has taken me so long to recognize him. Even though it's less than ten days since I saw him bury Isaiah.

135

"Occasionally I still step into the role. Assist Pastor Chemnitz when he's busy. But in the last forty years it's been mostly languages. My teacher at the university was Louis Hjelmslev. He was a professor of comparative linguistics. He had a solid knowledge of forty or fifty languages. And he had learned and forgotten just as many. I was young then and as surprised as you are. When I asked him how he had learned so many languages, he replied" – and now he imitates a man with a severe overbite – "'The first thirteen or fourteen take a long time. After that, it goes a lot faster.'"

He roars with laughter. He's in a terrific mood. He has demonstrated his brilliance and earned money for it. It strikes me that he is the first Greenlander I've ever met who used the formal *De* with me and expected me to do the same.

"There's one more thing," he says. "Since I was twelve years old, I've been totally blind."

He enjoys my sudden stiffness.

"I make my eyes follow your voice. But I can't see a thing. Under certain circumstances, blindness sharpens the sense of hearing."

I shake the hand he offers me. I ought to keep my mouth shut. It's really very wrong to harass a blind man. And a fellow countryman at that. But for me there's always been something mysterious and provocative about genuine, sincere greed.

"Mr Curator," I whisper, "you should be careful. At your age. With all the money you have on you. Surrounded by these treasures. On a ship that's screaming like an open bank vault. Sydhavnen is crawling with crooks. You know the world is full of people unscrupulously striving to obtain the possessions of their fellow human beings."

He tries to swallow his Adam's apple.

"Goodbye," I say. "If I were you, I would barricade the door after I leave."

The last golden rays of sunshine have settled on the flat paving stones of the dock. In a few minutes they'll be gone, leaving behind a raw, damp cold.

There's not a soul in sight. I use a key to slit the white plastic on the sign. Just a rip, just enough to see inside. It was painted by a sign painter. Black letters on a white background. "Copenhagen University, the Polar Centre, and the Cultural Ministry are here establishing the ARCTIC MUSEUM". Then a list of the foundations paying for the fun. I don't bother to read it. I start walking along the dock.

The Arctic Museum. That's where Isaiah's ship was bought. I pull the curator's receipt out of a deep pocket. It's impeccably composed, and yet another miracle, considering that he's blind. He signed it. His signature is illegible. But he has also stamped it. I can read the stamp.

It says, "Andreas Fine Licht, Ph.D. Professor of Eskimo Languages and Cultures".

I stand still until the shock subsides. Then I consider going back.

I decide to keep going. The tape is a copy. And when you're hunting, it's sometimes beneficial to make yourself visible, to stop and wave the butt of your rifle.

$$4$$

I ARRIVE JUST ABOUT ON TIME. The little blue Morris is parked on Hans Christian Andersens Boulevard, in front of Tivoli.

The mechanic looks like a man who's been waiting, and while waiting thinking too many gloomy thoughts.

I get in beside him. The car is cold. He doesn't look at me. His face reveals his pain like an open book. Together we stare straight ahead in silence. I'm not in the police force. I have no reason to press him for a confession.

"The Baron," he says finally, "he *remembered*. He never forgot."

I've had the same thought myself.

"S-sometimes three weeks would pass without him coming to the basement. When I was a kid and went away to summer camp for three weeks, I had practically forgotten my parents by the time I came home. But the Baron *did* little things. If I'm on my way home and he's at the playground playing, he stops. And then runs up to me. And then just walks along with me for a while. As if to show me that we know each other. Just up to the door. There he stops. And nods to me. To show that he hasn't forgotten me. Other children forget. They like anyone, and they forget anyone."

He bites his lip. I have nothing to add. There's relatively little that words can do for grief. Words can do relatively little about anything. But what else do we have?

"We're going to a café," I say.

On our way through the city I tell him nothing about my visit to Berth 126. But I do tell him about my phone call afterwards, from a phone booth, to Benedicte Clahn.

La Brioche d'Or is on Strøget, near Amagertorv, on the second floor, a couple of buildings past the Royal Porcelain shop.

In the doorway there are photographs of the cornucopia, a metre in diameter, that the patisserie delivered to the royal court with a crane. On our way up the stairs there is a display of particularly memorable cream cakes that look as if they've been given a coat of hairspray and will remain there for all eternity. The entrance is guarded by a life-sized model of the boxer Ayub Kalule that was made out of dark chocolate when he became European Champion, and inside there is a long table covered with cakes that look capable of anything except flying.

The ceiling is decorated with plaster curlicues like whipped cream, and there are chandeliers, and on the floor is a carpet as thick and plush and the same colour as a sponge cake drenched in sherry. Elegant ladies are sitting at small tables with white table-cloths, helping down a second piece of Sachertorte with half-litre cups of hot cocoa. To alleviate the expected shock of the bill and the encounter with the bathroom scales, a pianist wearing a toupee is sitting on a platform absentmindedly playing a Mozart potpourri, which turns downright sloppy when he attempts to wink at the mechanic at the same time.

In one corner, sitting alone, is Benedicte Clahn.

Certain people don't seem to match their voices. I can still remember my own surprise when, for the first time, I stood face to face with Ulloriannguaq Christiansen, who had read the news for twenty years on Greenland Radio. The voice had created expectations of a god. He turned out to be merely a human being, only slightly taller than I am.

The voices of other people mirror their appearance so precisely that once you've heard them speak, you're bound to recognize them when you see them. I spoke to Benedicte Clahn on the phone for one minute, and I know that's her. She's wearing a blue suit, she has kept her hat on indoors, she's drinking mineral water, and she's as beautiful and skittish and unpredictable as a racehorse.

She's in her mid-sixties, with long reddish-brown hair partially pinned up under her hat. She is straight-backed, pale, with an aggressive chin and flaring nostrils. She's a complex person if I've ever seen one.

The time it takes to cross the floor is all I have to make a few crucial decisions.

*　　　*　　　*

Some hours earlier I called her from a phone booth at Enghave Station. Her voice is deep, hoarse, almost lazy. But underneath the calm I think I can sense a pair of bellows. Or maybe I'm hearing a mirage. After spending an hour at Berth 126, I don't trust my ears any more.

When I tell her that I'm interested in her work in Berlin in 1946, she refuses to discuss it.

"It's absolutely out of the question. Completely impossible. It's a matter of military secrets, you know. And, by the way, it was Hamburg."

She is quite determined. But at the same time there is a touch of curiosity strictly reined in.

"I'm calling from Svanemølle Army Base," I say. "We're putting together a publication in honour of Danish participation in the Second World War."

She does an about-turn.

"Are you really? So you're calling from the base. Are you from the Women's Corps, perhaps?"

"I have a master's in history. I'm editing this commemorative publication for the army's historical archives."

"Are you really? A woman! I'm pleased to hear that. I think I'd better speak to my father first. Do you know my father?"

I haven't had the pleasure. And if I'm going to meet him, I'd better hurry. According to my calculations, he must be about ninety. But I don't say this out loud.

"General August Clahn," she says.

"We would like the publication to be a surprise."

She understands perfectly.

"When would you be free to talk to me?"

"That will be difficult," she says. "I'll have to look at my calendar."

I wait. I can see my reflection in the steel wall of the phone booth. It shows a big fur hat. Dark hair underneath. Beneath the hair a smirking smile.

"I might just be able to find time this afternoon."

That's what I remember on my way through the café. As I look at her. A general's daughter. A friend of the military. But also a hoarse voice. The way she looks at the mechanic. An explosive person. I reach a decision.

"Smilla Jaspersen," I say. "And this is Captain Peter Føjl, Ph.D."
The mechanic freezes.

Benedicte Clahn laughs radiantly at him. "How exciting. Are you a historian, too?"

"One of the best military historians in northern Europe," I say.

His right eye starts to twitch. I order coffee and raspberry tarts for him and myself. Benedicte Clahn orders another mineral water. She doesn't want any cake. She wants Dr Peter Føjl's undivided attention.

"There's so much. I don't know what you're interested in."

I take the plunge. "Your collaboration with Johannes Loyen."

She nods. "You've spoken to him?"

"He and Captain Føjl are close friends."

She nods girlishly. That's natural. That one sheik would know the other.

"It's so long ago, you know."

The coffee arrives in a bistro coffeepot. It's hot and aromatic. Meeting the mechanic is what has lured me out onto the slippery slopes of injurious intoxicants.

He leaves his cup untouched. He hasn't yet grown accustomed to his academic distinction. He's sitting there looking down at his hands.

"It was in March of 1946. The Royal Air Force had taken over Dagmar House on Rådhuspladsen from the Germans. I found out that they were looking for young Danish men and women who could speak German and English. My mother was Swiss. I had gone to school in Grindelwald. I'm bilingual. I was too young to join the Resistance. But I saw this as an opportunity to do something for Denmark."

She's talking to me. But everything is directed at the mechanic. A large part of her life has probably been directed towards men.

She laughs hoarsely. "To be quite honest, I had a boyfriend, a second lieutenant who had gone down there six months earlier. I wanted to be wherever he was. Women had to turn twenty-one within the first three months they were there. I was eighteen. And I wanted to leave at once. So I lied that I was three years older."

Maybe, I think to myself, this was also your chance to escape from Daddy General in a legal way.

"I was interviewed by a squadron-leader in the blue-grey uniform of the RAF. There was also a test in English and German. And in reading Gothic German handwriting. They said they wanted to check my conduct during the war. They could not have done that, or they would have found out about my age."

The raspberry tart has a bottom layer of almond custard. It tastes of fruit, burnt almonds, and heavy cream. Combined with the surroundings, it is for me the quintessence of the middle and upper classes in Western civilization. The union of exquisitely sophisticated crowning achievements and a nervous, senselessly extravagant consumption.

"We took a special train to Hamburg. Of course, Germany was divided among the Allied powers. Hamburg was British. We worked and were housed in a large Hitler Jugend barracks. Count Goltz Barracks in Rahlstedt."

Being the untalented listeners that they are, most Danes cheat themselves out of experiencing a fascinating law of nature. The one now taking effect in Benedicte Clahn, the transformation of the speaker the minute she becomes absorbed in her story.

"We were housed in double rooms with two beds across from the buildings where we worked. It was a large hall. We sat twelve to a table. We wore uniforms, khaki-coloured battledress with skirts, shoes, stockings, and a cape. We had the rank of sergeant in the British Army. At every table there was a *Tischsortierer*. At our table this was a female British captain."

She pauses for a moment. The pianist is working his way into Frank Sinatra. She isn't listening.

"Purple Bols," she says. "I got drunk for the first time in my life. We could buy things at the PX on the base. For a carton of Capstan cigarettes we could get as much on the black market as a German family spent on living expenses for a month. The man in charge was Colonel Ottini. An Englishman in spite of his name. About thirty-five. Charming, with a face like a good-natured bulldog. We read all mail going out and coming into the country. Letters and envelopes looked the way they do today. But the paper was worse. We would cut open the envelope, read the letter, stamp it CEN-SORED, and then tape it closed. All photographs and drawings were to be removed and destroyed. All letters with gossip about Nazis who had positions in the reconstruction of Germany were to be reported. If, for example, it said, 'Just imagine, once he was a *Sturmbannführer* in the SS, and now he's a manager . . . , etc.' It was quite common. But mostly they were looking for the Nazi underground organization called *Edelweiss*. You see, the Germans had burned a large part of their own archives during the retreat.

The Allies were in desperate need of information. That must be why they hired us. There were six hundred of us Danes. And that was just in Hamburg. If a letter mentioned the word *Edelweiss*, if it contained a pressed flower, if letters were underlined that might form the word *Edelweiss*, then we were supposed to stamp it – we each had our own rubber stamp – and send it on to *der Tischsortierer*."

As if by telepathy the pianist is now playing "Lili Marlene". With a march tempo, the way Marlene Dietrich sang one of the verses. Benedicte Clahn closes her eyes. Her voice has changed.

"That song," she says.

We wait until it comes to the end. It slips over into "*Ich hab' noch einen Koffer in Berlin*".

"The worst thing was the hunger," she says. "The hunger and the destruction. It was twenty minutes by a kind of metro from Rahlstedt to the centre of Hamburg. We were off every Saturday afternoon and Sunday. And with our sergeants' uniforms, we had access to the officers' mess halls. We could get champagne, caviar, chateaubriand, ice cream. Fifteen minutes from the centre of town, near Wandsbek, the piles of rubble started. You can't possibly imagine it. Rubble as far as the eye could see. All the way to the horizon. A plain of ruins. And the Germans. They were starving. They walked past on the street, pale, hollow-cheeked, famished. I was there for six months. Never, not once, did I ever see a German hurry."

She has tears in her voice. She has forgotten where she is. She grips my arm hard.

"War is horrible!"

She looks at us, realizes that we are representatives of the armed forces, and for a brief moment a number of planes of consciousness collide for her. Then she returns to the present, cheerful and sensual. She smiles at the mechanic.

"My second lieutenant went home. I was ready to follow him. But one day I'm called into Ottini's office. He makes me an offer. The next day I'm transferred to Blankenese. On the Elbe. There the British had taken over all the big mansions. We worked in one of them. There were forty of us in the house. Mostly British and Americans. The twenty who worked on the top floor listened in on the telephone network. Downstairs there were several different groups. Of course we were never told what the others were doing. In Rahlstedt we had also been sworn to secrecy. But there we talked to each other all the same. We showed each other funny letters. In Blankenese it was completely different. That's where I met Johannes Loyen. At first it was just myself and two others. An English mathematician and a Belgian teacher of choreographic notation systems. We worked with coded letters and telephone conversations. Mostly letters."

She laughs.

"I think they were testing us in the beginning. Gave us things that weren't important. We often cracked two letters a day. They were usually love letters. I arrived in July. In August something happened. The letters changed character. Many of them were written by the same people. A new censor was also attached to our group, a German who had worked for von Gehlen. I never understood it. That the Americans and the British took over parts of the German intelligence apparatus. But he was a kind and gentle man. You can never really tell about people, can you? – they say that Himmler played the violin. His name was Holtzer. He somehow had a special knowledge of the case we were working on. That's what I gradually came to understand. That it was a case. The other three knew about it. They never said anything. But they kept on asking me about specific phrases. Gradually a picture began to emerge."

We've vanished for her again. She is in Hamburg, on the Elbe, in August 1946.

"There was one word they kept asking about. It was 'Niflheim'. One day I looked it up. It means 'world of mists'. It's the outermost part of 'Hel', the realm of the dead. By the end of August they must have narrowed down what they were looking for, because from then on we only received letters exchanged by the same four people. We never saw the envelopes. We only knew their names, never their addresses. At first we had eight letters. About two new ones arrived each week. The code was rather sloppy, like something learned in a hurry. But still complicated to break, because it didn't build on normal language but on a series of agreed-upon metaphors. It ostensibly dealt with the transport and sale of goods. It was at this time that Johannes – Dr Loyen – joined the group. He was in Germany as a forensic medicine expert, to participate in the closure of concentration camps."

She squints her eyes, which makes her look like a schoolgirl.

"A very handsome man. And quite vain. Give him my greetings and tell him I said that, Captain."

The mechanic nods and crushes his napkin in his hands.

"He was bitter because the forensic odontologists were the big stars in the identification process, not himself, also in connection with the Nuremberg trials. With our group he was supposed to serve as a consultant on medical matters. There was no need for that. At that time I discovered that Niflheim had to be an expedition to Greenland. Loyen knew something about Greenland. Perhaps he had been there. He never told us. But he was good at German. He ended up working on an equal footing with the rest of us. At the end of September we had a breakthrough. I was the one who broke the code. A letter mentioned, as a prognosis, the price of beans during the current week. Figures that rose slightly each day, culminating on Friday. I looked up the week in the *Write and Travel Calendar* that my mother had sent me. There was a full moon on Friday. I had sailed the English Channel in the Admiral's Cup on Father's big Colin Archer several times. It seemed to me that the numbers resembled tide tables. We looked them up in the big almanacs of the British fleet. It was the ebb and flow of the Elbe. After that it was easy. It took us three weeks to decipher our way backwards through the letters. They were about finding a ship, and sailing it to Greenland. Operation Niflheim."

"For what?" I ask.

She shakes her head.

"I never found out. I don't think the others knew, either. The letters were about negotiating for a ship – which was quite complicated because of the state of emergency. And about the possibility of sailing to Kiel and north through Danish waters. About which passages had been mine-swept. About the British blockade of the Elbe and the Kiel Canal. But all the people who wrote them knew what it was about. That's why they never mentioned it."

All three of us lean back at the same moment. Back to the patisscrie, the Golden Brioche, back to the smell of coffee, back to the present, to "Satin Doll".

"I would like a small tart," says Benedicte Clahn.

She has earned it. It arrives, looking like summer. With whipped cream so fresh and soft and yellowish white, as if they keep a cow at the back of the bakery.

I wait for her to taste it. It's difficult for people to be on their guard at the same time as their senses are being caressed.

"Have you talked about this to anyone else?"

She's about to deny it indignantly. Then her reawakened

memories and her trust in us and maybe even the taste of the raspberries do something to her.

"I was brought up taking discretion for granted," she says.

We nod reassuringly.

"Perhaps Johannes Loyen and I have discussed these things one or two times. But that was over twenty years ago."

"Was it possibly in 1966?"

She looks at me with surprise. For a moment I'm in the danger zone. Then she tells herself that, of course, we knew this from Loyen.

"Johannes worked for a company that was organizing a trip to Greenland. He wanted us to sit down together and try to reconstruct some of the information from the letters of '46. It was mainly route descriptions. A lot about anchoring conditions. We were not successful. Even though we spent a lot of time on it. I even think I received a fee for it."

"And again in '90 and '91?"

She bites her lip. "Helen, his wife, is very jealous."

"What was he interested in?"

She shakes her head. "He has never told me anything. Have you tried to ask him yourself?"

"We haven't had the opportunity," I say. "But we will."

Something about my reply distracts her. I search for something reassuring to divert her attention. She thinks of something herself. She looks from me to the mechanic and back again.

"Are you married?"

Surprisingly enough, he blushes. It starts at his throat and creeps upward, like a shellfish allergy. A flaming, helpless blush.

I notice a brief wave of heat along my inner thighs. For a moment I think someone has put something warm in my lap. But there's nothing there.

"No," I say. "It's difficult to devote yourself to the army's archives and have a family at the same time."

She nods sympathetically. She knows everything about the dichotomy between war and love.

"Two men meet," I say, "possibly in Berlin. Loyen and Ving. Loyen knows something, knows about something in Greenland worth finding. Ving has an organization that they can use as a cover for getting it, because he's the director of the Cryolite Corporation and its real leader. Then there's Andreas Fine Licht. About him we know only that he is familiar with conditions in Greenland."

I have no intention of telling him about Berth 126.

"They organize an expedition, under the guise of the corporation, in 1966. Something goes wrong. Maybe there was an accident involving explosives. At any rate, the expedition fails. So they wait twenty-five years. And then try again. But this time something is different. Outside money pays for the transportation. It seems as if they've got help and allied themselves with someone. But something goes wrong again. Four men die. One of them is Isaiah's father."

I'm sitting on the mechanic's sofa. Under a woollen blanket. He's standing in the middle of the room, about to open a bottle of champagne. There's something disconcerting to me about the expensive wine here in this room. He puts it down unopened.

"I talked to Juliane this afternoon," he says.

I noticed at the patisserie, and afterwards on the way home, that something was wrong.

"The Baron was examined every month at the hospital. She got f-fifteen hundred kroner every time. Always the f-first Tuesday of the month. They picked him up. She never went along. The Baron never said anything."

He sits down and stares at the cold bottle. I know what he's thinking. He's considering putting it away again.

He has put tall, fragile glasses in front of us. First he washed them in hot water without soap, and then dried them with a clean dishcloth until they were totally transparent. In his big hands they seem as fragile as cellophane.

In Nuuk the waiting list for housing is eleven years. Then you get a cupboard, a shed, a shack. All money in Greenland is stuck to the Danish language and culture. Those who master Danish get the lucrative positions. The others can languish in the fish factories or in unemployment lines. In a culture that has a homicide rate comparable to a war zone.

Growing up in Greenland has ruined my relationship to wealth for good. I see that it exists. But I could never strive for it. Or seriously respect it. Or regard it as a worthy goal.

Often I feel like a dustbin. Circumstances have dumped into my life the excesses of a technological culture: differential equations, a fur hat. And now: a bottle of wine chilled to 0 °C. Over the years it has become harder for me to enjoy it wholeheartedly. If it were all taken away in a flash, I wouldn't mind.

I no longer make an effort to keep Europe or Denmark at a distance. Neither do I plead with them to stay. In some way they are part of my destiny. They come and go in my life. I have given up doing anything about it.

It's night. The last few days have been so long that I've been looking forward to my bed, and to a sleep as all-consuming as in my childhood. In a moment, after merely moistening my lips with the wine, I will get up and leave.

He opens the bottle almost soundlessly. He pours, slowly and carefully, until the glasses are a little more than half full. They are instantly frosted with a matte mist. From invisible irregularities on the inner, curved sides, small beaded rows of bubbles rise to the surface.

He puts his elbows on his knees and gazes into the bubbles. His face is remote, absorbed by the sight and, at that moment, as innocent as a child's. The same way I so often saw Isaiah view the world.

I leave my glass untouched and sit down in front of him on the low table. Our faces are now at the same level.

"Peter," I say, "you know the old excuse that she was drunk so she didn't know what she was doing."

He nods.

"That's why I'm doing this before I drink anything."

Then I kiss him. I don't know how much time passes. But while it lasts, my whole body is in my mouth.

Then I leave. I could stay, but I don't. It's not because of him or me. It's out of respect for what has taken hold of me, for what hasn't been there for years, for what I don't think I recognize any more, for what is foreign to me.

It takes me a long time to fall asleep. But that's mostly because I don't have the heart to abandon the night and the silence, and the alert, hypersensitive consciousness that he is lying downstairs, somewhere below me.

When sleep finally comes, I dream that I'm in Siorapaluk. There are several of us children lying on the bed. We've been telling stories, and now the others have fallen asleep. Only my voice is left. I hear it from outside myself, it's trying to keep on going. But at last it staggers, wobbles, falls to its knees, spreads out its arms, and allows itself to be gathered up in a net of dreams.

THE ADDRESS OF THE TRADE COMMISSION is 1 Kampmannsgade, and it appears well maintained, newly painted,
efficient, reliable, helpful, and exclusive without being pretentious.

The man who helps me is a mere boy. He is twenty-three at most,
with a double-breasted, custom-made suit of thin Harris tweed, a
white silk tie, white teeth, and a broad smile.

"Where have I seen you before?" he asks.

The papers have been put in a spiral notebook, the pile is as
thick as an illustrated Bible and stamped *Annual Report of the
Cryolite Corporation Danmark for Fiscal 1991.*

"How can you tell who controls the corporation?"

His hands brush mine as he turns the pages.

"It doesn't say directly. But according to corporate law, all
shareholdings above five per cent must be listed on the first page.
Was it at a party at the Business School?"

The list is fourteen lines long, with individual and company
names mixed together. Ving is there. And the National Bank. And
Geoinform.

"Geoinform. Could you show me their annual report?"

He sits down at the terminal. While we wait for the computer
he smiles at me.

"I'll remember where it was," he says. "You didn't study law,
did you?"

He has been reading a French newspaper. He follows my gaze.

"I've applied to get into the foreign service," he says. "So
it's important to keep up on things. We don't have anything on
Geoinform. It's probably not a public corporation."

"Is it possible to find out who's on the board of directors?"

He gets out a volume as big as two telephone books called
Green's Danish Foundations. He looks it up for me. There are three
people on Geoinform's board. I write down their names.

"Can I take you to lunch?"

"I have to go for a walk in the Dyrehaven," I say.

"I could go, too."

I point at his loafers. "There's seventy-five centimetres of snow."

"I could buy a pair of wellies on the way."

"You're working," I say. "On your way into the diplomatic service."

He nods dejectedly.

"Maybe when the snow melts," he says. "In the spring."

"If we live that long," I say.

I go out to the Dyrehaven. It snowed in the night. I've taken my *kamiks* along. Well past the entrance, I put them on. The soles of *kamiks* cannot stand much wear. When we were kids we were never allowed to dance with them on if there was sand on the floor. You could wear them out in a single night. But on the snow and ice, where the friction is different, their durability is astounding. The new snow is light and cold. I walk as far away from the paths as possible. For an entire day I wade slowly and heavily among black branches glittering with snow. I follow the lurching tracks of a deer until I know its rhythm. The animal's sudden hopscotching every hundred metres, its habit of scattering urine in small portions, a little to the right of its tracks. The regularity with which it scratches an open, heart-shaped area down to the dark earth to find leaves.

After three hours I find it. A buck. White, wary, interested.

I find an out-of-the-way table at Peter Liep's Restaurant and order hot chocolate. Then I lay out the paper with the three names in front of me:

Katja Claussen
Ralf Seidenfaden
Tørk Hviid

I take out Moritz's envelope with the copies of the newspaper clippings. I'm looking for a specific one.

The room fills up with a group of children and adults. They've parked their skis and sleighs outside. Their voices are loud and full of glee. Full of the snow's mysterious warmth.

The clipping is from an English-language newspaper. Maybe that's why I've latched on to it. It was cut out crooked, so part of the headline is missing. It has then been added back on by hand, with a green ballpoint. The date is 19 March 1992. First Copenhagen Seminar on Neocatastrophism. Professor Johannes Loyen, MD, member of the Royal Danish Academy of Sciences, giving the opening lecture.

Loyen is standing on the stage, apparently without a script or podium. It's a large hall. Behind him sit three men at a table that curves like an arc of a circle.

"Behind him Ruben Giddens, Ove Nathan, and Toerk Hviid, the . . ."

The text has been cut off, the rest of the sentence is gone. Their typesetting machines didn't have an ø for his name. That's why it had caught my eye. That's why I remembered it.

The setting sun is glowing as I set off for home. My heart is pounding.

The minute I step through the door, the telephone rings.

It takes forever to get the red tape off. I think it must be the mechanic. He must have tried calling dozens of times.

"This is Andreas Fine Licht."

The voice is weak, as if he has a cold. "I suggest that you come at once."

I feel a surge of annoyance. Some of us never learn to take orders. "You mean today?"

There's a strangled sound, as if he's suppressing a laugh. "You're interested, aren't you? . . ."

He hangs up.

I'm standing there with all my outdoor clothes on. In the dark, because I didn't have time to turn on the light. Where did he get my phone number?

I detest being rushed. I had other plans for the day.

I put down the *kamiks* and go back out into the Copenhagen evening.

On my way down the stairs, I stop outside the mechanic's door. I feel tempted to take him along. But I recognize the feeling as a form of weakness.

I have a felt-tip pen in my pocket but no paper. On a fifty-krone note I write: "Sydhavnen, Svajerbryggen, Berth 126. Back later. Smilla."

This message is a compromise between my need for protection and my belief that the plans you keep secret are the ones most likely to succeed.

I take a taxi to the Sydhavnen power plant. Maybe it's the mechanic's paranoia about phones that has infected me, but I don't want to leave a clear trail.

It's a fifteen-minute walk from the plant.

Even the machines are asleep now. The city seems far away. But in the deserted streets I pass through there is still a shimmer of light. Now and then scattered fireworks etch trails of light across the blue-black sky and explode. The distant boom takes a moment to reach me. It's New Year's Eve.

There are no streetlights. The cranes are silent silhouettes against the lighter sky. Everything is closed, dimmed, resigned.

Svajerbryggen is a white surface in the dark. The new snow on the ice gathers the scant light in the air and gleams dully. Only a solitary car has been here before me, and I walk in its tracks.

The sign on the post is still covered with plastic. With the little rip I left behind. The dock, the gangway, and part of the deck have been cleared of snow. A couple of crates have been moved to make room for a pallet of red barrels. Aside from the snow and the barrels and the darkness, everything is the same as yesterday.

There is no light on board.

On my way up the gangway I start thinking about the car tracks. In snow, tyre tread makes a slight backward slide inside the track itself. The track I had followed went down to the harbour. There was no return track. There are no other roads to or from Svajerbryggen than the one I came along. But the car is nowhere to be seen.

The lacquered door is shut but not locked. Inside, there is a faint light.

I know that the fibreglass Eskimo will be there. The light is coming from somewhere behind the screen.

A little reading lamp is on the desk. Behind the desk sits professor and museum curator Andreas Fine Licht with his head cocked, smiling at me broadly.

When I walk around the desk, the smile does not leave his face.

He is gripping the seat of his chair with both hands. As if to hold himself upright.

Close up I can see that his lips are pulled back from his teeth in a grimace. And he isn't gripping the chair. His hands are bound with thin cords of copper wire. I touch him. He's warm. I put my fingers on his neck. There's no pulse. He has no heartbeat, either. At least none that I can feel.

He has cotton in the ear facing me. Like a small child with an earache. I walk around him. He has cotton in the other one too.

My curiosity is exhausted. Now I want to go home.

At that moment the hatch door over the stairs is shut. There is no warning, no sound of footsteps. It is simply closed, quietly and calmly. Then it is locked from the outside.

Then the light goes out.

Only now do I realize why there was so little light in the room. Blind people have no need for light. It's absurd to think about that now, but that's my first thought in the dark.

I get down on my knees and crawl under the desk. That may not be a good idea. That may be the ostrich's strategy. But I have no desire to stand there towering in the darkness. Down on the floor I can feel the curator's ankles. They are warm, too. And they are also bound to the chair with wire.

There's a movement on the deck above my head. Something being dragged. I fumble around in the dark and get hold of a telephone cord. I follow it and suddenly wind up with the end in my hands. It has been ripped out of the receiver.

Then the ship's engine starts up, a big diesel engine's slow awakening. It remains idling.

I run out into the darkness. Twenty-four hours ago I found my bearings in the room. So I know where there's a door. I reach the bulkhead right next to it. It's not locked. As I step through, the engine noise grows louder.

The room has small portholes high up and facing the dock. A faint light shines through them. This room explains how the curator solved his commuting problem. He lived on board. It has been furnished as a bedroom for him. A bed, a nightstand, a built-in wardrobe.

The engine room must be behind the far wall. It's insulated, but there is still a distinct thudding. As I try to look out of the porthole, the noise becomes a roar. The ship slowly swings away from the dock. The engine has been put into gear. There's not a soul in sight. Only the black contour of the disappearing wharf.

There's a spark on the dock. Only a glint of light, like someone lighting a cigarette. The glow rises and floats in an arc towards me. Trailing a dripping tail of embers after it. It's a flare.

It explodes not far above my head with a muted bang. The next instant I am blind. A vicious white flash flings itself at me from the wharf and the water. At the same moment the fire sucks all the oxygen out of the air, and I throw myself to the floor. It feels as if I have sand in my eyes, as if I'm breathing in a plastic bag at which someone is blowing with a hair dryer. It's the barrels of petrol, of course. They poured petrol over the ship.

I crawl over and open the door to the room I came from. Now there is all the light you could ask for. The covering over the sky-lights has burned away, and the room is illuminated by what seems like a gigantic sun lamp.

On the deck there is a series of muffled explosions, and the light outside flickers blue and then yellow. Then the air is filled with burning epoxy paint.

I creep back to the bedroom. It's as hot as a sauna. Against the whiteness of the portholes I can see the smoke that has started to seep inside. The fire vanishes from one of the panes for a moment. The silo of the soya bean factory lights up as if it's sunset, the windows along Islands Brygge glow like molten glass. It's the reflection from the fire all around me.

Then the glass is splintering from the heat and the view vanishes.

I wonder whether diesel oil burns. I remember that it requires a high temperature. At that instant the diesel tank blows up.

There isn't any explosion, it's more like a whistle that turns into a roar, that grows and turns into the shrillest sound that ever existed on earth. I press my head against the floor. When I look up, the bed is gone. The wall to the engine room is gone, and I'm looking into a world of fire. In the middle of this world the engine is a black rectangle with a tooled network of pipes. Then it starts to sink. It breaks away from the ship. When it reaches the sea, it causes explosive boiling. Then it vanishes. Over the water tongues of burning diesel fuel weave a tapestry of flames.

The stern of the boat now forms an open gateway facing Islands Brygge. As I stand there looking out, the whole ship slowly turns, away from the burning oil.

The wreck starts to list. The water has made its way into the hull and is pulling it backwards. I'm standing in water up to my knees.

The door behind me bangs open, and the professor comes in. The careening of the ship has made his office chair roll. He slams into the bulkhead next to me. Then he rides through what once was his bedroom and plunges into the water.

I take off my clothes. The suede coat, sweater, shoes, trousers, shirt, knickers, and finally my socks. I touch my hat. I have only a circle of fur on my head. The flames from the diesel engine must have burned it away. I feel blood on my hands. The top of my skull has been singed bald.

It's about two hundred metres to the dock at Svajerbryggen. I have no choice. On the other side is the fire. I jump.

The shock of the cold forces me to open my eyes while I'm still underwater. Everything is gleaming green and red, lit up by the fire. I don't look back. In water less than 6 °C you can survive only for a few minutes. The number of minutes depends on your condition. Swimmers of the English Channel were in good shape. They could last a long time. I'm in very poor shape.

I swim almost vertically, so that only my lips are above water. The problem is with the weight of the part of your body that's above water. After a few seconds the shaking starts. While your body temperature drops from 38 to 36 °C you shake. Then the shaking stops. That's when your temperature falls to 30 °C. This temperature is critical. That's when apathy sets in. That's when you freeze to death.

After a hundred metres I can't straighten out my arms any more. I think about my past. That doesn't help. I think about Isaiah. That doesn't help. I suddenly feel as if I'm not swimming any more but standing on a slope and leaning into a stiff wind, and that I might just as well give up.

Around me the water is a mosaic of bits of gold. I remember that someone has tried to kill me. And that they're now standing somewhere and congratulating themselves. We got her. Smilla. The fake Greenlander.

That thought carries me over the last stretch. I decide to take ten more strokes. At the eighth one I bang my head against a tractor tyre hung as a bumper on the berth of the *Northern Light*.

I know that I have only a few seconds of consciousness left. Next to the tyre is a platform right over the water. I try to scream myself up on to it. Not a sound comes out. But I manage to pull myself up.

If you fall into the water in Greenland, you run when you get out, to keep from freezing. But there the air is cold. Here it's wonderfully mild, like in the summer. At first I don't understand why. Then I realize it's because of the fire. I lie there on the platform. The *Northern Light* is now in the middle of the harbour entrance, a coal-black skeleton of wood in a white ball of fire.

I crawl up the stairs on my hands and knees. The dock is deserted. There's not a soul around.

I'm about to let go, basking in the warmth of the burning ship. I can see my own naked skin glowing. The little hairs, singed black and curling. Then I start walking. I have hallucinations, fragmentary, incoherent. From when I was little. A flower I found, knotweed, with buds. A convulsive fretting about whether Eberlein's has more brocade like the kind my hat was made of. The feeling of being sick and wetting my bed.

There are headlights, and I don't care. The car stops, and it doesn't make any difference. Something is wrapped around me. Nothing could interest me less. I lie down. I recognize the holes in the roof. It's the little Morris. It's the back of the mechanic's neck. He's driving the car.

"Smilla," he says. "Smilla, damn it . . ."

"Shut up," I say.

In his apartment he wraps me up in wool blankets and massages me until it hurts too much. Then he makes me drink one cup of milky tea after another. The cold won't go away. It feels as if it's penetrated my whole skeleton. At some point I also accept a glass of spirits.

I cry a lot. Partly out of self-pity. I tell him about Isaiah's hiding place. About the cassette tape. About the professor. About the phone call. About the fire. I feel as if my mouth is going while I stand somewhere else looking on.

He doesn't comment.

At some point he fills the bathtub with water for me. I fall asleep in the tub. He wakes me up. We lie side by side in his bed and sleep. A few hours at a time. I don't really feel warm until it starts to get light.

It's morning when we make love. It would seem I'm not quite myself.

THE CITY

3

I CHANGE TAXIS TWICE and get out at Farumvejen. From there I take the path through Utterslev Marsh, and I look back two hundred and fifty times.

I call from Tuborgvej.

"What is Neocatastrophism?"

"Why do you always call from those unbearable phone booths, Smilla? Is it money? Have they disconnected your phone? Shall I get it hooked up again?"

For Moritz, a New Year's Eve party is the king of all parties. He suffers from a cyclical, recurrent delusion that it's actually possible to start afresh, that you can build a new life on resolutions. On New Year's Day the pounding in his head is so bad that it's audible over the phone. Even a pay phone.

"There was a conference on the topic in Copenhagen, in March of '92," I say.

He stifles a groan as he tries to make his brain function. What finally gets it going is the fact that my question turns out to have something to do with him.

"I was invited," he says.

"Why didn't you go?"

"There was too much to read."

He has been saying for years that he has given up reading. First of all, it's a lie. Second, it's an insufferable way of intimating that he has grown so smart that the rest of the world has nothing more to teach him.

"Neocatastrophism is a collective term. It was coined by Schindewolf sometime in the sixties. He was a palaeontologist. But all kinds of scholars in the natural sciences have taken part in the debate. What they agree on is that the earth – and, in particular, its biology – has not evolved at an even pace but in leaps, which have been directed by great natural catastrophes that favour the survival of specific species. Meteor showers, comets, volcanic eruptions, spontaneous chemical disasters. The core of the debate has always been the question of whether these catastrophes occur at regular intervals. And if they do, what determines the frequency? An international association was established. Their first meeting was in Copenhagen. At the Falkoner Conference Centre. Opened by the Queen. They spared no expense. They get money from left, right and centre. The unions contribute because they think it's research about environmental disasters. Those in the industrial sector contribute because they think that at least it's *not* about environmental disasters. The research councils contribute because the association has some big names to flaunt."

"Does the name Hviid mean anything in that connection? Tørk Hviid?"

"There was a composer named Hviid."

"I don't think he's the one."

"You know I can't remember names, Smilla."

That's true. He can remember bodies. Titles. He can reconstruct every golf stroke in every sizable tournament he has played in. But he regularly forgets the name of his own secretary. It's symptomatic. For the truly self-centred person, the surrounding world pales and becomes nameless.

"Why didn't you go to that conference?"

"It was too much of a hotchpotch for my taste, Smilla. With all the opposing interests, all the politics. You know I avoid politics. They didn't even dare use the word 'catastrophe' when it came right down to it. They called it the 'Centre for Developmental Research'."

"Can you find out who Hviid is?"

He takes a deep breath, full of his unexpected power. "Then I can count on you coming out here tomorrow," he says.

I'm about to tell him to send the information to me. But I'm feeling weak and rather soft. He can tell.

"You can meet me and Benja at the Savarin tomorrow."

It sounds like an order, but it's meant as a quick compromise.

One of the children opens the door.

I'm among the first to admit that a cold weather climate is unpredictable. But I'm still momentarily surprised. Outside, it's five o'clock in the evening. The first stars have appeared in the navy-blue, cloudless sky. But inside, around the child, it's snowing. A fine layer covers her red hair, her shoulders, her face, and her bare arms.

I follow her. In the living room there is flour everywhere. Three children are kneading dough right on the hardwood floor. In the kitchen their mother is greasing biscuit tins. On the kitchen table a little girl is kneading something that looks like pastry dough. Now she's trying to knead an egg yolk into it. With her hands and feet.

"The bottom fell out of the bag of flour in the living room."

"I see. The floor will be wonderfully clean."

"He's out in the conservatory. I've forbidden him to smoke in here."

She has an authoritative strength, like my childhood image of God. And an unflappable gentleness like Santa Claus in a Disney film. If you want to know who the real heroes of world history are, just look at the mothers. In the kitchens, with the biscuit tins. While the men are sitting on the lavatory. Out in the hammocks. Out in the conservatory.

He's brushing off the cacti. The air is thick with cigar smoke. He has a little brush, as narrow as a toothbrush but with long bristles, curved, and maybe thirty centimetres long.

"It's so the pores won't clog up. That would prevent them from breathing."

"All things considered," I say, "that might be an advantage."

He gives me a guilty look. "My wife won't let me smoke around the children."

He shows me the stump of his cigar.

"Romeo and Giulietta. A classic Havana. And it tastes damn good. Especially the last couple of centimetres. When you're just about to singe your lips. That's where it's saturated with nicotine."

I hang my yellow down jacket over the back of one of the white wrought-iron chairs. Then I take the scarf off my head. There's a piece of gauze underneath. I take that off, too. The mechanic cleaned the wound and rubbed chlorhexidine ointment on it. I bend my head down so he can see it.

When I lift my head up, his eyes are hard.

"A burn," he says thoughtfully. "You were in the vicinity, perhaps?"

"I was on board."

He washes his hands in a deep stainless-steel sink.

"How did you manage to survive?"

"I swam."

He dries his hands and comes back. He touches the wound. It feels as if he's sticking his hands into my brain.

"It's superficial," he says. "You're not likely to go bald."

I called him at University Hospital earlier that day. I didn't give my name, but it wasn't necessary, anyway.

"The ship that burned in the harbour," I say. "There was a man on board."

It was the lead story on the radio. The newspapers had it on the front page. The photo was taken at night, in the light of the fire brigade's spotlights. In the middle of the harbour three charred masts loom out of the water. The rigging and yardarms are gone. But nothing was mentioned about any casualties.

He says very slowly, "Is that correct?"

"I must have the results of the autopsy."

He's silent for a long time.

"Hell and damnation," he says. "I have a family to feed."

I have nothing to say to that.

"This afternoon. After four."

He sits down across from me, taking off the cellophane and paper ring of a cigar. He has a box of extra-long matches. He uses one to bore a hole in the conical, curved end of the rounded, rolled tobacco leaf. Then he lights it, carefully and meticulously. When it's burning evenly, he fixes his gaze on me.

"It wasn't you, by chance, who killed him, was it?" he says.

"No."

While he talks, he continues to stare at me, as if trying to examine my conscience.

"If a person drowns, the first thing to happen is that he tries to hold his breath. When he can't hold it any longer, he takes a couple of deep, desperate breaths. That pumps water into the lungs. This motion creates whitish protein material in the nose and throat, based on the same principle as when you beat egg whites. It's called froth. This person – whom I ought not to discuss, and particularly with someone who might be involved in the crime – this person has no trace of it. So he didn't drown, at any rate."

He carefully taps the ash from his cigar.

"He was already dead when I went on board."

He barely hears me. His thoughts are still on that morning and the autopsy.

"First they tied him up. With pieces of copper wire. He put up a hell of a fight, but they finally got him trussed up. There must have been a couple of them. He was a strong man. An elderly gentleman, but strong. Then they bent his head to one side. You're familiar with sodium hydroxide – lye. An extremely caustic base. One person held him by his hair. Several clumps were torn out. And then they dripped lye into his right ear. Nice and easy, just like that, damn it all."

He regards his cigar thoughtfully. "You can't be in my business without running into torture now and then. It's a complicated subject. A hell of a subject. The legal definition, by the way, says that it has to be carried out by an organization. The important thing for the torturer is to find the victim's weak point. And this man was blind. That's not something I discovered. I didn't know that until we got his medical records. But they knew it. So they concentrated on his hearing. Damned inventive, you have to give them that. It's psychopathic. But it has a creative streak. What you can't help wondering is what they were after."

I think about the curator's voice on the telephone, about what I had thought was a muffled laugh. They had already broken him by then.

"He had cotton in his ears."

"Glad to hear it. It was gone when he was fished out. But I guessed about the cotton. When I found the little burns. At some point they reached the end of the line with him. Whenever that might have been. And so they did something quite clever. They moistened some cotton, maybe with lye, since it was handy. They then split an electrical cord and put one pole in each ear. And plugged it in. And then calmly turned on the switch. Dead on the spot. Quick, cheap, clean."

He shakes his head. He's a doctor, not a psychologist. He finds the world in which we live beyond comprehension.

"A couple of fucking professionals. But if I believed in New Year's resolutions, mine would be to make them pay."

I wake up around one a.m. One second I'm sleeping, the next I'm awake.

He's lying next to me. On his stomach with his hands down at

163

his side. Asleep, one side of his face is pressed flat against the sheet. His mouth and nose vibrate gently, as if he were sniffing at a flower. Or were about to kiss a child.

I lie quietly and look at him in a way I haven't been able to before. His hair is brown, with a few grey streaks. It's thick, like the bristles of a broom. Burying your fingers in it is like grabbing a horse's mane.

There in bed, happiness comes over me. Not like something that belongs to me, but like a wheel of fire rolling through the room and the world.

For a moment I think I'll manage to let it pass and be able to lie there, aware of what I have, and not wish for anything more.

The next moment I want to hang on. I want it to continue. He has to lie beside me tomorrow, too. This is my chance. My only, my last chance.

I swing my legs on to the floor. Now I'm panic-stricken.

This is what I've been working to avoid for thirty-seven years. I've systematically practised the only thing in the world that is worth learning. How to renounce. I've stopped hoping for anything. When the practice of humility becomes an Olympic discipline, I'll be on the national team.

I've never had any patience for other people's unhappy love affairs. I hate their weakness. I watch them find a man at the end of the rainbow. I watch them have children and buy a Silver Cross royal-blue pram and walk along the embankment in the spring sunshine and laugh condescendingly at me and think, Poor Smilla, she doesn't know what she's missing, she doesn't know what life is like for those of us who have babies and a marriage certificate.

Four months later there's a reunion for their old prenatal care group, and her dear Ferdinand has a little relapse and lines up a few hits on a mirror, and she finds him in the bathroom where he's rolling around with one of the other happy mothers, and in a nanosecond she's reduced from the great, proud, sovereign, invulnerable mama to a spiritual gnome. At one stroke she falls to my level and below, and becomes an insect, a worm, a centipede.

And then they take me out and dust me off. Then I'm supposed to listen to how hard it is to be a single mother after the divorce, how they had a fight over splitting up the stereo, how her youth is being sucked out by the child, who is now a machine that uses her and gives nothing in return.

I've never wanted to listen to that. "What the hell do you want?"

I've said to them. "Do you think I edit some kind of agony column? Do you think I'm your diary? An answering machine?"

There's one thing that is forbidden on journeys by sleigh, and that is whimpering. Whining is a virus, a lethal, infectious, epidemic disease. I refuse to listen to it. I refuse to be saddled with these orgies of emotional pettiness.

That's why I'm scared now. Standing there on his floor, next to his bed, I can hear something. It's coming from inside me, and it's a whimper. It's the fear that what has been given to me won't last. It's the sound of all the unhappy love stories I've never wanted to listen to. Now it sounds as if they're all contained within me.

But I can still be saved. I can gather up my clothes and put them under my arm. I don't even have to take time to get dressed. I can just walk out and run up the stairs. In my apartment I'll pack the essentials, or not even that much. I'll call a removals company and arrange to have my furnishings moved out and put in storage, and then I'll put my money box in one pocket and Isaiah's tape in the other, and I'll move into a hotel, so that I'm gone when he wakes up and I'll never have to look him in the eye again.

He opens his eyes and looks at me. He lies there quite still, trying to determine where he is. Then he smiles at me.

I remember that I'm naked. I turn my back to him and walk sideways over to my clothes. He folded them for me; they haven't been folded that way since I bought them. I put on my underwear. Modesty is part of the fundamental nature of human beings. It makes me sick to think of the European idea that they can solve all their own self-induced sexual neuroses by laying the meat on the table and putting it under a microscope.

I go into the living room. I have no idea what to do with myself.

He comes in a moment later. He's wearing boxer shorts. They're white and reach down to his knees and they're big enough to be made out of an eiderdown cover. He looks like a half-naked cricket player.

I notice them now, and remember that I saw them yesterday too. He has narrow black lines around his wrists and ankles. They are scars. I don't want to ask him about it.

He comes over to me and kisses me. Even though we have not at any time been drunk, it makes sense to say that this is our first sober embrace.

Not until now do I remember yesterday. So clearly it's as though the glow of the fire were on the walls of the apartment, right now.

We set the table together. He has a juicer. He squeezes apple and pear juice into tall glasses. The apple juice is green with a reddish sheen, the pear juice is yellowish. For the first few minutes. Then they start changing taste and colour.

We eat virtually nothing. We drink a little juice and stare at the china and the butter and cheese and the toast and the marmalade and raisins and sugar.

There's no traffic in the harbour, and very little on the bridge. It's a national holiday.

He's several metres away, but he feels as close as if our bodies were still wrapped around each other.

By the time I kiss him goodbye and go up to my apartment, still in my underwear with my clothes under my arm, we haven't exchanged a single word that morning.

Back at my place, I decide not to shower. There are so many reasons for not washing. In Qaanaaq, one mother didn't wash her child's left cheek for three years because Queen Ingrid had kissed it.

I get dressed and go down to the phone booth on the square. I call University Hospital, Institute of Forensic Medicine, Autopsy Centre of Copenhagen, and ask to speak with Dr Lagermann.

He has aired out the room. In order to get enough oxygen so his next cigar will burn. But for a brief moment there is fresh, cool air.

"Can they stand all this fresh air – the cacti?"

With Lagermann, irony won't really get you any return on your investments.

"In the Sahara, in the hollows of Niger, it gets down to −7 °C at night. In the daytime it's 50 °C in the sun. That's the biggest temperature difference within a twenty-four-hour period on the earth's surface. Sometimes it doesn't rain for five years in a row."

"But does anyone breathe at them through a cigar?"

He sighs. "In there I can't smoke because of my family. Out here I'm harassed by my guests."

He puts the cigar back in the box. A flat wooden box with a picture of Romeo kissing Giulietta on the balcony.

"Now," he says, "I want an explanation, damn it."

I have to collect my thoughts. But they're stuck on the kiss on the cigar box.

"Do you know Euclid's *Elements*?" I ask.

Then I tell him everything in detail. About Isaiah's death. About the police. About the Cryolite Corporation Danmark. About the Arctic Museum. About Andreas Fine Licht. A little about the mechanic.

As soon as I start, he forgets and fishes a cigar out of the box.

It takes two cigars for me to finish.

When I stop talking he moves away, as if to put some distance between us. Slowly he strolls along the short narrow paths among the plants. He has a trick of smoking the cigar down to the last centimetre, until he's standing there with a glowing ember between his fingers. Then he drops the last flecks of tobacco into the cactus beds.

He comes towards me.

"I've broken my vow of confidentiality. I'm committing a criminal offence if I don't tell the police what you've told me. I'm up against one of Denmark's most influential scientists, the district attorney, the police commissioner. People have been fired for even thinking half of what I've actually done. And I have a family to feed."

"And the cacti must be watered," I say.

"But what pride would children have in a father who lets his arse get kicked the first time his job is threatened?"

I say nothing.

"Assistant chief pathologist can't be the only decent way to make a living. My grandmother was Jewish. Maybe I can take care of the lavatories at the Mosaic Cemetery."

He's thinking out loud. But he has already made up his mind.

In the kitchen he stops short.

"Year and date of the two expeditions?"

I give them to him.

"It might be instructive to look at the forensic medical reports," he says.

The first pastries have come out of the oven. One is shaped like a naked woman. They used raisins for the nipples and pubic hair.

"Look," a little boy says to me, "it's supposed to be you."

"Yes," says another one. "Take off your clothes so we can see if it looks like you."

"Shut up," says Lagermann.

167

He helps me with my coat. "My wife thinks that no circumstances warrant giving one's children even two of the best."

"In Greenland," I say, "they don't hit children, either."

He looks disappointed. "But it must, by God, be human to feel tempted."

The mechanic is waiting in the street. The two men shake hands. In an attempt to reach each other, the forensics expert stretches up in the air while the mechanic hunches down towards the ground. They meet in the middle, with the awkwardness of a silent film. As so often before, the question blows in the wind about why men so seldom stay in one piece. How can it be that they can be virtual equilibrists at an autopsy table, in a kitchen, behind a dog sleigh, but as soon as they have to shake hands with a stranger, they sink into infantile helplessness?

"Loyen," says Lagermann.

He turns away from the mechanic, as if to keep him out of the conversation. A last, failed attempt to preserve his professional discretion and protect a colleague.

"He went in early that morning. He comes and goes as he pleases. But the security guard saw him. I looked it up in the work schedule. He had no other reason to be there. He took that biopsy. He just couldn't damn well resist. The guard says that the cleaners were there at the same time. Maybe that's why he was so sloppy."

"How did he know the boy was dead?"

He shrugs.

"Ving." It is the mechanic.

Lagermann gives him a hostile look.

"V-ving. Juliane called him. And he must have called Loyen."

He has the little Morris parked outside. We sit next to each other without saying a word. When he speaks, he stutters badly.

"I f-followed you out here. Stopped near T-tuborgvej and saw you go through the m-marsh."

I don't have to ask why. In some ways we are equally frightened.

I open our clothes, straddle him, and place him inside me. We sit like that for a long time.

He puts tape on my front door. He has that kind of opaque white tape that graphic artists use. With scissors he cuts two thin strips and places them over the upper and lower hinges. They're invisible. If you know where they are, you can just make them out.

"Just for now. Every time you go inside, make sure they're there. If they've come unstuck, you wait for me to arrive. But it's best to spend as little time there as possible."

He avoids looking at me.

"If you want to, you c-could stay with me for the time being."

It's never clear what that "for the time being" means.

At the university they had a lot of funny ethnological clichés. One of them was about how much European mathematics was indebted to ancient folk culture; just look at the pyramids, whose geometry commands respect and admiration.

This, of course, is idiocy disguised as a pat on the back. Technological culture is superior in the very reality it defines. The seven to eight rules of thumb of the Egyptian surveyors is abacus mathematics compared to integral calculus.

In *The Last Kings of Thule*, Jean Malaurie writes that a significant argument for studying the interesting Polar Eskimos is that you can thus learn something about human progression from the Neanderthal stage to the people of the Stone Age.

It's written with a certain amount of affection. But it's a study in unconscious prejudices.

Any race of people that allows itself to be measured on a grade scale designed by European science will appear to be a culture of higher primates.

Grading is meaningless. Every attempt to compare cultures with the intention of determining which is the most developed will never be anything other than one more bullshit projection of Western culture's hatred of its own shadows.

There is one way to understand another culture. *Living* it. Move into it, ask to be tolerated as a guest, learn the language. At some point understanding may come. It will always be wordless. The moment you grasp what is foreign, you will lose the urge to explain it. To explain a phenomenon is to distance yourself from it. When I start talking about Qaanaaq, to myself or to others, I again start to lose what has never been truly mine.

Like now, on his sofa, when I feel like telling him why I feel a connection to the Eskimos. That it's because of their ability to know, without a shadow of a doubt, that life is meaningful. Because of the way, in their consciousness, they can live with the tension between irreconcilable contradictions, without sinking into despair and without looking for a simplified solution. Because of their short, short path to ecstasy. Because they can meet a fellow human being and see him for what he is, without judging, their clarity not weakened by prejudice.

I feel the need to tell him all this. Now I let this need grow. I feel it pressing on my heart, my throat, behind my forehead. I know it's because at this moment I am happy. Nothing corrupts like happiness. It makes us think that since we share this moment, we can also share the past. Since he's strong enough to meet me in the present, he must be able to contain my childhood as well.

Then I release the impulse. It's a feeling of tension. Now it rises up and disappears through the ceiling, and he will never have any idea that it existed.

He's cooking bananas. He leaves them in the oven until the skin is black. In the meantime, he roasts hazelnuts. On the toaster. He assures me that it p-produces a m-more even roasting.

There is no urge whatsoever to laugh. He's as solemn as a priest. He makes a single cut in the bananas. They are yellow and viscous. He puts heather honey and a few drops of liqueur into the cut.

As far as I'm concerned, the world could stop right now. No one needs to say anything more.

He dabs his lips with the napkin. Sensual lips and a wide mouth. A rather thick upper lip.

"They go up there in 1966. And then they're quiet for twenty-five years. They go up there again. Then they're quiet for a year and a half. Then the Baron dies. The police are very interested. The museum burns."

We each want the other person to say it.

"Seems like something's up, Smilla."

"You're right."

"They're getting ready to go back up there. Winter would be the right time to make preparations. So they c-could sail in early spring."

That's what I've been thinking, too.

"But how are they d-doing it? They can't organize the trip and the ship and the equipment through the Cryolite Corporation. Because it's practically shut down."

I feel like looking at the stars, so I turn off the light. The glow from outside is slightly different here than in my apartment.

"Loyen, Licht, Ving," I say. "They discovered it. Whatever it is. They found out it was there. Maybe in Hamburg. They were in charge of the first expeditions. But they're old now. They couldn't do it again. And someone has killed Licht. Behind the three of them is something else, something bigger, something more ruthless."

He comes over and puts his arm around me. I can lean my head against his armpit.

"They need a ship," he says thoughtfully. "I have a friend who knows something about ships."

I feel like asking him questions, to find out a small part of all that I don't know about him. But I stop myself.

"I was at the Trade Commission. Geoinform has three people on its board."

I mention the three names. He shakes his head. Outside the window the Pleiades are barely visible. I point to them.

"The Pleiades. In my language they're called *qiluttuusat*."

He pronounces it slowly and carefully. The way he cooks. His breath is aromatic and tangy. From nuts roasted on the toaster.

Standing in the middle of the bedroom, we take off each other's clothes.

He has a light, fumbling brutality, which several times makes me think that this time it'll cost me my sanity. In our dawning, mutual intimacy, I induce him to open the little slit in the head of his penis so I can put my clitoris inside and fuck him.

2

FIRST WE ENTER THE SALOON. The portholes are brass, the walls and ceiling mahogany. The chairs have light-coloured leather cushions and are bolted to the floor with brass rivets and furnished with bronze holders mounted on gimbals for whisky glasses, and they are so deep that even during an Arctic typhoon you could sit and enjoy the clinking of the ice cubes in your triple Laphroaig.

The next room is a promenade of twenty-five metres along the keel through more mahogany and past more polished portholes, and past ship's clocks and opulent desks bolted to the floor where a dozen people are working as if everything has to be finished in the next thirty seconds. The women are typing on word processor keyboards, the men are talking on three telephones at once, and the ceiling has disappeared in a cloud of cigarette smoke and frenzy.

Then comes a reception area. A middle-aged woman is sitting there, wearing makeup and a lace blouse and tailored jacket. She has the forearms of someone who has signed on as a blacksmith. She would have scared me if I hadn't had the mechanic along.

He knows her. They shake hands and it looks as if they're going to arm wrestle, and we continue on into the captain's cabin. Along the way we pass glass cabinets with models of tankers so long that the crew has to set up camp three times on a trip from one end to the other.

Inside, the portholes are as large as well covers, placed lower down on the wall so you can see the shrubs of the little park in the middle of Sankt Annæ Plads and be reminded that this entire maritime mirage is located on the third floor of a mansion house with its back to Amalienborg Palace, and is the worst interior architectonic extravaganza I have ever seen.

Behind the desk, which has a rim around the edge so the gold ballpoint pens won't roll on to the floor during an imaginary sea voyage, sits a boy who looks fourteen at most, newly confirmed, his sandy-coloured hair plastered down, and freckles on his nose.

When he speaks, it's in a thin, light alto, full of dignity. "I know what you want to say, sweetheart. You want to say: 'Where's your father, little boy, because he's the one we've come to talk to.' But you're mistaken. I'll be thirty-three next month. If a child molester accidentally happened to kill me, there would be twenty-five million kroner for my wife and my three kids after the business was sold."

Then he gives me a wink.

His name is Birgo Lander. He's the mechanic's friend. He is the owner and director of this shipping firm. He spent his youth in practically all the Danish reform schools; he's an orphan, rich, totally without scruples, even more dyslexic than the mechanic, addicted to gambling, and a drunkard; with his face he could ride the bus on a child's ticket, but that's not necessary since he owns a custom-made Jaguar.

Part of this I know, along with everyone in Denmark, from newspapers and magazines. The mechanic told me the rest on the way over here.

He takes the mechanic's hand in both of his. He doesn't say anything, but he looks at him as if he has been reunited with a long-absent big brother. Then we sit down. The mechanic pushes his chair back a little and withdraws from the conversation. I'm the one who's going to explain.

"If I wish to rent a ship of about 4,000 tons to transport a cargo that I have no intention of discussing, to a place that I am not going to reveal either, how would I go about it? And if I were already in the process of looking for the right ship, could anyone trace my efforts?"

He stands up. He's wearing high-heeled cowboy boots. They don't really do much for his height. From a cupboard on the wall he takes out a double bottle of clear fruit brandy. The mechanic and I decline. He pours himself one in a tall, cylindrical tumbler.

The whole room smells of fresh pears. Lander sips at his drink. Seven times in a row. Then he looks at me to see whether I'm shocked.

"I'm drunk from ten in the morning on," he says. "And I can afford it."

His eyes are swimming, but his voice is clear. "If you tried to find a ship, you could be traced. But only by someone who was friends with a ship broker. And you're friends with one now, dear."

Somehow I already like him. A disposable child, someone who

173

has always had a hard time dealing with the world and hasn't actually wanted to learn how.

He takes a thousand-kroner bill out of a drawer and puts it on the desk.

"Everything has a front and a back. Normally, they are of equal size."

He tenderly turns over the bill. "But in the shipping industry, things are arranged so cunningly that the back is much bigger than the front."

He throws out his hand. "The front is this location on this expensive square. It's all the cigar-box wood and the suites you walked through to reach this office."

He taps his thin hair. "The back is inside here. You don't 'rent' a ship, darling. You 'charter' it. From a shipowner. It's handled by contract. A contract has a front side which – if worst comes to worst – can be presented in maritime court. On the front it says where the ship is sailing and what it's sailing with."

He tastes a sip of the brandy. "But you are reticent with information about the destination and cargo. So you request a contract in which the destination is listed as 'the entire world', and the freight as 'unspecified'. That would make any shipowner unhappy. His ships are his children. He wants to know where they're going to be playing. Preferably avoid bad company. But no trouble is so great that you can't buy your way out of it. So you suggest that a so-called side letter, or side contract, be prepared. The Danish shipping business is full of side contracts. During the past fifteen years practically every Danish shipping company has transported coal from South Africa and ammunition to the Middle East, even though this is against the law. It takes side contracts many metres long. And they're not for the maritime court. They're just as sensitive to light as undeveloped film. That's what you would ask for. It says that you will pay the shipping company a kind of bonus in order to continue to be a discreet and secretive young lady. Let's play a game. Let's say that I'm the shipowner that you want to charter a ship from. Ninety-eight per cent of all deals in this business are made in private. So you confide to Uncle Birgo, person to person, where your little boat is really going."

"To the west coast of Greenland."

"That will make it more difficult for the person who wants to do the chartering, and easier for the one who wants to trace the transaction. A ship has to be classified 'ice class' to sail to Greenland. The Maritime Inspection Board of Denmark requires all ships to be classified every fourth year in terms of the hull, once a year for safety equipment and engines. If a ship is not approved, it cannot put to sea at all. Since last year, ships sailing to Greenland must have a double hull."

"The crew?"

"Normally a ship is chartered with crew. Or you go to one of the international companies that deal exclusively with supplying full crews. But in this particular situation, you would probably prefer a 'bare boat charter'. Which means that you hire a ship and nothing else. Then you find a captain. He has to be a special kind of person, the kind you can take aside and, over a full glass, tell him that in this case his wages will be a little out of the ordinary. On the other hand, you need all his tact and sensitivity. Along with him, you find the rest of the crew. For a ship of 4,000 tons, you need eleven to twelve men."

Now I have to ask him something. Requests are always difficult.

"If a customer had put out a feeler for that sort of ship and that sort of captain, would you be able to find out about it, Uncle Lander?"

He looks at me sadly. "The heading at the top of the page for everything in this business says: 'Any negotiations whatsoever to be kept strictly private and confidential.' The shipping industry is one of the most discreet in the world."

He solemnly wraps his hands around his glass. Then he gives me a wink. "But for you, my little G-string, I would go to great lengths."

He looks at the mechanic and then back at me. "If I may call you that?"

"You may call me whatever comes into your little shrivelled head," I say.

He blinks once. He's so unused to anyone standing up to him that he has forgotten what it feels like.

He hides his face in his hands for a moment to collect his thoughts. "This business may not look very good on the front side. But on the back it is full of what they call ethics. And the two most important rules are: You don't cheat a customer. And you never cheat a fellow shipowner."

He swallows. We are face to face with his philosophy of life.

"You cheat the shit out of the state and the authorities if an opportunity presents itself. With a big smile you break Minister Espersen's currency legislation, and travel to Cape Town with a briefcase with a million in cash to bribe a Bushman who's the harbour master, who's holding a 500,000-ton tanker at the shipyard under the pretence of a quarantine. You buy five companies a year in Panama for a thousand dollars apiece to avoid sailing under a Danish flag and regulations. You reroute a cargo that's allergic to customs to a Spanish port where you've paid the local customs officers to reinvoice your crates. But you don't cheat a customer. Because you need customers to come back. And above all, you never cheat a broker. We shipping folks stick together. The way it works is, I have a customer who has a ship and you have a customer who has a cargo, and we bring them together. Next time it's the other way around. A ship broker lives off other ship brokers, who live off other ship brokers . . ."

He's filled with emotion. "It's one big brotherhood, darling."

He takes a drink and waits until he has regained control of his voice.

"That means that we have a network. We know other brokers from Guadeloupe to Tierra del Fuego, from Rangoon to the Outer Hebrides. And we talk to each other. Little conversations, and when you've been talking for several years, and if you have a flair for it, you end up making 100,000 kroner every time you pick up the phone and open your mouth. In every large port Lloyd's and the other big companies have an observer on the staff who reports all arrivals and departures. And after a while you get to know the observers. If anyone has tried to hire a 4,000-ton ice class to carry a secret cargo to a secret destination, and if you're interested in who and how, then you've come to the right man, sweetheart. Because Uncle Birgo is going to find out for you."

We stand up. He shakes hands across the desk.

"It was nice to meet you, dear."

He really means it.

We go out past the lace blouse. In the next office I turn around.

"I forgot something."

He's sitting at his desk. He's still laughing. I go up to him and give him a kiss on the cheek.

"What would Føjl say?" he asks.

I give him a wink.

"Any negotiations whatsoever are to be kept strictly private and confidential."

*   *   *

Every other day Moritz picks up Benja after her afternoon rehearsals and they eat together at the Savarin in Nyhavn.

Moritz goes there because of the food, and because the prices stimulate his ego, and because he likes having a good view of people on the street through the plate-glass windows that stretch the entire height of the building façade. Benja goes because she knows that through those same windows people on the street have a good view of her.

They have their own table next to the window and their own waiter and they always eat the same thing. Moritz has lamb kidneys and Benja a bowl of the kind of fodder you give rabbits. Today there's a family sitting near them that has sneaked a little child into this otherwise child-free area. Moritz looks at the child.

"You've never given me any grandchildren," he tells me.

"Little children smell of pee," says Benja.

Moritz looks at her with astonishment.

"Lamb kidneys do, too," he says.

I think about the mechanic waiting outside in the car.

"Won't you sit down, Smilla?"

"Someone is waiting for me."

Through the windows Benja can see the Morris, but not who's sitting inside.

"It looks like someone your own age," she says. "Somewhere in his forties. Judging from his fancy car."

If I reply, I'll end up hurting Moritz. So I let it pass uncontested.

I lean over the edge of the table. It has always been like this. Benja and Moritz sit comfortably, leaning back. They belong here. I stand with my overcoat on, feeling as if I've come in from the street to peddle something.

Moritz is holding two envelopes in his hands. One is grey and spotted with what looks like red wine. In the silence between us he tries to use them to force me into a chair. He doesn't succeed.

"This makes me uncomfortable," he says.

I don't know what he means.

"Hviid is not an ordinary name. There *was* a composer, Jonathan Hviid. I called Victor Halkenhvad."

Benja lifts her head. Even she has heard of that name.

"I didn't know he was still alive."

"I'm not sure he is, either."

He hands me the envelope. I hold it up to my nose. The spots *are* red wine. Moritz sticks a finger inside his turtleneck collar and moves it around.

"It wasn't pleasant. He's not the man he used to be. At one point he slammed down the receiver. While I was in the middle of a sentence. But he did write, after all."

It's a rare experience to see Moritz uncomfortable. Not until I'm out in the car do I understand why.

He catches up with me at the door. "You forgot this."

It's the second envelope.

"A single clipping about Tørk Hviid. From the Danish Press Service."

A clipping service he subscribes to. They collect any mention in the press about him.

He wants to touch me. He doesn't dare. He wants to say something. He doesn't manage it.

In the car I read the letter out loud. The handwriting is almost illegible.

"Jørgen, you cheap little barber's assistant."

The mechanic looks puzzled.

"My father's first name is Jørgen," I say. "And Victor has always been temperamental."

It must be fifteen years since I saw him last. The opera had given him an honorary residence on Store Kannikestræde. He was sitting in an armchair positioned next to the piano. He was wearing a dressing gown; I had never seen him in anything else. His legs were naked and swollen. I don't know whether he could stand up any more. He must have weighed over a hundred and fifty kilos. Everything sagged on him. He was looking at me, not Moritz. Those weren't bags under his eyes, they were hammocks.

"I don't like women," he said. "Move further away."

I moved away.

"You were cute when you were little," he said. "That time is past."

He signed an album cover and handed it to Moritz.

"I know what you're thinking," he said. "You're thinking now that old idiot has recorded another album."

It was *Gurrelieder*. I still have the record. It's still an unforgettable recording. I've sometimes thought that the body, our very physical existence, puts a limit on how much pain a mind can bear. And that Victor Halkenhvad, on that record, reaches that limit. So that afterwards the rest of us can listen and make that journey without walking the distance ourselves.

Even if, like me, you know nothing about European cultural history, you can still hear a world collapsing in that music, on that record. The question is whether anything has taken its place. Victor didn't think so.

> I've looked it up in my journal. That's all I have left of my memory. It's ten years since you last visited me. Let me tell you that I have Alzheimer's. Even a money doctor like you must know what that means. Every new day a piece of my brain peels away. Soon, thank God, I won't even be able to remember all of you who betrayed me and yourselves.

It was his indifference that did it. At the same time as he sang, trembling, ready to burst, unbearably full of romanticism and its feelings, there was a sense of distance, a place inside him that didn't give a damn.

> Jonathan Hviid and I went to the Conservatory together. We started in 1933. The year that Schönberg converted to Judaism. The same year as the Reichstag fire. Jonathan was just like that. The most buggered awful timing. He composed a piece for eight flutes and called it 'Silver Polyps'. In the midst of the flatulent postwar Danish narrow-mindedness which even regarded Carl Nielsen as too controversial. He wrote a brilliant concerto for piano and orchestra. The piano was supposed to have old-fashioned iron hot plates placed on top of the strings because they produced a very special sound. He never got it performed. Never, not once. He married a woman about whom even I have a difficult time finding anything negative to say. She was in her early twenties when they had the boy. They lived in Brønshøj, in a neighbourhood that doesn't exist any more. Garden sheds with tin roofs. I visited them there. Jonathan wasn't making a penny. They washed their hands of the boy. Holes in his clothes, red-eyed, never had a bicycle, was beaten at the local proletarian school because he was too weak from hunger to defend himself. Because Jonathan was supposed to be a great artist. You've all betrayed your children. And it takes an old queen like me to tell you.

The mechanic has pulled over in order to listen.

"The sheds in Brønshøj," he says. "I remember them. They were behind the cinema."

> He broke off ties with me. At some point I heard that they had gone to Greenland. She had taken a job as a teacher. Provided for the family while Jonathan composed for the polar bears. After they came back I visited them only once. The son was there, too. Handsome as a god. Some sort of scientist. Cold. We talked about music. He asked about money the whole time. Permanently scarred. Like you are, Moritz. For ten years you haven't visited me. I hope your fortune suffocates you. There was a certain stubbornness about the boy, too. Like Schönberg. Twelve-tone music. Pure stubbornness. But Schönberg wasn't cold. The boy was ice. I'm tired. I've started peeing in my bed. Can you stand to hear that, Moritz? It'll happen to you some day, too.

He hadn't signed it.

The clipping in the other envelope is a single paragraph: "On 7 October 1991, the police in Singapore arrested Tørk Hviid, a Danish citizen. The Consulate, on behalf of the Foreign Ministry, has lodged a protest." It doesn't mean anything to me. But it reminds me that Loyen was once in Singapore, too. To photograph mummies.

We drive out to Nordhavnen. Outside the Cryolite Corporation Danmark he slows down, and we look at each other.

We leave the car near the Svanemølle power plant and stroll towards the harbour, along Sundkrogsgade.

There is a dry wind with barely visible, blowing ice crystals that sting your face.

Now and then we hold hands. Now and then we stop to kiss with cold lips and warm mouths, now and then we walk on separately. We're wearing boots. Snowdrifts have piled up on the pavement. And yet we feel like two dancers, gliding in and out of an embrace, a swoop into a lift. He doesn't hold me back. He doesn't weigh me down to the ground, he doesn't urge me forward. One moment he's at my side, the next he's a little behind me.

There's something honest about an industrial harbour. There are no royal yacht clubs here, no promenades, no energy wasted on façades. There are silos for raw materials, warehouses, container cranes.

Inside an open doorway there is a steel hull. We go up a wooden ladder and reach the deck. We sit on the bridge and look out across the white deck. I lay my head on his shoulder. We're sailing. It's summer. We're sailing north. Maybe north along the coast of Norway. Not very far from shore, because I'm afraid of the open sea. Past the mouths of the great fjords. The sun is shining. The sea is blue and clear and deep, as if we had a huge mass of fluid crystal beneath the keel. There's a midnight sun, a reddish, almost leaping disc of light. A faint song of the wind in the rigging.

We walk out to the quay. Men in overalls ride past on bicycles, turning around to stare at us, and we laugh at them, knowing that we are radiant.

We wander along the quiet docks until we're frozen stiff. We eat in a little café that's built on to a smokehouse. Outside, the clouds bow for a brief moment to an extraordinary red sunset that makes the colours on the hulls of the fishing vessels shift from blue-white to rose to purple.

He tells me about his parents. About his father, who never says anything, who is a carpenter and one of the last people in Denmark who knows how to make a winding staircase that twists up towards the sky in a perfect wooden spiral. About his mother, who invents recipes for the food pages of women's magazines, cakes that she can't even taste because she's diabetic.

When I ask him how he came to know Birgo Lander, he shakes his head and falls silent. Across the table I caress the side of his jaw, marvelling at the way life can suddenly allow us to experience happiness and ecstasy with someone who is a complete stranger.

Outside, night has fallen.

Even in the dark, even in the winter, the wealthy suburb of Hellerup belongs to another dimension than Copenhagen. We've parked the car on a quiet, now silent road. The snow gleams white along the kerb and along the high walls surrounding the villas. In the gardens evergreen trees and shrubs form dense black surfaces, like the edge of a forest or the side of a mountain, above a white carpet of snow.

There are no streetlights. And yet we can see the house. A tall white villa standing where the road on which we've parked dwindles down to a lane.

There is no hedge or fence around the house. From the pavement you can step directly on to the lawn. Upstairs, on the third floor, there's a light in a window. Everything seems well kept, newly painted, expensive, and discreet.

A few steps from the pavement there's a sign on the lawn lit by a lamp. The sign says GEOINFORM.

We were just going to drive by to look at the building. We've been here for an hour now.

It has nothing to do with the house. We could have parked anywhere. And for any length of time.

A police car stops alongside us. It has passed us twice before. Now they've become curious.

The officer addresses the mechanic across me.

"What's going on here, mate?"

I stick my head out of the window towards the police car.

"We live in a one-room apartment, Mr Commissioner. A basement apartment on Jægersborggade. We have three children and a dog. Sometimes we just need a little private life. And it mustn't cost anything. So we drive out here."

"All right, ma'am," he says. "But drive somewhere else for your private life. This is the embassy district."

They're gone. The mechanic starts the car and puts it into gear. Then the light goes out in the house in front of us. He slows down. We creep down towards the lane with our headlights off. Three figures come out on to the stairway. Two of them are merely dark spots in the night. But the third instinctively seeks out the light. A fur coat and a white face catch the light. It's the woman I saw talking to Andreas Fine Licht at Isaiah's funeral. She tosses her head, and the dark hair flows into the night. Now that I see this gesture repeated, I realize that it's an expression not of vanity but of self-confidence. A garage door goes up. The car comes out in a flood of light. Its headlights sweep over us and then it's gone. Behind it the door slowly closes.

We're following the car. Not close, because the lane is deserted, but not far behind either.

If you drive through Copenhagen in the dark and allow the surroundings to slip out of focus and blur, a new pattern appears that is not visible to the focused eye. The city as a moving field of light, as a spider's web of red and white pulled over your retina.

The mechanic is relaxed when he drives, almost introspective, as if he were about to fall asleep. He makes no sudden movements, and there is no sudden braking, no real acceleration; we simply float through the streets and the traffic. And the whole time, somewhere ahead, like a wide, low silhouette, is the car that is leading us.

The traffic grows more sporadic and finally vanishes altogether. We're on our way out towards Kalvebod Brygge.

We drive out to the wharf very slowly, our headlights off. Several hundred metres ahead, on the dock itself, a pair of red rear lights wink off. The mechanic parks beside a dark wooden fence.

The relative warmth of the sea has created a mist that swallows up the light. Visibility is about a hundred metres. The opposite side of the harbour has vanished in the darkness. The waves are languidly slapping against the wharf.

And something is moving. No sound, but a black crystallization of a point in the night. A field of blackness systematically moving between the parked cars. Twenty-five metres away from us the movement stops. A person is standing next to a light-coloured refrigerated lorry. Above the figure there is a lighter spot, as if from a white hat or a halo. He doesn't move for a long time. The mist grows a little thicker. When it disperses, the figure is gone.

"He was feeling the c-car bonnets. To see if they were warm."

He's whispering, as if his voice could be heard in the night.

"A c-cautious man."

We sit quietly, letting time pass through us. In spite of this place, in spite of the unknown we're waiting for, it feels like a flood of happiness to me.

By his watch about half an hour passes.

We don't hear the car. It appears out of the fog, its headlights turned off, and passes us with an engine sound that is merely a whistle. Its windows are dark.

We get out of the car and walk along the dock. The two dark contours that we could barely make out are ships. The closest one is a sailing ship. The gangway has been removed, and the ship is dark. A white plaque on the superstructure says, in German, that it's a Polish training ship.

The next one is a tall black hull. An aluminium companionway leads upward amidships, but it all seems empty and deserted. The ship's name is *Kronos*. It's about 125 metres long.

We walk back to the car.

"Maybe we should go on board," he says.

I'm the one who has to make the decision. For a moment I'm

tempted. Then comes the fear and the memory of the burning profile of the *Northern Light* against Islands Brygge. I shake my head. Right now, at this moment, life seems too precious to me.

We call Lander from a phone booth. He's still at work.

"What if the name of the ship was *Kronos*?" I say.

He goes away and then returns. A few minutes pass as he turns the pages.

"*Lloyd's Register of Ships* lists five: a chemical tanker based in Frederiksstad, a sand dredger in Odense, a tugboat in Gdansk, and two 'general cargo' ships, one in Piraeus and one in Panama."

"The last two."

"The Greek one is a 1,200-ton ship, the other 4,000 tons." I hand the ballpoint pen to the mechanic. He shakes his head.

"I'm no good at numbers, either."

"Any pictures?"

"Not in *Lloyd's*. But quite a few statistics. One hundred and twenty-seven metres long, built in Hamburg in '57. Reinforced for ice."

"The owners?"

He goes away from the telephone again. I look at the mechanic. His face is in darkness; now and then car headlights make it appear, white, anxious, sensual. And under the sensuality, something inflexible.

"*Lloyd's Maritime Directory* lists the shipowner as Plejada, registered in Panama. But the name looks Danish. A Katja Claussen. Never heard of her."

"I have," I say. "*Kronos* is our ship, Lander."

3

WE'RE SITTING ON HIS BED with our backs against the wall. In this light, against his naked whiteness, the scars around his wrists and ankles are as black as iron bands.

"Do you think that people determine their own lives, Smilla?"

"The details," I say, "but the big things happen on their own."

The telephone rings.

He removes the tape and listens to a brief message. Then he hangs up.

"You might want to find your high-heeled shoes. Birgo wants to meet us tonight."

"Where?"

He laughs secretively.

"A seedy dive, Smilla. But put on your good clothes."

He carries me up the stairs. I kick in his arms, and we laugh quietly so as not to attract attention. In Qaanaaq, when I was little, the bridegroom would drag the bride out to the sleigh on their wedding night, and they would drive off followed by hooting guests. Sometimes they still do that. The hour I'm going to spend alone getting dressed already seems long. I'd rather ask him to stay so I could keep on looking at him. He's still not completely anchored in reality for me. His raw sweetness, his massive bulk and awkward politeness are still like a vivid dream. But only a dream. I reach out, grab hold of the door frame, and resist being set down. I let my fingers slide along the top hinge. The two pieces of tape have been broken, the ragged edges prick my fingertips.

I take his hands and move them up to the tape. His face grows sombre. He puts his mouth against my ear. "We'll sneak off . . ."

I shake my head. My apartment is sacrosanct. You can take

anything away from me, but I must have a corner somewhere to myself.

I try the door. It's not locked. I step inside. He has to follow me. But he's not happy about it.

The apartment is cold. That's because I always turn down the heat when I leave. I'm stingy about energy. I seal windows. I shut doors. It comes from living in Thule. From a healthy experience of how precious and scarce petroleum is.

That's why I naturally turn off all the lights behind me, too. And turn on only what's absolutely necessary. Now a light that I did not turn on is shining from the living room out into the hallway.

The swivel desk chair is pulled over to the window. A coat with wide shoulders is hanging over the back. A hat is floating on the shoulders. A pair of shiny black shoes is resting on the windowsill.

I don't think we've made any noise. But the shoes come down all the same, and the chair slowly turns around to face us.

"Good evening, Miss Smilla," he says. "And Mr Føjl."

It's Ravn.

His face is ashen with weariness, and there's a shadow of a beard on his cheeks, which I can't possibly imagine that the district attorney for special financial crimes would approve of. His voice sounds groggy, like someone who hasn't had any sleep for a long time.

"Do you know what the first requirement is for establishing a career in the Ministry of Justice?"

I take a look around. But he seems to be alone.

"The first requirement is *loyalty*. You also had to have a high score on your exams. And a desire to achieve which is far beyond the ordinary. But in the long run, the important thing is whether you were loyal. Common sense was not a prerequisite, on the other hand. Might even be a drawback."

I sit down on a chair. The mechanic leans against the desk.

"At some point one had to choose. Some became deputy judges and, eventually, judges. They often had a natural faith in justice, in the system. Faith in the possibility of healing and rebuilding. The rest of us became assistant detectives, investigators, and later assistants to the district attorney. With time, maybe assistant prosecutors. We were the suspicious ones. We believed that a statement, a confession, an incident was seldom what it purported to be. This suspiciousness was an excellent tool for us. As long as it wasn't directed at our work or at the Ministry itself. Never must a bureaucrat in the prosecutor's office doubt that he is right. Any impertinent question from the press must be referred to higher-ups. Any article you publish with even a hint of criticism – well, virtually any article at all – will be interpreted as disloyalty towards the Ministry. In some ways you no longer exist as an individual in the Ministry of Justice. Most comply with this demand. I can tell you that most people secretly find it a relief to have the state divest them of the trouble of being an independent person. The few who can't comply are separated out at an early stage."

I've seen it on long journeys. When someone is burned out, he suddenly discovers within himself a landscape of cheerful cynicism.

"And yet once in a while a slippery character happens to stay in the system. Someone who can hide his true nature until it's too late. Until he's made himself relatively indispensable, so it would be difficult for the Ministry to do without him. This type of person will never reach the top. But he can get part way up. Maybe even as far as the position of investigator for the district attorney. By that time he would be too old – and maybe even too competent – to be dispensable. But he has made too much trouble to be promoted upward. This kind of person would be a pebble in the Ministry's shoe. It doesn't really hurt, but it's annoying. With time, they would try to put this kind of person into a niche. Where they could draw on his stubbornness and memory, but where they could keep him out of the public eye. Maybe he would end up taking on special assignments. Like intelligence work, where staying out of the spotlight is part of the job. In his lap there might even end up a complaint about the investigation of a little boy's death. If it turned out that there was already a report on file about the case."

He doesn't look at either of us. He's talking to the room.

"It happens that word comes from higher up that the person who filed the complaint must be reassured. 'Pacified', as they say at the Ministry. They have a good deal of experience in this. But this time the case is more difficult. A child's death. Photographs of his footprints on the roof. It could easily turn into an embarrass-ment. So I voice the idea that there's some irregularity in the boy's death. But I don't get any support, either from the police or from Slotsholmen."

He gets up from the chair with difficulty.

"Then that deplorable fire occurs. Unfortunately, it too has some-thing to do with Greenland. And the name of the gentleman who perishes is listed in the aforementioned report. Yesterday morning

I was taken off the case. 'Due to its complex nature', etc."

He straightens his hat and walks over to the desk. He taps lightly on the red tape on the phone.

"Very clever," he says. "There's no end to the trouble these apparatuses cause innocent citizens. But it would have been even better not to answer the phone at all, or not to give out your number. The ship was almost totally destroyed by the fire, but the telephone must have been made of a non-flammable material. Furthermore it was lying on the deck. It had a built-in memory that stored the last number called. The last number was yours. My guess is that you will soon be invited in for a little talk."

"Wasn't it risky for you to come here?" I ask.

He has a key in his hand. "We borrowed a key from the caretaker during the initial investigation. I took the liberty of making a copy. So I went through the basement rooms. I'm planning to go back out the same way."

For a fleeting moment something happens to him. A light goes on in his face, as if a pinch of humour and humanity is burnt off behind the lava. The fossilized memory of the pumice stone, of the time when everything was hot and flowing. It's this light that makes me ask the question.

"Who is Tørk Hviid?"

The light goes out, his face becomes expressionless, as if his soul had left his body.

"Is that someone's name?"

I pick up his coat and help him into it. He's a little shorter than me. I brush off a speck of dust from his shoulder. He looks at me.

"My home number is in the book. Think about calling me, Miss Smilla. But from a phone booth, if you wouldn't mind."

"Thanks," I say.

But he's already gone.

The chimes of Our Saviour's Church are ringing. I look at the mechanic. I have my hands behind my back. The room is full of what Ravn brought with him and left behind: candour, bitterness, insinuations, and a kind of human warmth. And something else.

"He was lying," I say. "He lied at the end. He knows who Tørk Hviid is."

We look into each other's eyes. Something is wrong.

"I hate lies," I say. "If any lying has to be done, I'll do it myself."

"Then you should have told him that. Instead of hugging him."

I can't believe my ears, but I see that I've heard correctly. In his eyes there is the gleam of pure, unadulterated, idiotic jealousy.

"I didn't hug him," I say. "I helped him into his coat. For three reasons. First, because it's a courtesy you ought to show towards a fragile, elderly man. Second, because he presumably risked his position and pension to come here."

"And the third?"

"Third," I say, "because it gave me the chance to steal his wallet."

I put it on the table, under the light, where Isaiah's cigar box once stood, a wallet made of heavy brown leather.

The mechanic stares at me.

"Petty theft," I say. "Considered a minor offence under the law."

I empty its contents on to the table. Credit cards, bank notes. A plastic case with a white card which states, under a black embossed crown, that Ravn has the right to park in the Ministry's car park at Slotsholmen. A bill from Andersen Brothers tailors. To the tune of 8,000 kroner. A small fabric sample of grey wool attached to the bill with a paper clip. "Gentleman's overcoat, Lewis tweed, delivered 27 October 1993." Until now I thought his coats were a mistake. A job lot he had bought secondhand. Now I see that they're intended to be that way. On the income of an ordinary bureaucrat he spends a fortune for the fragile illusion of an extra half-metre across his shoulders. For some reason this puts him in a conciliatory light.

There's a pouch for coins. I shake them out. Among them I find a tooth. The mechanic bends over me. I lean back against him and close my eyes.

"A baby tooth," he says.

In the back there is a bundle of photographs. I lay them out like playing cards in a game of solitaire. On a mahogany buffet there is a samovar. Next to the buffet a shelf full of books. The word "cultivated" is one of those Danish words that I've never been able to regard as anything but a linguistic truncheon to hit people over the head with. But maybe it could be used to describe the woman in the foreground. She has white hair, rimless glasses, a white wool suit. She must be in her mid-sixties. In the other photos she sits surrounded by children. Grandchildren. That explains the baby tooth. She pushes a child on a swing, cuts a cake at a table out in the garden, takes a baby being handed to her by a younger woman who has her jaw but Ravn's gauntness.

These pictures are in colour. The next one is black-and-white. It looks as if it's been overexposed.

"These are Isaiah's footprints in the snow," I say.

"Why does it look like that?"

"Because the police don't know how to photograph snow. If you use a flash or lights at more than a 45° angle, everything disappears in the glare. It has to be done with Polaroid filters and lights down at the level of the snow."

The next photo shows a woman standing on the pavement. The woman is me, the pavement is in front of Elsa Lübing's building. The picture is blurred, taken from a car window – part of the car door blocked the lens.

They were luckier with the mechanic. His hair seems too short, but otherwise it's a likeness. There is both a profile and a full-face photo.

"From the service," he says. "They got out the old pictures from when I was in the service."

The last picture is another colour photo; it looks like a holiday snap, with sunshine and green palm trees.

"Why t-take pictures of us?"

Ravn doesn't take notes and wouldn't need photographs to prod his memory.

"To show around," I say, "to other people."

I put the papers and the tooth and the coins back. I put everything back. Except the last photo. Palm trees beneath an undoubtedly intolerable sun. Humidity guaranteed close to one hundred per cent. But the man in the photograph is still wearing a shirt and tie under his lab coat. He looks cool and comfortable. The man is Tørk Hviid.

4

I'VE CHOSEN A DINNER JACKET with wide lapels of green silk. Black breeches that come to just below my knees, green stockings, and green daisy duck shoes, and a little velvet fez over my bald spot.

The problem for a woman with a dinner jacket is always what to wear over it. I have a thin white Burberry raincoat over my shoulders. But I've also told the mechanic that I want to be driven right into the hall.

We drive along Østerbrogade and then along Strandvejen. He's in a dinner jacket, too. In a different mood I might have noticed that it's the largest size you can buy off the rack, and thus five sizes too small, and it also looks like something from the Salvation Army and does more harm than good. But we've grown too close to each other. Even now, squeezed into his jacket, he reminds me of a butterfly on his way out of a black cocoon.

He doesn't look in my direction. He looks in the rearview mirror. His driving is still fluid and relaxed. But his eyes are memorizing the cars behind and in front of us.

We turn down Sundvænget, one of the little side roads off Strandvejen, towards the Sound. At one time it led to a garden gate leading out to the beach. Now it ends at a high yellow-brick wall and a white crossing gate with a glass booth. A man in uniform takes our passes and calls up our names on a screen and opens the gate and lets us drive to the next gate, where a woman in a similar uniform accepts 250 kroner apiece and admits us into a car park, where we pay an attendant 75 kroner for him to sneer shamelessly at the Morris, which he now takes care of so that we can walk through a revolving door in a marble façade, up to a cloakroom where we sacrifice another 50 kroner apiece so that a blonde, who carries herself so that we can look right up her nose, will take our coats.

In front of a mirror that covers an entire wall, I repair a little damage with lipstick, grateful that I used the bathroom at home. At least I won't have to find out how much it costs to pee.

The mechanic stands next to me, gazing at his own reflection as if it belonged to some stranger. We're in the foyer of Casino Øresund, Denmark's twelfth, newest, and most prestigious casino. A place that I've heard about but never expected to set foot in.

This is where Birgo Lander has summoned us, and now he appears. Dressed in white shoes, white trousers with a pale blue stripe down the leg, dark-blue blazer, grey turtleneck sweater, silk scarf with little embroidered anchors, and a little white yachting cap. His eyes are glassy, his walk slightly unsteady, and he's as radiant as the sun. With both hands he carefully straightens my white bow tie.

"You look unusually delicious tonight, sweetie."

"You don't look so bad yourself. Is that your Sea Scout uniform?"

He stiffens for a second. Only twelve hours have passed since we last met. But he has already forgotten the sensation.

Then he smiles at the mechanic. "She has a blank cheque to my heart."

They shake hands, and once again I note the almost imperceptible change in the shipowner. For a moment, while he's holding the mechanic's hand, his drunkenness and his self-styled, meticulously cultivated vulgarity give way to a gratitude bordering on adoration. Then he shows us inside.

I will never learn to be comfortable in ritzy places. With every step I take, I have the feeling that someone might appear at any moment to tell me that I have no right to be here. The mechanic isn't coping much better. He is slinking along several metres behind us, trying to pull his head down between his shoulders. Birgo Lander saunters along as if he owns the place.

"Did you know that I own a piece of the pie, sweetie? Don't you read the papers? Together with Unibank, which financed Marienlyst, and Casino Austria, which runs the casino at the Hotel Scandinavia and the ones in Århus and Odense. I did it to keep myself from gambling. The owners are never allowed to play in their own casinos. The same goes for the croupiers and the dealers. Austria puts out a book with their photographs, and none of them can gamble at any of the company's other casinos, either."

He leads us through the restaurant. It's a large round room with a dance floor in the middle. In the background there's a long, dimly lit bar. On a raised platform a jazz quartet is playing, soft and anonymous. The tablecloths are pale yellow, the walls cream-coloured, the bar stainless steel. All the walls are decorated with rivets, and the door frames are a metre thick and furnished with bolts. The whole thing is designed to resemble a safe, and it's solid, expensive, and as oppressively cold and alienating as an end-of-the-season dance in a bank vault. Part of one wall has windows facing the water. You can see the lights of Sweden and the other wing of the casino with the gambling rooms, illuminated like glass cages, jutting out into the water. Beneath the windows you can make out the grey ice floes along the frozen shore.

The mechanic falls behind. Lander takes my arm. Past us glide women in décolleté gowns and gentlemen in tuxedos, gentlemen in lavender shirts and white dinner jackets, gentlemen in chamois T-shirts with gold Rolex watches and sun-bleached sailor hairstyles.

The room is an oval shape, one side of which is glass, like a black wall, facing the water. The only light comes from the dim lamps over the gaming tables. There are four curved blackjack tables and two big roulette wheels. A velvet rope hangs between the tables creating an enclosure. Behind it sit three chief croupiers, one at the card games, the others each in a tall chair, one at the end of the French roulette table and one at the American. There is an inspector for every two tables, a croupier at each table.

There is such a crowd of people that you can't see the playing surfaces. The only sounds are the voices of the croupiers and the soft clicking of the chips being stacked up.

The gamblers are all men. A few Asian women are sitting at the tables. A few European women are watching without playing. The room vibrates with deep concentration. The players' faces are pale in the light, absorbed, enraptured.

Occasionally a figure tears himself away from the table and dis-appears past us. Several with bowed heads, others with shining eyes, but most of them neutral, preoccupied. Several say hello to Lander; no one notices me.

"They don't see me," I say.

He squeezes my arm. "You've been to school, honey, you remem-ber what men look like inside. Heart, brain, liver, kidneys, stomach, testicles. When they come in here, a change takes place. The moment you buy your chips, a little animal takes up residence inside you, a little parasite. Finally there's nothing left but the attempt to remember what cards have been dealt, the attempt to feel where the ball will fall, the probability of certain card combinations, and the memory of how much you have lost."

We look at the faces around the table he has led me to. They're like empty shells. At that moment it's practically impossible to imagine that they have any life outside of this room. Maybe they don't.

"That parasite, it's the gambling bug, darling. One of the most voracious creatures in the world. And I know what I'm talking about. I've lost everything several times over. But I got back on my feet again. That's why I had to buy into it. It's different now that I'm an owner, now that I've looked behind the scenes."

The crowd opens up a bit, and the green baize comes into view. The croupier is a young blonde woman with long red fingernails who speaks perfect, slightly nasal English.

"Buying in? Forty-five thousand goes down. One, two, three . . ."

A few of the guests have mineral water in front of them. No one is drinking alcohol.

"That bug comes in various sizes, sweetheart. For some it's a canary. For me it's a corn-fed duck. For that guy over there it's an ostrich . . ."

He's been speaking in a low whisper and he doesn't point, but I know he's talking about the man sitting to one side of us. He has a perfect Slavic face, like a defected ballet dancer from the seventies. High cheekbones, straight black hair. His hands are resting on stacks of coloured chips. He doesn't move a muscle. His attention is directed towards the card shoe next to the dealer, as if he is now focusing all his energy to influence the outcome of the game.

"Thirteen, Black Jack, insurance, sir? Sixteen. Do you want to split, sir? Seventeen, too many, nineteen . . ."

"An ostrich that has eaten him up from the inside and now takes up more room than he does. He comes here every night until he's lost everything. Then he works for six months. Then he come back and loses it all."

He leans his mouth to my ear. "Captain Sigmund Lukas. Last week he lost the last of it. Had to borrow money from me for a pack of cigarettes and a taxi home."

His age is indeterminate. He might be in his mid-thirties to mid-forties. Maybe he's fifty. As I watch him, he wins and rakes a tall stack of chips towards him.

"Each chip is worth 5,000 kroner. We had them made last

month. Each table has a different limit. This is the high-roller table. Minimum bet 1,000 kroner, maximum 20,000. With the right to double down, and with an average playing time of a minute and a half per deal, it means that you can win or lose 100,000 kroner in five minutes."

"If he's broke, whose money is he playing with today?"

"Today he's playing with Uncle Lander's money, honey."

He pulls me along with him. We stand with our backs to the bar. A tall, frosted glass is placed next to him. It has been in the freezer and is covered with a thin layer of ice, which now melts and starts to slide off. It's full of a clear, amber-coloured liquid.

"Bullshot, honey. Eight parts vodka, eight parts beef bouillon."

He ponders something.

"Take a look at our customers. There are all kinds of people. A lot of lawyers come here. Quite a few contractors. Several boys who have a fat allowance from home. The heavy artillery of the Danish underworld. They can walk right up and exchange whatever they want for chips. And we haven't given in to the vice squad's demands to record the serial numbers on the bills. That's why this shop is one of the most important money-laundering centres for drug money. And then there's the little yellow-skinned ladies who run the organized prostitution with Thai and Burmese girls. There are quite a few businessmen and several doctors. There are some who travel around the world gambling. Last week a Norwegian shipowner was here. Today he might be in Travemünde. Next week Monte Carlo. In one day he won four and a half million. It was in the newspapers."

He empties his glass and pushes it aside. It's replaced with a full one.

"Such different people. But they have one thing in common. They're losers, Smilla. In the long run they all lose. This shop has two winners, the owners and the state. We have eight bureaucrats from the tax authorities here at all times. They change – like our croupiers – from the day to the evening shift, and finally to a 'count' shift when the accounts are reconciled from three in the morning onwards. There are also plainclothes police and plainclothes inspectors from the Internal Revenue Service who, like our own security people, make sure that the croupiers don't cheat, don't mark the cards, and don't make side bets with the guests. We're taxed according to our turnover by one of the world's toughest tax regulations on gambling. And yet in the casino's gambling rooms alone we have two hundred and ninety employees: managers, dealers, head croupiers, security people, technical staff, and inspectors. In the restaurant and the nightclub there are an additional two hundred and fifty: cooks, waiters, bartenders, hostesses, bouncers, cloak-room attendants, show managers, inspectors, and the full-time hookers we also control. Do you know why we can afford to pay salaries to so many people? Just between you and me, it's because we make such a huge amount of dough off the people who gamble. For the government this sewer is the biggest sucker game since they started taking a toll on every ship passing the Sound in the Middle Ages. On the following day the Norwegian shipowner lost what he had won. But we didn't leak *that* to the newspapers. There was a Thai bordello madam who dropped 500,000 kroner three times last week. She comes here every night. Every time she sees me she begs me to have the place closed down. As long as it exists, she won't have any peace. She *has* to come here. Before us there were illegal joints, of course. But that wasn't the same thing. It was mostly poker, which is slower and requires some knowledge of odds. Legalization has changed that. It's like an infectious disease that was once under control but has now been let loose. Here comes a young man who has built up a painting company. He never gambled until someone brought him in here. Now he's losing everything. It cost a hundred million kroner to build and furnish this place. But it's a gilded piece of shit."

"But you've got money in it," I say.

"Maybe I'm a rotten apple myself."

I've always been fascinated by the melancholy shamelessness with which Danes accept the enormous gap between their common sense and their actions.

"It's a business like this one that creates a case like Lukas. A very, very skilful seaman. Sailed his own little coaster in Greenland for years. After that he was responsible for building up a fishing fleet near Mbengano in the Indian Ocean off the coast of Tanzania, as part of the biggest Scandinavian project to aid developing countries. Never drinks. Knows the North Atlantic like no one else. Some people say he's even fond of it. But he gambles. That little bug has emptied him out. He no longer has a family or a home. And now he's reached the point where he's for sale. If the amount is big enough."

We go over to the table. A man who looks like a butcher is sitting next to Captain Lukas. We stand there for maybe ten minutes. In that time he loses 120,000 kroner.

A new dealer comes up behind the woman with the red nails and taps her lightly on the shoulder of her black coatdress. Without turning around she finishes the game. Sigmund Lukas wins – as far as I can tell, about 30,000 kroner. The butcher loses the last of the chips in front of him. He gets up, his face expressionless.

Red Nails introduces her successor. A young man with the same superficial charm and politeness that she possesses. "Ladies and gentlemen, here is a new dealer. Thank you."

"Would you like to play, sweetheart?"

He's holding a stack of chips between his thumb and forefinger.

I think about the 120,000 that the butcher lost. The annual net salary for one of us ordinary Danes. Five times the annual salary of one of us ordinary Arctic Eskimos. Never in my life have I seen such disrespect for money.

"You can flush them down the lavatory," I say. "At least there you have the pleasure of hearing the flush."

He shrugs. For the first time Captain Lukas lifts his cat eyes from the baize and looks at us. He scrapes up his chips, stands up, and leaves.

We slowly follow him.

"Are you doing this for my sake?" I ask him.

He takes my arm, and now his expression turns serious. "I like you, darling. But I love my wife. I'm doing this for Føjl's sake."

He thinks for a moment.

"You can't say much good about me. I drink too much. I smoke too much. I work too much. I neglect my family. Yesterday, as I was lying in the bathtub, my oldest came in and stared at me and said, 'Dad, where do you live?' My life isn't worth much. But whatever it's worth, I owe to that little Føjl."

Captain Lukas is waiting in a small glass veranda that juts out over the water. I sink down on to the bench on the other side of the table; the mechanic materializes out of the blue and slips in next to me. Lander remains standing, leaning against the table. Behind him a female waiter closes a sliding door. We're alone in a little glass box that seems to be floating on the Sound. Lukas has turned away from us. In front of him there is a cup with a black fluid that smells strongly of coffee. He's chain-smoking. Not once does he look at us. The words drip bitterly and reluctantly from his lips, like the juice from an unripe lime. He has a slight accent. My guess would be Poland.

"One night in the winter they come to me here, maybe at the end of November. A man and a woman. They ask me how I feel about the sea north of Godthåb in March. 'Just like everybody,' I say. 'I think it's hell.' Then we part. Last week they came back. Now my situation has changed. They ask me again. I try to tell them about the pack ice. About the 'Iceberg Cemetery'. About the waters along the coast that are so full of drift ice and calving icebergs and ice avalanches that go straight from the glaciers into the sea that even the Americans' nuclear-powered icebreaker *Northwind* from the Thule base ventures through only every third or fourth winter. They pay no attention. They already know all about it. 'How much do I think I can manage?' they ask. I say, 'What does your cheque book think it can manage?'"

"Any name? Any company?"

"Only the ship. A coaster. Four thousand tons. *Kronos*. Docked in Sydhavnen. They bought it and had it revamped. It's just come from the shipyard."

"Crew?"

"Ten men, I hire them."

"Cargo?"

He looks at Lander. The ship broker doesn't move. The situation is unclear. Up until now I thought he was telling me this because Lander had pressured him. Now that I see him close up, I drop that idea. Lukas doesn't take orders from anyone. Except maybe that bug inside.

"I don't know the cargo."

Bitterness bordering on self-hatred makes him rock back and forth for a moment.

"Equipment?" It's the mechanic who has spoken all of a sudden. He holds off answering for a long time.

"An LMC," he says. "I've bought one of the navy's discards for them."

He puts out his cigarette in the coffee.

"The shipyard has equipped her with large booms. A crane. Special reinforcement in the forward cargo hold."

He stands up. I follow him. I want to get him out of earshot, but the glass cage is so small that we've reached the wall almost at once. We stand so close to the glass that our breath forms fleeting white circles.

"Can I come aboard?"

He thinks for a moment. When he answers I realize that he misunderstood the question.

"I still need a stewardess."

The door slides open. In the opening stands a man with broad grey shoulders in a coat that a guest with less authority would have been forced to leave in the cloakroom.

It's Ravn.

"Miss Smilla. May I have a few words with you?"

Everyone stares at him, and he bears their glances the way he presumably bears everything else, with rock-hard equanimity.

I walk several paces behind him. No one would be able to tell that we know each other. He leads me down a wide corridor with plants and clusters of leather sofas. At the end is a hall full of slot machines. They're all in use.

A young man gives up his machine for us. He takes up a position some distance away and stands there.

Ravn takes a roll of twenty-kroner coins out of his coat pocket. "I would be glad of my wallet back."

He's standing with his back to me, playing the machine.

"I have a regular shift here one day a week," he says. I can just barely hear his voice over the hum of the machine.

"So someone saw us to our party?"

At first he doesn't answer. "They're looking for you. The word went out fifteen minutes ago."

Now it's my turn to say nothing.

"There are always a dozen plainclothes officers on duty at this place. Plus our own representatives. If you stay here, you only have a few minutes of freedom. If you leave right now, I might be able to delay things a little."

I hand his wallet in front of him, along with a photograph and a newspaper clipping. He takes them without moving his eyes from the machine. His wallet disappears into one pocket and he glances at the photo and clipping. When he reaches back to hand me the clipping, the photo is gone. He shakes his head.

"I've done what I could," he says. "And what you haven't been given, you've taken yourself. Now it has to stop."

"I want to know," I say. "I'll do anything. Including selling you to the Nail."

"The Nail?"

"That flat, hard detective who keeps turning up."

He laughs for the first time. Then his smile is gone, as if it had never existed. His image in the glass in front of him is a lifeless reflection against the machine's multicoloured, wildly spinning cylinders. But when he speaks I know that I've hit home somehow.

"Chiang Rai, on the border between Cambodia, Laos, and Burma. The region is dominated by feudal princes. The most powerful is Khum Na. A standing army of six thousand men. Offices all over the Far East and in major Western cities. Regulates the entire world trade in heroin. Tørk Hviid worked in Chiang Rai."

"Doing what?"

"He's a microbiologist, specializing in radiation mutations. All the processing of opium poppies is located up in that area. They're said to have the most modern laboratories of their kind in the world. In the middle of the jungle. Hviid worked on the irradiation of the poppy seed in an attempt to improve yield. There were rumours that he had created a new type, *mayam*, which – in its raw, boiled-down, but not yet crystallized state – was twice as strong as any heroin known."

"How does this concern you, Ravn? Is the fraud division interested in narcotics?"

He doesn't answer.

"Katja Claussen?"

"Originally an antiques dealer. Sometime in 1990 or '91 it was discovered that throughout the eighties most of the heroin coming into the US and Europe had been smuggled inside antiques."

"Seidenfaden?"

"Transport. An engineer specializing in transport assignments. Arranged for the transport of antiques from the Far East for various companies. For a while he was in charge of a veritable airlift from Singapore via Japan to Switzerland, Germany, and Copenhagen. In order to avoid the risky air space over the Middle East."

"Why aren't they in prison?"

"The powerful and the talented are seldom punished. Now you have to go, Miss Smilla."

I stay put.

"What was Freia Film?"

His hand freezes on the chrome handle. Then he nods wearily.

"A film company that was a cover for German intelligence activities both before and during the occupation of Denmark. Under the pretext of filming footage to support Hörbinger's Thule theory, they organized two expeditions to Greenland. Their real purpose was to investigate the feasibility of occupying Greenland, especially the two cryolite quarries, to secure for Germany the production of aluminium, which was so crucial to the aircraft industry. They also did surveys with the intention of establishing air bases that could serve as supply links for a possible invasion of the US."

"Was Loyen a Nazi?"

"Loyen was and is obsessed with fame. Not politics."

"What did he discover in Greenland, Ravn?"

He shakes his head. "Nobody knows. Put it out of your mind."

Now he looks at me. "Go visit a girlfriend. Think up a plausible explanation for why you were on board that boat. Then turn yourself in to the police. Get a good lawyer. You'll be free in two days. Forget about the rest."

He sticks his hand out behind him. In his palm there is a cassette tape. "I took this from your apartment. To protect you in case of a search."

I reach for it, but he hides it away.

"Why are you doing this, Ravn?"

He gazes at the machine's spinning wheels. "Let's just say that I don't care for the insufficiently explained deaths of little children."

I wait, but nothing more comes from him. Then I turn around and leave. At that moment he wins. Like a metallic vomiting, the robot emits a stream of coins with a spitting clink that goes on and on behind me.

I pick up my coat from the cloakroom. My temples are pounding. Now everyone seems to be staring at me. I look around for the mechanic. I hope he has a plan. Most men know everything about sneaking around, making excuses, taking off. But the foyer is empty. Except for me and the cloakroom woman, who looks more serious than she ought to, considering that she takes fifty kroner for hanging people's coats on a hanger.

At that moment I hear the laughter. Loud, harrowing, sonorous. It segues right into the trumpet, a wild, plangent bleating that drops at once to a lower pitch, more suitable to the setting. But by then I've recognized the sound.

The time I have is so short. I make my way through the tables and cross the empty dance floor. The three white musicians behind him are wearing pale yellow tuxedos and have faces like white dumplings. He's wearing tails. He is gigantically fat, his face a black orb of sweat, his big eyes bloodshot and protruding, as if they were trying to escape the lethal proportion of alcohol in his skull. He looks like what he is: a colossus on a pedestal that has already dissolved and disappeared.

But the music is undiminished. Even now, when he is playing with a mute, it has an overwhelmingly dense, golden, warm tone, and even in the midst of the jingle they're playing, its sound is searching, profound, teasing. I stand right in front of the low circus ring.

When they finish, I step up on to the stage. He smiles at me. But it's a smile without warmth; it's merely a drunken pose for the world around him which he probably retains even in his sleep. If he ever sleeps. I put my hand around his microphone and turn it away from us. Behind us people stop eating. The waiters freeze in mid-stride.

"Roy Louber," I say.

His smile grows broader. He takes a drink from a big glass standing next to him.

"Thule. You once played in Thule."

"Thule . . ."

He pronounces it tentatively, searching his memory as if hearing it for the first time.

"In Greenland."

"Thule," he repeats.

"On the American base. At the Northern Star. What year was it?"

He smiles at me, mechanically shaking his trumpet. I have so little time to spare. I grab hold of his lapels and pull the big face down towards me.

"'Mr PC'. You played 'Mr PC'."

"They're dead, darling." His Danish is so thick that it's almost American English. "A long time ago. Dead and gone. Mr PC – Paul Chambers."

"What year? What year was it?"

His gaze filters through glassy eyes, drunken and uncommunicative.

"Dead and gone. Me too, darling. Any time. Any time now."

He smiles. I let him go. He straightens up and pours spit out of the trumpet. Then I feel myself gently lifted down to the floor. The mechanic is standing behind me.

"Start walking, Smilla."

I start walking. He vanishes again. I keep going straight ahead. In front of me is the door to the foyer.

"Smilla Jaspersen!"

We remember people by their clothes and by the places where we've seen them, so at first I don't recognize him. The dark-blue suit and the silk tie don't go with his face. Then I realize that it's the Nail. There's nothing shrill about him; his voice is low and commanding. Equally discreet and inescapable, they will follow me out to the car in a few minutes. I start walking faster. I've turned off my brain. On either side a man like him is now approaching, a self-confident and insistent figure.

I reach the foyer. Behind me the door slams shut. It's a large door, also made to resemble a bank vault door, so tall and heavy that it looks as if it serves merely a decorative purpose. Now it slams like the lid of a cigar box. The mechanic leans casually against it. It shuts out all noise. There is only a faint thud when someone sets his shoulder against it.

"Run, Smilla," he says. "Run. Lander's waiting out on the road."

I take a look around. There are no guests in the foyer. Behind the kiosk's magazine and cigarette displays a sales assistant yawns widely. Behind the information counter a girl is about to fall asleep over her computer. Behind me a man is nonchalantly leaning his two-metre frame against a steel door being jolted by small thuds. Everything is calm and quiet at Casino Øresund. A place with class. With style and cultured excitement and diversion at the green baize tables. The place where you make new friends and meet old ones.

Then I take off. I'm out of breath by the time I get to the car park.

"Your car, madam."

It's the same attendant as when we arrived.

"I've decided to have it scrapped. After the look you gave it."

There is no path for pedestrians. They hadn't catered for the eventuality that the casino might have guests arriving on foot. So I run along the road, duck under the two white crossing gates, and come out on Sundvænget. A hundred metres ahead waits a red Jaguar with its rear lights on.

Lander doesn't look at me as I get in. His face is tense and pale.

It's night and freezing cold. I don't remember ever seeing a big city gripped by frost like this. There is something defenceless and powerless about Copenhagen, as if a new ice age were on its way.

"What's an LMC?"

He drives stiffly and slowly, unused to the white, crystalline coating that the cold has spread on the asphalt.

"Landing Mobile Craft. A flat-bottomed landing vessel. The kind used during the invasion of Normandy."

I make him drive me to Havnegade. He parks between the hydrofoil jetty and the old dock for the Bornholm boat. I ask him for his shoes and his cap. He gives them to me with no questions asked.

"Wait an hour," I say. "But no longer."

The ice is dark bottle-green in the night, with a thin layer of snow that must have just fallen. I make my way down a vertical wooden ladder built into the wharf. It's very cold on the mirror of ice. My Burberry seems oddly stiff, Lander's shoes feel as thin as eggshells. But they're white. Along with my coat and the cap, they make me one with the ice. Just in case someone might be posted at the White Cells.

Along the bulwark small packs of ice have formed. I estimate the thickness to be over ten centimetres. Thick enough for the harbour authorities to open an ice rink. The problem is the dark, coagulated slush in the open passage.

People live so close together in Northern Greenland. Sleeping many to a room. Hearing and seeing everyone else at all times. The community is so small. There were six hundred people spread among twelve settlements the last time I was home.

In contrast to this is nature. Every hunter, every child is gripped by a wild delirium whenever he walks or rides away from the settlement. First there's the feeling of a rising energy bordering on madness. Then comes a peculiar glass-clear sense of clarity.

I know it's funny. But here in Copenhagen Harbour, at two in the morning, this feeling of expansiveness comes over me. As if it somehow came from the ice and the night sky and the relatively open space.

I think about what has happened to me since Isaiah's death.

I see Denmark before me like a spit of ice. It's drifting, but it holds us frozen solid inside the ice masses, each in a fixed position in relation to everyone else.

Isaiah's death is an irregularity, an eruption that produced a fissure. That fissure has set me free. For a brief time, and I can't explain how, I have been set in motion, I have become a foreign body skating on top of the ice.

The way I am now skating across Copenhagen Harbour, dressed in a clown hat and borrowed shoes.

From this angle a new Denmark comes into view. A Denmark that consists of those who have partially wrested themselves free of the ice.

Loyen and Andreas Fine Licht, driven by different forms of greed.

Elsa Lübing, Lagermann, Ravn, bureaucrats whose strength and dilemma is their faith in a corporation, in the medical profession, in a government apparatus. But who, out of sympathy, eccentricity, or for some incomprehensible reason, have circumvented their loyalty to help me.

Lander, the rich businessman, driven by a desire for excitement and a mysterious sense of gratitude.

That is the beginning of a social cross-section of Denmark. The mechanic is the skilled worker, the labourer. Juliane is the dregs. And I – who am I? Am I the scientist, the observer? Am I the one who has been given the chance to get a glimpse of life from the outside? From a point of view made up of equal parts of loneliness and objectivity?

Or am I only pathetic?

In the channel the grease ice is held together with a thin, dark, disintegrating crust of ice, what's called "rotten ice", dissolving and crumbling from below. I walk along the dark edge, down towards the White Cells, until I find a floe that's big enough. I step on to it and then on to the next. There's a slight movement with the current, down through the harbour, of maybe half a knot, rocking, lethal. I leap the last part of the way from floe to floe. I don't even get my feet wet.

The windows of the White Cells are dark. The entire complex seems to be in a sleep that also encompasses the walls, the play-ground, the stairways, the naked trunks of the trees. From the canal I come up behind the bicycle sheds, slowly and cautiously. I stop there.

I look at the parked cars. At the dark entryways. There is no movement. Then I look at the snow. The thin, fine layer of newly fallen snow.

There is no moon, so it takes time before I notice them. A single row of footprints. He came across the bridge and went behind the building. On this side of the playground the footprints are visible.

A Vibram sole under a large person. They lead in under the shed roof in front of me, and they don't come back out.

Then I can feel him. There's no sound, no smell, nothing to see. But the tracks have made me resonant to his presence, to the certainty of an imminent threat.

We wait for twenty minutes. When the cold makes me shake I pull away from the wall so I won't make any noise. Maybe I should give up and go back the way I came. But I stay. I detest fear. I hate being scared. There is only one path to fearlessness. It's the one that leads into the mysterious centre of the terror.

For twenty minutes there is only soundless waiting. At −13 °C. My mother could handle that. Most Greenlandic hunters can manage it any time. I can pull it off on rare occasions. For most Europeans it would be unthinkable. They would shift their weight, clear their throat, cough, rustle their overcoat.

The man whose presence I sense less than a metre away must be convinced that he's alone, that no one can hear or see him. And yet he is as soundless as if he never existed.

But not for one second am I tempted to move, to give in to the cold. Like one long, internal shriek my senses tell me that someone is waiting there. That he's waiting for me.

I don't even hear him leave. I close my eyes for a moment because the cold has made them run. When I open them, a shadow has torn away from the shed roof and is moving off. A tall figure with a quick, fluid gait. And above his head, like a halo or a crown, something white, maybe a hat.

There are two ways to tag polar bears. The usual way is to stun them from a helicopter. The machine drops down directly over the bear, you lean out of the cockpit, and the instant that the air pressure from the rotor strikes the animal, it falls to the ground and you shoot.

Then there's the other method that we used on Svalbard. From a snowmobile – the Viking way. You shoot with a custom air rifle made by Neiendamm in southern Jutland. This method requires you to get close, fewer than fifty metres. Less than twenty-five is better. The moment the bear stops and turns around, you get a good look at it. Not one of those living carcasses that amuse you at the zoo, but a *polar bear*, the one from the Greenlandic coat of arms, colossal, three-quarters of a ton of muscle, bone, and teeth. With an extreme, lethal ability to explode. A wild animal that has existed for only twenty thousand years, and in that time has known only two types of mammals: its own species and its prey, the food.

I have never missed. We used bullets in which a gas device injected a large dose of Zolatil. The bear fell almost instantaneously. But not once did I escape the panicky, hair-raising fear.

It's the same feeling now. What is moving away from me is only a shadow, a stranger, a person who is not aware of my presence. But the down on my skin, which is numb from the cold, stands on end like spines on a porcupine.

I reach the stairway through the basement rooms. The mechanic's door is locked, and the tape is in place.

The door of Juliane's apartment is open. As I pass, she comes out on to the stairs.

"You're going away, Smilla."

She looks weak and helpless. I hate her anyway.

"Why didn't you tell me about Ving?" I say. "That he came and picked up Isaiah?"

She starts to cry. "The apartment. He gave us the apartment. He's a big shot with the housing authority. He could take it away again. He said that himself. Aren't you coming back?"

"Of course I am," I say.

It's true. I'll have to come back. She's the only thing left of Isaiah. Just as, for Moritz, I'm his only connection with my mother.

I walk up to my own floor. The tape hasn't been touched. I let myself in. Everything is the way I left it. I gather up only the most essential clothes. They fill two suitcases, which weigh so much that I would have to call a moving van. I try to repack them. It's difficult, because I don't dare turn on a light but work by the reflection from the city's lights on the snow outside. Finally I limit myself to one large duffel bag. But not without heart-rending sacrifices.

Standing in the middle of the room, I take one last look around. I pick up Isaiah's cigar box and put it in the bag. I say a brief mental farewell to my home.

Then the phone rings.

Of course I should just let it ring. I promised the mechanic not to come up here. And I wouldn't want to talk to the police. Everything else can wait. I should just let it ring. I have everything to lose and nothing to gain.

I loosen the tape and pick up the receiver.

"Smilla . . ."

The voice is slow, almost absent-minded. But at the same time golden and resonant, like in a TV commercial. I have not heard it before. The hairs on the back of my neck stand on end. I know that it belongs to the person who was standing less than a metre away from me only moments ago. I know it with certainty.

"Smilla . . . I know you're there."

I hear his breathing. Deep, calm. "Smilla . . ."

I put down the receiver, not on the phone, but on the table. I have to use both hands so I won't drop it. I sling my bag over my shoulder. No time to change shoes. I race out the door and down the dark stairway, out the front door and along Strand Boulevard, across the bridge, and up Havnegade. We can't control ourselves every second of our lives. There comes a time, for each of us, when panic takes the upper hand.

Lander is waiting with the engine running. I throw myself into the passenger seat and cling to him.

"This is a good start," he says.

Slowly I get my breathing down to a tolerable level.

"It was purely a one-time acknowledgment of sympathy," I tell him. "Don't let it go to your head."

I let him drive me all the way up to the house. For tonight, anyway, I've lost all desire to be alone in the dark. And I don't know where else to go. Moritz opens the door himself. Wearing a white towelling robe, white silk shorts, his hair rumpled, his eyes sleepy.

He looks at me. He looks at Lander, who is carrying my bag. He looks at the Jaguar. Amazement, jealousy, old rage, temper, curiosity, and unctuous indignation roam and struggle through his half-asleep brain. Then he rubs the stubble on his face.

"Are you coming in?" he says. "Or should I just hand the money through the letter box?"

5

THE RIB BONES are the closed ellipses of the planets, with their focus in the sternum, the breastbone, the white centre of the photograph. The lungs are the grey shadows of the Milky Way against the black leaden shield of space. The heart's dark contour is the cloud of ashes from the burned-out sun. The intestines' hazy hyperboles are the disconnected asteroids, the vagabonds of space, the scattered cosmic dust.

We're standing in Moritz's consultation room at the light box, on which three X-rays have been clipped. In the technical reduction of photon photography it's more apparent than ever that the human being is a universe, a solar system seen from another galaxy. And yet this person is dead. With a jackhammer someone dug him a grave in the permafrost of Holsteinsborg, put stones on top, and poured cement over it to keep the Arctic foxes away.

"Marius Høeg, dead on the Barren Glacier, Gela Alta, July 1966."

Moritz and forensics expert Dr Lagermann and I are standing in front of the light box. In a wicker chair Benja is sitting sucking her thumb.

The floor is yellow marble, the walls are covered with light-brown fabric. There is wicker furniture and an examination table painted avocado green and covered with undyed leather. There is an original Dalí on the wall. Even the X-ray machine looks as if it feels comfortable with this attempt to make advanced technology seem homey.

This is where Moritz earns a portion of the money which helps to make his life's late afternoon golden, but right now he is working for free. He is examining the X-rays which Lagermann, in defiance of six paragraphs of the law, has taken from the archives of the Institute of Forensic Medicine.

"The report from the expedition in '66 is missing. It has simply been removed. Damn."

I told Moritz that they are looking for me and that I have no intention of turning myself in to the police. He detests illegalities but he acquiesces because, with or without permission from the police, it's better for me to be here than not.

I told him that I'm going to have a visitor and that we will need the light box in his clinic. His clinic is his inner sanctum, as private as his investments and his bank accounts in Switzerland, but he agrees.

I said that I wouldn't tell him what it was all about. Again he acquiesces. He's trying to pay back some of his debt to me. It's thirty years old and fathomless.

Now that Lagermann has arrived and unpacked and hung up the pictures with little clips, the door opens, and Moritz slouches in.

Standing there in front of us he is three people in one.

He is my father, who still loves my mother and possibly me as well, and is now sick with anxiety that he can't control.

He is the great doctor, MD, and international injection celebrity who has never been excluded, always the one who knew things before anyone else did.

And he is the little boy who has been shut out of the room in which something is happening that he's dying to take part in.

It's the latter person that I, on sudden impulse, allow into the room and whom I introduce to Lagermann.

Of course he knows my father; he shakes his hand and smiles broadly at him; he has met him two or three times before. I should have realized what would happen now: that Lagermann would pull him over to the light box.

"Just have a look at this," he says. "Because there's something here that'll knock the socks off you."

The door opens and Benja pads in. With her woollen socks and her turned-out prima-donna feet and her demand for undivided attention.

The two men are glued to the transparent star chart on the box. They are explaining it to me. But their words are directed at each other.

"There are few dangerous bacteria in Greenland."

Lagermann doesn't know that Moritz and I have forgotten more about Greenland than he will ever learn. But we don't interrupt him.

"It's too cold. And too dry. That's why poisoning from tainted food is extremely rare. With the exception of one kind: botulism, anaerobic bacteria that produce a very dangerous form of meat poisoning."

"I'm a lactovegetarian," says Benja.

"The report is in Godthåb, with a copy in Copenhagen. It says that they found five people on the same day, 7 August 1991. Healthy young people. Botulism, *Clostridium botulinum*, is anaerobic, just like the tetanus bacteria. And not dangerous in and of itself. But its waste products are exceedingly toxic. Attack the peripheral nervous system where the nerves innervate the muscle fibres. Paralyse the lungs. Just before death, it's spectacular, of course. Hypoventilation, acidosis like hell. The victim turns blue in the face. But when it's over, there's not a trace. Naturally the *livores* are slightly darker, but what the devil, they are with a heart attack, too."

"So there is nothing externally visible?" I ask.

He shakes his head. "Nothing. Botulism is determined by a process of elimination. Something you come to suspect because you can't find any other cause of death. Then you take a blood sample. And samples of the food under suspicion. You send them to the Serum Institute. Queen Ingrid's Hospital in Godthåb has a medical laboratory, of course. But no facilities to trace the less common toxins. So blood samples were sent to Copenhagen. In the samples they found the toxin from *botulinum*."

He takes out one of his big cigar matches. Moritz's eyebrows shoot up. It's forbidden, under penalty of death, to smoke in the clinic. Smokers are shown to the smoking salon, which means a walk in the garden. Even there he doesn't like it much. He thinks that the sight of someone smoking, even from a distance, might affect his golf swing. It was one of his few, great, miraculous triumphs over my mother that he got her to go outside to smoke in Qaanaaq. It was one of his many defeats that she smoked indoors in the summer tent at Siorapaluk.

With the unsulphured end of the match Lagermann points at a row of tiny numbers on the bottom edge of the X-ray. "X-rays cost a damn fortune. We only use them to search for hardware that has been stuck into people. No pictures were taken in '91. It wasn't thought necessary."

He takes out a cellophane-wrapped cigar from his breast pocket.

"You're not allowed to smoke in here," says Benja.

He gives her a faraway look. Then he gently taps the photo with the cigar.

"But in '66 they had to take pictures. There was some doubt about identification. They were severely maimed by the explosion. There was nothing to do but take X-rays. To look for old bone fractures and the like. The negatives were supposedly sent round to all the doctors in Greenland. Along with a full dental shot of what was left of their teeth."

It's not until now that I realize there are no thighbones beneath the pelvis in the X-ray.

Lagermann carefully places two more negatives next to the first. In one of them almost the entire spine is intact. The other is a chaos of bone fragments and dark shadows, a pulverized universe.

"These prompt various professional questions. Such as the location of the bodies in relation to the detonation. It looks as if they were sitting right on top of the charge. That it was not – as is normal when you use plastic explosives on rock or ice – placed in a bored-out channel, or kneaded to an upside-down can, which concentrates the explosion in one particular spot. It practically blew up right under their arse, so to speak. Which rarely happens when professionals are involved."

"I'm leaving," says Benja. But she stays in her chair.

"All of this is speculation based on very little evidence, of course. But *this* isn't."

He hangs two larger X-rays under the first ones. "Enlargements from the negative of these areas."

He points with the cigar. "You can see the remains of the liver, the lower oesophagus, and the stomach. The bottom rib is stuck here, right above the *vertebra lumbalis*, which is here. This is the heart. Here it's damaged, there it's intact. Do you notice anything?"

To me it seems a chaos of black and grey nuances. Moritz leans forward. Curiosity wins out over vanity. From his inside pocket he takes out the glasses which only we, the women in his life, have ever seen him wear. Then he puts a fingernail on each picture.

"There."

Lagermann straightens up.

"Yes," he says, "that's the spot. But what the hell is it?"

Moritz picks up a magnifying glass from an aluminium tray. Even when he shows it to me, I don't understand. Only when he shows it to me on the second negative can I make it out. Just like in glaciology. One occurrence is an accident. It's the repeat occurrence that creates a structure.

It's a needle-thin, whitish line, uneven, crooked. It wanders up along the smashed vertebrae, disappears at the ribs, reappears at the tip of one lung, vanishes, and shows up again near the heart, outside and partly inside of it, in the large ventricle, like a white thread of light.

Lagermann points at the second X-ray. Through the liver, into the left kidney.

They stare through the magnifying glass.

Then Moritz turns around. He picks up a shiny, thick journal from his desk.

"*Nature*," he says. "A special issue from 1979. Which you, Smilla, directed my attention to."

There's a photograph on the right-hand side. An X-ray photo, but using a technique that makes the soft organs visible too, so that the body almost imperceptibly merges into the skeleton.

"This", says Moritz, "is a man from Ghana."

He points with his fountain pen along the left side of the photograph. There is a light winding line moving from one hip up through the abdominal cavity.

"*Dracunculus*," he says. "Guinea worm. Transmitted via *Cyclops* crustaceans, in the drinking water. Can also bore its way through the skin. A truly nasty parasite. Up to a metre long. Works its way through the body with a speed of up to one centimetre a day. Finally sticks its head out through the thigh. That's where the Africans catch it and roll it up around a stick. Every day they wind up a few more centimetres. It takes a month to get it out. That month and the months before are one continuous period of suffering."

"That's revolting," says Benja.

We put our heads up close to the X-rays.

"I thought so," says Lagermann. "I thought it must be some kind of worm."

"The article in *Nature*", says Moritz, "is about diagnosing this sort of parasite by X-ray. It's quite complicated if it's not calcified in the tissue. Because the heart is no longer beating, it's very difficult to make the contrast fluids disseminate through the body."

"But this is about Greenland," I say. "Not the tropics."

Moritz nods.

"But you had underlined the article in your letter. Loyen wrote it. It's one of his main specialities."

Lagermann taps on the negative. "I don't know anything about tropical diseases. I'm a forensics specialist. But something has bored its way into these two people. Something that might be a worm or might be something else. Something that has left a channel forty centimetres long and at least two millimetres in diameter. Straight through the diaphragm and the soft organs. Something that stops in areas exploded by infection. For these two gentlemen the TNT didn't make any difference. They were already dead. They died because something – whatever the hell it was – had stuck its head into the heart of one man and the liver of the other."

We stare at the X-rays in bewilderment.

"The right man to solve this problem," says Moritz, "might be Loyen."

Lagermann regards him with his eyes narrowed.

"Yes," he says, "it would be interesting to hear what he has to say. But if we wanted to be sure of an honest answer, it looks as if we'd have to tie him to a chair, give him sodium pentothal, and hook him up to a lie detector."

6

I WOULD LIKE TO *understand* Benja. At this moment more than ever.

It wasn't always this way. I didn't always have to understand things. At least I tell myself that it wasn't always this way. When I came to Denmark for the first time, I *experienced* phenomena. In all their gruesomeness, or beauty, or grey drabness. But without feeling any great need to explain them.

Often there was no food when Isaiah came home. Juliane would be sitting at the table with her friends, and there were cigarettes and laughter and tears and massive alcohol abuse, but there wasn't so much as five kroner to go out and buy a portion of chips. He never complained. He never yelled at his mother. He never sulked. Patient, silent, and watchful, he would wrench himself away from the outstretched hands and go on his way. In order to find, if possible, some other solution. Sometimes the mechanic was at home, sometimes I was. He could sit in my living room for an hour or more without telling me he was hungry. Persisting in an extreme, almost stupid, Greenlandic politeness.

When I had cooked for him, when I had boiled a mackerel and had given him the whole fish, weighing a kilo and a half, on a newspaper on the floor because that's where he preferred to eat, and he, using both hands, without uttering a word, with methodical thoroughness ate the eyes and sucked out the brain and licked the backbone and crunched on the fins, that is when I occasionally got the urge to explain. I would try to understand the difference between growing up in Denmark and growing up in Greenland. To comprehend the humiliating, exhausting, monotonous emotional dramas with which European children and parents are bound together in mutual hatred and dependence. And to understand Isaiah.

Deep inside I know that trying to fathom things out leads to blindness, that the desire to understand has a built-in brutality that erases what you seek to comprehend. Only experience is sensitive. But perhaps I'm both weak *and* brutal. I've never been able to resist trying.

Benja seems to have been given everything. I've met her parents. They're trim and subdued and play the piano and speak foreign languages, and every year, when the Royal Theatre's school closed for the summer and they went south to their house on the Costa Smeralda, they always took the best French ballet tutor along to chivy Benja on the terrace between the palm trees every morning, because that's what she herself wanted.

You might think that someone who has never suffered or lacked anything worth mentioning would be at peace with herself. For a long time I misjudged her. I thought she and Moritz were playing a game when she walked through the room in front of us, dressed only in her little knickers, and placed red silk scarves over the lamps because the light hurt her eyes, and made an endless series of appointments with Moritz and then cancelled them because, she said, today she needed to see someone of her own age. I thought that on some mysterious wave of self-confidence she was testing her youth and beauty and attractiveness on Moritz, who was almost fifty years older than her.

One day I witnessed her ordering him to move the furniture so that she would have room to dance, and he refused.

At first she didn't believe him. Her pretty face and slanted, almond-shaped eyes and smooth brow beneath corkscrew curls glowed with the awareness of a victory already won. Then she realized that he was not going to yield. It may have been the first time in their relationship. First she turned pale with rage, and then her face cracked. Her eyes became despairing, empty, abandoned; her mouth closed on smothered, infantile, despairing tears which refused to flow.

Then I realized that she loved him. That under that appealing coquettishness was a love like a military operation that would tolerate anything and fight any necessary tank battles and demand the world in return. Then I realized, too, that she might always hate me. And that she had lost in advance. Somewhere inside Moritz there is a landscape she will never reach. The home of his feelings for my mother.

Or perhaps I'm wrong. Right now, at this very moment, it occurs to me that she might have won, after all. If that's the case, then I'll grant her that she put her nose to the grindstone. She didn't just leave it at wiggling her little arse around. She didn't settle for sending lovesick glances from the stage to Moritz in the first row, hoping that it would all work out in the long run. She didn't put her trust in her influence at home in the bosom of her family. If I didn't realize it before, I know it now. That there is a raw energy in Benja.

I'm standing in the snow, pressed up against the wall of the house, peering down into the pantry. There Benja is pouring a glass of milk. Enchanting, lithe Benja. And she's handing it to a man who now steps into view. It's the Nail.

I'm walking along Strandvejen from Klampenborg Station, and it's a wonder that I notice it at all, because I've had a hard day.

That morning I couldn't stand it any longer; I got up, tucked my hair and bandage – which is now only a Band-Aid over the wound – under a ski hat, put on sunglasses and a Loden coat, and took the train to the terminus, and there I call the mechanic's number, but no one answers.

Then I stroll along the docks, from the Toldkajen to Langelinie, trying to gather my thoughts. At Nordhavnen I make several purchases and pack up a box that they will deliver to Moritz's villa, and from a phone booth I make a call that I know is one of the crucial actions in my life.

And yet it's strange that it means so little. Under certain circumstances the fateful decisions in life, sometimes even in matters of life and death, are made with an almost indifferent ease. While the little things – for instance, the way people hang on to what is over – seem so important. What's important today is to see Knippels Bridge once again, where I rode with him, and the White Cells, where I slept with him, and the Cryolite Corporation, and Skudehavnsvej, where we walked together, arm in arm. I call him again from the phone booth at Nordhavnen Station. A man answers. But it's not him. It's a controlled, anonymous voice.

"Yes?"

I hold the receiver to my ear. Then I hang up.

I page through the phone book. I can't find his car repair shop. I take a taxi out to Toftegårds Plads and walk along Vigerslev Allé. There is no garage. From a phone booth I call the mechanics' association. The man I talk to is friendly and patient. But there has never been a car repair shop registered on Vigerslev Allé.

I've never noticed until now how exposed phone booths are. Making a call is like putting yourself on display for instant recognition.

The phone book lists two addresses for the Centre for Developmental Research, one at the August Krogh Institute and one at Denmark's Technical High School on Lundtoftesletten. At the latter address it says that there is apparently a library and office.

I take a taxi to Kampmannsgade, to the office of the Trade Commission. The boy's smile and tie and naïveté are unchanged.

"I'm glad you came back," he says.

I show him the newspaper clipping. "You read foreign papers. Do you remember this one?"

"The suicide," he says. "Everybody remembers that. The consular secretary jumped off a roof. The man they arrested had tried to talk her out of it. The case raised a fundamental question about the legal rights of Danes abroad."

"You don't happen to remember the secretary's name, do you?"

He has tears in his eyes. "We studied international law at the university together. A wonderful girl. Ravn was her name. Nathalie Ravn. She applied for a job with the Ministry of Justice. They said – in local circles – that she might become the first female police commissioner."

"There's nothing 'local' left any more," I say. "If something happens in Greenland, it's connected to something else in Singapore."

He gazes at me, uncomprehending and mournful.

"You didn't come here to see *me*," he says. "You came about this."

"I'm not worth getting to know," I say, meaning it.

"You remind me of her. Secretive. And not someone you would picture behind a desk. I couldn't understand why she suddenly became a secretary in Singapore. That's a different Ministry."

I take the train to Lyngby Station and then catch a bus. In a way, it feels like when I was seventeen. You think that the despair will stop you cold, but it doesn't; it wraps itself up in a dark corner somewhere inside and forces the rest of your system to function, to take care of practical matters, which may not be important but which keep you going, which guarantee that you are still, somehow, alive.

Between the buildings the snow is a metre high; only narrow corridors have been cleared.

They haven't finished fitting up the Centre for Developmental Research yet. In the lobby they've put in a counter, but it's covered up because they're in the process of painting the ceiling. I tell them what I'm looking for. A woman asks me whether I have computer time reserved. I say no. She shakes her head, the library isn't open yet, the centre's archives are kept on UNI C at Denmark's Data Processing Centre for Research and Training, the computer system for institutes of higher learning, which is not accessible to the general public.

I walk around among the buildings for a while. I was here many times in my student days. Our classes on surveying were held here. Time has changed the area, made it harsher and more alien than I remember it. Or perhaps it's the cold. Or just me.

I walk past the computer building. It's locked, but when a group of students comes out, I go in. In the central room there are about fifty terminals. I wait for a while. When an elderly man comes in, I follow him. When he sits down, I stand behind him and pay attention. He doesn't notice me. He sits there for an hour. Then he leaves. I sit down at a free terminal and press a key. The machine prompts: *Log on user ID?* I type *LTH3* – just as the elderly gentleman did. The machine replies: *Welcome to the Laboratory for Technical Hygiene. Your password?* I type *JPB*. The way the elderly gentleman did. The machine replies: *Welcome Mr Jens Peter Bramslev.*

When I type *Centre for Developmental Research* the machine responds with a menu. One of the topics is Library. I type in *Tørk Hviid*. There is only one title: "A Hypothesis on the Eradication of Submarine Life in the Arctic Sea in Conjunction with the Alvarez Incident".

It's a hundred pages long. I scroll through them. There are timelines. Pictures of fossils. Neither the pictures nor the captions are legible in the poor resolution of the screen. There are various charts. Some diagrammatic, geological maps of the present-day Davis Strait in various stages of its creation. The whole thing seems altogether incomprehensible. I press on to the end.

After a long list of references there is a brief abstract of the article.

This article is based on the theory of physicist and Nobel Prize-winner Luis Alvarez from the 1970s. He proposed that the iridium content in a layer of clay between the chalk and tertiary sediments at Gubbio in the northern Apennines and at Stevns Klint in Denmark is too big to be anything but the result of an extremely large meteor impact.

Alvarez theorizes that the impact occurred sixty-five million years ago, that the meteor was between six and fourteen kilometres in diameter, and that it exploded on impact, releasing energy comparable to a hundred million megatons of TNT. The resultant ash cloud totally blocked out the sun for a period of at least several days. During this period several food chains collapsed. The result was that a large proportion of the marine and submarine microorganisms was annihilated, which in turn prompted further consequences for the large carnivores and herbivores. On the basis of discoveries made by the author in the Barents Sea and Davis Strait, the article discusses the possibility that the radiation resulting from the explosion on impact might explain a series of mutations among marine-based parasites in the early Palaeocene periods. The article also discusses whether such mutations might be the reason for massive extinctions of the larger sea animals.

I scroll through it again. The language is clear, the style concise, almost transparent. But sixty-five million years still seems like a very long time ago.

It's dark by the time I take the train back. The wind carries a light snow with it, *pirhuk*. My mind registers it as if through an anaesthetic.

In a big city you adopt a particular way of regarding the world. A focused, sporadically selective view. When you scan a desert or an ice floe, you see with different eyes. You let the details slip out of focus in favour of the whole. This way of seeing reveals a different reality. If you look at someone's face in this manner, it starts to dissolve into a shifting series of masks.

With this way of seeing, a person's breath in the cold – that veil of cooled drops that forms in the air in temperatures under 8 °C – is not merely a phenomenon fifty centimetres from his mouth. It's something all-encompassing, a structural transformation of the space surrounding a warm-blooded creature, an aura of minimal but definite thermal displacement. I've seen hunters shoot snow hares in a starless winter night at a distance of two hundred and fifty metres by aiming at the fog around them.

I am not a hunter. And I'm asleep inside. Maybe I'm close to giving up. But I sense him when I'm fifty metres away, before he hears me. He's standing between the two marble pillars which flank the gate leading from Strandvejen to the stairs.

In the city, in the Nørrebro district, people stand on streetcorners and in doorways; it doesn't mean anything. But on Strandvejen it *is* significant. And besides, I've grown hypersensitive. So I shrug off the resignation, take several steps backwards, and slip into next door's garden.

I find the hole in the hedge that I used so often as a child, squeeze my way through it, and wait. After several minutes I see the other one. He's positioned himself at the corner of the porter's lodge, where the drive curves up towards the house.

I walk back to the place where I can approach the kitchen door from an angle so I'm not visible to either of them. The visibility has started to deteriorate. The black soil beneath the roses is hard as a rock. The birdbath is swathed in a big snowdrift.

I walk along the wall of the house, and it occurs to me that although I have so often felt persecuted, I actually might not have had anything to complain about until now.

Moritz is alone in the living room; I can see him through the window. He's sitting in the low oak chair, his hands gripping the armrests. I continue round the house, past the main entrance, along the back to where the bay window juts out. There's a light on in the pantry. That's where I see Benja. She's pouring a glass of cold milk. Refreshing on a night like this, when you have to stand guard and wait. I take the fire escape. It leads up to the balcony outside what was once my room. I go inside and feel my way forward. They've delivered the box; it's on the floor.

The door to the hallway is open. Downstairs in the hall Benja is seeing the Nail out.

I can see him walking across the gravel, like a dark shadow. Over to the garage and in through the little door.

They're parked in the garage, of course. Moritz moved his car a little so there would be room for them. Citizens must assist the police in every way possible.

I tiptoe down the staircase. I know it well, so I don't make any noise. I reach the hall, go past the cloakroom and into the small parlour. There is Benja. She doesn't see me. She stands looking out across Øresund. Towards the lights at Tuborg Harbour, towards Sweden and Flakfort. She's humming. Not particularly cheerful or relaxed. But intent. Tonight, she's thinking, tonight they'll nab Smilla. The fake Greenlander.

"Benja," I say.

She twirls around in a flash, like when she's dancing. But then she freezes.

I don't say a word, just motion with my hand, and with bowed head she precedes me into the living room.

I remain standing in the doorway, where the long curtains prevent me from being seen from the road.

Moritz raises his head and sees me. His expression doesn't change. But his face becomes flatter, more careworn.

"It was me." Benja has gone over to stand next to him. He is hers.

"I was the one who called," she says.

He rubs his hand across the whiskers on his chin. He hasn't shaved tonight. The stubble is black with flecks of grey. His voice is low and resigned.

"I never said I was perfect, Smilla."

He's said that thousands of times, but I don't have the heart to remind him. For the first time ever, I see that he is old. That some day, perhaps in the not so distant future, he's going to die. For a moment I fight it, then I give up and am filled with sympathy. At this pathetic moment.

"They're waiting for you outside," says Benja. "They're going to take you away. You don't belong here."

I can't help admiring her. You find some of this same madness in female polar bears defending their cubs.

Moritz doesn't seem to hear her. His voice is still low, introspective. As if he's talking mainly to himself. "I wanted peace and quiet so badly. I wanted to have my family around me. But I never achieved that. It never worked out. Things got out of control for me. When I saw that box they delivered this afternoon, I realized that you were leaving again. Like all the times you ran away. I'm too old to bring you back home again. Maybe it was wrong to do it in the past."

His eyes are bloodshot when he looks at me. "I don't want to let you go, Smilla."

Every life contains within it a potential for clarification. He has lost that opportunity. The conflicts that are now pressing him down in his chair are the same ones he had in his thirties, when I got to know him, when he became my father. The only thing age has done is to whittle away his ability to confront them.

Benja licks her lips.

"Will you go out to them yourself," she says, "or should I go and get them?"

For as long as I can remember, I have been trying to escape this house, this country. Each time, life has used him as its unresisting instrument to call me back. At this moment it becomes more obvious than it has ever been since I was a child that freedom of choice is an illusion, that life leads us through a series of bitter, involuntarily comical, and repetitive confrontations with the problems that we haven't resolved. At some other time I might have smiled at this. Right now I'm too tired. So I bow my head and prepare to give up.

Then Moritz stands up.

"Benja," he says. "Stay here."

She gives him a startled look.

"Smilla," he says, "what can I do?"

We measure each other with narrowed eyes. Something has slipped inside him.

"Your car," I say. "Drive your car up to the back door. As close as possible, so you can put the box in it without them seeing you. So that I can get in and lie on the floor in the back."

When he leaves the room, Benja sits down in his chair. Her face is expressionless and remote. We hear him start up the car and drive it out; we hear the crunching of the tyres on the gravel in front of the door. The sound of the door. Moritz's cautious, burdened steps as he carries the box out.

When he returns, he's wearing rubber boots, an oilskin coat and cap. He simply stands in the doorway for a moment. Then he turns on his heel and leaves.

When I get up, Benja slowly follows me. I go into the little parlour where the telephone is and dial a number. It's answered instantly.

"I'm coming," I say. Then I hang up.

When I turn round, Benja is standing behind me. "After you drive off, I'll go out and send them after you."

I step closer to her. With my thumb and forefinger, through her leotard, I grab her mound of Venus and squeeze. When she opens her mouth, I put my other hand around her throat and cut off her windpipe. Her eyes grow big and terrified. She falls to her knees and I go with her, so we are both kneeling across from each other

223

on the floor. She is taller and heavier than I am, but her level of energy and treachery are of a different kind. At the Royal Theatre they don't learn to express their anger physically.

"Benja," I whisper. "Leave me alone."

I pinch harder. There are beads of sweat on her upper lip.

Then I let her go. She doesn't utter a sound. Her face is empty with fear.

The door to the hall is open. The car is waiting right outside. I crawl in the back on the floor. My box is on the back seat. A blanket is pulled over me. Moritz gets into the front seat.

Outside the garage the car stops. The window is rolled down.

"Thank you so much for your help," says the Nail.

Then we drive off.

Skovshoved Water Ski Club has a wide wooden ramp that slopes down into the water from a high dock. That's where Lander is waiting. He's wearing a one-piece, watertight sailing outfit tucked into his boots. It's black.

Black, too, is the tarpaulin on the roof of his car. It's not the Jaguar but a Land Rover with the body high off the ground.

The dinghy tied on under the tarpaulin is also black. A Zodiac made of heavy rubberized canvas with a wooden bottom. Moritz wants to help but doesn't move fast enough. With a swift jerk the small man tips the boat off the car, catches it on his head, and shoves it down the ramp with one fluid movement.

He takes an outboard motor out of the back of the car, lands it in the boat, and fastens it to the stern.

All three of us lift the boat to get it into the water. In my box I find rubber boots, a balaclava, thermal gloves, and a sou'wester that I pull on over my sweater.

Moritz does not go out on the ramp with us but stays at the railing. "Can I do anything for you, Smilla?"

It's Lander who answers. "You can get out of here fast."

Then he pushes off and starts up the motor. An invisible hand takes hold of the boat from below and pulls us away from land. The snow is falling heavily. After a few seconds Moritz's figure disappears. Just as he turns around and goes back to the car.

Lander has a compass strapped to his left wrist. In a corridor of visibility momentarily appearing in the snowfall, we can see Sweden. The lights of Tårbæk. And, as lighter, floating spots in the dark, two ships at anchor between the shore and the central navigation channel. Northwest of Flakfort.

"The starboard one is *Kronos*."

I'm having a hard time separating Lander from his office, his liquor, his high heels, his elegant clothes. The authority with which he manoeuvres the boat between the swells, which get bigger the further we are from shore, is unexpected and foreign.

I try to orient myself. It's one sea mile out to the channel. Two booms along the way. The channel lights to Tuborg Harbour. To Skovshoved Harbour. The masthead lights on the hills above Strandvejen. A container ship on its way south.

When the snowfall blocks out the view, I correct his course twice. He gives me a searching glance, but he obeys. I don't try to explain anything to him. What would I say?

A slight wind comes up. It blows cold, hard drops of salt water into our faces. We huddle in the bottom, leaning against each other. The heavy Zodiac dances on the choppy waves. He puts his mouth to my balaclava, which I've pulled up.

"Føjl and I were in the Marines together. In the frogman corps. We were in our early twenties. If you're a thinking person, then you have to be young to put up with that kind of shit. For six months we would get up at five a.m. and swim a kilometre in ice-cold water and run for an hour and a half. We had parachute jumping at night over the sea, five kilometres off the coast of Scotland, and I'm practically night-blind. We lugged that bloody rubber boat around on our heads through the Danish woods while the officers pissed on us and tried to rearrange our psyches to make fighting men out of us."

I put my hand on his arm holding the throttle and correct the course. Five hundred metres ahead the container ship cuts across our course in the form of a green starboard light and three running lanterns up high.

"It's usually the small ones who do best. Guys my size. We were the ones who could keep it up. The bigger guys could manage one lift and then they were finished. We had to put them in the rubber boat and carry them along. But Føjl was different. Føjl was big. But as fast as if he were small. They couldn't wear him out. They never cracked him in the interrogation courses. He would just give them that friendly stare; you know how he is. And then he wouldn't budge an inch. One day we were diving under ice. It was winter. The sea was frozen solid. We had to dynamite a hole in it. There was a strong current that day. On my way down I passed through a cold belt. That happens sometimes. The condensed water from the exhaled air freezes to ice and blocks the small valves in the air tank. I hadn't attached the safety line yet. That's how you can find your way back to the hole in the ice. That's what diving under ice is like. From two metres away the hole is a dark edge. From five metres away you can't see it any longer. So I'm seized with panic. I lose the line. I don't think I can see the hole any more. Everything is green and brilliant and neon-coloured under the ice. I feel as if I'm being sucked into the realm of the dead. I can feel the current grabbing me and carrying me down and away. They tell me that Føjl was watching. So he picks up a lead belt in one hand and jumps into the water without any oxygen tanks. With only a line in his hand. Because there wasn't time. And he dives down to me. He catches me twelve metres down. But he's diving in a dry suit. This means that the water pressure drives the rubber against his skin. With an additional one atmosphere of pressure for every ten metres. About ten metres down the rubber edge cut through the skin of his wrists and ankles. What I remember about our passage up to the surface was clouds of blood."

I think about the scars around his wrists and ankles.

"He was also the one who forced the water out of my lungs. And gave me artificial respiration. We had to wait a long time. They only had a little gas turbine helicopter, and the weather was bad. He gave me heart massage and oxygen all the way back."

"Back to where?"

"To Scoresbysund. We were on exercises in Greenland. It was cold. But that suited him fine."

The snow closes around us in a chaotic gridwork, a wild confusion of slanted stripes.

"He's disappeared," I say. "I tried to call him. Some stranger answered the phone. Maybe he's in gaol."

One minute before the ship appears, I can sense its presence. The pull of the hull against the anchor chains, the slow shifting of the entire vast, floating hulk.

"Forget about him, honey. That's what the rest of us have had to do."

On the port side there is a short floating platform at the bottom of a steep ladder beneath a single yellow light. He doesn't turn off the motor but steadies the boat by holding on to an iron girder.

"You can go back with me, Smilla."

226

There's something touching about him, as if he hadn't realized until now that we stopped playing games a long time ago.

"The thing is," I say, "that I don't have anything in particular to go back to."

I sling the box on to the platform myself. When I step up on to it and turn around, he stands there for a moment, gazing at me, a small figure, rising and sinking, the big rubber boat lending him a dancing movement. Then he turns away and pushes off.

THE SEA

1

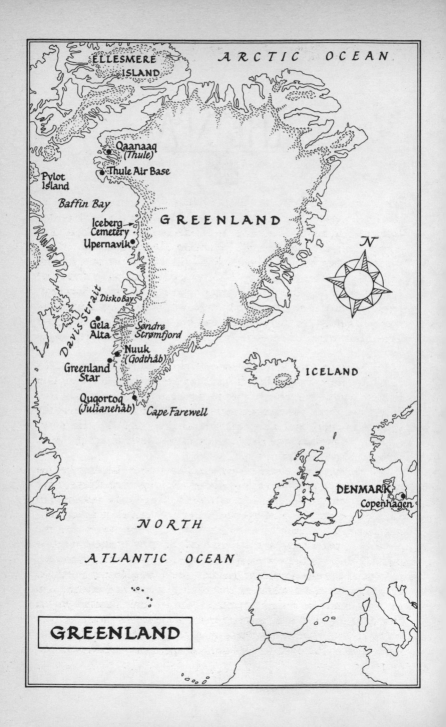

ARCTIC OCEAN

ELLESMERE
ISLAND

Qaanaaq
(Thule)

Thule Air Base

Pylot
Island

Baffin Bay

GREENLAND

Iceberg
Cemetery

Upernavik

N

Davis Strait

Disko Bay

Gela
Alta

Søndre
Strømfjord

Nuuk
(Godthåb)

Greenland
Star

Quqortoq
(Julianehåb)

Cape Farewell

ICELAND

DENMARK

Copenhagen

NORTH

ATLANTIC OCEAN

GREENLAND

1

MY CABIN IS TWO AND A HALF by three metres. But they've still found space for a sink and mirror, a cupboard, a bunk with a reading light, a shelf for books, and under the porthole a little desk with a chair, and on the table *Aajumaaq*, the big dog.

He stretches from one bulkhead all the way across to the bunk and is about two metres long. His eyes are sad, his paws dark, and with every list of the ship, he tries to touch me. If he succeeds, I will instantly disintegrate. My flesh will fall off my bones, my eyes will run out of their sockets and evaporate, my intestines will force their way out through my skin and explode in clouds of methane.

He doesn't belong here. He doesn't belong in my world at all. His name is Aajumaaq and he's from East Greenland, and my mother brought him home from a visit to Ammassalik. After seeing him once down there, she realized that he must have always been in the Qaanaaq region, and after that she saw him regularly. He never touches the ground, and here, too, he floats a little above the desk. He's here because I'm at sea.

I've always been afraid of the sea. Never once did they get me into a kayak, though it was my mother's greatest wish. Never have I set foot on the deck of Moritz's Swan. One of the reasons I'm fond of ice is that it covers the water and makes it solid, safe, negotiable, classifiable. I know that, outside, the waves and the wind have picked up, and far forward the bow of the *Kronos* is pitching through the waves, splintering them, and sending roaring cascades of water along the gunwale until, outside my porthole, they disperse into a whistling mist shining white in the night. On the open sea there are no landmarks, there is only an amorphous, chaotic shifting of directionless masses of water that loom up and break and roll, and their surface is, in turn, broken by subsystems that interfere and form whirlpools and appear and disappear and finally vanish without a trace. Slowly this confusion will work its way into the labyrinth of my ear and dissolve my sense of orientation; it will fight its way into my cells and displace their salt concentrations and the conductive power of my nervous system as well, leaving me deaf, blind, and helpless. I'm not afraid of the sea merely because it wants to strangle me. I'm afraid of it because it will take away from me my orientation, the inner gyroscope of my life, my awareness of what is up and down, my connection to Absolute Space.

No one can grow up in Qaanaaq without going to sea. No one can live as I have done, as a professional student and expedition advance party and guide in North Greenland, without being forced to go to sea. I've been on more ships and for much longer periods of time than I care to remember. If I'm not actually standing on a deck, I've usually managed to repress it.

From the moment I came on board several hours ago, the process of disintegration has begun. There's already a boiling in my ears, strange, spontaneous slides of fluids against my auricular membranes. I can no longer with certainty identify the points of the compass. On my desk Aajumaaq is waiting to catch me off guard.

He waits immediately inside the doorway leading to sleep, and every time I hear my own breath grow deeper and know that now I'm asleep, I don't slip into that peaceful obliteration of reality that I need, I fall into a new dangerous clarity beside the auxiliary spirit, the dog with three claws on each paw, magnified and intensified in my mother's imagination and from there, ever since I was a child, he has been grafted into my nightmares.

It's been perhaps an hour since the engines were started, and from a great distance I sensed rather than heard the play of the windlass and the clattering of the anchor chain, and I'm too tired to stay awake and too tense to sleep, and in the end I just wish for some form of diversion.

It comes with the opening of my door. There's no knock, and there are no warning footsteps. He has tiptoed up to the door, and now jerks it open, and sticks his head inside.

"The captain wants to see you on the bridge."

He remains standing in the doorway, to make it difficult for me to get out of bed and put on my clothes, to force me to expose myself. With the eiderdown round my shoulders I slide down to the foot of the bunk and give the door a kick so that he just manages to pull back his head in time.

Jakkelsen. His name is Jakkelsen. He might have a first name, too, but on the *Kronos* only surnames are used.

I stand there in the rain until the rubber dinghy with Lander's silhouette disappears. Since there's no one in sight, I try to lift my box by myself, but have to abandon any thought of getting it up the ladder. I leave it behind and climb into the darkness beyond the single light.

The steps end at an open cargo door. Inside, a night light illuminates a green passageway on a level with the second deck. Sheltered from the rain, with his feet up on a cable-end box, a boy sits smoking a cigarette.

He's wearing black steel-tipped shoes, blue trousers, and a blue wool sweater, and he's too young and much too gaunt to be a sailor.

"I've been waiting for you. Jakkelsen. We use last names here. Captain's orders."

He scrutinizes me. "Stick with me, because I can do things for you, know what I mean?"

He has a dusting of freckles across his nose, his hair is red and curly. His eyes, above the cigarette, are half-closed, lazy, inquisitive, insolent. He could be seventeen.

"You can start by getting my baggage."

He gets up reluctantly, letting his cigarette fall to the deck, where it continues to glow.

He barely manages to get up the ladder with the box. He puts it down on the deck. "I have a bad back, know what I mean?"

He walks on ahead, sauntering, with his hands behind his back. I follow with the box. Through the hull passes a deep, continuous vibration of giant engines as a reminder that departure is imminent.

A companionway brings us to the level of the upper decks. Here the smell of diesel fuel evaporates and the air tastes of rain and cold. One passageway has a white wall on the right, a long row of doors on the left. One of them is reserved for me.

Jakkelsen opens it, steps aside so I can enter, follows me in, closes the door, and stands in front of it.

I shove the box aside and sit down on the bunk.

"Jaspersen. According to the crew list, your name is Jaspersen."

I open the cupboard.

"How about a quick screw?"

233

I ponder whether I've heard right.

"Women are wild about me."

A certain eagerness and excitement has come over him. I stand up. One must avoid being caught by surprise.

"That's a good idea," I say. "But let's wait until your birthday. Your fiftieth birthday."

He looks disappointed. "By then you'll be ninety. So I won't be interested."

He gives me a wink and goes out the door. "I know the sea, remember. Stick with me, Jaspersen."

Then he shuts the door.

I unpack. The bathroom is down the passage. The water from the hot-water tap is scalding. I stand under the shower for a long time. Then I rub my skin with almond oil and put on a tracksuit. I lock the door and lie down under the eiderdown. The world can come and get me if it needs me. I close my eyes and sink down. Through the big gate. On the desk Aajumaaq slowly appears. In my dreams I know that it's a dream. It's possible to reach a certain age and a point in your life when even your nightmares start to have a halfway soothing and familiar sense to them. That's about the stage that I've reached.

Then the engine noise grows louder and they weigh anchor. Then the *Kronos* sails. And Jakkelsen opens my door.

I'm positive that I locked it. I make a note that he must have a key. It's a small thing worth remembering.

"Your uniform," he says outside the door. "We wear uniforms here."

In the cupboard there are blue trousers that are too big, blue T-shirts that are too big, a blue tunic that's too big and as shapeless as a flour sack, and a blue woollen sweater. On the floor there's a pair of short rubber boots with plenty of room to grow into. About five or six sizes, if I'm going to fit them.

Jakkelsen is waiting for me outside. He inspects me over his cigarette but doesn't say a word. His fingers drum against the bulkhead; there's a new restlessness about him. He walks on ahead.

At the end of the passage he turns left to the companionway leading to the upper levels. But I take a right, out on to the deck, and he has to follow me.

I stand by the rail. The air is dripping with ice-cold moisture, the wind is strong and gusty. But you can see lights to port.

"Helsingør–Hälsingborg. The world's busiest channel, you know. Swedish ferries, Danish ferries, a giant marina, container traffic. Every three minutes a ship crosses. There's no other place like it. The Strait of Messina, for instance, I've been there lots of times, it's nothing. This is really something. And in this kind of weather there are disturbances on the radar, it's like taking a submarine through buttermilk soup."

His fingers are drumming nervously on the rail, but his eyes are staring out into the night with what looks like enthusiasm.

"We came through here when I was in the merchant marine school. On a squarerigger. Sunshine, Kronborg Castle on the port side, and the little girls in the marina got all excited when they saw us."

I go first. We climb up three levels to reach the navigation bridge. To the right of the companionway is the chart room behind two big glass windows. It's dark, but faint red bulbs glow above spread out charts. We step inside the wheelhouse.

The room is dark. But below us, in the light of a single deck lamp, seventy-five metres forward in the night, lies the deck of the *Kronos*. Two twenty-metre masts with heavy cargo booms. At each mast four cargo winches; at the entrance to the short, elevated foredeck a control box for the winches. Between the masts, on the deck, is a rectangular shape under a tarpaulin where several small blue figures are working to secure long rubber straps across it. Maybe it's the LMC, the navy's surplus landing vessel. On the foredeck, a huge windlass and a hatch in four sections over a cargo hold. Every metre along the sea rail there's an upright white floodlight. In addition, fire hydrants, foam fire extinguishers and rescue equipment. Nothing else. The deck is clear, shipshape and Bristol fashion.

And now empty, as well. While I've been watching, the blue figures have disappeared. The light is turned off, the deck vanishes. Far forward, where the bow chops through the waves, sudden white wings of atomized water appear. On both sides of the ship, surprisingly close, the lights of the shores can be seen. Immediately fore and aft the little ferries cross. In the rain the yellow floodlights make Kronborg Castle look like a drab modern prison.

Out of the darkness of the bridge glow two slowly rotating green radar images. A red dot of dull light in a binnacle compass. In front of the window, with one hand on the manual tiller, stands a man, his back partly turned towards us. It's Captain Sigmund Lukas. Behind him a straight-backed, motionless figure. Next to me Jakkelsen is rocking restlessly on the balls of his feet.

"You can go." Lukas has spoken softly, without turning around. The figure behind him slips out the door. Jakkelsen follows him. For a moment his movements show no reluctance.

Slowly my eyes grow used to the dark, and out of nothingness appear the instruments; some I recognize, some I don't, but I've always kept my distance from all of them because they belong to the open sea. And because, for me, they symbolize a culture that has inserted a layer of lifeless instruments between itself and its attempt to determine one's location.

The liquid crystal display on the Satnav computer, the short-wave radio, the Loran, a radio location system that I've never understood. The depth-sounder. The clinometer. A sextant on a tripod. Instrument panels. The phone to the engine room. A radio direction-finder. The auto pilot. Two panels full of volt meters and control lights. And above all of it Lukas's alert, expressionless face.

The VHF emits a continuous crackle. Without shifting his gaze, he reaches over and turns it off. There is silence.

"You're on board because we needed a cabin attendant. A stewardess, as it's now called. Not for any other reason. That conversation we had was an employment interview, nothing else."

In my floppy sea boots and much too large sweater I feel like a little girl being disciplined in school. Not once does he look at me.

"We haven't been able to find out where we're going. We'll be told later. Until then we're following our noses due north."

There's something different about him. It's his cigarettes. They're gone. Perhaps he doesn't smoke at sea. Perhaps he sails to get away from the gambling tables and the cigarettes.

"First Mate Sonne will show you around and point out your work areas. Your duties include light cleaning, and you're responsible for the ship's laundry. You will also occasionally wait on the officers."

The question is why he's taken me along at all.

When I reach the door he calls after me, his voice bitter and low. "You heard what I said, didn't you? You understand that we're sailing without knowing our destination?"

*　　*　　*

Sonne is waiting for me outside the door. Young, polite, his hair close-cropped. We go down one level to the boat deck. He turns towards me, lowers his voice, and looks at me gravely.

"We have representatives of the ship's owners with us on this trip. They live in the fo'c'sle on the boat deck. There's no admittance whatsoever. Unless you're called on to serve a meal. Otherwise no. No cleaning, no little errands."

We continue down. The laundry, the drying room, and the linen supply area are located on the promenade deck. On the upper deck, where my cabin is, there are living quarters, offices for the engineer and electricians, the galley and the crew's mess. On the second deck are the cold storage rooms and freezer for foodstuffs, storerooms, two workshops, the CO_2 room. All of this is located in and below the superstructure; just in front of it and further forward are the engine room, tanks, tunnels, and the cargo holds.

I follow him up to the upper deck. Along the passageway past my own cabin. Farthest aft on the port side is the mess. He pushes open the door and we step inside.

I take my time and count eleven people in that little room. Five Danes, six Asians. Two of the latter are women. Three of the men look like little boys.

"Smilla Jaspersen, the new stewardess."

It's always been this way. I stand alone in the doorway, the others in front of me. Sometimes it's a school, sometimes a university, sometimes it's some other kind of gathering. They may not have anything in particular against me, they might be more or less indifferent, but almost every time they look as if they'd rather not be bothered.

"Verlaine, our bosun. Hansen and Maurice. The three of them are in charge of the deck. Maria and Fernanda, ship's assistants."

In the doorway to the galley stands a tall, heavy-set man with a full reddish-brown beard, wearing a white cook's outfit.

"Urs. Our cook."

There's something subdued and disciplined about all of them. With the exception of Jakkelsen. He's leaning against the wall, under the NO SMOKING sign, with a cigarette in his mouth. He has one eye closed against the smoke while the other regards me quizzically.

"That's Bernard Jakkelsen," says the first mate. He hesitates for a moment. "He also works on deck."

Jakkelsen ignores him. "Jaspersen will keep our cabins clean," he says. "There'll be plenty of work mucking out for eleven men and four officers. *I* seem to have a tendency to just drop things all over the floor, if you know what I mean."

Because my rubber boots are too big my socks have slipped down around my heels. It is impossible to live like a human being when your socks are drooping. When you're tired and scared besides. And now they're laughing, not a hearty laughter. But a feeling of dominance emanates from the gaunt figure of Jakkelsen, affecting everyone in the room.

I lose my temper. I grab hold of his lower lip and pinch it hard. I pull it away from his teeth. When he takes hold of my wrist, I grab his little finger with my left hand and bend back the top joint. He drops to his knees with a whimper like a woman. I increase the pressure.

"Do you know how I'm going to clean your cabin?" I say. "I'll open the porthole. And then I'll pretend that I've opened a big cupboard. And then I'll put all your things inside. And then I'll wash down your cabin with salt water."

I let him go and step aside. But he doesn't try to grab me. He stands up slowly and goes over to a framed photograph of the *Kronos* in front of a flat-topped iceberg in the Antarctic. He mournfully examines his face in the glass.

"I'll get a blood blister, damn it, a blood blister."

No one in the room has moved.

I straighten up and look around at them. People don't say "I'm sorry" in Greenlandic. I've never bothered to learn the phrase in Danish.

In my cabin I pull the desk over to the door and wedge Bugge's Greenlandic dictionary under the door handle. Then I go to bed. I have a fair hope that tonight the dog will leave me in peace.

IT'S SIX-THIRTY IN THE MORNING, but they've already eaten and the mess is empty except for Verlaine. I drink a glass of juice and follow him to the storage room for work clothes. He looks me over and then hands me a pile of clothes.

Perhaps it's the work clothes, perhaps it's the surroundings, or it may be the colour of his skin. But for a moment I feel the urge for some contact.

"What's your native language?"[1]

"You mean, what's *your* native language?" he corrects me gently, substituting the formal form of address.

His Danish has a faint lilt to each word, the way it's spoken on the island of Fyn.

We look each other in the eyes. In one breast pocket he has a plastic bag. From this he takes a pinch of rice. He stuffs it in his mouth, chews it slowly and thoroughly, swallows, and rubs his palms together.

"Bosun," he adds. Then he turns around and leaves. There's nothing under the sun as grotesque as cold European courtesy manifested in the third and fourth worlds.

In my cabin, I change into work clothes. He has given me the correct size. As much as work clothes can ever be the right size. I try putting a belt around the smock. Now I no longer look like a postbag. Now I look like an hourglass one metre sixty tall. I put a silk scarf over my hair. I have to clean, and I don't want to get dust in the fine down that is starting to cover my bald spot. I take out a vacuum cleaner. I put it down in the corridor, and then I quietly drift into the mess. Not to resume my breakfast – I couldn't get a bite down. During the night the sea outside my porthole has

[1] In Danish, as in French, there are two forms, both of which are transcribed as you or your. Smilla has used the more familiar.

seeped down into my stomach and joined forces with the smell of diesel fuel, with the awareness of being on the open sea, and coated my insides with tepid nausea. There are those who claim that you can fight seasickness by standing on deck in the fresh air. That may work if the boat is docked or on its way through the Falsterbo Canal, where you can go up and look at the solid land that you will soon have under your feet. When Sonne wakes me up this morning by knocking on my door to give me a key, and I get dressed and stand on deck wearing a down jacket and ski cap, and gaze out into the pitch dark of winter, and realize that now I will have to continue because I'm on the open sea and there's no way back, that's when I first feel truly sick.

In the mess the two tables have been cleared and wiped off. I stand in the doorway to the galley.

Urs is stirring a pot of boiling milk. I reckon he's about 115 kilos. But solidly built. All Danes are pale in the winter, but his face borders on green-tinged. Covered with a light mask of sweat in the heat of the galley.

"A superb breakfast."

I didn't touch it. But you have to start a conversation some-where.

He gives me a smile and turns back to the milk as he shrugs his shoulders. "I am *Schweizer*."

I've had the privilege of learning foreign languages. Instead of merely speaking a watered-down form of my mother tongue, like most people, I'm also helpless in two or three other languages.

"*Frühstück*," I say. "*imponierend. Wie ein erstklassiges Restaurant.*"

"*Ich hatte so ein Restaurant. In Genf. Beim See.*"

He has prepared a tray with coffee, steamed milk, juice, butter, and croissants.

"Can I take it to the bridge?"

"*Nein.* Breakfast isn't served. It's sent up in the dumbwaiter. But if you come back at eleven-fifteen, Fräulein, there's the officers' lunch."

"How do you like cooking on a ship?"

The question is an excuse to stay there. He has put a tray into the dumbwaiter and pushed a button labelled BRIDGE. Now he's preparing the next one. This is the one that interests me. It consists of tea, toast, cheese, honey, jam, juice, and soft-boiled eggs. Three cups and three plates. On the boat deck, to which the stewardess

240

is forbidden access, the *Kronos* has three passengers. He puts the tray in the dumbwaiter and presses BOAT DECK.

"*Nicht schlecht. Desuden var det eine Notwendigkeit. Also elf Uhr fünfzehn.*"

The scenario for the end of the world is firmly established. It will begin with three deep frozen winters and then the lakes, the rivers, and the seas will freeze over. The sun will grow cooler so that it can no longer establish summer, the snow will keep falling for a white merciless eternity. Then one long endless winter will come and, finally, the wolf Skoll will devour the sun. The moon and stars will be extinguished, and a fathomless darkness will reign. The Fimbul winter.

In school they taught us that this was the way northerners imagined the end of the world before Christianity taught them that the universe will perish in fire. I've always remembered this, not because it was less irrelevant to me than so much else I learned, but because it dealt with snow. When I heard it for the first time, I thought that it was a distorted picture created by people who had no understanding of the nature of winter.

Opinion was divided in North Greenland. My mother, along with many others, preferred winter. Because of the hunting on the new ice, because of the deep sleep, because of the handicrafts, but most of all because of the visiting. Winter was a time for community, not for the end of the world.

In school they also told us that Danish culture had made great progress since ancient times and the theory of a Fimbul winter. There are moments when it's difficult for me to believe this is true. Like now, when I'm wiping down the sunbed in the ship's gym with alcohol.

The ultraviolet lights from a sunbed split small amounts of the oxygen in the air, creating the unstable gas ozone. Its sharp smell of pine needles is also found in Qaanaaq in the summer, with its almost painfully bright sunshine over the reflectors of the snow and sea.

One of my duties is to wipe off this thought-provoking apparatus with alcohol.

I've always enjoyed cleaning. Even though they tried to teach us laziness in school.

For the first six months we were taught in the village by the wife of one of the hunters. One summer day they came from the boarding school and wanted to take me to the town. A Danish pastor and a West Greenlandic catechist. They issued orders without looking at our faces. They called us *avanersuarmiut*, people from the north.

Moritz forced me to go. My brother had grown too big and too obstinate for him. The boarding school was in Qaanaaq, in the town itself. I stayed for five months, until my fighting spirit had matured sufficiently for me to refuse.

In school we had all our meals served to us. We had a hot bath every day and clean clothes every other. In the village we had bathed once a week, much less often when hunting or travelling. Every day, from the glacier above the cliffs, I had collected *kangirluarhuq*, big blocks of freshwater ice, and carried them home in sacks and melted them over the stove. At the boarding school you turned on a faucet. When the summer holidays came, all the students and teachers went out to Herbert Island and visited the hunters, and for the first time in a long while we had boiled seal meat and tea. That's when I noticed the paralysis. Not just in me but in everybody. We could not pull ourselves together any more; it was no longer a natural thing to reach out for some water and brown soap and the package of Neogene and start rinsing the skins. We had lost the habit of washing clothes, we couldn't pull ourselves together to cook. At every break we would slip into a daydreaming state of waiting. Hoping that someone would take over, would relieve us, free us from our duties, and do what we ourselves ought to have done.

When I understood where things were heading, I rebelled against Moritz for the first time and went home. It was also a return to relative contentedness with my work.

This same contentedness comes over me now as I'm vacuuming the cabins in the crew's quarters on the upper deck of the *Kronos*. The same sense of calm as when I used to repair nets as a child.

Strict order reigns in each of the cabins. Those who like me survived the boarding schools in my life understood that when you have only a very few cubic metres to yourself and your innermost feelings, that private space must be subjected to the severest discipline if it is to withstand the dissolution, destruction, and pressure to yield coming from all sides.

In his own way Isaiah had this fastidiousness, too. The mechanic had it. The crew of the *Kronos* has it. Surprisingly enough, Jakkelsen has it, too.

On his walls Jakkelsen has banners, postcards, and little souvenirs from South America, the Far East, Canada, and Indonesia. All the clothes in the cupboard are meticulously folded and piled.

I feel around among the piles. I take off the mattress and vacuum out the cubbyhole for the bed linen. I pull out the desk drawers, I get down on my knees and look under the desk, I carefully examine the mattress. His cupboard is full of shirts. I touch every one of them. Some of them are handwashed silk. He has a collection of aftershave lotions and eau de toilette that smell expensive and sweetly alcoholic; I open them and put a dab of the fragrance on a paper napkin, which I then roll into a ball and put in the pocket of my smock, to flush down the lavatory later on. I'm looking for something specific, but I don't find it. Or anything else of interest, either.

I put the vacuum cleaner back and go below, past the second deck, past the cold storage and the supply rooms, and on down the companionway, bordered on one side by the smokestack housing and on the other by a wall labelled DEEP TANK. At the bottom of the companionway is the door to the engine room. I'm carrying in my hand as a ready excuse a scrubbing brush and bucket, and if that's not enough, I can always fall back on the tried and true story that I'm a stranger who's got lost.

The door is heavy and insulated, and when I open it the noise is at first deafening. I come out on to a steel platform from which a gallery extends, running around the entire perimeter of the room.

On the deck ten metres below me on a slightly raised platform in the middle of the room, the engine looms up. It's in two sections: the main engine with nine exposed cylinder heads and a six-cylinder auxiliary engine. The shiny valves move rhythmically like parts of a beating heart. The entire engine block is about five metres high and twelve metres long, and the whole thing gives the impression of an overwhelming, tamed savagery. There's not a soul in sight.

The steel of the walkway is perforated, my canvas shoes are walking right over the drop beneath me.

Everywhere signs prohibit smoking in five languages. Several metres up ahead there's an alcove. A blue veil of tobacco smoke is seeping out. Jakkelsen is sitting on a folding chair with his feet up on the worktable smoking a cigar. A centimetre under his lower lip there's a blood blister running the whole width of his mouth. I lean against the table, in order to put my hand discreetly on the thirteen-inch monkey wrench lying there.

He takes his feet off the table, puts down the cigar, and gives me a big smile. "Smilla. I was just sitting here thinking about you."

I let go of the wrench. His restlessness has been temporarily stowed away.

"I've got a bad back, you know. On other ships they take it easy while they're at sea. Here we start at seven a.m. Chipping off rust and splicing mooring cables and painting and scraping off oxide scale and polishing brass. How am I supposed to keep my hands looking presentable if I have to splice cable every single day?"

I don't reply. I try silence on Bernard Jakkelsen. He has very little tolerance for it. Even now when he's in good spirits, you can sense his underlying nervousness.

"Where are we off to, Smilla?"

I simply wait.

"I've been sailing for five years, and I've never seen anything like this before. Alcohol prohibited. Uniforms. No one allowed on the boat deck. And even Lukas says that he doesn't know where we're going."

He puffs on his cigar again. "Smilla Qaavigaaq Jaspersen. That must be a Greenlandic middle name . . ."

He must have looked at my passport. Which is in the ship's safe. That's something worth thinking about.

"I've had a good look at this ship. I know everything about ships. This one here, she's got a double hull and icebreaker cables running the whole length of the ship. Up front the plates are thick enough to withstand an anti-tank grenade."

He gives me a sly look. "In the stern, over the propeller, there's an ice cutter. That engine produces at least 6,000 i.h.p., enough to sail at sixteen to eighteen knots. We're on our way up to the ice. I'm sure about that. You don't think we're heading for Greenland, do you?"

I don't have to reply to keep him talking.

"Then there's the crew. They're a pile of shit. And they stick together. They all know each other. And they're scared; can't get them to talk about why. And there are the passengers that we never see. Why are they coming along?"

He puts down his cigar. He hasn't really been enjoying it. "Then there's you, Smilla. I've sailed on lots of 4,000-ton ships. None of them ever had a cabin attendant. Certainly not one who acts like she's the Queen of Sheba."

I pick up his cigar and drop it in my bucket. It goes out with a little hiss.

"I'm cleaning up," I say.

"Why did he let you on board, Smilla?"

I don't give him an answer. I don't know what to say.

It's not until the door to the engine room shuts behind me that I realize how enervating the noise was. The silence is refreshing.

Verlaine, the bosun, is standing on the lowest platform, leaning against the wall. I involuntarily turn sideways as I go past him.

"Lost?"

He pulls a pinch of rice from his breast pocket and puts it in his mouth. He doesn't drop a single grain, and nothing sticks to his hands; the whole movement is clean and experienced.

Perhaps I should make up an excuse, but I hate being interrogated. "Just took a wrong turn."

Several steps up, I happen to remember something.

"Mr Bosun," I add. "Just took a wrong turn, Mr Bosun."

3

I HIT THE ALARM CLOCK with the side of my hand. It shoots through the cabin like a projectile, slams against the hooks on the door, and drops to the deck.

I don't do well with phenomena that are supposed to last for life. Prison sentences, marriage contracts, lifetime appointments. They're attempts to pin down segments of life and exempt them from the passage of time. It's even worse with things that are supposed to last forever. Like my alarm clock. My "eternity clock". That's what they called it. I prised it out of the smashed instrument panel of the second NASA moon vehicle after it was written-off on the ice cap. The vehicle was as incapable as the Americans of withstanding − 55 °C and winds that went way off the Beaufort scale.

They didn't notice me taking the clock. I took it as a souvenir, to prove that there is no such thing as everlasting flowers where I am concerned, that even the American space programme will not last three weeks with me.

The clock has survived for ten years. Ten years in which it has received nothing but brutality and harsh words. But they expected great things from it back then. They said you could stick it in the flame of a blowtorch and boil it in sulphuric acid and sink it to the bottom of the Philippine Trench and it would keep time as if nothing had happened. This claim was a flagrant provocation for me. In Qaanaaq we thought that wristwatches were cute. Some of the hunters wore them for decoration. But we would never dream of being guided by them.

That's what I told Gil, who was driving. (My job was to sit in the observation cockpit and report when the colour of the firn got too dark or too white, which means that it won't hold but will open up, allowing the earth to swallow a fifteen-ton, idiotic American dream of reaching the moon, letting it fall into a thirty-metre-deep, brilliantly blue-and-green crevasse, which narrows at the bottom and wedges everything that falls in into a tight embrace at −30 °C.) In Qaanaaq we go by the weather, I told him. We go by the animals. By love. And death. Not by a piece of mechanized tin.

I was only in my early twenties. At that age you can lie – you can even lie to yourself – with greater self-confidence. In reality, European time had come to Greenland a long time ago, long before my birth. It came with the Greenland Trading Company's opening and closing times, payment schedules, church hours, and wage labour.

I've tried pounding on the clock with a sheet-metal hammer. It made dents in the hammer. By now I've given up. Now I make do with knocking it on to the deck, where it lies, electronically beeping, unperturbed, saving me from showing up on the bridge without having splashed some cold water on my face and put something around my eyes.

It's two thirty a.m. It's the middle of the night in the Northern Atlantic Ocean. At ten p.m., with no prior warning except a green wink of light, Lukas's voice issued from the loudspeaker over my bunk. Like an invasion of my little room.

"Jaspersen. Tomorrow at three I want coffee served on the bridge."

Not until the clock hits the floor does it give out any sound. I woke up of my own accord, roused by a feeling of unusual activity. Just twenty-four hours has made the ship's rhythm my own. A ship at sea is quiet at night. The engine thuds, of course, the long, high swells slosh against the side, and now and then the stern crushes a block of fifty-tons of water into a fine powder of fluid. But those are regular sounds, and when sounds are repeated often enough, they become silence. The watch is changed on the bridge, some-where a ship's clock strikes. But the people are asleep.

Against this familiar backdrop there is now commotion. Boots in the corridor, doors slamming, voices, sounds on the loudspeaker, and a distant rumbling from hydraulic winches.

On my way up the companionway to the bridge, I stick my head out on deck. It's dark. I can hear footsteps and voices, but no light is on. I make for the darkness.

I'm wearing no outdoor clothes. The temperature is about freezing point, the wind is blowing astern, the cloud cover is low and unbroken. The waves are visible only right next to the ship, but the troughs of the waves seem as long as a soccer field. The deck is slippery and slick with salt water. I duck under the sea rail to seek shelter and make myself as unobtrusive as possible. Near the tarpaulin I pass a figure in the dark. Up ahead there is a faint light. It's coming from the cargo hold farthest forward. The hatches have been pulled open and a railing put up around the opening. Two wires extend through the opening from the two aft-facing cranes on the forward mast. Over the railing, both in front and in back, lies a heavy blue nylon hawser. There's no one in sight.

The cargo hold is surprisingly deep and illuminated by four fluorescent lights, one on each bulkhead. Ten metres down, on the lid of a huge metal container, sits Verlaine. At each of its four corners there is a white fibreglass pod, like the ones for inflatable life rafts.

That's all I manage to see. Someone grabs my clothes from behind.

I yield, not out of resignation, but to retaliate with even greater force. At that moment the ship rolls on an oblique swell, and we lose our balance and fall backwards into the control panel for the winches and a waft of aftershave that I recognize.

"Idiot! You idiot!" Jakkelsen fights to catch his breath after his exertion. There's something in his face and voice that wasn't there before. The seeds of fear.

"This ship is run like in the old days – you keep to your own area." He gives me an almost pleading look. "Beat it. Get lost."

I walk back. He half whispers, half shouts after me into the wind. "Do you want to end up in the big wet cupboard?"

The tray rams into one side of the door frame and then the other before I manage to get my bearings and stand there clattering in the dark room.

No one speaks to me. After a moment I push my way backwards and find room for the cups and the pastry on the table among rulers and callipers.

"Two minutes, eight hundred metres."

He's merely an outline in the dark, but it's an outline that I haven't seen before. He's bending over the green digits of the electronic log.

The pastry dough smells of butter. Urs is a meticulous cook. The aroma is whisked away because the door is ajar. On the bridge wing I can make out Sonne's back. Above a sea chart, a faint red bulb is turned on and Sigmund Lukas's face appears out of the darkness.

"Five hundred metres."

The other man is wearing overalls with the collar turned up. Next to him, on the navigation table, there is a flat box the size of a stereo amplifier. Two slender telescope antennas stick up out of the sides of the box. Nearby stands a woman, wearing the same kind of overalls as the man. Against her work-clothes and her concentration there is something almost out of place about the long, dark, brushed hair which is flowing loosely down over her turned-up collar and curling down her back. It's Katja Claussen. Instinctively I know that the man is Seidenfaden.

"One minute, two hundred metres."

"Hoist it up."

The voice comes from the intercom on the wall. I release my grip on the tabletop behind me. My palms are sweaty. I've heard that voice before. On the phone in my apartment. The last time I was there.

The red light goes off. Out of the night a grey shape rises up, emerging from the forward cargo hold, and swings, swaying slowly, over the side of the ship.

"Ten seconds."

"Lower it, Verlaine."

He must be sitting in the enclosed crow's nest at the top of the forward mast. What we hear are his orders to the hands on deck.

"Pull it tight. Slack off now."

"Five seconds. Four, three, two, one, zero."

A ray of light behind us bores a tunnel through the night. The container is lying in the water, five metres from the stern. It's apparently riding a bow wave. From one of its corners, a blue hawser runs forward along the side of the ship. At the rail stand Maria and Fernanda, Hansen, and the deckhands. They're keeping it away from the hull with what looks like a very long boathook. In the light I can see that there are two narrow, inflatable white rubber strips along its sides.

"Verlaine. Release it."

I move over to the bridge wing. The light is coming from one of the spotlights mounted on the sea rail. Sonne is manning it. He searches with the spotlight across the water. The container is free of the hawser now, already forty metres astern, and is starting to sink.

There's a smack. The five fibreglass shells on the surface of the water are cast off, and like five enormous lily pads, five self-inflating grey flotation balloons spread out above the big metal container. Then the spotlight goes out.

"One metre, two thousand litres."

It's the woman's voice.

"Three thousand, four thousand. Two metres, five thousand litres. Two metres. Two and a half. Two point three. Five thousand litres, and two point three."

I stand next to the serving tray. In my place. On the instrument in front of her several displays are now lit up red.

"I'm letting it out. Forty thousand seven hundred and two and a half. Three, three twenty, four, four and a half, five. Fifty-seven hundred litres and five metres. List zero. Temperature −0.5 °C."

She turns a dial and in the bridge a sound grows, as if they had fetched my alarm clock.

"Directional signal, ten-four."

She switches off the intercom. The man in front straightens up from the log. A tension has been released. Sonne enters the room and shuts the door. Lukas is standing right next to me.

"You can go back to bed."

I gesture towards the coffee. He shakes his head. They don't even want me to pour it. I've been summoned up here to carry a tray six metres from the galley dumbwaiter to the bridge. It doesn't make sense. Unless he wanted me to see what I've just witnessed.

I gather up the tray. The woman in front of me puts out her hand to caress the man. She doesn't look at him. Her hand rests for a moment on the back of his neck. Then she twists a little strand of his hair around her fingers and pulls it out. They haven't noticed me at all. I wait for him to react to the pain. But he stands there, motionless, his back erect.

Urs's face is shiny with sweat. He tries to gesture with his hand and balance the big ten-litre pot at the same time.

"*Feodora, die einzige mit sechzig Prozent Cacao. Und die Schlagsahne muss ein bisschen gefroren sein.* Ten minutes *im frostboks*," he says to me.

All eleven of them are here. There are no questions hovering in the air. As if I'm the only one who has not understood what's been going on. Or as if they have no need to understand.

I slurp up the scalding chocolate through the lightly frozen whipped cream. The effect is like instant intoxication, starting in my stomach and rising up, hot and pulsating, to the top of my skull. I wonder what a wizard like Urs is doing on board the *Kronos*.

Verlaine stares at me thoughtfully. But I avoid his eyes.

I'm the next to the last to leave. In a corner Jakkelsen is brooding over a cup of black coffee.

Maria is in the bathroom, standing in front of the mirror. At first I think they are some kind of prosthesis, then I see that they're little hollow aluminium cones. She has one on each fingertip, and now she cautiously removes them. Underneath her nails are red, four centimetres long, and perfect.

"I support my family," she says. "In Phuket. On my salary. I came to Denmark as a whore. In Thailand you're either a virgin or a whore."

Her Danish is darker than Verlaine's, less distinct.

"Sometimes I had thirty customers a day. I've worked my way out of that."

She stretches out her forefinger, puts her nail on my cheek, and rests it against my skin.

"I once scratched out the eyes of a policeman."

I stand there, leaning against her fingernail. She gives me a searching look. Then she lowers her hand.

I'm waiting inside my cabin with the door slightly ajar. Jakkelsen appears a moment later. His cabin is a little further down the corridor. He locks his door behind him. Barefoot I walk over to his door. Inside, he's working on something. There's a faint scraping noise, the door handle is pulled upwards. He's wedging his desk chair under the door handle.

He's barricading himself in. Maybe he's scared of the door being forced by some of the women who long for him.

I tiptoe back to my cabin. I get undressed, take my pink towelling bathrobe and my loofah out of my box, and noisily walk to the bathroom, whistling. I scrub myself with the loofah, dry myself off, rub my skin with lotion, and go back down the corridor, my bath slippers slapping. Then I creep back to Jakkelsen's door.

It's quiet inside. Maybe he's manicuring his nails or tending to his delicate hands in some other manner. But I doubt it.

I knock on the door. There's no reply. I knock harder. Total silence. In my bathrobe pocket I have my own key. I unlock his door. But I still can't open it. I start wiggling the door handle up and down. After a minute the chair falls to the deck. I wait for the panic to subside. Then I push open the door, only after having had a quick look in both directions. The situation might be mis-understood.

I stand there in the dark. Not a sound. I decide that the cabin must be empty. Then I turn on the light.

Jakkelsen is sleeping in Thai silk pyjamas of delicate pastel colours. His skin looks waxen. There are bubbles of saliva at the corners of his mouth and they move with every faint, laboured breath. One arm protrudes over the edge of the bunk. His wrist sticking out of the pyjama sleeve is frighteningly skinny. He looks like a sick child — and in a way, that's what he is.

I give him a shake. His eyelids open slightly. His eyeballs roll upwards so that the whites of his eyes give me a blind, dead look. He doesn't utter a sound.

The ashtray next to his bunk is empty. There's nothing on the table. Everything is neat and tidy.

I roll up his pyjama sleeve. Along the inside of his arm there are between forty and sixty little yellowish-blue pricks with a black centre, a fine pattern along his swollen veins. I pull out the drawer for the bed linen. He has let it fall in there. Silver foil, matches, an old-fashioned glass hypodermic, fast-drying glue, syringe, an open penknife, plastic containers for sewing-machine needles, and a piece of black rubber packing cord.

He's not planned to wake up for a while. He's sleeping the com-pletely relaxed, worry-free powder sleep.

Before Home Rule, there were no customs officers in Greenland. The police and the harbour authorities were in charge of customs matters. The year I was posted at the meteorological station in Upernavik I met Jørgensen.

He was the harbourmaster. But he was rarely at work. He might be in Thule for the Americans or on board one of the navy's inspec-tion ships. He held the Greenland record for helicopter rides.

Jørgensen would be the one who was sent for whenever they had found something but didn't know where it was. When they had a suspicion but couldn't quite place it. The narcotics patrol at Thule Air Base had dogs and metal detectors and a team of lab assistants and technicians. In Holsteinsborg the navy had several search experts, and in Nuuk they had a mobile X-ray apparatus from the Welding Centre.

And yet they would all send for Jørgensen. He'd been a licensed welder at Burmeister & Wain, and since then he had studied to get his First Mate's ticket in the merchant navy, and had now ended up as a harbourmaster who never showed his face in the harbour.

He was a little grey man, bent, his hair bristly like a badger's. He spoke the same nasal, one-syllable Danish to Greenlanders and Russians and all the military people, regardless of rank.

They would bring him on board the seized ship or plane, and he would mumble a little at the crew and captain, and gaze around with his nearsighted eyes, and rather absentmindedly rap a knuckle on the iron plates here and there, and then they'd call over one of the navy's locksmiths, who would bring an angle grinder and remove the plate. Behind it they would find 5,000 bottles or 400,000 cigarettes, and as the years passed, more and more often, stacked up blocks of paraffin-coated white powder.

Jørgensen told us that when you're tracking something, a systematic approach will take you only so far. "Whenever I lose my glasses," he said, "first I use a little systematics. I look in the john and next to the coffee machine and under the newspaper. But if they're not there, I stop thinking and sit down on a chair and survey the scene to see whether an idea will come to me, and it always does; an idea always comes to me. We can't just go around breaking everything into pieces whether we're looking for a pair of glasses or for bottles of spirits; we have to think and take note, we have to discover the crook inside ourselves and decide where we might have stashed them."

In February 1981 he was shot on one of the outposts in Diskobugten by four young Greenlanders who, on his recommendation, had been given unreasonably harsh sentences for smuggling alcohol. For some reason he was fond of me. Greenlanders in general he never tried to understand.

Now I'm reminded of Jørgensen, and try to find the junkie in myself.

I would take my time hiding the stuff. I wouldn't be sloppy. I would be tempted to hide it outside my cabin. But I wouldn't be able to tolerate not having it near my own body. The way mothers are said to feel about their little ones.

There's the air conditioning. The *Kronos* has a high-pressure ventilation system that even now is humming softly. The intake vent is behind the perforated panels on the bulkhead. There are at least forty screws in each panel. Forty screws would seem too much every time I wanted to get to my baby.

For the second time today I go through his drawers. Still no results. They contain writing paper, Blu-tack to stick up postcards, a few thick glitzy issues of *Playboy*, an electric razor, several decks of cards, a box of chess pieces, four clear plastic boxes each containing a flashy silk bow tie, quite a lot of foreign currency, a clothes brush, and a few extra gold chains like the one he wears around his neck.

On the shelf a Spanish—Danish dictionary, Berlitz Turkish phrasebook, a handbook on contract bridge published by British Petroleum, a couple of books on chess. A dog-eared paperback with an illustration of a naked corn-fed blonde on the cover, entitled *Flossy — Sweet Sixteen*.

I've never been seriously interested in books that aren't reference books. I've never claimed to be particularly cultured. On the other hand, I've always thought that it's never too late to start a new life of learning. Maybe I should start with Flossy — sweet sixteen.

I take the penknife out of the drawer. On the edge of the blade are a few specks of bottle-green material. I open the cupboard and go through the clothes one more time. There's nothing of that particular colour. In his bunk, Jakkelsen gurgles softly.

From the drawer I take the box of chess pieces. I pick up a white king and a black queen and put them on the desk. They are exquisitely carved out of some kind of heavy wood. The chessboard is on the desk, covered with a thin metallic plate. On board a ship it must be practical having a chessboard that's magnetic. The magnets are on the bottom of the chess pieces, a lead-coloured disc at the base with a piece of green felt stuck on to it. I force the knife blade in between the metal disc and the base of the king. It resists, but it comes off. A little dab of glue has been applied on each side. I put the disc on the desk. A little speck of felt remains on the knife, a few minuscule green fibres that you wouldn't notice unless you were looking for them.

The chess piece is hollow. It's about eight centimetres tall and for its full length has been drilled a cylinder one and a half centimetres in diameter. It's probably not been done by Jakkelsen; they have been produced this way. But he has taken advantage of it. On top is a lump of putty. Underneath are three clear plastic tubes. I shake them out. There are four more under them.

I put them back in place, seal them up with the putty, and glue the magnet on to the chess piece. I could have examined the rest of the pieces. To see whether two or three phials would fit into each of the pawns. To determine whether he has enough for four or six months' use. But I feel like getting out of there. A single woman shouldn't stay too long in a strange gentleman's cabin.

4

"THAT WAS MY FIRST TRIP. So I went to see a colleague. 'How do I navigate to Greenland?' I asked him. He said, 'You sail to Skagen and turn left. When you get to Cape Farewell, turn right.'"

I twist the corkscrew into the cork. It's a bottle of white wine, its colour yellowish-green, and Urs has let it travel alone in the dumbwaiter at the last minute, as if it were a temperature-sensitive icon. When I pry up the corkscrew, half the cork stays in the bottle. I'll have to screw it in again. Then the cork disintegrates and falls into the liquid. Urs said that Montrachet is a great wine. So such a little cork shouldn't hurt.

"Then he took out a chart, placed one end of a ruler at Skagen, turned it on its edge, bent it, making the other end touch Cape Farewell, and drew a line along the curve. 'Follow this,' he said, 'and you'll be sailing the Great Circle route. And the last forty-eight hours before you reach the cape you don't sleep. You drink black coffee and keep a look out for icebergs.'"

Lukas is doing the talking. Turned away from his audience. But his authority holds their attention.

There are three people besides him in the officers' mess: Katja Claussen, Seidenfaden, and engineer Kützow.

This is the first time in my life that I'm waiting at table.

"In those days we sailed in April. We tried to hit the so-called Easter easterly. With luck, you'd have a tail wind the whole way. It was unheard of for anyone to actually choose the period between November and the end of March."

There are rules about the sequence in which you're supposed to serve wine. Unfortunately, I'm not familiar with them. So I take a chance and serve the woman. She swirls the two centimetres of liquid around in her glass, but her eyes are fixed on Lukas and she doesn't taste what she's tasting.

I try alternating from the right side to the left as I serve. To make sure everybody's happy.

They've dressed for dinner. The men are wearing white shirts, the woman is wearing a red dress.

"We can expect the first ice twenty-four hours out of Cape Farewell. That's where the Greenland Trading Company's *Hans Hedtoft* went down in 1959, and ninety-five passengers and crew perished. Have you ever seen an iceberg, Miss Claussen?"

I serve the cauliflower and Urs's sourdough bread. Everything goes tolerably well at the table. But out by the dumbwaiter I drop the rest of the cauliflower all over the poached salmon. It's lying there whole, its skin still on, staring at me expectantly. Urs explained that a Japanese chef taught him not to poach the eyes but to set them aside and then put them back in after the flesh is tender. And then lightly brush the whole fish with egg whites so that it has a slimy sheen, as if it has come straight from the net to the table. I don't think much of this technique. I think the fish looks as though it died of old age.

I scrape off the cauliflower and carry in the fish. They're not looking at what they eat, anyway. They're looking at Lukas.

"Icebergs are pieces of glaciers that float down from the ice cap to the open sea and break off. If they're solid, the relationship between the part above water and the part below is one to five. If they're hollow, it's one to two. The latter are the most dangerous kind, of course. I've seen icebergs forty metres tall, weighing 50,000 tons, that could be capsized by the vibrations from a ship's propeller."

I burn my fingers on the potatoes *au gratin*. Lukas hasn't seen anything yet. In a rubber raft near the Antarctic, I've slipped past partially melted table icebergs that were ninety metres tall, weighed a million tons, and might explode if you whistled the first few bars of "In the Lovely, Joyful Summertime".

"The *Titanic* struck an iceberg in 1912, southeast of Newfoundland, and sank three hours later. Fifteen hundred people died."

In my cabin I have placed a piece of newspaper in the sink, leaned over it, and cut twenty centimetres off my hair so that it has all the same length as the part that has grown out after the fire. For the first time since I came on board, I have taken off my scarf. That's all I can do to prevent the woman from recognizing me.

I could have spared myself the trouble. I'm a fly on the wall; she doesn't see me. The man is looking at Lukas, the engineer is looking at his glass, and Lukas isn't looking at anyone or anything. For a moment the woman's eyes fall on me, giving me an appraising look. She's at least twenty centimetres taller and five years younger than me. She's dark and wary, and there's a slight tension around her mouth that tells a story – possibly the story of what it costs, contrary to popular opinion, for a woman to look good.

I hold my breath. It was dark at Isaiah's funeral. There were twenty other women there. And she was there for a different reason. She was there to warn Andreas Fine Licht. He should have listened to that warning.

It takes her a fraction of a second to categorize me. Internally, she opens the drawer labelled "servant" and "one metre sixty" and drops me inside and forgets about me. She has other things to think about. Under the table she has put her hand on the man's thigh.

He hasn't touched the fish.

"But we have radar on board," he says.

"The *Hans Hedtoft* had radar on board, too."

No experienced captain or expedition leader would consciously frighten his fellow travellers. If you're familiar with the risks of travelling in ice, you know that once a trip has started, you can't afford to increase the external risk with inner fear. I don't understand Lukas.

"And then the icebergs are the least of our problems. They're the layman's image of the Arctic seas. Much worse is the field ice, a belt of pack ice that floats along the east coast, rounds Cape Farewell in November, and stretches all the way up past Godthåb."

I've managed to get the cork out in one piece from the second bottle. I fill Kützow's glass. As he drinks he absentmindedly studies the label on the bottle. What interests him is the percentage of alcohol.

"Where the pack ice stops, the western ice begins. It's formed in Baffin Bay and forced down into Davis Strait, where it joins and freezes with the winter ice to form an ice field that we'll run into near the fishing grounds north of Holsteinsborg."

Travelling tends to magnify all human emotions. Whenever we left Qaanaaq to set out hunting, to go visiting, or to go to Qeqertat, the latent feelings of love, friendship, and animosity would all explode. In the air between Lukas and his two passengers and employers, a mutual, solid feeling of antagonism rises up.

I look at Lukas. He hasn't said or done anything. And yet without a word he demands that they look at him. Once again I have that vague, uneasy feeling of having witnessed a performance that has been staged partially for my benefit, but which I don't understand.

"Where's Tørk?" the captain asks.

"He's working," replies the woman.

If you fly from Europe to Thule, you'll step out of the plane and think that you've entered a freezer that's under several atmospheres of pressure, as an invisible icy cold is now forcing its way into your lungs. If you fly in the opposite direction, you'll think you've landed in a Finnish sauna when you arrive in Europe. But a ship sailing for Greenland does not sail north; it sails west. Cape Farewell lies on the same latitude as Oslo. The cold doesn't come until you round the cape and sail due north. The wind that picks up during the day is raw and damp, but no colder than a storm in the Kattegat. The waves, on the other hand, are the long, deep swells of the North Atlantic.

The deck is swimming in water. The hatch to the forward cargo hold is now closed. I pace it off. It's five and a half by six metres. It wasn't originally that size. At both ends there's a white, newly painted border three quarters of a metre wide. And there's a welding seam on the deck. The opening has recently been enlarged by almost a metre in both directions.

For Europeans the sea symbolizes the unknown, and sailing is both a journey and an adventure. This image bears no relation to reality. Sailing is the movement that comes closest to standing still. To feel that you are actually moving requires landmarks, it requires fixed points on the horizon and ice heaves that disappear beneath your sleigh runners, and the sight of mountains seen across the *napariaq*, the upright at the back of the sleigh, ice formations that loom up and pass by and vanish on the horizon.

All this is missing at sea. A ship seems to stand still, to be a fixed platform of steel, framed by a permanent cyclorama with a cold grey winter wind blowing across it, placed on top of a moving yet always uniform abyss of water. Convulsed by the monotonous exertion of its engines, the ship pounds in vain on one spot.

Or else it's just me who's grown too old for travelling.

With the fog from outside, depression drifts in over me.

To travel you have to have a home to leave and come back to. Otherwise you're a refugee, an outcast, a *qivittoq*. At this very moment in North Greenland they're all huddling together in their shanty huts in Qaanaaq.

I ask, as I have so many times before, why I have ended up here. I can't bear the whole responsibility, it's too heavy a burden. I must have had bad luck as well. The universe must have somehow pulled away from me. When my surroundings give way, I retreat into myself like a live mussel sprinkled with lemon juice. I can't turn the other cheek, I can't face hostility with yet more faith.

Once I hit Isaiah. I had told him that when we were children and the ice broke up near Siorapaluk, far inside the bay, we would leap from one ice floe to another, knowing full well that if we slipped we would slide under the ice and the current would carry us to Nerrivik, the mother of the sea, never to return. The next day he wanted to wait outside the co-op, near the Greenlander statue on the square, and when I came out, he was gone. And when I went over to the bridge, I saw him down there on the ice – thin, new ice, disintegrating from below because of the current. I didn't shout, I couldn't shout. I walked over to the urinal by the bulwark and called gently to him, and he came, hesitantly, skipping over the ice, and when he was standing on the cobblestones, I hit him. The blow was probably a distillation of my feelings for him, the way violence sometimes is. He barely managed to stay on his feet.

"You are hitting me," he said, looking around through his tears for a weapon to slit me open with.

Then, in one simple but enormous leap, he found his way back to the unlimited reserves of his character.

"*Naammassereerpoq*, one can get used to that," he said.

I don't possess such depths. Maybe that's one of the reasons why things have gone the way they have.

There's no sound, but I know that someone is standing behind me. Then Verlaine leans against the sea rail, following my gaze out across the sea. He takes off his work glove and pulls a pinch of rice out of his breast pocket.

"I thought Greenlanders had short legs and fucked like pigs and only worked when they were hungry. Once when I was on a ship up there we were taking paraffin to a town somewhere in the north. We pumped it straight into the tanks standing on shore. At one point a little man in a boat came over and fired a rifle and shouted something at us. Then they all ran to their huts and came back with rifles and set off in their dinghies or fired their guns from shore. If I hadn't been watching, the pressure would have blown the hoses off the tanks. It turned out to be because of a school of some kind of fish."

"What time of year was this?"

"Maybe July or the beginning of August."

"Beluga," I say. "A small whale. It must have been near the trading stations south of Upernavik."

"We telegraphed the trading company that they had stopped work and had gone fishing. We received the reply that this happened several times a year. That's the way it is with primitive people. When their stomachs are full, they don't see any reason to work."

I nod in agreement. "In Greenland they say that Filipinos are a nation of lazy little pimps, who are only allowed on ships because they don't ask for more than a dollar an hour, but you have to keep on feeding them vast amounts of steamed rice if you don't want a knife in your back."

"That's true," he says.

He leans towards me so he won't have to yell. I look up towards the bridge. We're in full view where we're standing.

"This is a ship with rules. Some are the captain's. Some are Tørk's. But not all of them. They're dependent on us; we're just the rats."

He smiles at me. His teeth are glazed pieces of chalk against his dark skin. He notices what I'm looking at.

"Porcelain crowns. I was in prison in Singapore. After a year and a half I didn't have a tooth left in my mouth. My jaw was held together with galvanized steel wire. Then we organized an escape."

He leans even closer to me. "That's where I found out how little I can stick cops."

When he straightens up and leaves, I stay there, staring out at the sea. It starts to snow. But it's not snow. It's coming from the deck. I look at myself. The whole way from my collar to the elastic at my waist, my down jacket has been cut open with a single slit. Without anything touching the lining, the padding was cut wide open so the down is now tearing loose and swirling around me like snowflakes. I take off the jacket and fold it up. On my way back across the deck it occurs to me that it must be cold. But I don't feel the cold.

$$5$$

THE WELFARE COUNCIL of the merchant navy sends out packages of nine videos at a time to subscribers. Sonne has arranged to show the first one on the enlarged screen in the exercise room. I sit at the back. When it fades in on a sunset over a desert landscape, I slip out.

On the second deck, arranged in two rows of cupboards facing each other, tools and spare parts are stored. I take out a Phillips screwdriver. I rummage aimlessly. In a wooden crate I find several grey, lightly greased ball bearings made of solid steel, each a little bigger than a golf ball, wrapped in oily paper. I take one of them.

I walk up the companionway and on to the quarterdeck. The light from the projector shines out of the two long windows up there. I crawl on my knees over to the bulkhead underneath the window and peer inside. Only after I've found both Verlaine's shiny black hair and the outline of Jakkelsen's curls do I return to the corridor. I let myself into Jakkelsen's cabin.

Now there is only bed linen in the drawer under the bunk. But the chess game is still in its place. I put the box under my sweater. I listen at the door for a while and then go back to my own cabin. Far away, from some indeterminate direction, the soundtrack of the film is discernible through the metal hull.

I put the box in a drawer. It's a peculiar feeling to be in possession of something that would probably bring its owner anywhere from three years unconditional to a death sentence, depending on the port where it was discovered.

I put on my tracksuit. I knot the steel ball into a long white bath towel that I've folded double. Then I hang it back on its hook. And I sit down to wait.

* * *

If you have to wait for a long time, you have to seize hold of the waiting or it will become destructive. If you let things slide, your consciousness will waver, awakening fear and restlessness, then depression strikes, and you're pulled down.

To keep up my spirits I ask myself, What is a human being? Who am I?

Am I my name?

The year I was born my mother travelled to West Greenland and brought home the girl's name Millaaraq. Because it reminded Moritz of the Danish word *mild*, which didn't exist in the vocabulary of his love relationship with my mother, because he wanted to transform everything Greenlandic into something that would make it European and familiar, and because apparently I had smiled at him – the boundless trust of an infant, which comes from the fact that she still doesn't know what's in store for her – my parents agreed on Smillaaraq. With the wear and tear that time subjects all of us to, it was shortened to Smilla.

Which is merely a sound. If you look beyond the sound, you will find the body with its circulation, its movement of fluids. Its love of ice, its anger, its longing, its knowledge about space, its weakness, faithlessness and loyalty. Behind these emotions the unlabelled forces rise and fade away, parcelled-out and disconnected images of memory, nameless sounds. And geometry. Deep inside us is geometry. My teachers at the university asked us over and over what the reality of geometric concepts was. They asked, Where can you find a perfect circle, true symmetry, an absolute parallel when they can't be constructed in this imperfect, external world?

I never answered them, because they wouldn't have understood how self-evident my reply was, or the enormity of its consequences. Geometry exists as an innate phenomenon in our consciousness. In the external world a perfectly formed snow crystal would never exist. But in our consciousness lies the glittering and flawless knowledge of perfect ice.

If you have strength left, you can look further, beyond geometry, deep into the tunnels of light and darkness that exist within each of us, stretching back towards infinity.

There's so much you could do if you had the strength.

It's two hours since the film ended. Two hours since Jakkelsen locked his door. But there's no reason to be impatient. You can't grow up in Greenland without being familiar with abuse. It's an erroneous cliché that narcotics make people unpredictable. On the contrary, drugs make them very, very predictable. I know that Jakkelsen will come. I have the patience to wait as long as it takes.

I lean forward to turn off the light so I can sit in the dark. The light switch is between the sink and the cupboard, so I have to lean forward.

That's the moment he chooses. He must have been standing with his ear to the door. I've underestimated Jakkelsen. He has sneaked up to my door and unlocked it, waiting for some audible movement inside – all this without my hearing him, even though I'm sitting right behind the door. Now he opens it so that it slams me on the side of the head and knocks me to the deck between the bunk and the cupboard. Then he's inside and has shut the door behind him. He's not going to rely on his own physical strength. He has brought along a big marline-spike with a wooden handle and a hollow tip of polished steel.

"Give it here," he says.

I try to sit up.

"Stay down!"

I sit up.

He shifts the marline-spike in his hand so the heavy end is pointing down, and with the same motion he strikes my foot. He hits the bone of my right ankle. For a moment my body refuses to believe the extent of the pain, then a white tongue of fire shoots through my skeleton to the top of my skull, and I slump back to the deck of my own accord.

"Give it here."

I can't say a word. But I put my hand in my pocket, pull out the little plastic container, and hand it to him.

"All of it."

"In the drawer."

He pauses for a moment. To reach the desk he'll have to step over me.

His nervousness is more pronounced than ever, but there's something determined about him. I once heard Moritz say that you can live a long healthy life on heroin. If you can afford it. The stuff itself has an almost preservative effect. What puts junkies in their graves are the cold companionways and liver infections and the contaminated additives and AIDS and the exhausting business of getting money. But if you can afford it, you can live with your dependency and stay healthy. That's what Moritz said.

I thought he was exaggerating. The cynical, ironic, distanced exaggeration of a professional. Heroin is suicide. I don't think it's any better because you drag it out over twenty-five years; no matter what, it's a form of contempt for your own life.

"You get it out for me," he says.

I pull myself into a squatting position. When I try to stand, my right leg buckles and I fall to my knees. I make the fall look a little worse than it is and use the sink to pull myself up. I take the white towel from the row of pegs and wipe the blood off my face. Then I turn around and hobble a step towards the desk and the drawers, with the towel still in my hand. I turn to face the cupboard.

"The key's in there."

As I turn, I start my swing. An arc that starts towards the porthole, climbs towards the bulkhead, and accelerates downward towards the bridge of his nose.

He sees it coming and takes a step back. But he's prepared only for the swat of a piece of fabric. The ball wrapped in the towelling strikes him right over the heart. He falls to his knees. Then I take another swing. He manages to put up his arm; the blow lands beneath his shoulder and throws him backwards on to the bunk. Now there is murder in his eyes. I swing as hard as I can, aiming for his temple. He does the right thing: moves towards the blow, puts up his arm so that the towel wraps around it, and jerks it towards him. I fly forward a pace. Then he swings with the marline-spike, low and sweeping, and it catches me in the abdomen. I seem to be watching myself from the outside as my body is lifted and flung backwards across the cabin, and I realize that it's the desk slamming into my back. He moves towards me across the bunk. I feel as if I have no body, so I look down. At first I think that a white fluid is running out of me. Then I see that it's the towel, which I pulled along with me when I fell. He moves over the edge of the bunk. I raise the ball off the deck, shorten the length of the towel by half, put my right hand over my left, and yank my outstretched arms upward.

It hits him right under the chin. His head snaps back, followed more slowly by his body, as he's thrown against the door. His hands fumble behind him briefly, trying to hang on to the door handle; he gives up and sinks to the floor.

I stay where I am for a moment. Then I scuttle across the three metres of floor space, leaning first on the bunk, next the cupboard and the edge of the sink, numb from my navel down. I pick up the marline-spike. I take the little phial out of his pocket.

It takes him a long time to come around. I wait, clutching the spike. He touches his mouth and spits blood into his hands, along with a few pieces of something more solid and a lighter colour.

"You've ruined my face."

Half of one of his front teeth has been knocked out. You can see it when he talks. The anger has ebbed out of him. He looks like a child.

"Give me that phial, Smilla."

I take it out and balance it on my thigh.

"I want to see the forward cargo hold," I say.

The tunnel starts in the engine room. A narrow companionway leads from the deck down between the steel beams of the engine platform. At the bottom a watertight fire door opens on to a narrow corridor less than a metre wide and just high enough to stand up in.

It's locked, but Jakkelsen opens it.

"Over there, on the other side of the engine, a tunnel like this one goes under the middle and lower rooms of the quarterdeck and down to the wing tanks."

In my cabin he poured a short, fat line of powder on to my pocket mirror and snorted it straight into one nostril. It has transformed him into a brilliant, self-confident guide. But he lisps because of the broken front tooth.

I can barely put any weight on my right foot. It has swollen up as if from a bad sprain. I stay behind him. I've stuck the point of the little Phillips screwdriver into a cork and put it inside the waist band of my trousers.

He turns on the lights. Every five metres there's a bare light bulb inside a wire cage.

"It's twenty-five metres long. Runs along the whole length of the ship, up to where the foredeck starts. Up above is a cargo hold that's 34,500 cubic feet, and above that another one of 23,000 cubic feet."

Along the sides of the tunnel the ribs of the ship form a tight gridwork. He puts his hand on it.

"Fifty centimetres. Between the ribs. Half the normal distance on a 4,000-tonner. Four-centimetre plates in the nose. That gives a localized strength that's twenty times greater than what the insurance companies and the ship inspectors require to approve sailing in ice, you know. That's how I knew we were on our way up to the ice."

"How do you know so much about ships, Jakkelsen?"

He draws himself up. All charm and effusiveness. "All Danish teenagers know the novel about the sailorboy Peder Most, don't they? I am Peder Most. I was born in Svendborg just like he was. I have red hair. And I belong to a bygone era. To the days when ships were made of wood and sailors were made of iron. Now it's the other way around."

He runs a hand through his red curls, fluffing them up. "I'm just as fashionably slim as he was, too. I've had several offers to be a male model. In Hong Kong there were two guys who signed a contract with me. They were in the fashion business. They had noticed my looks from far away. I was supposed to be at the first photo session the next day. That was when I had signed on board ship as a galley boy. I didn't have time to do the dishes. So I threw all the cutlery and plates out the porthole. When I got to their hotel, they had left, unfortunately. The skipper deducted 5,000 kroner from my wages to pay the diver who retrieved the dishes."

"It's an unfair world."

"It sure is, man. That's why I'm only a sailor. I've been sailing for seven years. I was supposed to go to navigation school lots of times. Something just always came up. But I know everything about ships."

"But that container we dropped into the water yesterday – you couldn't suss that out, could you?"

His eyes narrowed. "So it's true, what Verlaine's been saying."

I wait.

He gestures with his hand. "I could be a valuable man to the police. They could put me on the narc squad. I know all about that world, you know."

There's a water pipe running above our heads. Every ten metres there are nozzles for the sprinkler system. Every nozzle is equipped with a dull red light. Jakkelsen takes a handkerchief out of his pocket and wraps it around the nozzle with a practised motion. Then he lights a cigarette.

"Each of them has a smoke detector. If you sit down in a corner to have a smoke, the alarm will go off if you don't take precautions."

He fills his lungs with pleasure, squinting at the pain from his tooth. "In Denmark it's hell getting rid of illegal cargo. The whole country is regulated; as soon as you approach a harbour you've got the police and the harbour authorities and the customs officials on your back. And they want to know where you're coming from and where you're going and who the shipowner is. And you can't find any people who will take bribes in Denmark – they're all bureaucrats and won't accept so much as a glass of mineral water. So you come up with the idea that one of your friends could come alongside in a smaller boat and take the crate and put it ashore on a dark beach somewhere. But that won't work, either. Because everybody knows that in Denmark the coastguard and the customs authorities work together. At the two big military bases on Anholt Island and in Frederikshavn the naval police assign a number to all the inbound and outbound ships in Danish waters and track them by computer. They would spot your friend with the boat right away. That's why you decide just to throw the crate overboard. With a buoy attached, or a couple of floats and a little battery-powered transmitter emitting a signal that could be located by whoever comes to pick it up."

I try to make some connection between what he's telling me and what I've seen.

He stubs out his cigarette. "But there's still something that doesn't fit. The ship came from a shipyard in Hamburg. She's been in Danish waters for two weeks. Docked in Copenhagen. It's a little too late to drop off the goods five hundred sea miles out in the Atlantic, isn't it?"

I agree. It seems incomprehensible.

"I don't think what happened yesterday had to do with smuggled goods. I know this business, I'm positive it had nothing to do with goods. You know why? Because I looked inside the container. You know what was in the container? Cement. Hundreds of fifty-kilo sacks of Portland cement. I took a look inside one night. There was a padlock on it. But the keys to the cargo area are always kept on the bridge. In case the tonnage should shift. So when I was on watch, I borrowed them. I was psyched, man. I opened the top. Nothing but cement. I tell myself it must be a joke. There must be something underneath. So I go all the way back to the galley and get a barbecue skewer. I'm about to shit my pants at the thought of Verlaine catching me. I spend two hours in that container. Moving the sacks around and sticking the skewer into them, trying to find something. My back's killing me. My hands are all cracking up. Cement dust is the worst. But I don't find a thing. I tell myself it's impossible, this whole trip. Everything is secret. Extra pay because we don't know where we're going, don't know what we're carrying. And then the only thing they take on board is a dustbin full of cement. It's too much. I can't sleep at night. I tell myself that it has to be dope."

"So you've given up."

"I think," he says slowly, "that yesterday was a test. The thing is, it's not that easy to drop a heavy cargo over the side. You want to hit the precise coordinates so you can find the goods later. You want to avoid getting it caught in the propeller. You don't want it to sway too much if there's a wind and a high sea, or you'll risk screwing it up. And you know that even small movements will change your relative speed on the coastguard's radar. It would be preferable to stop and carefully ease the container into the water. But that won't work. They make a note of all changes in speed. You'd have the customs people on the VHF immediately. So if you really want to put something big and heavy into the water and do it discreetly and without drawing attention, you'd need to do a trial run. To test your flotation balloons and your transmitting equipment, and to give the sailors a chance to rehearse their manoeuvres on deck. To set up the boom and the winch and the forward guy wire properly. That container yesterday was a test, a dummy. It was dropped at that point to make sure we were out of radar range. It was really just a preview."

"For what?"

"For the real goods, what we're on our way to get. Take my word for it. I know everything about the sea. This is costing them a fortune. The only thing that would pay so much as the interest on the investment would be dope."

At the end of the tunnel a narrow spiral companionway winds around a steel girder no thicker than the base of a flagpole. Jakkelsen places his hand on the white enamel. "This supports the forward mast."

I think about the loading boom and winch. They're both marked for a maximum weight of forty-five tons.

"It's so flimsy."

"Vertical pressure. The weight on the mast produces a pressure downwards. There's no lateral pressure of any significance."

I count fifty-six steps, and estimate that we've ascended to a height comparable to a three-storey house. My injured foot only just manages to make it.

We come to a landing on the stairs against a bulkhead. There's a circular hatch on the bulkhead, one and a half metres in diameter. There are two compression wheels on it, making it look like the entrance to a bank vault in a cartoon. The hatch doesn't fit in with its surroundings. The *Kronos* looks as if it was built about the same time as the Lauritzen Shipping Company's *Kista Dan*, which was my first encounter with a big diesel ship as a child — an overwhelming experience. That was in the early sixties. This hatch looks as if it was made the day before yesterday.

It hasn't been screwed tight. Jakkelsen turns both wheels half a revolution and pulls. It must be heavy, but it moves outwards without resistance. Inside, a heavy, three-ply, black rubber flange acts as a seal.

Behind the door is a platform jutting out over dark nothingness. From somewhere next to the door Jakkelsen fetches a big battery lantern. I take it from him and turn it on.

From the sound — the distant echo from the walls far away — I already had a sense of the room's size. Now the beam of light strikes the bottom, which seems sickeningly far below us. In reality it's about ten or twelve metres down. The hatchway is about five metres above us. I move the light all the way around its perimeter. It has the same kind of rubber flange. I shine the light on the bottom. It's a stainless-steel grating.

"It's lower now," he says. "When the container was in here, it was higher up."

Under the grating the deck slopes down towards a drainage outlet.

I find a corner and move the light all the way up the wall.

The walls are of polished steel. Part way up, light falls on something jutting out. It looks like a shower head. But it's pointed straight down. A little higher up there's another one. And then another. The same on the opposite wall. A total of eighteen in the room.

I examine the wall. In the middle, at the top, and at the bottom of each wall there's a built-in fifty-by-fifty-centimetre grating.

The platform we're standing on sticks out half a metre into the room. On the left there's some sort of instrument panel. It has four lights, a power switch, a meter labelled OXYGEN %, another labelled AIR PRESSURE, a thermostat with a scale from +20°C to −60°C, and a hygrometer.

I hang the lantern back in its place. We go out, and I close the hatch. There's a white door in the wall to the left. I try Jakkelsen's key, but it won't open. That doesn't matter too much. I can guess what's behind it. A panel identical to the one inside the tank. Plus some control buttons.

We walk back, Jakkelsen in front. His energy is waning. He's almost burned out.

I make him wait in his cabin while I get his chess pieces for him. There's no one around. My alarm clock says it's three thirty a.m. I feel as if I've aged.

I take a shower. When I come out of the bathroom, he's standing in the doorway. Full of energy. With a transfigured look on his thin young face.

"Smilla," he whispers, "how about a quick fuck?"

"Jakkelsen," I say, "tell me something. Was that Peder Most a junkie, too?"

$$\textcircled{6}$$

I STICK MY HEAD inside the dryer and bury my hands in the dish towels, still burning hot. I can feel the skin on my face and hands start to dry out at once.

If you're homeless, you're always looking for connections, similarities, little smells and colours and sensations that remind you of a place where you felt at home, where you once felt settled. The air inside a clothes dryer is desert air. I once felt at home in a desert.

We were walking across a plain at the bottom of a valley; around us stretched flat, lifeless steppes; overhead was the hot sun. As if a mercilessly curious god had pointed his microscope and laboratory light at us because we were the only living creatures in an otherwise dead world. We walked through sand dunes and across salt pans, through a yellowish-brown and ashen-grey and yet incredibly beautiful hell of heat. At the end of the day a sandstorm came up and we had to lie flat on the ground with scarves over our faces. We didn't have any water left, and one of the participants, a young man, became delirious and screamed that he was going to die of thirst. When the storm let up, a curtain of blowing sand hung between us and the sun for a moment. It shone from inside, as if it had encircled the sun, as if a great, glowing swarm of bees was about to rise up into the sky with it. I felt clear-headed and happy, for no explainable reason.

The time was eleven-thirty at night, the burning light was the midnight sun, and the place was Schuckerdt Valley in Northeast Greenland, an Arctic desert where, during a very brief summer, the polar sun heats up the cliffs to 35 °C, creating a mosquito-plagued landscape of dried-out riverbeds and a rocky surface shimmering with heat. It took two days to cross it, and ever since I've often wished I could go back. My brother was on the expedition as a hunter. That was the last time he and I took a long journey together. We felt like children, as if the time when Moritz forced me to go to Denmark had never existed, as if we had never experienced twelve years of separation. At this moment, in front of the clothes dryer, I hang on to that inexplicable memory of my youth, whose sweetness I will never again share with anyone. The bad thing about death is not that it changes the future. It's that it leaves us alone with our memories.

I pull the screwdriver out of its cork and rip open the big black dustbin bag.

It was the night before last that Jakkelsen showed me the cargo hold. Since yesterday I haven't gone anywhere without the screwdriver.

Yesterday around noon I left the laundry room to go back to my cabin and change my clothes.

My life as a whole might seem rather messy. But my clothes are always neat. I've brought along hangers for my trousers, inflatable hangers for my blouses, and I always fold my sweaters in a special way. One's clothes will stay new and yet familiar if they're properly ironed, folded, hung up, brushed, or neatly piled in their place.

There's a T-shirt in my cupboard that's not folded the way it should be. I examine the whole stack. Someone has gone through it.

I sit down next to Jakkelsen in the mess. I haven't seen him since the night before. For a moment he stops eating, then he bends over his plate.

"Did you," I ask him quietly, "search my cabin?"

A touch of fear appears in his eyes, like a slight fever. He shakes his head. I ought to eat something, but I've lost my appetite. Before I report for work in the laundry room after lunch, I put two thin strips of tape on my door.

When I come back before dinner, they're broken. Since then I've carried the screwdriver with me everywhere. It might not be a rational reaction, but people use so many odd objects to bolster their courage. A Phillips screwdriver is no worse than so many other things.

A pile of men's clothing spills out of the bag on to the floor. String vests, shirts, socks, jeans, underpants, and a pair of heavy trousers made of cavalry twill.

What I have here is the first batch of laundry from the off-limits boat deck.

A small amount of women's clothing. A cardigan, stockings, a cotton skirt, towels labelled THE JUTLAND DAMASK MILLS and made of thick towelling, embroidered with the name Katja Claussen. She hasn't sent me anything else. I understand her quite well. Women don't like having others see or handle their laundry. If I wasn't the only one in charge of the laundry, I'd wash my own clothes in the sink and dry them over the back of a chair.

There's one other heap of men's clothing: T-shirts, shirts, sweat-shirts, linen trousers. There are three things worth noting. That everything is new, that it's expensive, and that it's size XL.

"Jaspersen."

The small black telephones of some man-made material that are in each and every room on the *Kronos*, and that can be activated from the bridge and thereby permit the person on watch, any time he fancies, to break in with an order – for me, this moment at any rate, are the image of and the result of the past forty years' ingenious, pettily terroristic, sophisticated and abnormally superficial technological development.

"Bring coffee to the bridge."

I don't like being watched. I hate punch cards and clocking on and off. I'm allergic to cross-referenced lists. I loathe passport control and birth certificates, obligatory school attendance, mandatory disclosure of information, alimony, legal liability, oaths of confidentiality – the whole rotten monstrosity of government controls and demands that fall on your head when you come to Denmark. All the things that I normally sweep out of my mind but which may still confront me at any moment, perhaps manifested in a little black telephone.

I hate it even more because I know that it's also a kind of back-handed blessing: all the Western mania for control and archives and cataloguing is intended as a protection.

In the thirties, when they asked Ittussaarsuaq – who as a child had wandered with her tribe and kinfolk across Ellesmere Island to Greenland during the migration when Canadian Eskimos had their first contact in 700 years with the Inuit of North Greenland – when they asked her, an eighty-five-year-old woman who had experienced the entire modern colonization process, moving from the Stone Age to the radio, how life was now, compared to the past, she said without hesitation, "Better – the Inuit very rarely die of hunger nowadays."

Emotions must flow freely if they're not to become confused. The problem with being able to hate the colonization of Greenland with a pure hatred is that, no matter what you may detest about it, the colonization irrefutably improved the material needs of an existence that was one of the most difficult in the world.

The intercom has been turned off. I lean against the wall next to it.

"I was just standing here," I say, "waiting for a chance to do my utmost."

On my way up, I step out on to the deck. The *Kronos* is rolling on long transverse swells, old seas created by some distant storm that has disappeared, leaving behind nothing but this moving, matte-grey carpet of energy bound in water.

But the wind is blowing from the bow, a cold wind. I breathe in the air, open my mouth, letting it find a resonance, a deep upright wave, like when you blow across the top of an empty bottle.

The tarpaulin has been taken off the landing vessel. Verlaine is working with his back to me. With an electric screwdriver, he's fastening long teak slats onto the bottom.

Lukas is alone on the bridge. With his hand on the tiller. The automatic pilot is off. Something tells me that he prefers to steer manually, even though it gives a less precise course.

He doesn't turn around when I come in. Until he speaks, there's no sign that he knows I'm here.

"You're limping."

He has developed an ability to see everything without looking directly at anything in particular.

"It's my varicose veins."

"Do you know where we are, Jaspersen?"

I pour his cup of coffee. Urs knows exactly how he likes it. Small and black and poisonous, like a thimble of boiling tar.

"I can smell Greenland. Today, out on the deck."

His back emanates suspicion. I venture an explanation. "It's the wind. It smells of earth. At the same time, it's cold and dry. There's ice in it. It's the wind coming down from the ice cap blowing along the coast and reaching us out here."

I put the cup down in front of him.

"I can't smell anything," he says.

"It's a scientific fact that chain smokers burn out their sense of smell. Strong coffee doesn't help, either."

"But you're right. Tonight, around two a.m., we'll pass Cape Farewell."

He wants something from me. He hasn't spoken to me since the day I came on board.

"It's customary that when you pass the cape, you make a report to Greenland Ice Centre," he says.

I've spent three hundred flying hours in the Ice Centre's Havilland Twin Otter, and three months in the barracks at Narsarsuaq drawing ice maps on the basis of aerial photos, which were then faxed to the Meteorological Institute, which in turn forward them to the shipping industry via Skamlebæk Radio. But I don't tell Lukas any of this.

"It's up to you," he says. "But everyone takes advantage of it. They check in and then report back every twenty-four hours."

He downs the coffee as if he's swallowing an aspirin. "Unless you're on a mission that's not legal. And you want to hide your movements. If you don't report to the Ice Centre, no word is sent to the Danish inspection vessels, either. Or to the police."

Everybody is talking to me about the police. Verlaine, Maria, Jakkelsen. And now Lukas.

"We've made an agreement with the shipowner that the telephone on board will not be used during the trip. I'm prepared to make one exception."

At first the offer takes me by surprise. I didn't think I'd given the impression that I needed to be on the phone all the time, whingeing with my relatives via Lyngby Radio.

Then it dawns on me. Too late, of course, but all the more obvious. Lukas thinks I'm from the police. Verlaine thinks so, too. And Jakkelsen. They think I'm here undercover. That's the only explanation. That's why Lukas took me aboard.

I glance over at him. There's nothing evident, but it must be there: fear. It must have been there at our first meeting, in the reflection of his face, turned away, in the windowpanes of the casino. He must have made quite a few questionable voyages in his life. But there's something special about this one. This one scares him. So much so that he took me on board, believing that I am on the trail of something. And that his reluctant cooperation will give him some sort of alibi if the hand of the law should fall on him and the *Kronos* and her passengers.

It is in his back. You can tell from the stiffness, from the way he tries to keep watch over everything, to be everywhere at once. In the discipline he maintains.

"Is there anything you . . . need on board?"

The question doesn't come to him naturally. He's not a welfare worker or a personnel manager. He's a man who gives orders.

I move up behind him. "A key."

"You have a key."

I'm so close that I can breathe on the back of his neck. He doesn't turn around.

"To the boat deck."

"It's been confiscated."

His bitterness lashes at me, at this. But mostly at the fact that they've taken away his omnipotence as the commander-in-chief of the ship.

Then I ask him, as Jakkelsen asked me: "Where are we bound?"

His finger jabs at the chart at his side. It's a map of South Greenland. On it a clear plastic overlay on which are marked lines, circles, cross-hatching, and inky black triangles of the transmitter at Julianehåb, indicating ice concentrations, visibility, and icebergs. A course has been marked out north along the coast, around Cape Thorvaldsen, and then north by northwest. The course stops near the Vestland, at a point in the middle of the ocean.

"That's all I know."

He hates them for this. For keeping him on a short rein like an infant.

"But the western ice stretches south to Holsteinsborg. And it's no picnic. A little north of Søndre Strømfjord. That's as far as they'll get me to take them."

I've sat down next to Jakkelsen. Fernanda and Maria are sitting at the other side of the table. They've joined forces once and for all against the male world surrounding them. They ignore me, as if they were rehearsing for the way it will be when, quite soon, I no longer exist.

Jakkelsen is staring at his plate. His bunch of keys is lying on the table next to him. I put down my knife and fork, stretch, put my right hand on his keys, slide them slowly across the table, and let them drop into my lap. Under the shelter of the table edge I move them through my fingers, one by one, until I find the key marked with three Ks and a seven. It's the standard issue key on the *Kronos*; I have one myself. But Jakkelsen's also has an H. The ship was repaired in Hamburg. The H stands for *Hauptschlüssel*.

I twist it off the key ring. Then I put the rest of the keys back on the table and stand up. Jakkelsen hasn't moved.

In my cabin I put on warm clothes, then I go out on the quarterdeck.

I saunter along with my hand on the sea rail. It's supposed to look as if I'm taking a stroll.

In North Greenland distances are measured in *sinik*, in "sleeps", the number of nights that a journey requires. It's not a fixed distance. Depending on the weather and the time of year, the number of *sinik* can vary. It's not a measurement of time, either. Under the threat of a storm, I've travelled with my mother non-stop from Force Bay to Iita, a distance that should have required two nights.

Sinik is not a distance, not a number of days or hours. It is both a spatial and a temporal phenomenon, a concept of space-time, it describes the union of space and motion and time that is taken for granted by the Inuit but that cannot be captured by any European everyday language.

The European measurement of distance, the standard metre in Paris, is something quite different. It's a concept for reshapers, for those whose primary view of the world is that it must be transformed. Engineers, military strategists, prophets. And mapmakers. Like me.

The metric system didn't really become part of me until I took a course in surveying at Denmark's Technical College in the autumn of 1983. We surveyed the Dyrehaven. With theodolites and tape measures and normal distribution and equidistances and stochastic variables and rainy weather and little pencils that had to be sharpened constantly. And we paced off areas. We had a teacher who repeated over and over that the alpha and omega of surveying is that the geodesist must know the length of his own stride.

I knew my own pace measured in *sinik*. I knew that when we ran behind the sleigh because the sky was black with pent-up explosions the space-time around us would be half the number of *sinik* required when we let the dogs pull us over smooth new ice. In fog the number would double, in a snowstorm it might be tenfold.

In the Dyrehaven I translated my *sinik* into metres. Ever since, no matter whether I'm walking in my sleep or secured to a line, whether I'm wearing boots and crampons or the tight little black number that reduces me to a five centimetre Japanese shuffle, I've always known exactly how much distance I'm covering when I take a step.

This is not a pleasure stroll I'm taking on the quarterdeck. I'm measuring up the *Kronos*. I'm gazing out across the water, but all of my disposable energy is focused on remembering.

I saunter twenty-five and a half metres past the mast furthest astern and its two winches, down to the aft superstructure. Twelve metres along the superstructure. At the rail I lean over and estimate the height of the freeboard to be five metres.

Someone is standing behind me. I turn around. Hansen fills the doorway to the metal shop. Massive, wearing huge, wooden-soled boots. In his hand he's holding what looks like a short dagger.

He regards me with that indolent, brutal satisfaction that physical superiority makes some men feel.

He raises his knife. Then he puts his left hand up to the blade and, with a circular motion, starts polishing it with a little rag. It leaves a white soapy film on the blade.

"Viennese chalk. You have to polish them with Viennese chalk. Or they won't hold an edge."

He doesn't look at the knife. His eyes are fixed on me as he talks.

"I make them myself. Out of old cold chisels. The hardest steel in the world. First I set the edge with a diamond wheel. Then I polish it with carborundum and oilstone. Finally I polish it with Viennese chalk. Very, very sharp."

"Sharp as razors?"

"Sharper," he says with satisfaction.

"More pointed than nail files?"

"Much more pointed."

"Why is it, then," I ask, "that you are so bloody unshaven, and you show up in the galley that I've just cleaned with such incredibly filthy nails?"

He glances up towards the bridge and then back at me. He licks his lips. But he can't come up with an answer.

Isn't this an example of history repeating itself? Hasn't Europe always tried to empty out its sewers into the colonies? Isn't the *Kronos* once more the convicts on their way to Australia, the Foreign Legion on its way to Korea?

Back in my cabin I take out the two folded pieces of paper that I've been carrying in my jacket pocket. I've stopped leaving anything important in my cabin. While I remember them, I set down the numbers I've paced off on to the sketch I'm in the process of drawing of the *Kronos*'s hull. In the margin I write down the other figures; some I know, the others I guess at.

Length overall: 105 metres
Length inboard: 97 metres
Width: 15 metres
Depth of upper decks: 9.5 metres
Depth of second deck: 6 metres
Cargo capacity (second deck): 100,000 cubic feet
Cargo capacity (in hull): 125,000 cubic feet
Total: 225,000 cubic feet
Cruising speed: 18 knots, comparable to 4,500 BHP
Diesel consumption: 14 tons per day
Range: 10,000 nautical miles

I look for an explanation for the restrictions that have been placed on the movements of the *Kronos*'s crew. When the Eskimo Hans sailed with Peary to the North Pole, the sailors were not allowed on the officers' deck. It was part of the exercise, an attempt to bring along the security of a feudal hierarchy to the Arctic. On ships today the crew is too small for these types of regulations. And yet they exist on the *Kronos*.

I start the washing machines. Then I leave the laundry room.
   When you're part of an isolated group of people – whether in a boarding school, on the polar ice cap, or on a ship – your individuality dissolves and is partially replaced by a sense of unity. Unconsciously, at any given moment, I can place everyone else in the universe of the ship. By their footsteps in the corridor, by their breathing when they're asleep behind closed doors, by their whistling, the rhythm of their work, and my knowledge of their work shifts.
   Just as they know where I am. That's the advantage of the laundry room. It sounds as if I'm there even when I'm not.

Urs is eating. He has pulled out a folding table next to the stove, spread a cloth over it, set the table, and lit a candle.

"*Fräulein Smilla, attendez-moi* one minute."

The crew's mess on board the *Kronos* is a Tower of Babel of English, French, Filipino, Danish, and German. Urs drifts helplessly among fragments of languages he has never learned to speak. I sympathize with him. I can hear that his mother tongue is disintegrating.

He pulls up a chair for me and puts down a plate.

He's a social eater. He eats as if he'd like to unite the peoples of the world around his pots and pans, with the optimistic knowledge that despite wars and rape and language barriers and differences in temperament and the Danish military's exercise of sovereignty over North Greenland, even after Home Rule, we have this in common, that we need to feed ourselves.

On his plate he has a portion of pasta big enough to serve a full table.

He gives me a melancholy look when I decline. "You are too thin, *Fräulein*."

He grates a big chunk of Parmesan cheese; the dry golden dust drifts down over the pasta like snow flurries.

"You are *ein Hungerkünstler*."

He has slit his homemade baguettes lengthwise and fried them with butter and garlic. He stuffs a hand's width at a time into his mouth, grinding slowly and with pleasure.

"Urs," I say, "how did you sign on?"

I can't imagine using the more formal term of address with him. He stops chewing. "Verlaine says that you're *Polizist*."

He considers my silence. "I was *im Gefängnis*. For two years. *In der Schweiz*."

That explains the colour of his skin. Prison pallor.

"I was on a holiday in Morocco, by car. I thought that if I took *Zwei Kilo* along, I'd have enough for two years. At the Italian border they pulled me over at random. *Ich bekam drei Jahre*. Released after two. In October of last year."

"How was prison?"

"*Die beste Zeit meines Lebens*." Emotion has made him switch over to German. "The best time of my life. No stress. Only *Ruhe*, peace. I did voluntary kitchen duty. That's why I got *Strafermässigung*."

"And the *Kronos*?"

Once again he weighs what I am after. "I did my military service in the Swiss Navy."

I look at him to see whether this is supposed to be a joke, but he stops me with a wave of his hand.

"*Flussmarine*. I was a cook. One of my colleagues has connections in Hamburg. He recommends the *Kronos*. *Ich hatte meine Lehrzeit teilweise in Dänemark, in Tønder gemacht.* It was difficult. It's hard to find work when you've been in prison."

"Who hired you?"

He doesn't answer.

"Who is Tørk?"

He shrugs. "I've only seen him *einmal*. He stays on the boat deck. Seidenfaden and *die Frau* are the ones who come out."

"What are we going to pick up?"

He shakes his head. "*Ich bin Koch. Es war unmöglich Arbeit zu kriegen. Sie haben keine Ahnung, Fräulein Smilla . . .*"

"I want to see the walk-in refrigerators and the storage rooms."

There is fear in his expression. "*Aber Verlaine hat mir gesagt, die Jaspersen will . . .*"

I lean across the table. In this way I force him away from his pasta, away from our previous intimacy, from his trust in me.

"The *Kronos* is a smuggler ship."

Now he's panic-stricken. "*Ahh, ich bin kein Schmuggler. Ich konnte nicht ertragen, noch einmal ins Gefängnis zu gehen.*"

"Wasn't it the best time of your life?"

"*Aber es war genug.*"

He takes me by the arm. "*Ich will nicht zurück. Bitte, bitte.* If we're caught, tell them I'm innocent, that I don't know anything."

"I'll see what I can do."

The food storerooms are right under the galley. They consist of a meat locker, a freezer for eggs and fish, a double refrigerator kept at 2 °C for other perishable goods, plus various cupboards. The whole area is well stocked, clean, orderly, functional, and subject to such constant use that it would be no good as a hiding place for anything.

Urs shows me the area with equal parts professional pride and fear. It takes ten minutes to inspect. I'm on a schedule. I go back to the laundry room, spin dry the clothes, stuff them in the dryer, and turn the dial back to Start. Then I sneak out again. And head below.

❊   ❊   ❊

I don't know a thing about engines. And what's more, I have no intention of learning about them, either.

When I was five years old, the world was incomprehensible. When I was thirteen, it seemed to me much smaller, much dirtier, and depressingly predictable. Today it still seems muddled, but again – although in a different way – as complex as when I was a child.

With age I have voluntarily chosen certain limitations. I don't have the energy to start over again. To learn new skills or fight my own personality or understand the workings of diesel engines.

I rely on Jakkelsen's off-hand remarks. This morning I surprised him in the laundry room, sitting with his back against the insulation on the hot-water pipe, with a cigar in his mouth and his hands in his pockets so the salt air won't sneak in and damage his peach-soft skin that's supposed to be used for stroking the ladies' inner thighs.

"Smilla," he says when I ask him about the engine, "it's enormous. Nine cylinders, and each is 450 in diameter, with a 720-millimetre-stroke Burmeister & Wain direct reversible, with supercharger. We're sailing at eighteen to nineteen knots. It's from the sixties, man, but it's been renovated. We're outfitted as an ice-breaker."

I stare at the engine. It's looming up before me; I have to walk past it, with its injection valves, fuel cocks, radiator pipes, springs, polished steel and copper, its exhaust manifold, and its lifeless yet dynamic motion. Like Lukas's little black telephones, the engine is a distillation of civilization. Something that is both taken for granted and incomprehensible. Even if I had to, I wouldn't know how to stop it. In a certain sense, maybe it can't be stopped. Temporarily interrupted perhaps, but not permanently brought to a standstill.

It may give this impression because, unlike a human being, it has no individuality; it's a replica of something else, the soul of the machine or the system of axioms underlying all engines.

Or maybe it's the mixture of loneliness and fear that's making me see phantoms.

But I still can't explain the essential thing: Why was the *Kronos* outfitted two months ago in Hamburg with a vastly oversized engine?

The hatch in the bulkhead behind the engine is insulated. When it falls shut behind me, the noise of the engine vanishes and my ears ring deafly. The tunnel goes down six steps. From there the corridor stretches twenty-five metres, straight as an arrow, lit by wire-wrapped bulbs – an exact copy of the stretch that Jakkelsen and I covered less than twenty-four hours ago, although now it feels like the distant past.

The diesel tanks below deck are marked with numbers on the deck. I pass numbers seven and eight. On the wall, next to the location of each tank, there is a foam extinguisher, a fire blanket, and an alarm button. It's not pleasant being reminded about the dangers of fire on board ship.

At the end of the tunnel a spiral companionway leads upwards. The first hatch is on the left-hand side. If my provisional measurements are correct, it will lead to the smallest cargo hold farthest aft. I move past it. The next hatch is three metres higher up.

The room is not at all like the one I'd seen earlier. It's no more than six metres high. The sides don't go all the way up to deck level but stop at the between decks, where the beam of my torch disappears in the darkness.

The room is a peeling, spotted, and much-used cargo hold. Wooden wedges, hemp ropes, and sacks used for moving and securing cargo are piled up against one bulkhead.

Against the other bulkhead about fifty railway sleepers are stacked and strapped down.

One level up, a door opens on to the between decks. My torch finds distant walls, the high ridge where the cargo hold juts up, the bracing under the spot where the aft mast must stand. Clusters of white-painted electrical cables and the outlets of the sprinkler system.

The between decks is as wide as the ship, and is actually a single vast low-ceilinged room supported by columns; behind one end of the room are the walk-in refrigerators and storage rooms. The opposite end vanishes aft into the darkness.

That's the direction I go in. After twenty-five metres there is a rail. Three metres down my light strikes bottom. The aft cargo hold. I remember Jakkelsen's statistics: 1,000 cubic feet, as opposed to the 3,500 in the hold I've just looked at.

I take out my sketch and compare it with the space beneath me. It seems somewhat smaller than I've drawn it.

I go back to the spiral companionway and down to the first door.

Seen from the floor of the hold, it's understandable why it seems smaller than in my drawing. It's half filled with a rectangular shape a metre and a half high under a blue tarpaulin.

With my screwdriver I make two punctures and a rip in the canvas.

Keeping in mind the railway sleepers, you might think we were on our way to Greenland to lay seventy-five metres of track and start up a railway company. Under the tarpaulin there is a stack of rails.

But you wouldn't be able to attach them to the sleepers. They're welded together in a huge, rectangular construction with an iron bottom.

It reminds me of something. Then I let the thought pass. I'm thirty-seven years old. With age everything starts reminding you of something else.

Back on the between decks I glance at my alarm clock. By now the laundry room must be quiet. Someone might have called me. Someone might have come by.

I walk further aft.

The vibrations in the hull tell me that the propeller must be somewhere below, right in front of my feet. According to my diagram, about fifteen metres away. Here the deck is cut off by a bulkhead with a door. Jakkelsen's key fits the lock. Inside, there is a red emergency light with a switch. I don't turn on the light. I must be on the floor beneath the low aft superstructure. It's been locked ever since I came aboard.

The hatch leads to a short passageway with three doors on either side. The key opens the first one on the right. No doors are closed to Peder Most and his friends.

Until not very long ago this room was one of three small cabins on the port side. Now the dividing walls have been torn down to create one room. A storeroom. Along the walls are rolls of blue 64-millimetre nylon hawsers. Woven polypropylene rope. Eight sets of 8-millimetre Kermantel double rope in bright alpine safety colours, an old friend from the ice cap. Every set costs 5,000 kroner, has a breaking strain of five tons, and it's the only rope in the world that can stretch twenty-five per cent of its own length.

Under straps are aluminium ladders, firn anchors, tents, lightweight shovels, and sleeping bags. Metal hooks screwed into the walls hold ice axes, climbing hammers, pitons, snap hooks, dynamic brakes, and ice screws – both the narrow ones that look like corkscrews and the wide ones: you screw a cylinder of ice into the core and they can hold an elephant.

Inside some metal cabinets along the wall, opened at random, I find wedges, glacier goggles, a crate of six Tommen altimeters. Frameless backpacks, Meindl boots, safety harnesses. Everything straight from the factory and wrapped in clear plastic.

The room to starboard was also formed by combining three cabins. There are more ladders and ropes and a fire chest marked EXPLOSIVES, which Jakkelsen's key unfortunately will not open. In three big cardboard boxes there are three identical examples of Danish quality craftsmanship: twenty-inch manual winches with three gears from Sophus Berendsen, Inc. I don't know much about mechanical gear ratios, but they're as big as barrels and look as if they could lift a locomotive.

I pace off the hallway at five and a half metres. At the end a companionway leads up to deck level, where there's a lavatory, a paint room, a metal workshop, and a little mess hall used as a shelter when they're working on deck. I decide to postpone my inspection to another time.

Then I change my mind.

I have left the door I came through on a latch. Perhaps because the hallway and the small rooms would feel like a rat trap otherwise.

Perhaps to see whether a light would be turned on behind me.

There's a sound now. Not much. Just a little noise that almost disappears in the sound of the propeller and the seething crash of the sea along the hull.

It's the sound of metal on metal. Cautious, but enhanced by the harsh echo of the room.

I head up the companionway to reach the deck. At the top there's a door. The key makes the latch click back, but the door doesn't open. It's battened down from the outside. I turn back.

In the darkness of the between decks, I withdraw to the side, squat down, and wait.

They arrive almost at once. There are at least two of them, maybe more. They move slowly, inspecting the space around them along the way. Discreet, but without making an effort to be quiet.

I put my torch on the deck. I wait for the *Kronos* to rip on a high swell. Then I turn on the torch and let it go. It starts rolling to starboard and its beam flickers across the pillars.

I run forward, along the side.

It doesn't distract them. In front of me is something that feels like a curtain. I try to push it aside, but it wraps itself around me. Then another flutters around my head and shoulders, and I scream, but the sound is muted by the heavy fabric and becomes merely a ringing in my own ears, along with the taste of dust and wool in my mouth. They've wrapped me up in fire blankets.

There has been no violence, everything has been gentle and undramatic.

They lay me down and put pressure on the blankets, and there is a new smell of mildew and jute. They've pulled a sack over the blankets, over my head – one of the sacks I saw so many of in the cargo hold.

They lift me up, still taking care; I'm lying across the shoulders of two men who carry me along the deck. Irrationally, the vain thought strikes me that I must look ridiculous.

A hatchway is opened and closed. On our way down the companionway they hold me stretched out between them. Blindness leads to an increased awareness in my body, but not once do I hit the stairs. If it hadn't been for the wrapping and the circumstances, they might have been carrying a patient on a stretcher.

A sound that is both muffled and close at hand tells me that we're outside the door to the engine room. The door is opened, we pass the engine room, and the sound dies out again. Time and distance seem longer. I feel as if we've been walking for an eternity before they take the first step upward. In reality, it can't have been more than the twenty-five metres to the bottom step.

Now there's only one shoulder under me. I try to get my arms free.

Gently, I'm placed on the deck; there's a slight vibration of metal somewhere above my head.

Now I know where we're going. The opened door doesn't lead anywhere; it opens on to the little platform where Jakkelsen and I stood, twelve metres from the bottom.

I don't know why, but I'm positive that they're going to throw me from that platform into the bottom of the tank.

I'm in a sitting position. A fold in the blankets allows me to pull my left arm up along my chest. I have the screwdriver in my hand.

When he lifts me up from the floor, my chest rests against his. I try to feel my way to where his ribs end, but I'm shaking too hard. Besides, the cork is still on the screwdriver.

He leans me against the rail and kneels in front of me, like a mother about to lift her child.

I'm sure that I'm going to die. But I push the thought aside. I refuse to accept this humiliation. There's a degrading coldness about the way they must have planned it. It was so easy for them, and now here I am: Smilla the Greenlander, about to go splat.

As he gets his shoulder underneath me, I shift the screwdriver into my right hand. As he slowly stands up, I put it to my mouth, bite down on the cork, and pull it off. He rolls me around ninety degrees to get me free of the edge. With the fingers of my left hand I find his shoulder. I can't reach his throat, but I can feel the soft, triangular hollow between his collarbone and trapezius muscle, where the nerves lie exposed beneath a thin layer of skin and tissue. That's where I jab the screwdriver. It goes through the blanket. Then it stops. The surprisingly elastic resistance and solidity of living cells. I put the palms of my hands together, and with a jerk I lift my body free so that all my weight rests on the handle of the screwdriver. It slides into place.

He doesn't utter a sound. But all movement ceases, and for a moment we stand there swaying together. I wait for him to release me; I'm already anticipating the impact with the grating in the darkness beneath me. Then he drops me on to the platform.

I hit my head on the rail. Dizziness spreads over me, increases, and then disappears. The sack and the woollen blankets protected my head enough for me to remain conscious.

Then a ram batters me in the stomach. He's kicking me.

My first impulse is to vomit. But since the pain keeps coming, I can't manage to catch my breath between each kick. I'm about to suffocate. I think that it's too bad I couldn't get any closer to his throat.

The next thing I notice is the screaming. I think it's him screaming. Someone takes me by the shoulders and I think that now I've used up all my own resources and my luck, and I just want to die in peace.

But he's not the one who's screaming. It's an electronic screech, the sine wave of an oscillator. I'm being dragged up the stairs. The small of my back thuds against every single step.

A feeling of coldness reaches me, along with the sound of rain falling. Then a hatch is opened and I'm released. Next to me an animal is coughing up its lungs.

I work the sack up over my head. I have to roll back and forth to get free of the blankets.

I emerge into a cold, pouring rain, to the electronic screech, a blinding electric light, and to the retching breathing of the creature beside me.

It's not an animal. It's Jakkelsen. Soaking wet and white as chalk. We're inside a room that I can't immediately identify. Above our heads the sprinkler system is sending wildly rotating cascades of water over us. The sound of the smoke alarm is rising and falling, monotonous and nerve-racking.

"What else could I do? I lit a cigar and put my mouth up to the sensor. Then the shit hit the fan."

I try to ask a question but can't manage a sound. He guesses what I want to ask.

"Maurice," he says. "His days as a pin-up are over. He didn't even notice me."

Somewhere overhead there's the sound of running footsteps. They're coming down the stairs.

I'm incapable of moving. Jakkelsen gets to his feet. He has dragged me up the companionway to the next level. We must be on the between decks, under the foredeck. The exertion had made him collapse.

"I'm not in very good shape," he says.

Then he runs unsteadily into the darkness.

The door flies open. Sonne steps in. It takes me a moment to identify him. He's carrying a big foam extinguisher, and he's dressed in full firefighting gear with an oxygen tank on his back. Behind him stand Maria and Fernanda.

As we gaze at each other, the alarm stops and the water pressure tapers off in the sprinkler system and finally halts altogether. Amid the trickling of drops along the walls and the murmuring of streams on the bulkhead and floor, the distant sound of waves breaking against the bows of the *Kronos* seeps into the room.

FALLING IN LOVE has been greatly overrated. Falling in love consists of forty-five per cent fear of not being accepted and forty-five per cent manic hope that *this time* the fear will be put to shame, and a modest ten per cent frail awareness of the possibility of love.

I don't fall in love any more. Just like I don't get the mumps.

But of course anyone can be attacked by love. The last few weeks I've allowed myself to think about him for a few minutes each night. I give my mind permission and then watch how my body yearns and how I still remember him from the time before I really noticed him. I see his solicitude, remember his stutter, his embraces, and the awareness of the solid core of his personality. When these images start to radiate too much longing, I cut them off. At least I try to.

I haven't fallen in love. I see things too clearly for that. Falling in love is a form of madness. Closely related to hatred, coldness, resentment, intoxication, and suicide.

Occasionally – not often, but occasionally – I'm reminded of the times in my life when I've fallen in love. That's what's happening now.

Across from me at the table in the officers' mess the man they call Tørk is sitting. If this encounter had taken place ten years ago, I might have fallen in love with him.

Sometimes a person's charisma is such that it slips right through our façades, our essential prejudices and inhibitions, and goes straight to our guts. Five minutes ago a clamp locked around my heart, and now it's getting tighter. This sensation is linked to a rising fever which is my body's response to the stress it's been under, and it brings on a piercing headache.

Ten years ago this headache might have led to a strong desire to press my mouth on his and watch him lose his self-control.

Today I can observe what is happening to me, full of respect for the phenomenon, but completely aware that it's nothing more than a short-lived, lethal illusion.

The photographs had captured his charm but made it lifeless, like a statue. They couldn't reproduce his personal presence, which has two sides to it. Both an emanation out into the room and an attraction towards him.

Even when he's sitting down, he's quite tall. His hair is almost metallic white, pulled back into a ponytail.

He looks at me, and the heavy pounding in my foot and my back and the base of my skull grows louder. A number of the boys and men in my life who have affected me in this way pass hazily through my mind like the patches of ice formations we were expected to recognize during exams at the university.

Then I take hold of reality and pull myself back on shore. The hairs on the back of my neck are standing on end, telling me that, no matter who else he might be, he's the one who stood a metre away from me in the cold night while we both waited in front of the White Cells. The halo around his head was his extraordinary white hair.

He gazes at me attentively.

"Why on the foredeck?"

Lukas is sitting at the head of the table. He's talking to Verlaine, sitting diagonally across from me, slouching and amenable.

"To get warm. Before I had to go back to working on the runners."

Now I remember. *Kista Dan* and *Maggi Dan*, the Lauritzen Line ships used for trips to the Arctic – the ships of my childhood. Before the American base, before the flights from South Greenland. For extreme conditions, such as a hard freeze, they were equipped with special aluminium lifeboats that had runners screwed on underneath so they could be pulled across the ice like sleighs. That's the kind of runners Verlaine had been attaching.

"Jaspersen."

He glances down at the paper in front of him. "You left the laundry room half an hour before your shift was over, at 1530 hours, to take a walk. You went down to the engine room, saw a door, opened it, and followed the tunnel to the companionway. What the devil were you doing there?"

"Wanted to find out what was down below."

"And?"

"There was a door. With two handles. I touch one of them, and the alarm goes off. I think at first that I am the one who did it."

He looks from Verlaine to me. Anger clouds his voice. "But you can barely stand up."

I look straight at Verlaine. "I fell. When the alarm went off, I took a step back and fell down the stairs. I must have hit my head on the steps."

Lukas nods, slowly and bitterly. "Any questions, Tørk?"

He doesn't shift his position. He simply cocks his head slightly. He might be in his mid-thirties or his mid-forties.

"Do you smoke, Jaspersen?"

I remember his voice clearly. I shake my head.

"The sprinkler system is turned on by section. Did you smell smoke anywhere?"

"No, I didn't."

"Verlaine. Where were your people?"

"I'm looking into that."

Tørk gets up. He stands there leaning on the table, looking at me thoughtfully.

"According to the clock on the bridge, the alarm went off at 1557 hours. It stopped three minutes and forty-five seconds later. During that time you were in the activated section. Why aren't you soaking wet?"

My previous feelings have vanished. The only thing I notice through the fever is that one more person with power is persecuting me. I look him straight in the eye.

"Practically everything I experience runs off me like water off a duck's back."

8

HOT WATER IS SOOTHING. I, who grew up with milky-white baths in glacial meltwater, have grown addicted to hot water. One of the few dependencies I acknowledge. Like my occasional need to drink coffee, or to see the sun shining on the ice.

The water from the taps on board the *Kronos* is boiling hot. I mix it with cold to just about scalding, and then I let the shower wash over me. It makes the flames burst out from my back, at the base of my skull, the bruises on my pelvis, and especially my foot, which is still swollen and sprained. The fever and shaking grow worse; I stand there until it all goes away, leaving me listless.

I get a thermos of tea from the galley and take it back to my cabin. In the dark, I put it down, lock the door, take a deep breath, and then turn on the light.

On my bunk, Jakkelsen is sitting, wearing a white tracksuit. His pupils seem to have receded into his brain, giving him a quartz-like gaze of artificial self-confidence.

"You realize that I saved your life, don't you?"

I wait for the terror to let go of my limbs so that I can sit down.

"Life at sea, I tell myself, is too brutal for Smilla. So I go down to the engine room and wait. If somebody wants to find you, he just has to go below. Sooner or later you'll come past on your way to the bottom. And right behind you come Verlaine and Hansen and Maurice. But I stay where I am. I'd locked the doors up to the deck, you know. You would all have to come back the same way."

I stir my tea. The spoon clatters against the cup.

"When they come back with you in a bag, I shall still be sitting there. I'm familiar with their problem. Dumping rubbish from the mess and tipping people you don't like overboard is a thing of the past. There are always two on watch on the bridge, and the deck is lit up. Anyone who drops something bigger than a toothpick over the rail will face trouble and a marine enquiry. We'd have to put in at Godthåb and have little bowlegged Greenlanders in police uniforms running around like ants."

It occurs to him that I'm one of those little bowlegged ants he's talking about.

"Sorry," he says.

Somewhere a clock strikes four double strikes, four bells, the measure of time at sea, a time that doesn't distinguish between night and day but only the monotone changeover of four-hour watches. These bells reinforce the feeling that we're at a standstill, that we've never left port but have remained stationary in time and space, merely twisting ourselves further down into meaninglessness.

"Hansen stays next to the hatch in the engine room. So I saunter up on deck and over to the port companionway. When Verlaine comes up, I see what's going on. Verlaine keeping watch on deck. Hansen at the hatchway. And Maurice alone with you down below. What does that mean?"

"Maybe Maurice wants a quick fuck," I say.

He nods thoughtfully. "That's possible. But he prefers young girls. An interest in mature women comes later, with experience. I'm positive that they're going to drop you into the cargo hold. What a great plan, man! It's twelve metres down. It'll look like you fell. All they have to do is take off the sack afterwards. That's why they were carrying you so carefully. So there wouldn't be any marks."

He beams at me. Pleased that he figured out their plan.

"I go down to the between decks and over to the companionway. Through the steps I can see Maurice lugging you through the door. He's not even breathing hard. But then it's every day in the weight room. Two hundred kilos on the bench press and twenty-five kilometres on the exercycle. I have to make a decision. You've never done anything for me, have you? In fact, you've been a pain. And besides, there's something about you that's so . . . so damned . . ."

"Old-maidish?"

"Exactly. On the other hand, I never could stand Maurice."

He pauses dramatically.

"I'm a fan of the ladies. So I light the cigar. I can't see you any more. You're out on the platform. But I put my mouth on the smoke detector and blow, and it goes off."

He gives me a searching look.

"Maurice comes towards the companionway, covered with blood. The sprinklers wash it down the steps. A small flood. It

294

makes me want to throw up. Why are they going to so much trouble? What have you done to them, Smilla?"

I need his help. "They've put up with me until now. Things started going wrong as soon as I got too close to the stern."

He nods. "That's always been Verlaine's territory."

"Now we're going to go up to the bridge," I say, "and tell Lukas all about this."

"No can do, man."

There are red patches on his face. I wait. But he can hardly speak.

"Does Verlaine know that you're a little needle freak?"

He reacts with that baroque cockiness you sometimes encounter in people who have almost hit bottom.

"I'm the one controlling the drug; the drug doesn't control me!"

"But Verlaine has seen through you. He's going to put the finger on you. Why would that be so bad?"

He meticulously studies his tennis shoes.

"Why do you have a pass key, Jakkelsen?"

He shakes his head.

"I've already been up on the bridge," I say. "With Verlaine. We agreed that the alarm went off by itself. That I fell down the stairs out of sheer astonishment."

"Lukas won't swallow that."

"He doesn't believe us. But there's nothing he can do. You weren't mentioned at all."

He's relieved. Then a thought occurs to him. "Why didn't you tell him what happened?"

I have to win his help. It's like trying to build something on sand. "I'm not interested in Verlaine. I'm interested in Tørk."

The panic is back in his eyes. "That's much worse, man. I know a creep when I see one, and he's bad news."

"I want to know what we're on our way to get."

"I've told you, man. We're on our way to get some dope."

"No," I say. "It's not dope. Narcotics come from the tropics. From Colombia. From Burma. From Pakistan. And it goes to Europe. Or the USA. It doesn't come to Greenland. Not in quantities that require a 4,000-ton ship. That forward cargo hold is specially built. I've never seen anything like it. It can be sterilized with steam. The air composition, temperature, and humidity can be regulated. You've seen all of this and thought about it. What did you come up with?"

His hands take on their own helplessly fluttering life on top of my pillows, like baby birds that have fallen out of the nest. His mouth opens and shuts.

"Something alive, man. Otherwise it wouldn't make any sense. They're going to transport something that's alive."

9

SONNE UNLOCKS the sick bay for me. It's nine o'clock at night.
I find a gauze bandage. He bolsters his uncertainty by standing at
attention. Because I'm a woman. Because he doesn't understand
me. Because there's something he wants to say.

"On the between decks, when we showed up with the fire-
extinguishing equipment, you were sitting there with a couple of
fire blankets."

At the spot where the skin is broken I dab on a diluted solution
of hydrogen peroxide. No simple disinfectant for me. I have to feel
it sting before I believe it's going to do any good.

"I went back, but they were gone," he says.

"Someone must have taken them away," I say. "It's good to keep
things tidy."

"But they forgot to take this away."

Behind his back he's been holding a wet, folded gunny sack.
Maurice's blood has left big purplish patches on it.

I put the bandage on the wound. The gauze has some kind of
adhesive on it that makes it stay on by itself.

I take along a big elastic bandage. He follows me through the
door. He's a nice young Dane. He ought to be on board an East
Asiatic Company tanker right now. He could have been on the
bridge of one of the Lauritzen ships. He could have been sitting
at home under the cuckoo clock with his mother and father in
Ærøskøbing, eating meatballs and gravy, praising Mama's cooking,
and basking in Papa's humble pride. Instead, he wound up here. In
worse company than he could ever imagine. I feel sorry for him.
He's a little piece of what's good about Denmark. The honesty, the
integrity, the enterprise, the obedience, the crew cut, and money
matters.

"Sonne," I say, "are you from Ærøskøbing?"

"Svaneke." He looks disconcerted.

"Does your mother make meatballs?"

He nods.

"Good meatballs? Crusty on the outside?"

He blushes. He wants to protest. Wants to be taken seriously. Wants to exert his authority. The way Denmark does. With blue eyes, pink cheeks, and honourable intentions. But all around him are powerful forces: money, development, abuse, the collision of the new world with the old. And he doesn't understand what's going on. That he will only be tolerated as long as he cooperates. And he has no imagination for doing anything else. Only enough to cooperate.

To say stop requires quite different talents. Something much more vulgar, much more clear-sighted. Much more embittered.

I reach up and pat his cheek. I can't resist. The blush rises up from his throat, like a rose beneath his skin.

"Sonne," I say, "I don't know what you're up to, but just keep on doing it."

I lock my door, place the chair under the door handle, and sit down on my bunk.

Those who have travelled enough in places where it's very cold will sooner or later find themselves in a situation where survival means staying awake. Death is built into sleep. The person who freezes to death passes through a brief state of sleep. The person who bleeds to death goes to sleep, and the one who is buried under an avalanche of compact, wet snow falls asleep before suffocating to death.

I need to sleep. But I can't, not yet. In this situation there's a certain respite in the hazy region between sleep and full consciousness.

During the first Inuit Circumpolar Conference we discovered that all peoples around the Arctic Sea shared the story of the raven, the Arctic creation myth: "Even the raven started out in human form, and he fumbled blindly, and his actions were haphazard until it was revealed to him who he was and what his purpose was."

To find out what your purpose is. Maybe that's what Isaiah has given me. The way every child can. A sense of purpose. Through me, and on through him, a wheel is turning – a vast and frail and yet necessary movement.

That is what has been violated. Isaiah's body in the snow is a violation. While he was alive, he brought purpose and meaning. And, as always, I didn't appreciate how important he was until he was gone.

Now my purpose is to understand why he died. To penetrate and illuminate the infinitesimal yet all-encompassing fact of his death.

I wrap the elastic bandage around my foot and try to get my circulation going. Then I let myself out and quietly knock on Jakkelsen's door.

He's still full of chemical bounce. But the effects are beginning to wear off.

"I want to go up on the boat deck," I say. "Tonight. You're going to help me."

He's on his feet and on his way out of the door. I don't try to stop him. Someone like that doesn't have any real freedom of choice.

"You must be insane. That's a restricted area. Jump overboard, man. Why don't you jump overboard instead."

"You have to help me," I say. "Or I'll be forced to go up on the bridge and tell them to come and get you. And in the presence of witnesses roll up your sleeves so they can admit you to the sick bay, strap you to the bed, and lock the door with a guard outside."

"You'd never do that, man."

"My heart would bleed at having to report a hero of the high seas. But I'd be forced to do it."

He struggles with his suspicions.

"I'd also let drop a few words to Verlaine about what you've seen."

That pushes him over the edge. He's shaking uncontrollably.

"He'd cut me up in little pieces," he says. "How could you do that, after I rescued you?"

Perhaps I could make him understand. But it would require an explanation that I can't give him.

"I want to know," I say, "I *have* to know what we're going to pick up. What that tank is designed to hold."

"Why, Smilla?"

It all began with a person falling off a roof. But before that's resolved, there is a series of connections that may never be untangled. And what Jakkelsen needs is to be reassured. Europeans need easy explanations; they will always choose a simple lie over a contradictory truth.

"Because I owe it to somebody," I say. "I owe it to someone I love."

It's not a mistake to use the present tense. It's only in a narrow, physical sense that Isaiah has ceased to exist.

Jakkelsen stares at me, disillusioned and gloomy. "You don't love anyone. You don't even like yourself. You're not a real woman. When I dragged you up the stairs, I saw that little point sticking out of the bag. A screwdriver. Like a little dick. You stabbed him, man."

His face is full of amazement. "I can't figure you out, man. You're the good fairy in the monkey cage. But you're cold, too, man. You're like a fucking banshee."

As we reach the covered area on the upper deck, the clock on the bridge strikes two bells; it's two in the morning, halfway through the middle watch.

The wind has died down, the temperature has dropped, and *pujuq*, the fog, has raised its four white walls around the *Kronos*.

Next to me, Jakkelsen has already started shivering. He has no resistance to the cold.

Something has happened to the contours of the ship, to the sea rail, the masts, the spotlights, and the radio antenna, which at a height of thirty metres stretches from the mast farthest forward to the one in the stern. I rub my eyes. But it's not my eyesight.

Jakkelsen puts his finger on the rail and lifts it again. It leaves behind a black spot where it has melted through the fine, milky layer of ice.

"There are two kinds of icing up, you know. The ugly kind, that comes from the waves slamming over the side and freezing solid. More and more, faster and faster, after the rigging and everything else upright starts to get thick with it. And then the truly bad kind of ice. The type that comes from the sea fog. It doesn't need any waves, it simply covers everything. It's just something that's there."

He gestures out towards the whiteness. "This is the start of the truly bad kind. Four more hours and we'll have to get out the ice clubs."

His movements seem feeble but his eyes are shining. He would hate having to hammer off ice. But somewhere inside him even this aspect of the sea ignites a wild joy in him.

I walk ten metres forward, to a spot where I won't be visible from the bridge, but where I can survey several of the windows on the boat deck. They're all dark. All the windows in the superstructure are dark, except for a faint light from the officers' mess. The *Kronos* is asleep.

"They're sleeping," I say.

He's been over to the quarterdeck to look at the windows facing astern. "We should fucking well all be asleep."

We go up the three levels to the boat deck. He continues on to the next landing. From there he'll be able to see whether anyone leaves the bridge. And whether anyone should happen to leave the boat deck. Inside a sack, for instance.

I'm wearing my black serving uniform. It's almost worthless as an excuse for anything at two o'clock in the morning, but I couldn't come up with anything else. I'm taking actions without stopping to think about them. Because forward is the only way to go, and it's impossible to stop. I put Jakkelsen's key in the lock. It slides in effortlessly. But it won't turn. The combination has been changed.

"It's a sign, man. We should drop this idea."

He comes back down and stands right behind me. I take hold of his lower lip. The blood blister hasn't gone down yet. He would have protested if I hadn't put my hand over his mouth.

"If it's a sign, then it means that behind that door there's something they've gone to a lot of trouble to keep us from seeing."

I whisper this in his ear. Then I let him go. He can think of a lot of things to say, but he restrains himself. He follows me with his head bowed. When the opportunity arises, he'll take his revenge and stomp on me, or sell me to whoever comes along, or give me the final kick from behind. But right now he feels cowed.

Rooms designed for some form of socializing always seem unreal when they're empty. Theatre stages, churches, dining rooms. The mess is dark and lifeless, but still populated with the memory of life and mealtimes.

In the galley there's a strong odour of sourdough, yeast, and alcohol. Urs told me that his bread rises for six hours, from ten o'clock at night until four in the morning. We have an hour and a half, two at the most.

When I open the two sliding doors, Jakkelsen realizes what I'm up to.

"I knew you were crazy, man. But I didn't know you were that far gone . . ."

The dumbwaiter has been cleaned, and inside there is a tray laden with cups and saucers, breakfast plates, cutlery, and napkins. Urs's token preparations for the next day.

I remove the tray and the china.

"I get the bends," says Jakkelsen.

"You're not the one who's going up in it."

"I get the bends for other people, too."

The box is rectangular. I get up on the counter and crawl in sideways. First I test whether it's even possible to put my head down far enough between my knees. Then I wriggle my upper body part way inside.

"You press the button for the boat deck. When I get out, leave the dumbwaiter there. So it doesn't make any unnecessary noise. Then go up to the companionway and wait. If anyone tries to send you away, refuse to leave. If they insist, go back to your cabin. Give me an hour. If I'm not back by then, wake up Lukas."

He wrings his hands. "I can't, man. I can't."

I have to stretch my legs, but I also have to watch that I don't put my hands down on the sourdough rising on the counter.

"Why not?"

"He's my brother, man. That's why I'm on board. That's why I have a key. He thinks I'm clean."

I take one last lungful of air, exhale, and squeeze myself into the little box.

"If I'm not back in an hour, wake up Lukas. It's your only chance. If you don't come to get me, I'll tell Tørk everything. He'll get Verlaine to take care of you. Verlaine is his man."

We haven't turned on the light. The galley is dark except for the faint glow from the sea and the reflection of the fog. But I can still tell that I've hit home. I'm glad I can't see his face.

I put my head between my knees. He pushes the doors closed. There's the soft hum of an electric motor beneath me in the dark as I move upward.

The movement lasts for about fifteen seconds. My only thought is one of helplessness. The fear that someone will be waiting for me up there.

I get out my screwdriver. So I'll have something to offer when they slam open the doors and pull me out.

But nothing happens. The dumbwaiter stops abruptly in its shaft of darkness, and I sit there with nothing but the pain in the back of my thighs, the movement of the ship on the sea, and the distant sound of the engine, which is now barely audible.

I stick the screwdriver in between the two sliding doors and force them apart and open. Then I wriggle on my back onto a countertop.

There's a faint light coming into the room. It's from the stern running lights shining into this level from a skylight overhead. The room is a kitchenette with a refrigerator, a sideboard, and a couple of hot plates.

The door leads to a narrow corridor. I crouch down in the corridor and wait.

People perish during transitional phases. In Scoresbysund they would shoot each other in the head with shotguns when the winter started to kill off summer. It's not difficult to ride on affluence, when a balance has been established. What's difficult is the new. The new ice. The new light. The new feelings.

I sit down. It's my only chance. It's everybody's only chance. To give yourself the necessary time to get settled.

The bulkhead in front of me is quivering from the distant engine beneath us. The smokestack must be just on the other side. This level of the ship has been built around the big, rectangular shape of the funnel.

To my left I can see a faint light at deck level. It's the night light on the stairs. That door is my escape route.

To my right there is silence at first. Then, in the stillness, I can hear someone breathing. It's much softer than the other sounds of the ship. But after six days on board, the daily noises have become a discreet background against which all deviations are evident. Even the light snoring of a sleeping woman.

This means that there is one cabin, or possibly two, here on the port side, and there will be one or two opposite. So the saloon and mess face the foredeck.

I stay seated. After a while a pipe gurgles distantly. The *Kronos* has high-pressure flushable lavatories. Somewhere either above or below us, a toilet was flushed. The movement in the pipes reveals that the bath and lavatories on this deck are in front of the smokestack, and built adjacent to it.

I've brought my alarm clock in my apron pocket. What else could I do? I look at it, and then I make my move.

The lock on the exit is a bolt. I pull back the bolt. So that I'll be able to get out fast. But mainly so that someone else will be able to get in.

Between the short corridor to the exit and what must be the saloon, I feel my way to a door. I put my ear against it and wait. The only thing I hear is the distant ship's clock that sounds the bells. The door opens into darkness more intense than the dimness behind me. Here, too, I wait. Then I turn on the light switch. It doesn't produce an ordinary light. It illuminates hundreds of aquarium lamps over hundreds of very small, sealed aquariums, set in rubber frames and attached to stands that cover all three walls. There are fish in the aquariums. More different kinds and greater numbers than in any tropical-fish shop.

Along one wall is a black-stained table with two large, flat porcelain sinks with an elbow-operated mixing apparatus. On the table there are two gas jets and two Bunsen burners, all with permanent copper pipe connections to a gas cock. An autoclave is mounted on a side table. A Mettler scale. A pH meter. A large bellows camera mounted on a tripod. A bifocal microscope.

Under the table there is a metal rack with small, deep drawers. I open a few of them. In cardboard boxes from Struer's Chemical Laboratory there are pipettes, rubber hoses, plugs, glass slides, and litmus paper. Chemicals in little glass flasks. Powdered magnesium, potassium permanganate, iron filings, powdered sulphur, copper sulphate crystals. Against the wall, in wooden crates lined with straw and corrugated cardboard, are little carboys of acid. Hydrofluoric acid, hydrochloric acid, and acetic acid in various concentrations.

On the opposite table are permanently attached plastic trays, developing baths, and an enlarging apparatus. I don't understand a thing. The room is furnished like a mixture of Denmark's National Aquarium and a chemical laboratory.

The saloon has double doors with panelling. A reminder that the *Kronos* was built for the long-vanished elegance of the fifties, old-fashioned even then. The room lies right below the navigation bridge and is exactly the same size – like a low-ceilinged Danish living room. There are six large windows facing the foredeck. All of them are iced over, and a faint bluish-grey light seeps through the ice.

On the port side unmarked wooden and cardboard boxes are stacked, held in place by a flag rope stretched between two heaters.

A table is bolted down in the middle of the room, and several thermoses are standing in the indentations of the tabletop. Long worktables with Luxo lamps have been put up along two of the walls. A small photocopier has been screwed on to the bulkhead. Next to it is a fax machine. A cupboard overhead is filled with books.

On my way over to the bookshelf I notice the sea chart. It has been placed beneath a sheet of non-reflecting Plexiglas; that's why I didn't notice it before. I turn on the lamp.

The text in the margin has been cut off, so it takes a few minutes for me to identify it. On sea charts, land is a detail, a mere line, a contour drowning in a swarm of numbers indicating depths. Then I recognize the promontory across from Sisimiut. Under the glass plate, at the edge of the map, there are several smaller photocopies of specialized maps: "Mean time lag from moon's transit (upper or lower) at Greenwich until onset of high tide in West Greenland"; "Overview of surface currents west of Greenland"; "Index map of sector divisions in Holsteinsborg region".

At the top, up against the bulkhead, lie three photographs. Two of them are black-and-white aerial shots. The third looks like a fractal detail of the Mandelbrot set, produced by a colour printer. All three photos have the same shape in the centre. A shape approximating a circle, curving around an opening. Like a five-week-old foetus which, fishlike, curls around the gills.

I try the filing cabinets, but they're locked. I'm about to look at the books when a door opens somewhere on the deck. I turn off the light and grow into the deck. A second door is opened and shut, and then there is silence. But the deck doesn't seem asleep any more. Somewhere someone is awake. I don't need to look at my clock. There's still time, but my nerves can't take it.

I have my hand on the exit door when someone comes up the companionway. I retreat backwards into the corridor. A key is put in the lock. There is a pause of surprise that the door isn't locked. I push open the door to the galley, step in, and close it behind me. Footsteps approach down the corridor. Maybe there's something cautious, hesitant about them, maybe someone is wondering why the door wasn't locked, maybe they're going to search the deck. It may be that I'm hearing things. I shove myself up on to the counter and into the dumbwaiter. I pull the doors shut, but they don't close properly from the inside.

The door to the hallway opens and a light is turned on. In the middle of the room, right in front of the slit I haven't been able to close, stands Seidenfaden, wearing his outdoor gear, still windblown from his walk on deck. He goes over to the refrigerator and disappears out of my field of vision. There's a hiss of carbon dioxide, and he comes back into view. He's standing there drinking beer out of a can.

At that moment, while his face has an expression of introspective pleasure and he seems about to cough, he's looking straight at me, but he doesn't see me. Suddenly the dumbwaiter starts to rumble with a loud clatter.

There's no room for me to react. All I can do is pull the cork off the screwdriver and get ready to be discovered in about two seconds.

Then the dumbwaiter descends.

Above me in the dark the doors are pulled aside. But I'm already gone; I'm on my way down.

I pray that it's Jakkelsen who has disobeyed my orders; perhaps he noticed some movement in the shaft and pushed the button to bring me down. I hope that it'll be dark when the doors open. And that Jakkelsen's trembling hands will be there to help me when I crawl out.

I stop, the door is cautiously pulled open. Outside, it's dark.

Something cold and wet is pressed against my thigh. Something is put in my lap. Something is shoved under my knees. Then the door is closed, the dumbwaiter hums, a motor starts up, and I ascend once more.

I shift the screwdriver into my left hand and find the torch with my right. For a moment I'm blinded, then I can see.

Leaning against me, five centimetres from my eyes, looms an upright, cold magnum bottle beaded with moisture: Moët & Chandon 1986 Brut Imperial Rosé. Pink champagne. In my lap there's a champagne glass. Under my knees I can feel the concave bottom of another bottle.

I take it for granted that when the doors open I will find myself bathed in light, face to face with Seidenfaden.

It doesn't turn out that way. I count two bumps and know that I've passed the boat deck. I'm on my way up to the bridge, to the officers' mess.

The dumbwaiter comes to a halt, and then there is silence; nothing happens. I try to open the doors. It's almost impossible because of the bottles.

Somewhere a door is opened and shut. Then a match is struck.

I wriggle the doors open a crack. There's a candle in a candlestick on the big dining-room table where I served dinner a few days ago. Now someone picks up the candle and moves towards me.

The doors slide back. I have a hand against the wall behind me in order to put as much force as I can into the blow. I'm expecting Tørk or Verlaine. I'm thinking of aiming for their eyes.

The light blinds me because it's so close. I can't make out anything except a dark outline, which removes one bottle and then the other. When the glass is removed, a hand fumbles over my hip for a moment.

There is a muffled sound of surprise.

Kützow's face is lowered towards me. We gaze into each other's eyes. Tonight his are bulging, as if he had been afflicted with acute Basedow's disease. But he isn't sick in the ordinary sense. He is enormously drunk.

"Jaspersen!" he says.

Then we both catch sight of the screwdriver. It's pointed at a spot between his eyes.

"Jaspersen," he repeats.

"A minor repair," I say.

It's difficult to talk because my scrunched-up position makes it hard to breathe.

"I'm the one in charge of repairs on board."

His voice is authoritative but slurred. I poke my head out the door. "I see you're also in charge of the wine cellar. Urs and the captain will be interested to hear that."

He blushes, a slow but pervasive change to a colour bordering on purple. "I can explain."

In ten seconds he'll start wondering. I get an arm out.

"I don't have time," I say. "I have to get on with my work."

At that instant the dumbwaiter starts down. At the last second I pull my head and shoulders inside. I manage to feel a burst of fury that there isn't some kind of safety device preventing it from operating when the doors are open.

In my mind I go through the entire discovery, confrontation, and catastrophic ending. By the time I reach the galley, my imagination has been used up.

The dumbwaiter doesn't stop there. It continues its descent.

Then it stops. Those final seconds have drained my last reserves. Now I have only the element of surprise on my side. I wrench open the doors and push them back. They slam into place with a bang. A sack marked 50 KILOS VILDMOSE POTATOES sways towards me. I swing both legs out, put them against it, and push. The sack stops swaying, pitches backward, and flies towards the farthest corner. It lands among the boxes labelled WIUFF'S LAM-MEFJORD CARROTS.

I regain my balance on the deck. My legs feel like rubber. But I have the screwdriver out in front of me.

Urs comes out from behind the sack.

I can't think of anything to say. When I stagger through the door, he's still on his knees.

"Bitte, Fräulein Smilla, bitte . . ."

Subconsciously I must have been expecting some kind of alarm. Armed men in wait for me. But the *Kronos* is wrapped in darkness. I walk up through three decks without meeting anyone.

The companionway from the bridge is empty. Jakkelsen is nowhere to be seen. I brazenly enter the bridge deck, go through the door marked OFFICERS' ACCOMMODATIONS, and open the door to the men's bathroom.

He's standing at the sink. He had been combing his hair. His forehead is pressed against the mirror, as if he wanted to make sure that the result will be really nice. He was in the process of combing back the hair over his ears. But he's asleep. Unconsciously and pliantly his body follows the rolling of the ship, holding itself upright. But he's snoring. His mouth is open and his tongue is hanging out slightly.

I stick my hand into the breast pocket of his work shirt. I take out a rubber tube. He slipped into the bathroom and had a little fix to keep up his courage. Then he tried to spruce himself up. And then he got tired.

I kick his legs out from under him. He falls heavily to the deck. I try to pull him up, but my back hurts. I only manage to lift up his head.

"You overlooked Kützow," I say.

A lascivious little smile appears on his face. "Smilla. I knew you'd come back."

I get him to his feet. Then I push his head into the sink and turn on the cold water. When he can stand up, I pull him over towards the companionway.

We're five steps down when Kützow comes out of the door behind us.

There's no doubt that he thinks he's sneaking around on cat's paws. In reality he manages to stay upright only by hanging on to whatever is at hand. When he catches sight of us, he stops abruptly, puts his hand on the board with the barometer, and stares at me.

I have Jakkelsen's weak-kneed body pressed up against the rail. I'm having difficulty walking myself.

Shock slowly penetrates his drunkenness, which now must be further enhanced by one or two pearly magnums.

"Jaspersen," he croaks. "Jaspersen . . ."

I feel so tired of men and their abuse. It's been this way ever since I came to Denmark. You always have to watch out not to trip over people who have poisoned themselves but think they're carrying it off with dignity.

"Piss off, Mr Engineer," I say.

He stares at me blankly.

We don't meet anyone else on our way below. I shove Jakkelsen into his cabin. He falls onto his bunk like a rag doll. I turn him on his side. Infants, alcoholics, and drug addicts all risk suffocating on their own vomit. Then I lock his door from the outside with his own key.

I lock and barricade my door. It's four fifteen a.m. I'm going to sleep for three hours and then report sick and sleep twelve more. Everything else will have to wait.

I manage to sleep for forty-five minutes. Then an electronic buzzer penetrates through the first nightmares, on the edge of sleep, followed by Lukas's command.

I'm working less than two metres away from Verlaine. He's using a hard rubber club as long as a woodman's axe.

I can tell from my chapped lips that it's just below − 10 °C. He's working in his shirtsleeves. With one hand he hangs on to the sea rail or the fencing around the radar scanners. With the other he raises the club in a graceful, gentle arc behind his back and then brings it down on the deckhouse roof with an explosion like a car windscreen being smashed. His face is covered with sweat, but his movements are easy and tireless. Each blow breaks off a plate of ice about a metre square.

There's no wind but a choppy sea in which the *Kronos* is pitching heavily. And there is fog, like big moist planes of whiteness in the dark.

Every time we emerge from one of the fog banks, which hang so

309

low that they give the impression of floating on the water, the layer of ice grows visibly thicker. I'm scraping the ice off the scanners with the handle of an ice pick. When I'm done with one of them I might as well go back to the one I just did. In less than two minutes a millimetre-thick layer of hard grey ice has covered it again.

The deck and the superstructure are alive. Not with the small, dark figures hammering at the ice, but with the ice itself. All the deck lights are on. Together, the ice and the light have created a mythological landscape. The riggings and mast stays are coated with thirty centimetres of ice festoons drooping from the masts to the deck like watchful faces. An anchor lantern on its mount shines through its shroud of ice, like the glowing brain inside the head of some fabulous beast. The deck is a grey, solidified sea. Everything upright looms in the air with inquisitive faces and cold grey limbs.

Verlaine is on the starboard side. Behind me is the sea rail, and beyond that a free fall of almost twenty metres to the deck below. In front of me, behind the radar pedestals and the low mast with the antennas, siren, and a mobile spotlight for harbour manoeuvres, Sonne is shovelling ice. The sheets of ice that Verlaine chops loose he tosses over the rail, where they fall on to the boat deck next to the lifeboat. From there Hansen, wearing a yellow hard hat, sends them on over the side of the ship.

On the port side Jakkelsen is chopping the ice free from the radar pedestals with a hammer. He's working his way towards me. At one point the scanners hide us from the rest of the roof.

He sticks the hammer in his jacket pocket. Then he leans back against the radar. He takes out a cigarette.

"As you predicted," I say. "The bad ice."

His face is white with exhaustion.

"No," he says. "That doesn't start until 5–6 Beaufort, at just about the freezing point. He's called us out on deck too soon."

He looks around. There's no one anywhere near.

"When I started sailing, you know, it was the captain who sailed the ship, and time was measured by the calendar. If you were on your way into an icy situation, you decreased your speed. Or you changed your route. Or turned and sailed with the wind. But in the last few years things have changed. Now it's the shipping companies that decide, now it's the offices in the big cities that are sailing the ships. And *this* is what you measure time by."

He points at his wristwatch. "But we're obviously supposed to get somewhere by a certain time. So they've given him orders to keep going. And that's what he's doing. He's losing his touch. Since we had to go through this, anyway, there was no reason to call us on deck right now. A smaller ship can withstand ice up to ten per cent of its displacement. We could sail with five hundred tons of ice and it wouldn't make much difference. He could have sent a couple of the boys up to chop the antennas free."

I scrape ice away from the directional antenna. When I'm working, I'm awake. As soon as I stop, I have brief lapses of sleep.

"He's afraid we won't be able to maintain cruising speed. Afraid we're going to blow something. Or that it'll suddenly get worse. It's his nerves. They're almost shot."

He drops his cigarette, half smoked, on to the ice. A new fog bank envelops us. The moisture seems to stick to the ice that has already formed. For a moment Jakkelsen is almost hidden.

I work my way around the radar. I make sure that I stay in both Jakkelsen's and Sonne's fields of vision at all times.

Verlaine is right next to me. His blows fall so close to me that they punch frozen air towards my face. They land at the foot of the metal pedestal with the precision of a surgical incision, tearing away a transparent plate of ice. He kicks it over to Sonne.

His face is next to mine.

"Why?" he asks.

I hold the ice pick slightly behind me. Only a short distance away, out of earshot, Sonne clears off the base of the mast with the handle of his shovel.

"I know why," he says. "Because Lukas wouldn't have believed it, anyway."

"I could have pointed to Maurice's wound," I say.

"A work accident. The angle grinder started going while he was changing the wheel. The chuck key struck him in the shoulder. It's been reported and explained."

"An accident. Just like the boy on the roof," I say.

His face is close to mine. Its only expression is one of incomprehension. He has no idea what I'm talking about.

"But with Andreas Licht," I say, "the old man on the ship, that's where things got a little more clumsy."

When his body stiffens, it gives the illusion that he's frozen, like the ship around us.

"I saw you on the dock," I lie. "When I swam in."

While he ponders the consequences of what I've said, he gives himself away. For one second a sick animal stares at me from somewhere inside his body. Like his teeth, a thin shell covers the torture that turned into sadism.

"There will be an investigation in Nuuk," I say. "Police and naval authorities. Attempted murder alone could get you two years. Now they'll look into Licht's death, too."

He grins at me, a big white-toothed smile.

"We're not putting in at Godthåb. We're going to the tankers' floating dock. It's twenty sea miles from land. You can't even see the coast."

He gives me a quizzical look.

"You put up a good fight," he says. "It's almost too bad that you're so alone."

THE SEA

2

"I'M THINKING," SAYS LUKAS, "about the little captain on the bridge up there. He no longer sails a ship. He no longer exercises any authority. He's just a gear-box that transfers impulses to a complex machine."

Lukas is leaning against the rail of the bridge wing. In front of the bow of the *Kronos* a skyscraper of red polyenamel blossoms up out of the sea. It looms over the foredeck and well beyond the tops of the masts. If you tip your head way back you can see that somewhere high in the grey sky even this phenomenon comes to an end. It's not a building; it's the stern of a supertanker.

When I was a child in Qaanaaq in the late fifties and early sixties, even the European clock time moved relatively slowly. Changes occurred at a rate that allowed a protest to rise against them. This rebellion first took form in the concept of the "good old days".

Nostalgia for the past was then a completely new feeling in Thule. Sentimentality will at any time be man's first revolt against development.

The times have made this reaction obsolete. Now a different kind of protest is needed than tearful homesickness. Things are happening so rapidly now that any moment the present we're living in will be the "good old days".

"For those ships," says Lukas, "the rest of the world doesn't exist any more. If you meet them on the open sea and try to raise them on the VHF to exchange weather reports and positions, or to ask about the ice conditions, they won't answer. They don't even have their radio on. When you displace 250,000 cubic metres of water and produce horsepower like a nuclear reactor and have a computer as big as an old-fashioned ship's chest to calculate your course and speed and maintain them or diverge from them slightly if necessary, then your surroundings cease to interest you. The only thing then left in the world is your departure point and your destination and who's paying you when you reach it."

Lukas has lost weight. He has started smoking.

He might be right anyway. One of the syndromes of development in Greenland is that everything seems to have happened recently. The Danish Navy's new heavily armed, high-speed inspection ships have recently been introduced. The vote to join the Common Market and the narrow majority to withdraw as of 1 January 1985. Renegotiations in November 1992 and rejoining in May 1993 (the greatest foreign policy flip-flop of all time) are all recent events. Not long ago the Defence Ministry restricted entry permits to Qaanaaq on military grounds. And at the spot where we're now standing – the large floating oil platform, the *Greenland Star*, outside of Nuuk, 25,000 linked metal pontoons anchored to the sea floor 700 metres below us, half a square kilometre of desolate, windblown, green-painted metal, ugly as sin, twenty sea miles from the coast – everything has just been built. "Dynamic" is the word the politicians use.

It has all been created with the goal of coercion in mind.

Not the coercion of Greenlanders. The presence of the army and the direct violence of civilization are almost at an end in the Arctic. Development has no need of it any longer. These days the liberal appeal to greed in all its aspects is sufficient.

Technological culture has not destroyed the peoples of the Arctic Ocean. Believing that would be to think too highly of culture. It has simply acted as a catalyst, a cosmic model for the potential – which lies in every culture and every human being – to centre life around that particularly Western mixture of greed and naïveté.

What they want to coerce is the Other, the vastness, that which surrounds human beings. It is the sea, the earth, the ice. The complex stretched out in front of us is an attempt to do just that.

Lukas's face is haggard with distaste.

"Previously, up until 1992, there was only Polar Oil at Færinge-havn. A small place. On one side of the fjord a communications station and a fish cannery. On the other the plant. Managed by the Greenland Trading Company. We could dock stern-fast, up to 50,000 tons. When we had the floating hoses laid out we would go ashore. There was only one building for living quarters, a galley, and a pumphouse. It smelled of diesel. Five men ran the whole place. We always had a gin and tonic with the manager in the galley."

316

This sentimental side of him is new to me.

"That must have been nice," I say. "Did they have clogging and concertinas, too?"

His eyes grow narrow.

"You're wrong," he says. "I'm talking about power. And about freedom. In those days the captain was the highest authority. We went ashore, and we took the crew along with us, except for the anchor watch. There was nothing at Færingehavn. It was just a desolate, godforsaken place between Godthåb and Frederikshåb. But in that nothingness, you could go for a walk if you wanted to."

He gestures towards the system of pontoons in front of us, and towards the distant aluminium barracks.

"Here they have three duty-free shops and a regular helicopter service to the mainland. Here there's a hotel and a diving station. A post office. Administrative offices for Chevron, Gulf, Shell, and Esso. In two hours they can put together a landing strip that can handle a small jet. The gross tonnage of that ship in front of us is 125,000 tons. Here there is development and progress. But no one is allowed ashore, Jaspersen. They come on board if you want anything. They tick off your requests on a list, and they bring a portable chute and load your order on board. If the captain insists on going ashore, a couple of security officers turn up with a gallery and hold your hand until you are back on board. They say it's because of the danger of fire. Because of the risk of sabotage. They say that when the piers are full, there are a billion litres of oil here."

He searches for a new cigarette, but the pack is empty.

"That's the nature of centralization. Under these conditions the shipmasters have virtually disappeared. Seamen don't exist at all."

I'm waiting. He wants something from me.

"Were you hoping to go ashore?" he asks.

I shake my head.

"Even if this was your only chance? If this was the end of the line? If we only had the return trip left?"

He wants to find out how much I know.

"We're not taking on any cargo," I say. "We're not unloading anything. This is nothing but a rest stop. We're waiting for something or other."

"You're guessing."

"No," I say, "I know where we're going."

His body is still relaxed. But now he's on guard. "Tell me."

"If I do, you have to tell me why we're docked here."

His complexion is not robust. It's very pale and chapped in the relatively dry air. He wets his lips. He's been counting on me as a form of insurance. Now he's confronted with a new, risky contract. It demands a trust in me that he doesn't feel.

Without a word he walks past me. I follow him inside the bridge. I shut the door behind us. He goes over to the slightly raised navigational table.

"Show me," he says.

It's a 1:1,000,000 chart of Davis Strait. To the west it just catches the outermost point of Cumberland Peninsula. To the northwest it includes the coast along Great Halibut Banks.

On the table, next to the chart, is the Ice Centre's map of ice formations.

"The field ice," I say, "has this winter, since November, been a hundred sea miles out and no further north than Nuuk," I say. "The ice forced further north by the West Greenland current has moved out to sea and melted because Davis Strait has had three mild winters and is relatively warmer than normal. The current, now free of ice, continues up along the coast. Disko Bay has the world's highest concentration of icebergs per square unit. During the last two winters the glacier at Jakobshavn has moved forty metres a day. That produces the largest icebergs outside of Antarctica."

I point to the map of ice formations.

"This winter the icebergs have been forced out of the bay as early as October and directed out along the coast with a ridge of turbulence between the West Greenland current and the Baffin current. Even in sheltered water there are icebergs. When we leave here, Tørk will set a northwesterly course until we're free of this belt."

His face is expressionless. But his concentration is the one that I saw at the roulette table.

"Since December the Baffin current has carried western ice down to the 67th parallel. It has frozen together with the new ice somewhere between two hundred and four hundred sea miles out in Davis Strait. Tørk wants us somewhere in the vicinity of that edge. From there we'll be given a course due north."

"You've sailed here before, Jaspersen?"

"I have hydrophobia. But I know something about ice."

He bends over the map. "No one has ever sailed further north than Holsteinsborg this time of year. Not even in sheltered waters. The current has packed field ice and western ice into a floor of cement. We might be able to sail north for two days. What does he want us to do at the edge of the ice?"

I straighten up. "You can't play without chips, Captain."

For a moment I think that I've lost him. Then he nods.

"It's as you said," he replies slowly. "We're waiting here. That's what they've told me. We're waiting for a fourth passenger."

Five hours earlier the *Kronos* shifts course. Outside the mess a dull sun hangs low in the sky; by its position I can tell for certain, but I had already sensed the change.

In the dining halls of the boarding schools, students seemed to take root in their chairs. In any unstable situation, the few fixed points take on special meaning. In the mess of the *Kronos*, we sit glued to our chairs. At the other table Jakkelsen is eating, introspective and wan, his head bowed over his plate. Fernanda and Maria try to avoid looking at me.

Maurice is eating with his back to me. He's only using his right hand. His left hand is in a sling that partially covers a thick bandage on his shoulder. He's wearing a work shirt with one sleeve cut off to make room for the bandage.

My mouth is dry with a fear that won't let up as long as I'm on board this ship.

On my way out the door, Jakkelsen comes up behind me. "We've changed course! We're on our way to Godthåb."

I decide to clean the officers' mess. If Verlaine follows me, he'll have to pass the bridge. If we're on our way to Nuuk, he'll have to come. They can't permit me to go ashore in a large port.

I stay in the mess for four hours. I clean the windows and polish the brass trim and finally rub the wooden panelling with teak oil.

At one point Kützow comes by. When he sees me, he hurries off. Sonne appears. He stands there for a while, rocking back and forth on the balls of his feet. I'm wearing a short blue dress. Maybe he takes that as an invitation to stay. He has misread me. I've put on the dress so I'll be able to run as fast as possible. When he gets no encouragement, he leaves. He's too young to make a move, and not old enough to have become pushy.

At four o'clock we drop anchor behind the red wall. Half an hour later I'm summoned to the bridge.

*   *   *

"At this time of year," says Lukas, "there's only one chance to get further north. Unless you have an icebreaker along. And even then the odds are against you. What you have to do is go further out to sea. Otherwise you'll get caught in a bay, and suddenly the ice will have closed around you, and there you'll sit."

I could lie to him. But he's just about the only straw I have left to cling to. He's a man on his way down. Maybe sometime in the near future he'll end up down there where our paths could cross.

"At 54° west longitude," I say, "the ocean floor drops off. That's where a branch of the western current turns away from the coast. There it meets the relatively colder northern current. There, west of the great fishing banks, comes an area of unstable weather."

" 'The Sea of Fog'. Never been there."

"A place where the largest chunks of ice from the east coast are carried and from where they can't escape. A parallel to the Iceberg Cemetery north of Upernavik."

With the corner of the ruler I find a dark area on the ice map. "Too small to be clearly marked. It often — maybe now as well — takes the form of a long bay, like a fjord in the pack ice. Risky but navigable. If the journey is important enough. Even the small Danish inspection cutters occasionally went in there, chasing British or Icelandic trawlers."

"Why sail a 4,000-ton coaster with a couple of dozen men up towards Baffin Bay to enter a dangerous opening in the pack ice?"

I close my eyes and call up an image of a magnified plant embryo, a little shape curved around its own centre. The same images that were superimposed on the sea chart on the boat deck.

"Because there's an island. The only island that far from the coast before Ellesmere Island."

Under my ruler it's a dot so small that it's almost invisible.

"Isla Gela Alta. Discovered by Portuguese whalers during the last century."

"I've heard of it," he says thoughtfully. "A bird reserve. The weather is too bad even for the birds. It's forbidden to go ashore. Impossible to drop anchor. No reason in the world to go there."

"I'll still bet that's where we're headed."

"I'm not sure," he says, "that you're in a position to make bets."

*　　*　　*

320

While I'm still on my way down from the bridge I think that the world may have lost a nice person in Sigmund Lukas. It's a phenomenon that I've often observed without understanding it. Inside someone another person can exist, a sterling, generous, and trustworthy individual who never comes to light except in glimpses, because he is encased in a corrupt, dyed-in-the-wool, recividist.

Out on deck, dusk has fallen. Somewhere in the dark a cigarette is glowing.

Jakkelsen is leaning against the rail. "This is incredible, fucking incredible!"

The complex below us is lit up by lights on poles lining both sides of the piers. Even now, bathed in this yellow light, painted grass green, with lights on in the distant buildings, and little electric cars and white traffic markings, *Greenland Star* looks like some thousands of square metres of steel plunked down in the Atlantic Ocean.

To me it seems so obviously a mistake. To Jakkelsen it's a magnificent union of the sea and high technology.

"Yes," I say, "and the best part about it is that the whole thing can be taken apart and packed up in twelve hours."

"With this place they've won out over the sea, man. Now it doesn't matter how, or what the weather's like. They can put down a harbour anywhere. In the middle of the ocean."

I'm no teacher or Boy Scout leader. I'm not interested in setting him straight.

"Why do they need to be able to take it apart, Smilla?"

Maybe it's nervousness that makes me answer him, after all. "They built it when they started bringing oil up from the sea floor off North Greenland. It took ten years from the time they discovered oil until they could extract it. Their problem was the ice. First they built a prototype of what was supposed to be the world's largest and most solid oil rig, the *Joint Venture Warrior*, a product of glasnost and Home Rule, a cooperative venture between the United States, the Soviet Union, and A. P. Møller Shipping Inc. You've sailed past oil rigs. You know how big they are. You see them fifty sea miles away, and they get bigger and bigger, like a universe floating on posts. They've got bars and restaurants and offices and workshops and cinemas and theatres and fire stations, the whole thing mounted twelve metres above the surface of the ocean so even the worst storm waves will pass underneath it. Just think of one of them. The *Joint Venture Warrior* was meant to be four times as big. The prototype was eighteen metres above the water surface. It was intended to provide jobs for fourteen hundred people. They erected the prototype in Baffin Bay. When it was standing there, finished, an iceberg came along. This had been foreseen. But this iceberg was a little bigger than usual. It was calved somewhere on the edge of the Arctic Ocean. It was a hundred metres tall and flat on top, the way icebergs are when they're that high. It had four hundred metres of ice below the surface, and it weighed about twenty million tons. When they saw it coming, they did get just a little nervous. But they had two big icebreakers on hand. They fastened them to the iceberg so that they could pull it on to a different course. There was very little current and no wind. Still, nothing really happened when they revved up the engines. Except that the iceberg continued straight ahead. It did not seem to notice anything was tugging at it. And it walked right over the prototype, and behind it, in the water, there were no traces of the proud model for the *Joint Venture Warrior* except for some patches of oil and pieces of debris. Since then, they've made all Arctic Ocean equipment so that it can be dismantled in twelve hours. That's how much warning the Ice Centre can give them. They drill from floating platforms that can scarper. This magnificent harbour is nothing more than a tin tray. If the ice came by, it would carry it off as though it had never been here. They only put it up during mild winters when the field ice doesn't reach this far north or the pack ice this far south. They haven't beaten the ice, Jakkelsen. The battle hasn't even begun."

He puts out his cigarette. He has his back to me. I don't know whether he's disappointed or indifferent.

"How do you know, Smilla?"

When they were still deliberating whether to put the *Joint Venture Warrior* on the ice, I was working for six months at the American Coldwater laboratory on Pylot Island, setting up models for measuring the elasticity of sea ice. We were an enthusiastic team of five. We knew each other from the first two ICC conferences. When we had parties and got drunk, we would make speeches about the fact that this was the first time five glaciologists of Inuit origin were gathered in one place. We told each other that we represented at this time the highest concentration of expertise anywhere in the world.

We gleaned our most important data from washing-up bowls. We would pour salt water into the bowls, put them in a laboratory freezer, and freeze the water to ice of a standard thickness. These sheets we would take outside, lay them over the gap between two tables, load them with weights, and measure how much they sagged before they broke. We made little electric motors vibrate the weights and proved that the vibrations from the drills wouldn't affect the structure or elasticity of the ice. We were full of pride and scientific pioneer enthusiasm. It wasn't until we were writing the final report, in which we advised A. P. Møller, Shell, and Gospetrol to commence exploiting the Greenland oil reserves from platforms built on the ice, that we realized what we were doing. By then it was too late. A Soviet company had designed the *Joint Venture Warrior* and won the concession. All five of us were fired. Five months later the prototype was pulverized. Since then they haven't tried anything more stable than floating platforms.

I could tell Jakkelsen all this. But I don't.

"Tonight I'm going to fix everything for us," he says.

"That will be wonderful."

"You don't believe me, man, but just wait and see. The whole thing is crystal clear to me. They've never been able to fool me. I know this ship. I've got it all worked out."

When he steps into the light from the bridge, I see that he's not wearing any overclothes. He's been standing here when it's −10 °C, making conversation with me as if we were indoors.

"Get your beauty sleep tonight, Smilla, and tomorrow everything will be different."

"The prison kitchen provided *einzigartige* opportunities for making sourdough."

Urs is leaning over a rectangular shape wrapped in a white dish towel.

"*Die vielen Faktoren*. The sourdough starter, the yeast, and finally the bread dough. How long should it rise, and at what temperature? *Welche Mehlsorten*? Oven temperature?"

He unwraps the bread. It has a dark-brown, shiny, glazed crust broken in places by whole grains of wheat. An overwhelming aroma of grain, flour, and pungent freshness. Under different circumstances I might have enjoyed it. But something else is interesting me. A time factor. Every event on a ship has its first portent in the galley.

"You are baking now, Urs? It's *ungewöhnlich*."

"The problem is the balance between the *Säuerlichkeit* and the rising power."

Since we lost contact, since he discovered me in the dumbwaiter, I've thought there was something rather doughlike about him. Something elastic, unspoiled, simple, and yet sophisticated. And at the same time much, much too soft.

"Are you serving an extra meal?"

He tries to ignore me.

"You'll end up in the slammer," I say. "Right back *ins Gefängnis*. Here in Greenland. No chance of a kitchen job. *Keine Strafermässigung*. They don't make much of a fuss about meals here. When we meet up again, in three or four years, we'll see whether you've hung on to your good humour. Even if you've lost thirty kilos."

He slumps like a deflated soufflé. He has no way of knowing that there aren't any prisons in Greenland.

"*Um elf Uhr. Für eine Person.*"

"Urs," I say, "what were you sentenced for?"

He gives me a stony look.

"It only takes one call," I say. "To Interpol."

He doesn't reply.

"I called them before we sailed," I tell him. "When I saw the crew list. It was heroin."

Beads of sweat form on the narrow edge between his moustache and his upper lip.

"It wasn't from Morocco. Where was it from?"

"Why do I always have to be tormented?"

"Where was it from?"

"The airport in Geneva. The lake is so close. I was in the military. We unloaded the crates along with the food supplies, via the river."

When he starts to talk, for the first time in my life I understand a little about the art of interrogation. Fear alone isn't what makes him talk. It's just as much a longing for contact, the burden of a guilty conscience, and the loneliness of the sea.

"Crates full of antiques?"

He nods. "From the Far East. On the plane from Kyoto."

"Who brought them out? Who was the shipping agent?"

"You must know that."

I don't reply. I know what he's going to say before he says it.

"*Der Verlaine, natürlich.*"

So that's how they've manned the *Kronos*. With people so

compromised that they had no choice. Not until now, after all this time, do I see the ship's mess for what it really is: a microcosm, an image of the network that Tørk and Claussen created earlier. Just as Loyen and Ving used the Cryolite Corporation, they have also made use of an organization that already existed. Fernanda and Maria from Thailand. Maurice, Hansen, and Urs from Europe. All part of the same organism.

"*Ich hatte keine Wahl. Ich war zahlungsunfähig.*"

His fear no longer seems exaggerated.

I'm on my way out, but he follows me.

"*Fräulein Smilla*, sometimes I think you're bluffing. That maybe you're not from the police, after all."

Even half a metre away, I can feel the heat from the bread. It must have just come out of the oven.

"And if that's the case, *wäre es kein besonderes Risiko*, if one day I served you a portion of trifle, shall we say . . . full of glass shards and bits of barbed wire."

He's holding the bread in his hand. It must be more than 200 °C. It may be that he's not so soft, after all. If he was exposed to high temperatures, he'd develop a crust as hard as glass.

A breakdown doesn't necessarily have to be a collapse; it can also take the form of a quiet slide into resignation.

That's the way it happens to me. On my way out of the galley, I decide to escape from the *Kronos*.

Back in my cabin I put on underwear made of new wool. On top of that my blue work clothes, blue rubber boots, blue sweater, and a thin navy-blue down jacket. In the dark it will be almost black, and it's the least conspicuous thing I can find at the moment. I don't pack a suitcase. I roll up my money, toothbrush, an extra pair of knickers, and a little bottle of almond oil in a plastic bag. I don't believe I will get away with anything more.

I tell myself that it's the loneliness that's getting to me. I grew up in a community. If I've desired and sought out brief periods of solitude and introspection, it has always been in order to return to the social group as a stronger person.

But I haven't been able to find that group. I seem to have lost it, sometime during that autumn when Moritz first brought me out of Greenland by plane. I'm still searching; I haven't given up. But I don't seem to be making any progress.

Now life on this ship has turned into a travesty of my existence in the modern world.

I'm no heroine. I have felt something for a child. I could have put my tenacity at their disposal, if anyone had wanted to understand his death. But there wasn't anyone. No one but me.

I go up on deck. At every corner, I expect to meet Verlaine. I meet no one. The deck seems deserted. I go over to the rail. The *Greenland Star* looks different to when I stood here some hours ago. Then I was still numb from the preceding days. Now it represents my way out, my escape route.

At least two of the piers are 800 metres long. They're strangely motionless in the long swells rolling in from the dark. Up near the buildings I can see small, illuminated electric cars and forklifts.

The gangway of the *Kronos* is down. Big signs on the dock say: ACCESS TO PIER STRICTLY FORBIDDEN.

At the bottom of the gangway I'll have to walk across six or seven hundred metres of pontoon dock bathed in light. There probably isn't any guard. The lights are out in the control towers, from which they monitor the pumping of the oil. But it's likely that they have the area under surveillance and that they'll see me and pick me up.

That's what I'm counting on. They may be obliged to return me to the ship, but first they'll take me somewhere to an officer and a desk and a chair. Then I'll tell them about the *Kronos*. Nothing bordering on the truth that I know. They wouldn't believe me. But something less. Something about Jakkelsen's drugs, and that I feel threatened by the rest of the crew and want to leave the ship.

They'll have to listen. Technically and legally, desertion no longer exists. A sailor and a cabin stewardess can go ashore any time they like.

I go down to the second deck. From there the gangway is visible. Where it joins the deck there's an alcove. That's where Jakkelsen once waited for me.

Now someone else is waiting. Hansen has propped his rubber boots up on the low steel box.

I could reach the bottom of the gangway before he was even out of his chair. I'd be the certain winner in a 150-metre sprint down the dock. But then I would run out of steam and collapse.

I retreat to the deck to reconsider my options. I've come to the conclusion that there aren't any, when suddenly the lights go out.

I had just closed my eyes, trying to find an answer in the sounds.

The rolling of the waves along the dock, the hollow sound of the water slapping against the fenders. The gulls screeching in the darkness, the wind howling low against the control towers. The sigh of the links of the pontoons rubbing against each other. A distant, faint hiss from great turbine generators. And more disheartening than all these sounds put together: the feeling that all noise is being sucked out into the emptiness above the vast Atlantic Ocean. That the entire complex, along with the docked ships, is a vulnerable miscalculation that will be swept away at any moment.

These sounds have no advice to give me. In a place like this, the only way to leave a ship is by means of the gangway. I'm a captive on the *Kronos*.

That's when the lights go out. When I open my eyes, they seem blinded by the darkness at first. Then a series of red lights materialize, approximately a hundred metres apart, on the dock. Emergency lights.

The lights have been turned off on the pier where the *Kronos* is moored and on the ship itself. The night is so dark that even things close at hand seem to vanish. The distant part of the platform lies like a yellowish-white island in the night.

I can see the dock. I can also see a figure down there. Heading away from the *Kronos*. The mixture of fear and hope and life-long habit stops me from hitting my head on the mast or a capstan. At the bottom of the companionway I pause for a moment. There's no one around. But even if there was, I wouldn't be able to see him. Then I take off, running.

Off the ship and down the gangway. I see no one, and no one calls after me. I turn and run along the pier. The pontoons seem alive and unsteady beneath my feet. Down here the emergency lights seem painfully bright. I keep to the side away from the lamps and increase my speed every time I approach a patch of light, catching my breath when I'm back in the dark. Only six days have passed since I watched Lander sail off into the fog, on his way back to Skovshoved, and in every sense of the word, I'm still at sea. But I share some of the joy a sailor must feel when he sets foot on land again after a long voyage.

A figure appears in front of me, moving with the faltering, swaying gait of a drunkard.

It has started to rain. The dock is marked off for traffic, like a boulevard, which is lined with the windowless sides of ships, rising up like skyscrapers forty-five metres high. In the distance the aluminium of the barracks glistens. Everything vibrates dully from big, invisible engines. The *Greenland Star* is a deserted town on the edge of the empty heavens.

The only living thing is the wobbly figure in front of me. It's Jakkelsen. The silhouette against the lamp is indisputably Jakkelsen. Far ahead of him there's someone else heading off somewhere. That's why Jakkelsen is wavering. Like me, he's trying to avoid the light. He's trying to keep himself invisible to the person he's following.

There doesn't seem to be anyone following me, so I fall back, not wanting to gain on the two in front of me, but still moving forward.

I make a turn at the last skyscraper. Before me lies a vast open area. A piazza in the middle of the ocean. In the dimness, the only light comes from a single fluorescent lamp way up high.

In the centre of the piazza, inside a series of concentric circles, slouches the outline of a large dead animal. A Sikorsky helicopter with four slightly bowed, drooping blades. Near one of the barracks someone has left a little pump wagon for extinguishing fires and an electric bus. Jakkelsen has vanished. It's the most desolate place I've ever seen.

As a child I sometimes dreamed that everybody was dead and had left me behind with the euphoric freedom of choice in an abandoned adult world. I've always thought of it as a pleasant dream. At this moment, on this piazza, I realize that it has always been a nightmare.

I walk forward towards the helicopter, and then on past it, into the faint light tinted dark-green by the non-skid surface of the pontoons. The entire place is so deserted that I cannot even be afraid of being discovered.

At the point where the platform seems to meet the water there are three barracks and an open shed. Jakkelsen is sitting in the shadow, just outside the light. For a moment I feel uneasy. Just minutes ago he was moving as fast as a monkey; now he's all hunched up. But when I put my hand on his forehead, I feel the heat and sweat from his run. When I try to shake some life into him, there's the clink of metal. I fish around in his breast pocket and pull out his syringe. I remember the expression on his face when he assured me that he could take care of himself. I try to pull him to his feet, but he's too limp. What he needs is two strong orderlies and a hospital trolley. I take off my jacket and put it over him, pulling it up over his forehead so that it won't rain on his face. I slip the syringe back in his pocket. You have to be younger or at least more idealistic than I am to try to pretty up people who are determined to kill themselves.

As I straighten up, a shadow glides away from the open shed and takes on a life of its own. It's not heading towards me; it's on its way across the piazza.

It's a person carrying a small suitcase and wearing a flapping overcoat. But it's not the suitcase that's small. It's the person that is big. From this distance I can't see very well, but I don't need to, either. It doesn't take much to trigger the recognition. It's the mechanic.

Maybe I knew it all along. Knew that he was the fourth passenger.

When I recognize him, I realize that I'll have to return to the *Kronos*.

Not because it suddenly doesn't matter whether I live or die, but because the problem has been taken out of my hands. It no longer has to do with Isaiah alone. Or with me. Or with the mechanic. Or even with what there is between us. It's something much bigger. Perhaps it's love.

When I walk back along the dock, the lights have come on again. There's no use trying to hide.

The tower in front of the *Kronos* is manned. The figure behind the glass looks like an insect. Close up you realize this is because of his hard hat with two short antennae attached.

Two hoses have been connected up. The *Kronos* is taking on fuel.

Hansen is sitting at the top of the gangway. When he sees me, he stiffens. He had been sitting there because of me. But he was expecting me to come from the other direction. He's not prepared for this situation. He slowly shifts gears; he's no improviser. He starts by blocking my way, trying to evaluate the risk of attempting an attack. I fumble for the screwdriver and put my hand into my plastic bag. On the companionway behind him Lukas comes into view. I stretch out my clenched fist towards Hansen.

"From Verlaine," I say.

His hand closes around what I give him. With the instinctive obedience prompted by the bosun's name. Then Lukas is standing right behind him. He surveys the situation with a single glance. His eyes narrow.

"You're wet, Jaspersen."

He stands in my path up the companionway.

"I had to run an errand," I say. "For Hansen."

Hansen tries to find words to protest. He opens his hand, looking for a possible answer there. On his broad palm there's a crumpled ball. It unfolds as we watch. It's a pair of knickers – tiny, with lace, pure white.

"They didn't have a bigger size," I say. "But I'm sure you can get them on, Hansen. They seem rather elastic."

I walk past Lukas. He doesn't try to stop me. All of his attention is directed at Hansen. His face is full of amazement. Having a hard time of it is Lukas. Nothing but unanswered questions all around him.

As I head up the companionway I hear him give up on this puzzle, too.

"First the baggage," he says. "Then the sternmost capstan. We sail in fifteen minutes."

His voice sounds hoarse, astonished, annoyed, and harried.

I take off my wet work clothes and sit down on my bunk. I think about Jakkelsen.

Through the hull I can tell that the oil pumps have stopped. The hoses have been rolled up, the hawsers taken in. The deck is being made ready for sailing.

Somewhere outside in the dark, about 800 metres from here, Jakkelsen is sitting. I'm the only one who knows that he's left the ship. The question is whether I should report his absence.

The gangway is raised. On deck the posts at the mooring lines are manned.

I stay on my bunk. Because Jakkelsen may have been on to something. There was something about his voice on the deck, something about his self-confidence and conviction that I keep going back to. If it's true that he's discovered something, there must be a reason why he wanted to go ashore. He must have thought that whatever had to be done, had to be done from there. So maybe he can still help me. Even though I have no idea how or why. Or by what means.

There is no blast of the siren. The *Kronos* leaves the *Greenland*

Star as unobtrusively as it arrived. I didn't even notice the engine increasing power. It's a change in the movements of the hull that tells me we are sailing.

Our cruising speed is eighteen knots. Four hundred to four fifty sea miles every twenty-four hours. This means that it will take about twelve hours for us to reach our destination. If I'm right. If we're on our way to the Barren Glacier on Gela Alta.

Something heavy is being dragged down the passageway. When the door to the quarterdeck closes, I go out into the passageway. Through the window in the door I can see Verlaine and Hansen moving the mechanic's baggage aft. Black cases, the kind that musicians keep their instruments in, placed on dollies. He must have had excess baggage on the flight over. It must have been expensive. I wonder who paid for it.

$$\boxed{2}$$

IF YOU REACH THE AGE of thirty-seven in a country like Denmark, and have regular intervals free of pharmaceuticals, haven't committed suicide, and haven't completely sold out the tender ideals of your childhood, then you've learned a little about facing adversity in life.

With instruments sent up in meteorological balloons we measured supercooled drops of water in Thule in the seventies. They live for a short time in very high clouds. The area surrounding them is cold but completely still. In a pocket of motionlessness their temperature will drop to -40 °C. They ought to freeze, but they don't; they remain stationary and stable and fluid.

That's the way I try to face adversity.

The *Kronos* hasn't yet settled down. There's a sense of invisible life and movement. But I can't wait any longer.

I could have gone through the engine room and across the between decks, if those places hadn't been associated with so many claustrophobic memories for me. At least I want to be able to see them when they come.

The quarterdeck is bathed in light. I take a deep breath and walk across the stage. Out of the corner of my eye I see the warping lines go by, and the railing around the base of the mast. Then I reach the aft superstructure and unlock the door. Inside, I stand at the window and look out at the deck.

This is Verlaine's domain. Even now, when there's not a soul in sight, his presence is palpable.

I lock the door behind me. My weapons have always been the small details that no one knows about. My identity, my intentions, Jakkelsen's passkey. They can't know that I have it. They must think it was an accident, an oversight on their part, that I got into the quarterdeck last time. They have been afraid that I was on to something. But about the key they can't know anything.

In the first room I let the beam of my torch play over tightly packed and battened down cans of red lead, primer paint, ship's lacquer, joint filler, special thinner, crates of face masks, epoxy tar, paintbrushes, and rollers. Everything is stacked up and clean and orderly. Verlaine's meticulousness.

The second door is the back entrance to a lavatory – the one opposite the double shower room. The next leads to the metal shop, where Hansen burnishes his knives with Viennese chalk.

The last room is the electrical workshop. You could hide a small elephant in the labyrinth of cupboards, shelves, and crates, and it would take me an hour to find it. I don't have an hour. So I close the door and head below.

The door to the between decks is locked now. And bolted shut. Someone has wanted to make sure that no one will get in this way. I switch on my light only for brief moments. I'm probably being overly cautious, since I'm in a windowless darkness, but my nerves can't take much more.

I stand still and listen. I have to force myself not to panic. I've never liked the dark. I've never understood the Danish penchant for wandering around at night. Taking a stroll in pitch darkness. Nightingale expeditions in the woods. Insisting on gazing at the stars. Night-time orienteering.

You have to respect the dark. Night is the time when space simmers with evil and peril. You can call it superstition. You can call it fear of the dark. But it's ridiculous to pretend that the night is just like the day, simply without light. Night is the time to huddle together indoors. If you don't happen to be alone and have other obligations, that is.

Sounds are more tangible than objects in the dark. The sound of water around the propeller somewhere beneath my feet. The muted trilling of the ship's wake. The engine noise. The ventilation system. The rotation of the propeller shaft on its bearings. A little electric compressor, its location almost impossible to pinpoint. Like trying to work out which neighbour has the noisy refrigerator in your apartment building.

There's a refrigerator here, too. I don't find it by the sound. I find it because the darkness makes me visualize my own sketch. I pace off the passageway. But I already know the results. Sheer nervousness prevented me from noticing it earlier. The passageway is two metres too short. According to Jakkelsen, somewhere behind

333

the wall at the end of the room is the hydraulic rudder system. But that doesn't explain the missing two metres.

I shine my light on the wall. It has been covered with the same veneer as the other walls. That's why I didn't see it before. But it's been recently applied. The veneer has been nailed down. It's a rather makeshift hiding place, hastily rigged up. But I wouldn't be able to open it on my own. Even if I had the proper tools.

I open the nearest door.

The black cases are standing against the wall. They're labelled: GRIMLOT MUSICAL INSTRUMENT FLIGHT CASES. I open the first one. It's rectangular and looks as if it might hold a medium-sized tweeter.

The manufacturer's guarantee under the two shiny blue tanks of enamelled steel says: SELF-CONTAINED UNDERWATER BREATHING APPARATUS. They're covered with a rubberized net to protect the paint from impacts.

I open another, smaller case. It contains what look like valves to screw on to the tanks. Bright and shiny. Nestled in custom-shaped foam. An oxygen gauge. But a type I've never seen before, which is supposed to be attached to the tanks instead of sitting directly on the mouthpiece.

In the next case there are pressure gauges and wrist compasses. A large suitcase contains goggles, three pairs of flippers, stainless-steel daggers in rubber sheaths, and two inflatable float collars to attach to the tanks.

In a duffel bag there are two hooded rubber suits with zip fasteners at the wrists and ankles. Wetsuits made of neoprene. At least fifteen millimetres thick. Underneath are two Poseidon dry suits. And under them are gloves, socks, two thermal suits, safety lines, and six different kinds of battery-powered lamps, two of which are attached to a helmet.

There's a case that looks as if it might contain an electric bass, but it's somewhat longer and deeper. It's leaning against the bulkhead. Inside it is Jakkelsen.

It wasn't quite big enough for him, so they had to press his head down against his right shoulder and bend his legs up behind his thighs so that he's kneeling. His eyes are open. He still has my jacket over him.

I touch his face. He's still moist and warm. The body temperature of a large animal drops a few degrees per hour after it's been shot, if it's lying outdoors in the summer. The rate is probably about the same for human beings. Jakkelsen is approaching room temperature.

I put my hand in his breast pocket. The syringe is gone. But there's something else in the pocket. I should have wondered about that before. Metal doesn't clink all by itself. It clinks against another piece of metal. Very cautiously, with my hand inside his pocket, I grab hold of a little triangle. It's growing out of his chest.

Rigor mortis spreads from the jaw muscles downwards. The same way neurotic tension does. He's stiff all the way to his navel. I can't turn him over, so I run my hand down along the inside of the case and up behind his back, inside his jacket. Sticking out from between his shoulder blades there's a piece of metal, only a few centimetres long, flat and no thicker than a nail file. Or the steel of a cold chisel.

The blade has been driven in between two ribs and then straight up. I guess that it went through his heart. Then the handle was removed, but the blade was left in. To prevent bleeding.

On any other person the blade would not have gone through the body. But Jakkelsen is fashionably slim.

It must have happened right before I reached him. Perhaps even while I was on my way across the square.

In Greenland I never had any cavities; now I have twelve fillings. Every year I need another one. I refuse to have Novocaine. I've developed a strategy for handling the pain. I breathe deeply from my abdomen, and right before the drill pierces the enamel into the dentine of the tooth, I think to myself that now something is happening to me that I have to accept. That's how I become an involved but not overwhelmed spectator to the pain.

I was present in the parliament, the Landsting, when the Siumut Party proposed that the planned withdrawal of American and Danish forces from Greenland should be preceded by the establishment of a Greenlandic army. But of course that's not what they called it. A decentralized coastguard, they said, initially manned by those Greenlanders who had served as constables in the navy during the past three years. And led by Grade A officers who would be trained in Denmark.

I thought it was impossible; they'd never agree to it.

It was voted down. "We are surprised by the results of the vote," said Julius Høeg, Siumut's foreign-policy spokesman, "considering that this parliament's committee on national security has

335

recommended a coastguard and established a preliminary work group made up of representatives from the Danish Navy, the Greenland police, the Sirius Patrol, the Ice Service, and other professionals."

Other professionals. The most important information always comes at the end. As if in passing. In a side letter. In the margin.

The security personnel on the *Greenland Star* were Greenlanders. Only now that it's behind us do I remember this fact. We no longer notice things that have become commonplace. It has become common to see armed Greenlanders in uniform. Common for us to wage war.

For me, too. The only other thing I have left is my ability to distance myself.

This is happening to me, the pain is mine, but it doesn't completely absorb me. Part of me remains a spectator.

I crawl into the dumbwaiter. It hasn't become any easier since yesterday. I'm not getting any younger, after all.

Now I'm glad that there's no safety device. This dangerous system allows me to press the UP button myself.

The rush of fear during the ascent of the shaft is still the same. The silence at the top. The empty galley.

The moon is shining through the skylight. On my way to the door I have a vision of myself as I must look from outside. Clad in black, but as pale as the white-painted clown.

There are the same sounds in the passageway. The engines, the lavatories, a woman's breathing. It's as if time has stopped.

The moonlight streaming into the saloon is blue and palpably cold, like a liquid against my skin. The rolling of the ship on the waves makes the silhouettes of the window ledges stretch out like living shadows across the walls.

I head for the books first.

The Greenlandic Pilot, the Geodetic Institute's mapbook of Greenland, the admiralty's sea charts of Davis Strait, reduced 4:1 and collected in a single volume. Colbeck's *Dynamics of Snow and Ice Masses*, on the movements of ice. Buchwald's *Meteorites* in three volumes. Issues of *Naturens Verden* and *Varv*. *The Review of Medical Microbiology* by Jawetz and Melnick. Rintek Madsen's *Parasitology – A Handbook*. Dion R. Bell's *Lecture Notes on Tropical Medicine*.

I put the latter two volumes on the deck and leaf through them with my right hand, holding my torch in my left. Under the heading *Dracunculus* so many passages are highlighted in yellow that it looks as if the paper has changed colour. I put the books back in place.

Out in the hallway I listen intently at each door. By sheer chance I locate Tørk's cabin on the first try. I open the door a crack. Moonlight is shining through the porthole and across the bunk. It's cold in the room, but he has pushed the eiderdown aside. His torso looks like blue-tinged marble. He's sleeping heavily. I step inside and close the door behind me. What complicates life is having to make choices. The person who has his choices made for him lives simply.

Everything takes care of itself. He had been working at the desk. The writing implements were put away, since on a ship everything that might roll around has to be stowed. But his papers are still lying there. A heap of them, but not too big for me to carry.

I stand there for a moment, looking at him. Like so many times before, ever since my childhood, I marvel at the chaste vulnerability of human beings in sleep. I could bend over him. I could kiss him. I could feel his heartbeat. I could slit his throat.

I suddenly realize that my life is such that I have often been awake while other people sleep. I've been through many late nights and many early mornings. I didn't plan it that way. But that's how it turned out.

I take the heap of papers out to the saloon. There won't be time to take them along when I leave.

I sit there for a moment without turning on the light. A sense of solemnity has come over the room. As if the moonlight had encapsulated everything in bluish-grey glass.

Everyone dreams of finding the key to oneself and one's future. The religious classes at Sunday school in Qaanaaq were taught by a catechist from the Moravian mission, an introverted and brutal Belgian mathematician who didn't know one word of the Thule dialect. The lessons were given in a grotesque hotchpotch of English, West Greenlandic, and Danish. He scared us but also fascinated us. We were brought up to respect the profundity that is sometimes found in madness. Sunday after Sunday he would dwell on two things: the newly discovered Nag Hammadi canon's commandment to know thyself and the idea that our days are numbered, that there is a divine arithmetic in the universe. We were all between five and nine years old. We didn't understand a word. Yet I still remembered various things later on. I especially thought that I'd like to see the cosmic calculation for my own life.

Every once in a while it feels as if that moment has arrived. Just like now. As if this heap of papers in front of me has something vital to tell me about my future.

My mother's forefathers would have been astounded that the key to the universe for one of their descendants would turn out to be in written form.

On top there is a copy of the Cryolite Corporation Danmark's report on the 1991 expedition to Gela Alta. The last six pages are not copies. They are the original, slightly blurry and technically flawed aerial photos of the Barren Glacier. It looks like its reputation: arid, cold, white, worn, windblown, and abandoned even by the birds.

Then there are a couple of dozen handwritten pages with figures and small pencil sketches that are incomprehensible.

Twelve photographs are reprints of X-rays. They might be the same people I once looked at on the light box in Moritz's consultation room. They might be anything at all.

There are more photos. These might have been taken by X-ray, too. But the images are not of the human body. Straight black and grey lines have been drawn across the pictures, as if made with a ruler.

The last pages are numbered from one to fifty and are all part of a single report.

The text is sparse, the numerous pen-and-ink drawings are sketchy; calculations have been added by hand in several places when the typewriter couldn't supply the proper symbols.

It's a compilation of data pertaining to the transport of large objects across ice. With sketches of the procedures and brief, illustrative equations regarding the mechanical specifications.

There's a summary about the use of heavy sleighs on expeditions to the North Pole. A series of drawings demonstrate the way ships were pulled across the ice to avoid being frozen solid in it.

Several sections of the report have short titles such as: "Ahnighito, Dog, Savik 1, Agpalilik". They concern the transport of the largest-known fragments of meteorites from the Cape York site, Peary's difficult salvage operations and voyage on the schooner *Kite*, Knud Rasmussen's logbook, and Buchwald's legendary transport of the 30-ton *Ahnighito* in 1965.

This last section contains copies of Buchwald's own photographs.

338

I've seen them many times before; they've been included in every article on the subject for the past twenty years. And yet it still seems as if I'm seeing them for the first time. The chutes made from railway sleepers. The winches. The crudely welded sleighs made of train tracks. The photocopies make the contrast too extreme and blur the details. And yet it's all so obvious. The *Kronos* is carrying a duplicate of Buchwald's equipment in the aft cargo hold. The meteorite that he transported to Denmark weighed 30.88 tons.

The last part of the report deals with the joint Danish, American, and Soviet plan for a drilling platform on the ice. The Pylot Report on the bearing capacity of ice is mentioned in the list of references. My name is in the list of authors.

At the bottom of the heap of papers there are six colour photos. They were taken with a flash in some kind of stalactite cave. Every student of geology has seen similar pictures. The salt mines in Austria, the blue grottoes in Sardinia, the lava caves in the Canary Islands.

But these are different. The light of the flash has been thrown back towards the lens in blinding reflections. As if it were a picture of a thousand small explosions. The photographs were taken in an ice cave.

The ice caves that I've seen have all had an extremely short lifetime, lasting only until the break in the glacier or the crevasse closed, or they were filled up by underground rivers of thawing ice. This one is not like anything I've ever seen before. Long, glittering stalactites hang from the ceiling everywhere, a colossal system of icicles that must have been formed over a long period of time.

In the middle of the cave is what looks like a lake. There's something in the lake. It could be anything. It's impossible to tell from the photo.

That it's at all possible to imagine the scale of things is because a man is sitting in the foreground. He's sitting on one of the mounds that the dripping water and the cold have made grow up from the cave floor. He's laughing triumphantly at the camera. This time he's wearing down trousers. But he still has *kamiks* on. It's Isaiah's father.

When I lift up the heap of paper, the last sheet stays on the table because it's thinner than the photographs. It's a sheet of writing paper with the rough draft of a letter. Only a few lines, written in pencil and crossed out in several places, then placed at the bottom of the heap. Like when you've written a diary, or a will, and you don't really want to own up to it. You don't feel that it should lie around, shouting your confessions to the wind. But you still want to have it close at hand. Maybe because it still needs some work.

I read it, then fold it up and put it in my pocket.

My throat is dry. My hands are shaking. What I need now is a problem-free exit.

I've just put out my hand to open the door to Tørk's cabin when there's a click inside and a strip of light falls into the passageway. I step back. The door starts to open. It opens towards me, giving me time to choose a door to my right, open it, and step inside. I pull the door behind me but don't dare shut it all the way.

It's dark. The tiles under my feet tell me that I'm in the bathroom. The light is turned on from the outside. I retreat behind a curtain into the shower stall. The door opens. There's no sound, but a pair of hands float into view in the vertical slit where the curtain isn't quite closed. They are Tørk's hands.

His face appears in the mirror. He's so groggy with sleep that he doesn't even see himself. He bends down, turns on the faucet, lets it get cold, and drinks from it. Then he straightens up, turns around, and leaves. He moves mechanically, like a sleepwalker.

The instant the door to his cabin closes, I'm out in the passageway. In a second he'll notice that the papers are missing. I want to get out before the search starts.

The light goes out. His bunk creaks. He has gone back to sleep in the blue moonlight.

A chance like this, such magnificent luck, occurs only once in a lifetime. I could dance all the way to the door.

A woman calls out in a low, commanding voice further along the hallway in the dark up ahead. I turn around and head in the other direction. A man giggles somewhere in front of me. At the same moment he passes the patch of light from the open doorway to the saloon. He's naked. He has an erection. They have not seen me. I'm caught between them.

I step back into the bathroom again, back into the shower stall. The light goes on. They come inside. He goes over to the sink. He waits for his erection to subside. Then he stands on his toes and urinates into the sink. It's Seidenfaden. The author of the report that I was just looking at about transporting massive weights across sea ice. The report in which he refers to an article that I wrote. And now we're this close to each other. We live in a world of compressed juxtapositions.

The woman is standing behind him. She has an intent expression on her face. For a moment I think that she has seen me in the mirror. Then she lifts her hands above her head. She's holding a belt with the buckle down. When she strikes, she does it with such precision that only the buckle hits him, leaving a long white stripe across one buttock. The stripe changes from white to flaming red. He takes hold of the sink, bends over, and urges his backside towards her. She strikes again; the buckle hits his other buttock. Romeo and Juliet come to mind. Europe has a long tradition of elegant rendezvous. Then the light goes out. The door closes, and they're gone.

I step out into the passageway. My knees are shaking. I don't know what to do about the papers. I take two steps towards Tørk's cabin. Can't make up my mind. Take one step back. Decide to leave them in the saloon. There's nothing else to do. I feel as if I'm trapped in a shunting yard.

A door opens in the dark. There's no warning this time, the light isn't turned on, and it's only because I've become familiar with my surroundings that I manage to step into the bathroom and hide in the shower stall in time.

Now the light doesn't go on. But the door is opened and then closed and locked. I take out my screwdriver. They've come to get me. I'm holding the papers behind my back. I'm going to throw them as I jab with the screwdriver. Once from below, up towards the abdomen. And then I'll run.

The curtain is pushed aside. I get ready to push off from the wall.

The water is turned on. The cold water. Then the hot. The temperature is adjusted. The shower has been directed towards the wall. Within three seconds I'm soaking wet.

The spray is diverted away from the wall. He gets in under the water. I'm ten centimetres away. Except for the splashing of the water, there's not a sound. And there's no light. But at this distance I don't need it to recognize the mechanic.

In the White Cells he never turned on the light on his way up the stairs. He always waited until the last minute to flip the switch in the basement. He likes peace and solitude in the dark.

His hand brushes mine when he fumbles for the soapdish. He finds it, steps back a little from the water, and soaps up. Puts the soap back and massages his skin. Searches for the soap again. His fingers brush mine and move on. Then they slowly come back. Touch my hand.

A gasp of surprise ought to be the minimum. A scream wouldn't be out of place. But he doesn't utter a sound. His fingers register the screwdriver, carefully take it out of my hand, and move up my arm to my elbow.

The water is turned off. The curtain is shoved aside; he steps out into the room. After a moment the light goes on.

He's put a big orange towel around his waist. His face is expressionless. All of his movements have been calm, deliberate, subdued.

He looks at me. And then he recognizes me.

His handle on the present dissolves. He doesn't move, his face hardly changes expression. But he's paralysed.

I now know that he didn't realize I was on board.

He looks at my wet hair, the clinging dress, the soaked papers that I'm holding in front of me. My sloshing rubber boots and the screwdriver that he's holding. He doesn't understand a thing.

Then he hands me his towel, with an awkward and perplexed gesture. Without thinking that he is exposing himself. I take it and hand him the papers. He holds them in front of his genitals while I dry my hair. His eyes never leave my face.

We're sitting on the bunk in his cabin. Close together, with a chasm between us. We're whispering, even though it's not necessary.

"Do you know what's going on?" I ask.

"M-most of it."

"Can you tell me?"

He shakes his head.

We've ended up just about where we started. In a morass of secrets. I feel a wild urge to throw myself at him and beg him to anaesthetize me and wake me up only after it's all over.

I've never got to know him. Until a few hours ago I thought that we had shared certain moments of silent solidarity. When I saw him walking across the landing platform of the *Greenland Star*, I realized that we've always been strangers. When you're young, you think that sex is the culmination of intimacy. Later you discover that it's barely the beginning.

"I want to show you something."

I put the papers in a pile on his desk. He hands me a T-shirt, underpants, thermal trousers, woollen socks, and a sweater. We get

342

dressed with our backs turned, like two strangers. I have to roll his trousers up above the knees and the sleeves of his sweater to the elbow. I ask him for a wool cap as well, and he gives it to me. From a drawer he takes out a flat, dark bottle and stuffs it into an inside pocket. I take the wool blanket off his bunk and fold it up. Then we leave.

He opens the case. Jakkelsen stares at us sadly. His nose is blue-tinged and sharp, as if it were frozen.

"Who's this?"

"Bernard Jakkelsen. Lukas's little brother."

I go over to him and unbutton his shirt and pull it away from the triangular steel. The mechanic doesn't move.

I turn off the light. We stand quietly in the darkness. Then we go aloft. I lock the door behind us. When we reach the deck, the mechanic stops.

"Who?"

"Verlaine," I say. "The bosun."

There are steps welded on to the external bulkhead. I crawl up first. He follows me slowly. We reach a small half-deck clothed in darkness. A motorboat is perched on two wooden trestles, and behind it there's a large rubber raft. We sit down between the two. From here we have a view of the quarterdeck, but we're shielded from the light.

"It happened on the *Greenland Star*. Just as you arrived."

He doesn't believe me.

"Verlaine could have heaved him over the side. But he was afraid the body would float up near the platform the next day. Or be sucked up into a propeller."

I think about my mother. Whatever is thrown into the Arctic Ocean never comes up again. But Verlaine wouldn't know that.

The mechanic still doesn't say a word.

"Jakkelsen followed Verlaine on to the docks. He got caught. The best solution was to make room in the cases and put him inside one of them. Load him on board and wait until we were free of the platform. And then let him slip overboard."

I try to keep my sense of desperation out of my voice. He has to believe me.

"We're far out at sea now. Every second he's on board is a risk for them. They'll come in a few minutes. They'll have to bring him

343

up on deck. There's no other way than over the side. That's why we're sitting here. I thought you should see for yourself."

There's a soft sigh in the dark. It's the cork coming out of the bottle, which he hands to me. I take a swallow. It's dark, sweet, strong rum.

I put the woollen blanket over us. It's about −10 °C, but I'm burning hot inside. Alcohol makes your capillaries expand and the surface of your skin ache slightly. It's this pain that you have to avoid at all costs if you don't want to freeze to death. I take off the woollen cap to feel the cold against my forehead.

"Tørk would n-never have permitted it."

I hand him the letter. He glances up towards the dark windows of the bridge, leans behind the hull of the motorboat, and reads the letter in the beam of my torch.

"It was with Tørk's papers," I say.

We take another drink. The moonlight is so bright that it's possible to distinguish different colours. The green deck, my blue thermal trousers, the gold and red of the label on the bottle. It's like sunlight, falling with a tactile warmth across the deck. I kiss him. The temperature is no longer important. At some point I kneel across him. We are no longer two bodies, just patches of heat in the night.

Later we sit leaning against each other. He's the one who pulls the blanket over us. I'm not cold. We drink from the bottle. It tastes heavy and fiery.

Are you from the police, Smilla? No, I answer. Are you from another firm? No, I say. Have you known all along? No, I say. Do you know now? I have an idea, I say.

We take another drink and he puts his arms around me. The deck must be cold under the blanket, but we don't notice it.

No one comes. There is no life on the *Kronos*. As if the ship had wrenched itself off its course and is now carrying us away, just the two of us.

At some point the bottle is empty. Then I stand up, because I realize that something is wrong. Aren't there any other openings in the hull, I ask. Some other way to get rid of him? Why are you talking about death, he asks. How should I answer him? How is the anchor lowered, he asks me.

We climb down to the between decks. The case is now full of life vests. Jakkelsen is gone. We go down the companionway, through the tunnel, the engine room, another tunnel, up the spiral staircase. He throws two bolts and opens a door that's one metre square. The chain of the anchor is stretched taut in the middle of the room. Up near the bulkhead it passes through a pipe; on either side the moonlight and the silhouette of the windlass are visible. Then the chain disappears downward through a hawser hole the size of a sewer cover. The anchor is pulled up to just below the hawser hole. That doesn't leave much of a gap. He stares at the opening.

"A grown man wouldn't fit through there."

I touch the steel. We both know that this is where Jakkelsen was shoved out during the night.

"He was fashionably slim," I say.

3

CAPTAIN LUKAS IS UNSHAVEN, he hasn't combed his hair, and he looks as if he has slept in his clothes.

"What do you know about electrical currents, Jaspersen?"

We're alone on the bridge. It's six-thirty in the morning, an hour and a half before his watch begins. His face is sallow and covered with a thin film of sweat.

"I can change a light bulb," I say. "But I usually burn my fingers."

"Yesterday, when we were docked, we lost power on the *Kronos*. And a section of the harbour area did, too."

He is holding a piece of paper. His hand and the paper are shaking.

"On ships all the wiring goes through circuit breakers. As a result, all power outlets are directly connected to a fuse. Do you know what that means? It means that it's damned hard to create electrical havoc on a ship. Unless you're too clever for your own good and go straight for the main feeder. That's what someone did yesterday. During the brief periods when Kützow is sober, he has his brighter moments. He tracked down the source of the accident. It was a darning needle. Yesterday someone stuck a darning needle into the supply cable. Presumably with an insulated pair of pliers. And then broke off the needle afterwards – an especially clever touch. The insulation contracts over the needle, making it impossible to pinpoint the problem unless you know a few tricks like Kützow does, with a magnet and a multimeter. And if you have some idea what you're looking for."

I think about Jakkelsen's excitement and the tone of his voice. "I'll take care of this for us, Smilla," he said. "Tomorrow everything will be different." I feel a new respect for his resourcefulness.

"During the blackout one of the sailors – Bernard Jakkelsen – apparently disobeyed orders not to go ashore and left the *Kronos*. This morning we received this telex from him. It's his resignation."

He hands me the paper. It's a telex from the *Greenland Star*. It's brief, even for a resignation.

To Captain Sigmund Lukas. As of now, I hereby resign my post on the *Kronos* due to personal reasons. Go to hell. B. Jakkelsen

I look up at Lukas.

"I have a strong suspicion", he says, "that you were also ashore during the blackout."

His demeanour cracks. Gone is the officer, gone is the sarcasm. All that remains is anxiety bordering on desperation.

"Tell me what you know about him."

Everything that Jakkelsen didn't tell me I can now see. Lukas's panicked concern, his desire to protect and rescue his brother and keep him sailing, out of gaol and away from bad company in the cities. No matter what the cost. Even if it meant taking him along on a voyage like this one.

For a moment I'm tempted to tell him everything. For a moment I see a reflection of myself in his torment. Our irrational, blind, and vain attempts to protect other people from something that we don't understand but that keeps reappearing no matter what we do.

Then I let my momentary weakness fade away and die out. There's nothing I can do for Lukas now. For Jakkelsen no one can do anything any more.

"I was standing on the quay. That's all."

He lights a new cigarette. The ashtray is already full. "I called the telex office. But the whole situation is impossible. It's strictly forbidden to put a man ashore in this way. And their internal system makes things even more difficult. You write a telegram and hand it in at a window. From there it's taken over to the post room. A third person takes it over to the teletype office. I talked to a fourth person. They don't even know whether it was delivered in person or called in. It's impossible to find out anything."

He takes hold of my arm. "Do you have the faintest idea why he would go ashore?"

I shake my head.

He waves the telegram. "This is so typical of him."

He has tears in his eyes.

It's exactly like something Jakkelsen would write. Brief, arrogant, secretive, and yet with an enthusiasm for the clichés of formal speech. But it wasn't Jakkelsen who wrote it. It's the same text that was on the piece of paper I took from Tørk's cabin last night.

Lukas gazes out across the water without seeing anything, absorbed in the first of many painful speculations that will start building from this moment on. He has forgotten that I'm there.

At that moment the fire alarm goes off.

There are sixteen of us gathered in the galley. Everyone on board except Sonne and Maria, who are up on the bridge.

Technically it's daytime, but outside it's dark. The wind has picked up and the temperature has risen, a combination that makes the rain sweep across the windows like the boughs of a tree. The waves strike the sides of the ship with the irregular blows of a sledgehammer.

The mechanic is leaning against the bulkhead next to Urs. Verlaine sits a little apart; Hansen and Maurice are with the rest of the crew. In the company of others, they always seem so inconspicuous. Inconspicuousness is part of Verlaine's attention to detail.

Lukas is sitting at the head of the table. It's an hour since I saw him on the bridge. He's practically unrecognizable. He's wearing a freshly ironed shirt and polished leather shoes. He's clean-shaven, and his hair has been slicked down with water. He's alert and gets right to the point.

Just inside the door stands Tørk. In front of him sit Seidenfaden and Katja Claussen. It takes a while before I can bring myself to look at them. They pay no attention to me.

Lukas introduces the mechanic. Then he reports that the fire alarm system is still malfunctioning. It was a false alarm this morning.

He briefly reports that Jakkelsen has deserted. He says everything in English.

I glance over at Verlaine. He's leaning against the bulkhead. His eyes bore into mine, attentive and searching. I can't lower my gaze. Someone else – a demon – is staring out of my eyes, promising Verlaine revenge.

Lukas announces that we're approaching the destination of the voyage. He doesn't say any more than that. In a day or two we'll be there. No one will be allowed ashore.

His lack of more precise details is absurd. In the age of Satnav, you can determine the exact time of sighting land with a margin of error of only a few minutes.

348

No one reacts. They all know there's something wrong with this trip. Besides, they're used to conditions on board big tankers. Most of them have been at sea for up to seven months without putting in to port.

Lukas looks across at Tørk. This meeting was arranged for Tørk's benefit. At his request. Maybe so that he could see all of us in one place. To gauge our reactions. While Lukas has been talking, Tørk's eyes have wandered from face to face, resting on each for a moment. Now he turns around and leaves. Seidenfaden and Claussen follow him.

Lukas adjourns the meeting. Verlaine exits. The mechanic pauses for a moment to talk to Urs, who is explaining in broken English about the croissants we've just eaten. I catch something about the importance of moisture. Both in the rising stage and in the oven.

Fernanda makes her departure, avoiding my eyes.

The mechanic leaves. He hasn't looked at me once. I'm going to see him this afternoon. But until then we have to pretend we don't exist for each other.

I think about what I have to work on in the meantime. Not some kind of glorious planning for the future, merely a dull, bare-bones strategy for survival.

I drift down the passageway. I have to talk to Lukas.

I have one foot up on the companionway as Hansen comes down towards me. I withdraw to the open deck area below the upper level.

This is where I first realize how bad the weather is. The rain is close to freezing, heavy and torrential. The gusts of wind whip up the rain as it falls. There are white stripes across the sea where the wind is chopping at the tops of the swells, pulling them along as spindrift.

The door opens behind me. I don't turn around; I walk over towards the exit to the quarterdeck. It opens and Verlaine comes out.

This narrow, covered section of open deck now seems different. My attention is usually diverted by the lights permanently on and the two doors, and by the windows of the crew cabins facing the deck. Now I realize that this is one of the most isolated spots on board. It can't be seen from above, and there are only two entrances. The windows behind me belong to Jakkelsen's cabin and my own.

In front of me is the sea rail. Beyond that, it's twelve metres down to the sea.

Hansen approaches while Verlaine stays where he is. I weigh fifty kilos. It will just be a quick lift and then the water. What was it Lagermann said? You hold your breath until you think your lungs are going to burst. That's when you feel pain. Then you exhale and take a deep breath. After that there's only peace.

This is the only place they could do it without being seen from the bridge. They must have been waiting for this opportunity.

I approach the rail and lean over. Hansen comes closer. We both move calmly and deliberately. On my right the drop to the sea is interrupted by the freeboard extending down to the rail. On the outside of the ship a row of rectangular iron rungs has been welded into recesses, vanishing up into the darkness.

I perch on top of the rail. Hansen and Verlaine freeze. The way people always freeze when faced with someone who's going to jump. But I don't jump. I grab hold of the iron rungs and pull myself out over the side.

Hansen can't work out what I'm up to. But Verlaine rushes to the rail and grabs for my ankles.

The *Kronos* is struck by a heavy swell. The hull shudders and lists to starboard.

He has hold of my foot. But the movement of the ship presses him against the rail, threatening to fling him into the sea. He has to let me go. My feet slip on the rungs, which are as slippery as soap from the rain and salt water. While the ship rolls back, I hang by my hands. Somewhere far below me the waterline shines white. I close my eyes and clamber up.

After what seems like an eternity, I open my eyes again. Below, Hansen is staring up at me. I've climbed only a few metres.

I'm outside the portholes of the promenade deck. On my left there are lights behind the blue curtains. I pound on the glass with the palm of my hand. When I give up and start climbing again, someone cautiously pushes the curtains aside. Kützow peers out at me. I have been pounding on the window of the engineer's office. He shields his face with his hands to block out the reflection, pressing his face against the window. His nose becomes a flattened, dull green spot. Our faces are only inches away from each other.

"Help," I scream. "Help, goddamn it!"

He looks at me. Then he pulls the curtains shut.

I keep on climbing. The rungs stop and I collapse on the boat deck next to the davits holding the aft lifeboat. The door is immediately to my right. It's locked. An outside ladder like the one I've just climbed leads up along the funnel to the platform outside the bridge.

Under different circumstances I would have had reason to admire Verlaine's foresight. At the top of the ladder, a few metres above, Maurice is standing, with his arm still in a sling. He's there to ensure that there are no witnesses on the upper decks.

I head for the companionway leading down. From the deck below Verlaine is coming up towards me.

I turn around. I think that I might be able to get the lifeboat lowered into the water. That it must have some kind of quick release to make it drop. That I could jump into the water after it.

But standing in front of the winches for lowering the boat, I have to give up. The system of snap hooks and cables is too complicated. I rip the tarpaulin off the boat, looking for something to defend myself with. A boathook or a flare.

The tarpaulin is made of heavy green nylon with elastic along the edge that fits around the gunwale of the boat. When I lift it up, the wind pulls it free and it flaps out over the side of the ship. It catches on an eyelet on the bow of the lifeboat.

Verlaine is up on deck. Hansen is right behind him. I grab the tarpaulin and step over the side. The *Kronos* rolls and I'm lifted free; wrapping my thighs around the tarpaulin, I lower myself down. At the end of the tarpaulin my feet dangle in midair. Then I fall. They've cut the tarpaulin loose. I fling out my arms and the sea rail catches me in the armpits. My knees strike the side of the ship. But I keep hanging there, momentarily paralysed because the breath was knocked out of me. Then I slide head-first on to the upper deck.

An absurd fragment of memory brings up images of the first time I ever played tag, right after I arrived in Denmark – my unfamiliarity with the game, which quickly eliminated the weak, and then, through a natural hierarchy, everyone else.

The door to the companionway opens and Hansen appears. I head across the quarterdeck, making it over to the companionway leading up to the boat deck. At eye level a pair of blue shoes is coming down the steps. I stick my hands under the rail and shove the shoes outward. It's a continuation of their own movement, so it doesn't take much force. The feet sail out into the air in a small arc, and Verlaine's head strikes the step next to my shoulders. Then he plummets down the last few metres and hits the deck without being able to break his fall.

I run up the companionway. On the boat deck I cross over to starboard and then climb up the ladder. Maurice must have heard me. As I climb he comes over to the ladder. Behind him the door to the bridge opens and Kützow appears. He's wearing a bathrobe and is barefoot. He and Maurice stare at each other. I walk past them into the bridge.

I fumble for the torch in my pocket. The beam catches Sonne's face. Maria is standing at the tiller.

"Let me into the sick bay," I say. "I've had an accident."

Sonne leads the way. Outside the map room he turns round and stops dead. I look down at myself. The knees of my trousers are gone; instead, there are two bloody holes. The palms of both hands are lacerated.

"I fell," I tell him.

He unlocks the sick bay. He avoids looking at me directly.

When I sit down and the skin tightens across my knees, I almost faint. A flood of tiny, painful memories washes over me: the first stairs in boarding school and falling on rough ice – flashes of light, numbness, heat, sharp pain, cold, and finally a dull throbbing.

"Could you clean it for me?"

He looks away. "I can't stand the sight of blood."

I clean it myself. My hands shake, the liquid runs down over my wounds. I put on sterile compresses and wrap gauze around them.

"Give me some Ketogan," I say.

"That's against regulations."

I stare up at him. He takes out a bottle.

"And amphetamines."

Every ship's pharmacy and every expedition has a supply of medicine to stimulate the central nervous system and relieve the feeling of exhaustion.

He hands me some. I crush five tablets into a paper cup with water. They taste bitter.

I'm having a hard time using my hands. He takes out a pair of white, tight-fitting cotton gloves, the kind worn by people with allergies.

As I go out the door he tries to smile bravely. "Feeling better now?"

352

He is the quintessential Dane, the fear, the iron resolve to repress what's happening around him. The untameable optimism.

The rain hasn't let up. It looks like threads of water slanting across the windows of the bridge. The dim grey of faint daylight is appearing.

"Where's Lukas?"

"In his cabin."

A man who hasn't slept for forty-eight hours is useless.

"He goes on watch in an hour," says Sonne. "In the crow's nest. He wants to see the ice for himself."

One of the radar screens is fixed on a radius of fifty sea miles. A short distance from the edge it shows a cross-hatched green continent. The beginning of the field ice.

"Tell him I'm coming up," I say.

The deck of the *Kronos* is deserted. It no longer resembles anything on board a ship. The faint daylight forms deep shadows, but they're not just shadows any more. In every patch of darkness an inferno is raging. When I was a child, this atmosphere accompanied every death. Somewhere women would start shrieking, and then we knew someone had died; this knowledge would transform the room. Even if it was May in Siorapaluk, with a bluish-green light flooding down, penetrating everything and making people crazy with the spring, even this kind of light would turn into the cold reflection of a realm of the dead that surfaced on earth.

A ladder goes up the front of the mast. The crow's nest is a flat aluminium box furnished with windows both fore and aft. Mandatory on any ship that sails in ice.

It's twenty metres to the top. It doesn't look like much on my sketch of the *Kronos*. But the climb up is terrifying. The ship pitches through the sea and rolls sideways; all the movements at the hull's fulcrum are magnified the higher I go, and the arc widens.

The rungs come to an end at a platform, above which the block of the derrick is attached. From there you step up on to a smaller platform and then through a little door into the metal shed.

It's just high enough to stand up. In the darkness I can make out an old-fashioned engine-room telegraph, a tilt gauge, a log, a large compass, a tiller, and the intercom to the bridge. When we enter the field ice, Lukas will steer the *Kronos* from up here. Only from here will there be sufficient visibility.

There's a seat along the back wall. When I come in, he moves aside and makes room for me. I see him as a denser shape in the darkness. I want to tell him about Jakkelsen. On every ship the captain has some type of weapon. And he still has his position of authority. It must be possible to hold Verlaine at bay, to turn the ship around. We should be able to reach Sisimiut within seven hours.

I slide on to the seat. He puts his feet up on the telegraph. It's not Lukas, it's Tørk.

"The ice," he says. "We're getting close to the ice."

It's barely visible, like a greyish-white light on the horizon. The sky is low and dark like coal smoke, with a few lighter patches.

The little cabin that we're in jolts from side to side. I roll towards him and then back against the wall. He doesn't move. With his boots up on the telegraph and his hand on his chair, he seems to be wedged tight.

"You went ashore on the *Greenland Star*. You were in the forward part of the ship when the first fire alarm went off. Kützow has seen you walking around at night several times. Why?"

"I'm used to being able to move freely aboard ship."

I can't see his face; I can barely make out his profile.

"What ship? You only gave the captain your passport. I faxed the Marine Transport Commission. They've never issued a discharge book in your name."

For a moment the temptation to give up is overwhelming.

"I sailed on smaller ships. They never ask for papers outside the merchant fleet."

"So you heard someone mention this job and contacted Lukas."

It's not a question, so I don't reply. He's studying me. He probably can't see any better than I can.

"This voyage wasn't mentioned anywhere. It was kept secret. You didn't contact Lukas. You got Lander, the owner of a casino, to set up a meeting."

His voice is low, interested. "You sought out Andreas Fine Licht and Ving. You're looking for something."

The ice seems to be slowly wandering towards us, across the sea.

"Who are you working for?"

It's the realization that he has known who I was from the very beginning that is so excruciating. Not since my childhood have I felt myself to such an extent in someone else's power.

He didn't tell the mechanic that I would be on board. He wanted to observe our encounter. In order to see what there was between us. That was his primary objective in gathering us all together in the mess. It's impossible to guess what he has decided.

"Verlaine thinks it's the Danish National Police. I was tending towards that opinion myself for a while. I had a look at your apartment in Copenhagen. And at your cabin here on board. You seem so alone. So unorganized. But maybe it's some corporation? A private client?"

For a moment I was about to sink back to await sleep, unconsciousness, and then oblivion. But the repetition of his question brings me out of my trance. He wants an answer. This, too, is an interrogation. He can't be a hundred per cent sure who I am. Whom I have contact with. Or how much I know. I'm still alive.

"A child in my building fell off a roof. I found Ving's address in his mother's apartment. She gets a pension from the Cryolite Corporation as the result of her husband's death. This led me to the company archives and to what information was available on the expeditions to Gela Alta. Everything else stemmed from that."

"Who helped you?"

All along there's been a sense of both urgency and indifference in his voice. As if we were discussing mutual friends or circumstances that have no real importance for us.

I've never believed that people could be truly cold. Strained perhaps, but not cold. The essence of life is warmth. Even hatred is warm when unleashed on its natural target. Now, here, I realize that I've been mistaken. A cold, overwhelming current of energy, physically real, emanates from this man next to me.

I try to picture him as a boy, try to hold on to something human, something understandable: a malnourished, fatherless boy in a shed in Brønshøj. Tormented, thin as a bird, and alone.

I have to give up; the image falters, shatters, and dissolves. The man beside me is rock solid, and yet fluid and cunning. A man who has risen above his past so there is no longer any trace of it.

"Who helped you?"

This last question is the key one. What *I* know is not important. The important thing is whom I've shared the information with. So he can work out what's in store for him. Maybe this is where his humanity lies, in the traces of growing up with a sense of unfathomable insecurity: the need to plan, to make his world predictable.

I remove all emotion from my voice. "I've always been able to handle things myself."

He pauses for a moment. "Why are you doing this?"

"I want to understand why he died."

An extraordinary feeling of confidence can come over you when you're standing at the end of the plank with a blindfold over your eyes. I know I've said the right thing.

He takes in my answer. "Do you know why I'm going to Gela Alta?"

The "I" in his question reveals great candour. Gone is the ship, the crew, me, and his colleagues. The whole extraneous machinery is moving for his sake alone. The question holds no arrogance. It is simply an expression of fact. We are all here, for one reason or another, because he wanted us here and was able to make it happen.

I'm walking on a knife edge. He knows I've lied, that I didn't get here without someone's help. The fact that I was allowed on board at all tells him as much. But he still doesn't know whether he's sitting next to an individual or an organization. His doubt is my opportunity. I remember the faces of the hunters when they came home; the more they had on their sleigh, the more remote their expression would be. I remember my mother's false modesty after fishing trips. It was her charade, but it was Moritz who pinned it down during one of his fits of rage: "It's best to underplay by twenty per cent; forty per cent is even better."

"We're going to pick up something," I say. "Something so heavy that it requires a ship the size of the *Kronos*."

It's impossible to tell what he's thinking. In the darkness, I sense only the presence of a force that registers and analyses, manifested in extreme alertness. And again the image of a polar bear comes to mind: the savage creature's awareness of its own hunger, the defensive capability of its prey, and the circumstances.

"Why did you call my apartment?" I hear myself ask him.

"I found out a lot from that phone call. No normal woman, no normal human being would have picked up that phone."

Together we step out on to the platform, which now has a light coating of ice. Every time a wave rams the hull, we can feel the engines labouring as the pressure on the propeller increases.

I let him go first. A person's power is usually diminished when he steps outdoors. But not Tørk's. He fills the space and the watery grey light around us with his own radiance. I've never been so afraid of anyone.

Out on the platform I suddenly know that he was up on the roof with Isaiah. That he saw him jump. This certainty comes to me like a vision, still without details, but absolutely unshakable. At that moment, across time and space, I share Isaiah's terror; at that moment I'm up on the roof, too.

Standing with his hands on the rail, Tørk looks into my eyes.

"Step back, please," he says.

Our mutual understanding is complete; words are hardly necessary. He has visualized a possibility – that he would take a step down the ladder and I would come forward, tear his hands away, and kick him in the face, letting him fall backwards, plunging the twenty metres to the deck, which looks so small from here, as if he might not even hit it.

I step back until I'm up against the rail. I'm almost grateful to him for taking this precaution. The temptation might have been too great.

Twice I've made trips to Greenland when I didn't look in a mirror for six months. On the trip home I would carefully avoid mirrors on the plane and in the airports. When I finally stood in front of a mirror in my apartment I clearly saw the physical manifestations of the passage of time. The first grey hairs, the network of wrinkles, the ever deepening and sharpening shadows of the bones beneath my skin.

Nothing was more reassuring to me than the knowledge that I would die. In these moments of clarity – and you see yourself clearly only when you see yourself as a stranger – all despair, all gaiety, all depression vanish and are replaced by calm. For me death was not so much something scary or a state of being or an event that would happen to me. It was a focusing on the now, an aid, an ally in the effort to be mentally present.

Sometimes on summer nights Isaiah would fall asleep on my sofa. I don't remember exactly what I would be doing; I probably sat there watching him. At some point I would touch his neck and feel that he was too hot. Then I would cautiously unbutton his shirt and pull it away from his chest. I would get up and open the window onto the harbour, and at that moment we would be somewhere else. We were at Iita, in the summer tent. Light seeps through the canvas, as if from a full moon. But it's the fabric of the tent that colours the light blue, because when I open the tent flap it's the dull red light of the midnight sun that falls over him. He doesn't wake up; he hasn't slept for twenty-four hours. We haven't been able to sleep in the endless light, but now he has collapsed. Maybe he's my child; that's how it feels. And I look at his chest and his throat, and watch his breathing and his rapid pulse beneath the brown flawless skin.

Then I would step in front of the mirror and take off my shirt and look at my own breast and neck and realize that some day it would all be over, even my feelings for him would one day die with me. But he would still be here, and after him would come his children or other children, a wheel of children, a chain, a spiral winding into eternity.

Such apprehension of the mortality and continuity of all things always made me happy.

I feel somewhat the same way now. I've taken off my clothes and stand in front of the mirror.

Anyone interested in death would benefit from looking at me. I've taken off my bandages. There's no skin on my kneecaps. Between my hips is a wide yellowish-blue patch of blood that has coagulated under the skin where Jakkelsen's marline-spike struck me. The palms of both hands have suppurating lesions that refuse to close. At the base of my skull I have a bruise like a gull's egg, and a spot where the skin is broken and contracted. I've been modest enough to keep on my white socks so you can't see my swollen ankle; and I won't even mention all the black and blue marks, or my scalp, which still throbs now and then from the burn.

I've lost weight, going from gaunt to emaciated. Lack of sleep has made my eyes sink into their sockets. And yet I smile at the stranger in the mirror. There's no simple arithmetic for life's distribution of happiness and sorrow, no such thing as a standard share. One of the few people who make life worth living is on board the *Kronos*.

He calls me at exactly five o'clock. This is the first time I feel affection for the intercom system.

"S-Smilla, meet you in the sick bay in fifteen minutes."

He feels the same way about telephones as I do. He barely manages to state his message before he's gone.

"Føjl," I say. I have never pronounced his last name before. It is a sweetness in my mouth. "Thanks for yesterday."

The system clicks off, the light goes out.

I put on blue work clothes. It's not a haphazard decision. There's nothing haphazard about the clothes I choose to wear. I could dress up, of course. Even here I could dress up. But the blue clothes are the uniform of the *Kronos*, symbolizing the fact that we are now meeting under different circumstances, that the world is against us more than ever before.

I listen at the door for a long time before I venture out into the passageway.

I can't imagine that anything like the Christian hell exists. But lately I've been wondering about the ancient Greenlandic realm of the dead. If you consider all the unpleasantness you encounter while you're alive, it seems improbable that it would all come to an end simply because you're dead.

If there are clandestine meetings between lovers in the realm of the dead, the prelude would be something like this. I move from doorway to doorway. I no longer see the *Kronos* merely as a ship, but rather as a minefield. I try to calculate in advance whether a specific danger might solidify into something life-threatening.

When someone comes out of the exercise room, I dash into the bathroom before the door has closed behind them. From the crack in the doorway I watch Maria go past. Swift and stony-faced. I'm not the only one who knows that the *Kronos* is doomed.

I meet no one on my way up the stairs. The door to the bridge is shut, the chart room empty.

In front of the sick bay I stop. I straighten my clothes. My face feels naked without makeup.

The room is dark, the curtains drawn. I close the door behind me and lean against it. I feel my lips. I want him to come out of the dark and kiss me.

A cool, delicate floral fragrance reaches me. I wait.

It's not the bulkhead light that someone turns on but the lamp above the bed, a kind of operating light. It makes yellow patches of light on the black leather, leaving the rest of the room in shadow.

Tørk is sitting on a chair, with his feet propped up on the bed. Near the wall, in semi-darkness, stands Verlaine. Katja Claussen is

359

sitting on the foot of the bed with her feet dangling. There's no one else in the room.

I watch myself from a distance. Maybe because it's too painful to be inside my own body. I don't care about the three in front of me; I don't care about myself. It was the mechanic that I talked to a moment ago. He was the one who summoned me here.

We all have our limits. A certain limit to our perseverance, to how many overtures we can make to life. And to how many rejections we can stand.

"Empty your pockets."

Verlaine does the talking. This is my first opportunity to observe the division of labour between the two men. Verlaine taking care of the physical violence.

I step towards the light and put my torch and keys down on the bed. I wonder what the woman is doing in the room. Next moment I have my answer. Verlaine nods to her, and she comes over to me. The men look away as she searches me. She's much taller than I am, but still agile. She starts below my knees, feeling my ankles and then working her way up. She finds the screwdriver and Jakkelsen's hypodermic case. Then she takes my belt away from me.

Tørk does not look at what she's found. But Verlaine weighs the objects in his hand.

How will it come? Will I see it coming?

Tørk stands up. "Formally, you are under arrest."

He doesn't look at me. We both know that any reference to formalities is part of the same illusion as our mutual courtesy. They are the only veil left.

He looks down. Then he slowly shakes his head, and something like amazement passes over his face.

"You're a spectacular bluffer," he says. "I'd much rather sit up in the crow's nest listening to your lies than walk around among all these mediocre truths."

All three of them stand there for a moment. Then they leave.

Verlaine is the one who locks the door. He stops in the doorway. He looks tired. There's something honest about his silence. It tells me that this isn't a cell and I haven't been arrested. This is the start of the finish, which will happen sometime soon.

THE ICE

IN SUNDAY SCHOOL they taught us that the sun was Our Lord Jesus, at boarding school we learned for the first time that it was supposed to be a continuously exploding hydrogen bomb.

For me it will always be the Heavenly Clown. In my first conscious memory of the sun, I have my eyes scrunched up and I'm looking right at it, fully aware that this is forbidden, and I'm thinking that the sun is menacing and laughing at the same time, like the clown's face when he paints himself with blood and ashes, sticks a length of wood in his mouth, and, alien, gruesome, and joyous, approaches us children.

Now, just before the sun's orb reaches the horizon, where momentarily it evades the black cloud cover, casting a fire of light across the ice and the ship, it is an image of the clown's strategy. To evade the darkness by ducking as low as possible. The dangerous striking power of humiliation.

The *Kronos* is on its way into the ice. I can see it in the distance, veiled by ten millimetres of safety glass fogged up by the salt crystallized on the outside. That doesn't make any difference. I feel it as if I were standing on it.

It's dense field ice, and at first everything is grey. The narrow channel the *Kronos* breaks is like a track of ashes. The ice floes – most of them as big as the ship – are like huge pieces of rock, slightly swollen and cracked by the cold. It's a world of absolute lifelessness.

Then the sun drops beneath the cloud cover, like ignited petrol.

The ice cover was formed last year in the Arctic Ocean. From there it was forced out between Svalbard and the east coast of Greenland, carried down around Cape Farewell, and pushed up along the west coast.

It was created in beauty. One October day the temperature drops thirty degrees in four hours, and the sea grows as motionless as a mirror. It's waiting to reflect a wonder of creation. The clouds and the sea now glide together in a curtain of heavy grey silk. The water grows viscous and tinged with pink, like a liqueur of wild berries. A blue fog of frost smoke detaches itself from the surface of the water and drifts across the mirror. Then the water solidifies. Out of the dark sea the cold now pulls up a rose garden, a white blanket of ice blossoms formed from salt and frozen drops of water. They may last for four hours or two days.

At this point the structure of the ice crystals is based on the number six. Surrounding a hexagon, like a honeycomb of solidified water, six arms reach out towards six other cells, which in turn – as seen in a photograph taken with a colour filter and greatly enlarged – dissolve into new hexagons.

Then frazil ice is formed, grease ice, and pancake ice, whose plates freeze together into floes. The ice separates out the salt, the seawater freezes from below. The ice breaks; packing, precipitation, and increased cold give it an undulating surface. Eventually the ice is forced adrift.

In the distance is *hiku*, the permanent ice, the continent of frozen sea which we are sailing alongside.

Everywhere around the *Kronos* – in the fjord which the local current conditions have created (only partially understood and recorded) – are different types of ice floes, *hikuaq* and *puktaaq*. The most dangerous are the blue and black floes, pure meltwater ice, which lie heavy and deep in the water, and because of their transparency take on the colour of the water surrounding them.

It's easier to see the white glacier ice and the grey sea ice, coloured by air particles.

The surface of the ice floes is a wasteland of *ivuniq*, packs of ice forced upwards by the current and the collision of the plates; of *maniilaq*, ice knolls; and of *apuhiniq*, snow which the wind has compressed into hard barricades.

The same wind that has blown *agiuppiniq* across the ice, snow-drifts that you follow with the sleigh when fog covers the ice.

For the moment, the weather and the sea and the ice are allowing the *Kronos* to slip through. Now Lukas is sitting up in the crow's nest, now he is coaxing his ship through the channels, looking for *killaq*, air holes, and letting the bow slide up on to the new ice, where it's less than thirty centimetres thick and then let the weight of the ship crush it. He's making progress. Because the current here is the way it is. Because the *Kronos* is built for it. Because he's had experience. But we're just barely making headway.

Shackleton's ice-reinforced ship, the *Endurance*, was crushed by pack ice in the Weddell Sea. The *Titanic* sank. The *Hans Hedtoft* did, too. And so did the *Proteus* when it was attempting to rescue Lieutenant Greely's expedition during the second International Polar Year. There are no complete records for losses on Arctic voyages.

There's too much resistance in the ice. It doesn't make any sense to try to conquer it. Right now I can see how the impact of collisions has splintered the edges of the floes, forcing them up into barriers twenty metres high; underneath, the floes extend thirty metres down in the water. It's freezing up all around us. At this moment I can feel how the sea wants to close us in, how it's merely a coincidental, passing constellation of water, wind, and current that allows us to continue. A hundred sea miles north, the pack ice forms a wall that nothing can penetrate. Towards the east stand the solidly frozen icebergs that have broken off from the Jakobshavn Glacier; in a single year it has calved a thousand icebergs, amounting to more than 140 million tons of ice, standing between us and the land like a rigid chain of mountains seventy-five sea miles from the coast. At any given time floating ice covers a fourth of the earth's ocean area. The drift ice belt in Antarctica is twenty million square kilometres; between Greenland and Canada it's between eight and ten million square kilometres.

Yet they still want to conquer the ice. They want to sail through it and build oil drilling platforms on it and tow table icebergs from the South Pole to the Sahara to irrigate the deserts.

These are schemes whose interim projections do not interest me. It's a waste of time calculating impossibilities. You can try to live with the ice. You can't fight it or change it or live instead of it.

In some ways ice is so transparent. It carries its history on its surface. Ice packs, knolls, and slush form when the ice melts and then freezes again. The blend of various ice ages in mosaic ice: the black fragments of *sikussaq*, ancient ice formed in protected fjords, released over time and forced out to sea. Now, in the last rays of the sun, a fine veil of *qanik*, snow flurries, falls from the clouds that the sun has ducked under.

A reed stretches from the white surface straight into my heart. Like an extension of the saltwater tree within the ice.

*   *   *

When I wake up, I realize I've been asleep for some time. It must be night.

The *Kronos* continues to move forward. Its movements tell me that Lukas is still having to break through new ice.

I try the drawers in the medicine cupboard. They're locked. I wrap my sweater around my elbow and push in the glass. On the shelves there are scissors, clips and tweezers. An otoscope, a bottle of ethanol, iodine, sterile-wrapped surgical needles. I find two disposable scalpels with plastic handles and a roll of Leuco bandages. I put the thin plastic handles together and wrap them with tape. Now they will not break so easily.

There are no warning footsteps. The door simply opens. The mechanic enters carrying a tray. He looks more tired and more stooped than when I saw him last. His eyes fix on the broken glass.

I hold the scalpel against my thigh. My palms are sweaty. He looks down at my hand. I lay the knife on the bed. He puts down the tray.

"Urs has outd-done himself."

I feel as if I'm going to throw up if I look at him. He goes over and shuts the door. I move away. Self-control is so fragile.

The worst thing is not the anger. The worst thing is the physical desire behind the anger. It's possible to live with pure emotion. It is my secret need to cling to him that truly frightens me.

"You've been on expeditions yourself, Smilla. You know there c-comes a time when you have to let it proceed, when you can't stop it any more."

Somehow I think that I don't know him, that I've never made love with him. On the other hand, there's a coldly dignified consistency in his lack of regret. As soon as the opportunity presents itself, I'm going to kick him out of my life. But right now he's my only frail, improbable chance.

"I want to show you something," I say. And then I tell him what it is.

He laughs. Not a happy laugh.

"Impossible, Smilla."

I open the door for him, so that he'll leave. We've been whispering, but now I give up talking softly.

"Isaiah," I say. "Now, in a way, you were in on this too. You as well, you were there on the roof behind him."

His hands grip my arms and he lifts me back towards the bed. "How c-can you be so sure, Smilla?"

His stuttering has become much worse. There's fear in his face. There may not be a single person now on board the *Kronos* who isn't afraid.

"You w-won't run away, will you? You'll c-come back with me afterwards?"

I almost laugh.

"Where would I go, Føjl?"

He doesn't smile.

"Lander told me that he saw you walk on water."

I take off my socks. Between my toes and the ball of my foot there's a piece of bandage. It holds Jakkelsen's passkey in place.

We don't meet a soul. The light above the quarterdeck is off. When I let us in, we both realize that we're standing a few metres away from the deck platform where we waited less than twenty-four hours ago to observe Jakkelsen's last journey. This awareness means nothing in particular. Love will grow when you have energy to spare, but when you need your energy simply to survive, to secure food and sleep and shelter, then it shrivels up.

On the lower level I turn on the light, a flood of light compared to the beam from my torch. Maybe I'm being rash, but there's no time for anything else. We'll reach our destination in a few hours at the most. Then the deck lights will be lit and these desolate rooms will be full of people.

We stop in front of the bulkhead at the end of the room.

I'm staking everything on my curiosity. I want to know why, according to my measurements, the wall has been moved more than a metre and a half away from the hydraulic rudder system. Why there's some sort of generator somewhere behind the wall.

I glance at the mechanic. Suddenly I can't understand why he's come with me. Maybe he doesn't know why, either. Maybe because of the lure of the improbable. I point at the door to the metal workshop.

"There's a mallet in there."

He doesn't seem to hear me. He seizes hold of the moulding around the edge of the wall and yanks it off. He examines the nail holes. It's fresh wood.

He slips his hands into the gap between the panelling and the bulkhead and pulls. It won't budge. There are about fifteen nails in each side. Then he yanks at it sharply and the wall comes away in his hands. It's a piece of plywood ten millimetres thick and six metres square. In his hands it looks like a cupboard door.

Behind it is a refrigerator that's two metres tall and one metre wide, made of stainless steel. It reminds me of the dairies in Copenhagen in the sixties, where for the first time I saw people using energy to keep something cold. It has been secured against the rolling of the ship with metal fittings that must have been attached to the original wall of the room and then screwed on to the base of the refrigerator. It has a cylinder lock on the door.

He gets a screwdriver. He unscrews the fittings. Then he takes hold of the refrigerator. It seems immovable. He relaxes completely. Then he jerks it half a metre into the room. There's something knowing about his movements, an experience that you should deliver your utmost only for fractions of a second. He tugs three more times, and the refrigerator now has its back to us. He has a Phillips screwdriver on his knife. There must be fifty screws all around the back covering. He inserts the screwdriver, supporting the screw with the forefinger of his left hand, turning in a continuous movement, not in spurts. The screws leave the holes of their own accord. It takes less than ten minutes for him to remove all of them. He carefully gathers them in his pocket. He lifts off the entire back covering with its cords, cooling grid, compressor, and fluid tank.

Even under these circumstances, I note that what we're looking at is both banal and out of the ordinary: we're looking into a refrigerator from behind.

It's full of rice. The square boxes are carefully stacked from bottom to top.

He takes out a box and opens it, lifting the sachet free of its container. I have time to think that I didn't have much to lose, after all. Then I notice the skin of his face contract. I take another look at the bag. It's dull, almost opaque. It's not rice. It's a vacuum pack around a substance that is dense and yellowish like white chocolate.

He opens a knife blade and cuts a slit in the bag. With a little sigh it takes in air. Then a lumpy dark powder sifts into his hand, as if melted butter is poured into the sand that measures time in an hourglass.

He chooses a few more boxes at random, opens them, looks inside, and then carefully returns them to their place.

He screws the back covering on and shoves the refrigerator back. I don't help him; I can't touch him any more. He puts up the plywood and presses the wall into position. He gets a hammer and meticulously pounds it into place. His movements are distracted and stiff.

Not until then do we look at each other.

"*Mayam*," I say. "A stage between raw opium and heroin. With a high oil content; that's why it has to be refrigerated. Tørk developed it. Ravn told me about it. It's part of the agreement between Tørk and Verlaine. It's Verlaine's piece of the pie. We're supposed to pull in to some port on our way back. Maybe Holsteinsborg, maybe Nuuk. Maybe he has connections on the *Greenland Star*. Only ten years ago they were smuggling liquor and cigarettes up here. That's already a thing of the past. That's already the good old days. Now there's lots of cocaine in Nuuk. There's a Greenland upper class who live like Europeans. It's the nicest market up here."

His eyes are dreamy, remote. I have to reach him.

"Jakkelsen must have discovered it. He must have found out about it. And then he gave himself away. He must have been high and he overestimated his own abilities. He put pressure on them. That forced them to act. Tørk took care of the telegram for them. He had to do it. But he and Verlaine hate each other. They come from two different worlds. They only work together because they can use each other."

He leans down towards me and takes my hands.

"Smilla," he whispers, "when I was a child I had a tank you could wind up – with caterpillar treads. If you put something down in front of it, it would climb straight over it because it had such low gears. If the object was perpendicular the tank would turn around and crawl along the edge until it found some other way over. You couldn't stop it. You're like that tank, Smilla. You were supposed to be kept out of all this, but you kept on getting involved. You were supposed to be left behind in Copenhagen, but suddenly you wound up on board. They lock you up – that was my idea, it was the safest thing for you. They lock the door; that's the end of Smilla. And then suddenly you're out again. You keep popping up. You're like that tank, Smilla."

Irreconcilable emotions are battling in his voice.

"When *I* was a child," I say, "my father gave me a teddy bear. Until then we'd only had dolls that we'd made ourselves. The bear lasted a week. First it got dirty, then the fur came off. It got holes in it and the stuffing fell out; and apart from that it was hollow inside. You're like that teddy bear, Føjl."

We're sitting next to each other on the bed in his cabin. On the desk is one of those flat flasks, but he's the only one drinking.

He's huddled up with his hands between his thighs.

"It's a meteorite," he says. "Some sort of stone. Tørk says that it's ancient. It's wedged into a kind of saddle in the cliff beneath the ice. We're going to pick it up."

I think about the photographs among Tørk's papers. I should have guessed then. The ones that looked like X-rays. The Widman-stätten structure. It's in every textbook. The visible manifestation of the relationship between nickel and iron in meteorites.

"Why this one?" I ask.

"Whoever finds something of interest in Greenland has to report it to the National Museum in Nuuk. From there they'll c-call the Mineralogical Museum and the Institute for Metallurgy in Copenhagen. The find will be registered as something of national interest and will be confiscated."

He leans forward.

"Tørk says it weighs fifty tons. It's the biggest meteorite ever found. They took along oxygen and acetylene in '91. They cut off several fragments. Tørk says there are diamonds in it. Substances not found on earth."

If it hadn't been for the cock-eyed situation, I might have almost thought there was something touching and boyish about him. A child's enthusiasm at the thought of the mysterious substances, the diamonds, the gold at the end of the rainbow.

"Isaiah?"

"He went along in '91. He was with his f-father."

Of course that's the way it happened.

"He ran away from the ship in Nuuk. They had to leave him behind. Loyen found him and sent him home."

"And you, Føjl?" I say. "What did you want with him?"

When he understands what I'm asking, his expression becomes stony and hard. Now, when it's all too late anyway, I manage to reach into the far corners of his soul.

"I never touched him, of course. Up there on the roof. I loved him, in a way I've n-never . . ."

His stuttering strangles his sentence. He waits for the tension to subside.

"Tørk knew that he had taken something. A c-cassette tape. The glacier had moved. They searched for two weeks without finding it. Finally Tørk chartered a helicopter and flew to Thule. To find the Eskimos who had been on the expedition in '66. He found them, all right. But they d-didn't want to come back. So he got a description of the route from them. That's the tape the Baron took. That's what you found."

"So how did you happen to move into the White Cells?"

I know the answer.

"Ving," I say. "It was Ving. He put you there to keep an eye on Isaiah and Juliane."

He shakes his head.

"The other way around, of course," I say. "You were there first. Ving moved Isaiah and Juliane in to have them near you. Maybe to find out how much they knew or remembered. That's why Juliane's request to move to a lower floor wasn't approved. They were supposed to be near you."

"Seidenfaden hired me. I had never heard of the other two. Not until you uncovered them. I had been a diver for Seidenfaden. He's a transport engineer. At that time he was dealing in antiques. I dived for idols for him, in Liai Lake in Burma, before the state of emergency."

I think about the tea he made for me, how it tasted of the tropics.

"Later I run into him in Copenhagen. I am unemployed. Have no p-place to live. He suggests that I keep an eye on the Baron."

There's not a single human being who doesn't find it a relief to be forced to tell the truth. The mechanic is not a natural liar.

"Tørk?"

His gaze becomes remote. "Someone who sets his mind on something, he does it."

"What does he know about us?" I ask. "Does he know we're sitting here right now?"

He shakes his head.

"And you, Føjl? Who are you?"

His eyes are empty. It's the one question he has never found an answer for. "Someone who wants to make a little money."

"I hope it's a lot of money," I say. "Enough to compensate for the death of two children."

His mouth tightens.

"Give me a swig," I say.

The flask is empty. He takes another one out of the drawer. I catch a glimpse of a round blue plastic container and a yellow cloth wrapped around something rectangular.

The alcohol has a real kick to it.

"Loyen, Ving, Andreas Fine Licht?"

"They were excluded from the start. They're t-too old. This was supposed to be *our* expedition."

I can hear Tørk's voice behind his clichés. There's something charming about naïveté. Until it's seduced. Then it's simply depressing.

"So when I started making trouble, all of you agreed that you should be the one to follow me?"

He shakes his head. "I never heard about any of this, or about Tørk and Katja. That came later. Everything you and I found out together was new to me."

Now I see him for what he is. It's not a disappointing sight. It's just a more complete picture than the one I saw at first. Infatuation always simplifies things. Like mathematics. Seeing him clearly means becoming objective, dropping the illusion of a hero and coming back to reality.

Or maybe I'm already drunk after a few sips. That's what comes from drinking so seldom. You get drunk as soon as the first molecules are absorbed by the mucous membranes in the mouth.

He stands up and goes over to the porthole. I lean forward. With one hand I pick up the bottle. With the other I pull out the drawer and touch the cloth inside. It's wrapped around a rounded, ridged metal object.

I look at him. I see his weight, his slowness, his vigour, his greed, and his simplicity. His need for a leader, the danger he represents. I also see his carefulness, his warmth, his patience, his passion. And I see that he is still my only chance.

Then I close my eyes and wipe my internal slate clean. Gone is our mutual lying, the unanswered questions, the justifiable and the morbid suspicions. The past is a luxury we can no longer afford.

"Føjl," I say, "are you going to dive near that stone?"

He has nodded. I didn't hear whether he said anything or not. But he nodded. For a moment this affirmation blocks out everything else.

"Why?" I hear myself ask.

"It's lying in a lake of meltwater. It's almost covered. It's supposed to be close to the surface of the ice. Seidenfaden doesn't think it will be difficult to get to it. Either through a meltwater tunnel or through the cracks in a crevasse right next to the saddle. The problem is getting it out. Seidenfaden thinks we should enlarge the tunnel that drains the lake and bring the stone out that way. It will have to be enlarged with explosives. It will all be underwater work."

I sit down next to him.

"Water", I say, "freezes at 0 °C. What explanation did Tørk give you for the water surrounding the stone?"

"Isn't there something about the pressure in the ice?"

"Yes. There's something about the pressure. The further down you go in a glacier, the warmer it gets. Because of the pressure of the ice masses above. The ice cap is −23 °C at a depth of five hundred metres. Five hundred metres further down it's −10 °C. Since the melting point depends on the pressure, water actually exists at temperatures below freezing. Maybe even around −1.6 °C. There are temperate glaciers in the Alps and the Rocky Mountains in which meltwater exists at a depth of thirty metres and below."

He nods. "That's what Tørk explained to me."

"But Gela Alta isn't in the Alps. It's a so-called 'cold' glacier. And it's quite small. At the present time its surface temperature will be −10 °C. The temperature at its base is about the same. The melting point under that pressure is around zero. Not one drop of liquid water can form in that glacier."

He looks at me as he takes a drink. What I've said doesn't bother him. Maybe he didn't understand it. Maybe Tørk provokes a sense of trust in people that locks out the rest of the world. Maybe it's just the usual problem: ice is incomprehensible to those who were not born to it. I try another approach.

"Did they tell you how they found it?"

"The Greenlanders found it. In prehistoric times. It was in their legends. That's why they got Andreas Fine Licht involved. In those days it might have still been on top of the ice."

"When a meteor enters the atmosphere," I say, "the first thing that happens, at about 150 kilometres out, is that a blast wave goes through it, as if it had rammed into a concrete wall. The outer layer melts off. I've seen black stripes of meteor dust on the ice cap. But this decreases the speed of the meteor and reduces the heat. If it reaches the earth without breaking up, it will typically have the earth's median temperature of 5 °C. So it doesn't melt its way down. But it doesn't just sit there either. The force of gravity calmly and quietly presses it down. No meteorites of any size have ever been found *on top* of the ice. And none ever will be. Gravity will press them down. They become encapsulated and with time are carried out to sea. If they get caught in a crevice underground, they'll be pulverized. There's nothing delicate about a glacier. It's a combination of a stonecrusher and a gigantic carpenter's plane. It doesn't create enchanted caves around objects of geological interest. It files them down, mashes them to powder, and empties the powder into the Atlantic Ocean."

"Then there must be warm springs around it," the mechanic says.

"There's no volcanic activity on Gela Alta."

"I've s-seen the photographs. It's lying in a lake."

"Yes," I say. "I've seen those photographs, too. If the whole thing's not a hoax, it's sitting in water. I sincerely hope that it's a hoax."

"Why?"

I wonder whether he'll be able to grasp it. But there's no alternative to telling him the truth. Or what I suspect is the truth.

"I can't know for sure, but it looks as if the heat might be coming from the stone. As if it's emitting some kind of energy. Maybe in the form of some kind of radioactivity. But there's also another possibility."

"What's that?"

I can tell by looking at him that these are not new ideas for him, either. He, too, knew that something was wrong. But he pushed the problem aside. He's a Dane. Always choose the comfort of suppressed information rather than the burdensome truth.

"The forward tank of the *Kronos* has been rebuilt. It can be sterilized. It's equipped with supplies of oxygen and compressed air. It's constructed as if they were going to transport a large animal. It has occurred to me that Tørk may believe that the stone you are going to pick up is alive."

The bottle is empty.

"That was a good idea with the fire alarm," I say.

He smiles wearily. "It was the only way to put the papers back and at the same t-time explain why they were wet."

We're sitting at opposite ends of the bed. The *Kronos* is moving more and more slowly. Inside my body rages an obscure and voluptuous battle between two kinds of poison: the crystal-clear unreality of the amphetamine and the fuzzy pleasure of the alcohol.

"It was when Juliane told you that Loyen had regularly examined Isaiah that I decided it might have something to do with a disease. But when I saw the X-rays, I was convinced. X-rays from the expedition in '66. Lagermann got them from Queen Ingrid's Hospital in Nuuk. They didn't die from the explosion. They had been invaded by some kind of parasite. Maybe some sort of worm. But bigger than any I've ever seen. And faster. They died within a few days. Maybe in a few hours. Loyen wanted to find out whether Isaiah had been infected."

He shakes his head. He doesn't want to believe me. He's on a treasure hunt. On his way to find diamonds.

"That's why Loyen has been involved right from the start. He's a scientist. Money is secondary. He was after the Nobel Prize. He's been anticipating a scientific sensation from the moment he found out about it back in the forties."

"Why didn't they tell me all this?" he asks.

We all live our lives blindly believing in the people who make the decisions. Believing in science. Because the world is inscrutable and all information is hazy. We accept the existence of a round globe, of an atom's nucleus that sticks together like drops, of a curving universe – and the necessity of interfering with genetic material. Not because we know these things are true, but because we believe the people who tell us so. We are all proselytes of science. And, in contrast to the followers of other religions, we can no longer bridge the gap between ourselves and the priests. Problems arise when we stumble on an outright lie. And it affects our own lives. The mechanic's panic is that of a child who for the first time catches his parents in a lie he had always suspected.

"Isaiah's father was diving," I say. "Presumably the others were, too. Most parasites go through a stage in water. You're going to dive, and you'll get others to dive. You're the last person they're going to tell."

Emotion drives him to his feet.

375

"You have to help me make a phone call," I say.

As I stand up, my hand closes over a piece of metal wrapped in a cloth in the drawer, and around a flat tin.

The radio room is located behind the bridge, across from the officers' mess. We manage to make it there without being seen. Outside the door I hesitate. He shakes his head.

"It's empty. The IMO requires it to be manned twice an hour, but we have no radio technician on board. Instead, they set the HF at 2182 Khz, the international emergency frequency, and then they connect it to an alarm which goes off when someone sends a distress signal."

Jakkelsen's key won't open the door. I feel an urge to scream.

"I *have to* get inside," I say.

The mechanic shrugs.

"You owe it to both of us," I say.

He still wavers for a moment. Then he carefully places his hands on the door handle and pushes the door in. There's no splintering of wood, only a scraping sound as the latch forces the steel frame inward.

The room is quite small and crammed with equipment. There's a little VHF, a double long-wave transmitter the size of a refrigerator, some kind of box that I've never seen before, with a Morse key mounted on top. A desk, chairs, telex machine, fax, and a coffee machine with sugar and plastic cups. On the wall there's a clock with paper triangles of different colours taped to its face, a mobile telephone, a calendar, equipment certificates in thin steel frames, and a licence certifying Sonne as a radio operator. On the desk there's a tape recorder that has been screwed down, manuals, and an open radio log.

I write the number on a piece of paper.

"This is Ravn," I say.

He stiffens. I take him by the arm, thinking that this is the last time in my life I'll ever touch him.

He sits down in the chair and is transformed into a different person. His movements become swift, precise, and authoritative, just as in his kitchen. He taps on the face of the clock.

"The triangles indicate the internationally established times when the channels have to be kept free and open for distress signals. If we go into that time, the alarm will go off. For the HF this means for three minutes past the hour and the half-hour. We have ten minutes."

He hands me a telephone receiver, taking the headphones himself. I sit down next to him.

"It's hopeless in this weather and this far from the coast," he says.

At first I can follow what he's doing, even though I couldn't have done it myself.

He selects the maximum output of two hundred watts. At that level the transmitter risks drowning out its own signal, but the bad weather and distance from shore make it necessary.

There's the crackling of empty space, and then a voice comes through.

"This is Sisimiut. What can we do for you?"

He decides to transmit on the carrier wave. The transmitter has analogue readouts and automatic settings. Now it will continue to adjust according to the carrier wave while the conversation is transmitted over a side band. It's the most efficient method, and probably the *only* one on a night like this.

Right before he sets the dials, the receiver picks up a Canadian station sending classical music over the short-wave net. For a moment I can't see the room around me for childhood memories. It's Victor Halkenhvad singing *Gurrelieder*. Then Sisimiut is back.

The mechanic doesn't ask for Lyngby Radio. He asks for Reykjavik. When the station responds, he asks for Torshavn.

"What's happening?" I ask.

He covers the microphone. "All the larger stations have an automatic directional finder that is switched on when they receive a call. They compute the costs for a conversation under the name of the ship you give. In case a false name is used, they take a bearing on the ship's position, so that a conversation can always be charged back to a set of coordinates. I'm c-creating a smokescreen. With every new station it'll be harder to trace the call. By the fourth link-up it'll be impossible."

He gets Lyngby Radio, tells them he's calling from the good ship *Candy 2*, and gives them Ravn's number. He looks into my eyes. We both know that if I demand a different procedure, a direct call that would make it possible for Ravn to track the position of the *Kronos*, he will break off the connection. I don't say a word. I've already pressed him hard. And we're not done yet.

He requests a security line, with no one listening in. Far away, in a different part of the world, a telephone rings. The signal is faint and intermittent.

"What's it like outside, Smilla?"

I try to remember the night and the weather. "Clouds with ice crystals."

"That's the worst. The HF beams arc along the atmosphere. When it's overcast or snowing, they can get caught in a reflection trap."

The telephone rings, monotone and lifeless. I give up. Hopelessness is a numbness that emanates from your gut.

Then someone picks up the phone.

"Yes?"

The voice is close, crystal clear, but groggy with sleep. It must be around five in the morning in Denmark.

I envision her the way she looked in the photos in Ravn's wallet. White-haired, wearing a wool suit.

"May I speak to Ravn?"

As she puts down the receiver, a child starts crying nearby. It must be sleeping in their bedroom. Maybe between them in the bed.

"Ravn speaking."

"It's me," I say.

"You'll have to call some other time."

Because his voice comes through so clearly, the rejection is quite clear as well. I don't know what has happened. But now I've gone too far to wonder about it.

"It's too late," I say. "I want to talk about what happens on the roofs. In Singapore and in Christianshavn."

He doesn't reply. But he's still listening.

It's impossible to visualize him as a private citizen. What does he wear in bed? How does he look right now, in bed next to his grandchild?

"Let's imagine that it's late afternoon," I say. "The boy is walking home alone from kindergarten. He's the only child who isn't picked up every day. He's walking along the way children do, wandering and skipping, with his eyes on the ground. Only aware of his immediate surroundings. The same way your grandchildren walk, Ravn."

I can hear him breathing as distinctly as if he were in the room with us.

The mechanic has pulled the headset away from one ear so that

378

he can follow the conversation and also listen for sounds in the passageway.

"That's why he doesn't see the man until he's right next to him. He was waiting in the car. The buildings have no windows facing the car park. It's almost dark. It's the middle of December. The man grabs him. Not by the arm, but by his clothes. By the bib of his dungarees, which won't tear, and where he won't leave any marks. But he miscalculates. The boy recognizes him at once. They've spent weeks together. But that's not why he remembers him. He remembers him from one of the last days. The day he saw his father die. It may be that he saw the man force the divers back into the water after one had died. At a time when they hadn't yet understood what was wrong. Or maybe it was the experience of death which the boy has come to associate with the man. At any rate, he doesn't see a human being in front of him. He sees a threat. The way only children can experience threats. It's overwhelming. At first he freezes. All children freeze."

"You're guessing," says Ravn.

The signal is getting fainter. For a moment I almost lose my train of thought.

"The child beside you," I say, "would freeze up, too. That's where the man miscalculates. The boy in front of him looks so small. He bends down towards him. He's like a doll. He is going to lift him on to the seat. For a moment he lets go. That is his mistake. He hadn't anticipated the boy's spirit. Suddenly the boy takes off. The ground is covered with packed snow. That's why the man doesn't catch him. He doesn't have the boy's training in running on snow."

Now they're paying attention, the man next to me and the man an infinite distance away. It's not so much me they're listening to. It's fear that binds us, the child's fear we all carry within us.

"The boy runs along the building. The man runs out into the street and blocks the way. The boy reaches the warehouses. The man comes after him, slipping and stumbling. But calmer now. There's no escape. The boy turns towards him. The man relaxes. The boy looks around. He has stopped thinking. But inside him an engine is spinning that will keep on going until all his strength is used up. It's this engine that the man hasn't counted on. Suddenly the boy is on his way up the scaffolding. The man follows. The boy knows what's behind him. It's terror personified. He knows that he's going to die. This feeling is stronger than his fear of heights.

He continues up to the roof. And then he runs forward. The man stops. Perhaps he wanted this to happen from the very beginning, maybe the idea first occurs to him now, maybe only up here he becomes aware of his own intentions. The possibility of eliminating a threat. To avoid having the boy ever tell anyone what he saw in a cave on a glacier somewhere in Davis Strait."

"You're guessing." Ravn's voice is a whisper.

"The man moves towards the boy. Watches him running along the edge, looking for a way down. Children can't grasp the whole picture, the boy probably doesn't even know where he is; he only sees what's a few metres ahead. At the edge of the snow the man stops. He doesn't want to leave any tracks. He's hoping it won't be necessary."

The signal disappears. The mechanic twists the dials. It comes back.

"The man waits. There seems to be an enormous amount of self-confidence in this waiting. As if he knows that his presence is enough. His silhouette against the sky. As in Singapore. Was it enough there, Ravn? Or did he push her because she was older and more rational than the boy? Because he could come right up to her? Because there wasn't any snow to leave tracks in?"

The sound is of such clarity that I think it's the mechanic, but he is silent.

It's there again, tormented. It's coming from Ravn.

I speak softly to him. "Look at the child, Ravn, the child next to you. That's the child on the roof. Tørk is behind him, a silhouette. He could stop the boy, but he doesn't, he drives him onward, as he did the woman. Who was she? What did he do?"

He disappears and then returns, far away.

"I have to know! Her name was Ravn!"

The mechanic puts a hand over my mouth. His palm is cold as ice. I must have screamed.

". . . was . . ." Ravn's voice fades out.

I grab the apparatus and shake it. The mechanic pulls me away. At that moment Ravn's voice comes back, clear, distinct, stripped of all emotion.

"My daughter. He pushed her. Are you satisfied, Miss Smilla?"

"The photo," I say, "did she take that photo of Tørk? Was she with the police?"

He says something. At the same time his voice is carried away through a tunnel of noise and vanishes. The connection is broken.

The mechanic turns off the light in the bulkhead. In the glow from the instrument panels his face is pale and tense. Slowly he takes off the headset and hangs it back in place. I'm sweating as if I'd been running.

"Testimony from a child wouldn't be valid in court, would it?"

"It would have weighed heavily with the jurors," I say.

He doesn't continue this line of thought; he doesn't have to. We're both thinking the same thing. There was something about Isaiah's eyes, a wisdom beyond his years, beyond anyone's years, a deep insight into the adult world. Tørk was familiar with that look. There are other kinds of accusations than the ones presented in court.

"What about the door?" I say.

He puts his hand on the steel frame and steadily bends it back into place.

He has accompanied me along the external companionway. At the sick bay he pauses for a moment in the doorway.

I turn away. The body's pain is so paper-thin and insignificant compared to that of the mind.

He spreads out his fingers and looks down at his hands.

"After we're done," he says, "I'm going to kill him."

Nothing could induce me to spend the night on an examining table – even such a short and bleak night as the one ahead of me. I pull off the sheets, remove the cushions from the chairs, and lie down right in front of the door. If anyone tries to come in, they'll have to push me aside first.

No one tries to get in. I have a few hours of deep sleep; then the hull scrapes against something and the deck is full of footsteps. I think I hear the rattling of the anchor chain, too; maybe the *Kronos* has put in at the edge of the ice. I'm too tired to get up. Somewhere close by, out in the darkness, lies Gela Alta.

○2

CERTAIN TYPES OF SLEEP are worse than no sleep at all. After the last two hours I wake up more tense, more physically depleted than if I had kept myself awake. It's dark outside.

I make a list in my mind. I ask myself whom I could recruit to my side. It's not an expression of hope. It's just that the mind won't quit. As long as one is alive, it will never stop looking for ways to survive. As if there were someone else inside, someone more naïve but also more tenacious than oneself.

I give up on the list. The crew of the *Kronos* can be divided into those who are already against me and those who will be, when the chips are down. I don't include the mechanic. I'm trying not to think about him at all.

When they bring my breakfast I'm lying on the bed. Someone fumbles for the light switch, and I ask him not to turn on the light. He puts the tray inside the door and leaves. It was Maurice. He wouldn't have seen the broken glass in the cupboard in the dark.

I force myself to eat a little. Someone is sitting outside. Now and then I can hear a chair scraping against the door. At some point the auxiliary engine and the big generators start up. Ten minutes later they start unloading from the quarterdeck. I can't see what it is. The sick bay portholes face aft.

The day is beginning. The dawn doesn't seem to bring light with it; it's more like a physical substance itself, like wisps of smoke drifting past the portholes.

The island isn't visible from this angle. But I can feel the ice. The *Kronos* is tied up astern. The edge of the ice is about seventy-five metres away. I can see one of the ropes passing through an anchor of packed ice, attached to a beacon of churned-up, solid ice floes.

The motorboat docks and is emptied. There's not enough light to identify the people or determine the baggage. At some point it

382

looks as if the boat has been abandoned, tied up at the edge of the ice.

I feel as if I've gone the whole way. You can't ask of anyone to go further than that.

Jakkelsen's key is inside the cushion that I'm using as a pillow. There is also a blue plastic container. And a duster wrapped around a piece of metal. I had expected him to find out right away, but he hasn't come.

It's a revolver. Ballester Molina Inûnángitsoq. Manufactured in Nuuk under an Argentine licence. There's a disparity between its purpose and its design. Surprising that evil can assume so simple a form.

Rifles can be excused by the fact that they're used for hunting. In certain types of snow a long-barrelled, large-calibre revolver may be necessary for self-defence. Because both musk oxen and polar bears can slip around the hunter and attack from behind. So swiftly that there's no time to swing a rifle around.

But for this snub-nosed weapon there's no excuse.

The bullets have a flat-tipped jacket of lead. The box is full. I load the cylinder. It holds six. I snap the cylinder into place.

I stick a finger down my throat, producing a rattling cough. I kick at the remaining shards of glass in the cupboard door. They fall to the deck with a crash. The door swings open and Maurice comes in. I lean against the bed, holding the revolver with both hands.

"Get down on your knees," I say.

He starts towards me. I aim the barrel downwards at his legs and press the trigger. Nothing happens. I've forgotten to release the safety catch. He makes a forward, upward jab with his good left arm. The blow catches me in the chest and throws me up against the cupboard. Pieces of glass from the broken window dig into my back with that typically cold pain of extremely sharp edges. I drop to my knees. He kicks me in the face. His foot breaks my nose and momentarily robs me of consciousness. When I come to, one of his feet is next to my head; he must be standing right over me. I take the scalpels wrapped in Band-Aids out of the tool pouch in my work trousers. I move forward a little and cut him behind his ankle. There's a tiny snap as his Achilles' tendon is severed. When I take the knife away there's a yellowish glimpse of bone at the bottom of the incision. I roll away from him. He tries to come after me, but he falls on his face. It's not until I stand up that I realize I'm still holding the revolver. He's down on one knee. Without haste he reaches inside his windcheater. I step over to him and hit him in the mouth with the barrel of the gun. He falls backwards against the cupboard. I don't dare approach him again. I go out of the door. His key is still sitting in the lock. I lock the door behind me.

The corridor is empty. But there's movement behind the door to the mess. I open it a crack. Urs is setting the table. I slip inside the door. He puts down a basket of bread. He doesn't notice me at first; then he does.

I unscrew the top of a thermos. Pour myself a cup, put in some sugar, stir it, and take a sip. The coffee is almost scalding, the burned taste of the beans is nauseating combined with the sugar.

"How long are we going to be here, Urs?"

He's staring at my face. I can't feel my nose, can only sense a diffuse heat.

"You're under arrest, *Fräulein Smilla*."

"I have permission to take a walk."

He doesn't believe me. He's hoping that I'll leave. Nobody likes a guaranteed loser.

"*Drei Tage*. Tomorrow the provisions will be taken ashore. Then we'll all work *im Schnee*."

They're going to help pull the stone down the chute made from railway sleepers. That means that it must be very close to the coast.

"Who has gone ashore?"

"Tørk, Verlaine, *der neue Passagier. Mit Flaschen*."

At first I don't understand him. He sketches them with his hands in the air: oxygen tanks.

I'm on my way out of the door when he comes after me. The situation is a repeat; we've stood this way before.

"*Fräulein Smilla . . .*"

Urs, the man who has never dared come too close, takes hold of my arm, insistent.

"*Sie müssen schlafen. Sie brauchen medizinische* treatment," he says.

I pull my arm away. I haven't succeeded in frightening him. Instead, I have awakened his compassion.

At sea, as a matter of principle, you lock a door only when leaving a room, to make the work easier during a rescue operation if there's a fire. Lukas sleeps with his door unlocked. He's sound asleep. I close the door behind me and sit down at the foot of his bunk. He opens his eyes. At first they're dull with sleep, then glassy with shock.

"I've temporarily discharged myself."

He tries to reach me. He's quicker than you might expect, considering that he's lying on his back and has just been sound asleep. I show him the revolver. He keeps coming. I bring the barrel up to his face and snap off the safety.

"I've got nothing to lose," I say.

He relaxes. "Go back. Being under arrest is your security."

"Oh, sure," I say, "having Maurice outside is so comforting. Put on your coat. We're going out on deck."

He hesitates. Then he reaches for his overclothes. "Tørk is right. You're sick."

Maybe he's right. In any case, a layer of numbness has come between me and the rest of the world. A crust in which the nerves are dead. I rinse off my nose at the sink. It's awkward because I have to hold the gun in my other hand and keep an eye on Lukas at the same time. There's not as much blood as I thought. Facial wounds always feel worse than they are.

He goes first. As we pass the companionway to the upper decks, Sonne comes down. I step close to Lukas. Sonne stops. Lukas waves him on. He hesitates, then his years of training school and in the navy, and all his inner discipline take over. He steps aside. We continue on across the deck. Over to the rail. I stand a few metres away. This means we have to speak loudly to hear each other. But it makes it more difficult for him to reach me.

I have spent so many days on the open sea that the island seems to me to have a dark, painful beauty about it.

It's so narrow and high that it looms up from the frozen sea like a tower. The rock is visible only in a few places; by and large it's covered with ice. Like a cold Arctic cornucopia, the ice spills over the edge of the bowl-shaped top and down the steep sides. A spit is protruding through the sea towards the *Kronos*: the Barren Glacier. If we could see the other sides, we'd see sheer rock faces, ravaged by crevasses and avalanches.

The wind is blowing off the island, a north wind, *avangnaq*. This crystallizes into another word, and at first there is only the internal sound, as if it were spoken by someone else, someone inside me. *Pirhirhuq*, snowstorm weather. I shake my head. We're not in

Thule; the weather is different here. My exhausted system is creating phantoms.

"Where will you go afterwards?"

He gestures around the deck and at the open water. At the motorboat over at the edge of the ice.

"Feel free, Miss Smilla."

Now that he drops all pretence of courtesy, I realize that it has never really been part of him. It belongs to Tørk. Along with the justice on board. Lukas has never been anything but a tool.

He starts walking away from me. He, too, is a loser. He has nothing more to lose, either. I let the heavy metal slip down into my pocket. Before, in the sick bay, I could have shot Maurice. Maybe. Or maybe I consciously didn't release the safety.

"Jakkelsen," I say to his back. "Verlaine killed Jakkelsen, and Tørk sent the telegram."

He comes back. He stands next to me, staring out across the island. He stays there, his expression never changing, as I talk. At one point the outlines of several large birds tear themselves away from high up on the slopes of ice: migratory albatrosses. He doesn't see them. I tell him everything, from the beginning. I don't know how long it takes. When I'm done, the wind has died down. The light also seems to have shifted, although I couldn't say exactly how. Now and then I glance over at the door. No one appears.

Lukas has lit one cigarette after another. As if lighting up, inhaling, and then exhaling the smoke must be done with great precision each time.

He straightens up and gives me a smile.

"They should have listened to me," he says. "I suggested that they give you an injection. Fifteen milligrams of Apozepam. I told them you would escape. Tørk was against the idea."

He smiles again. This time there is madness in his smile. "It's almost as if he wanted you to come. He left the rubber dinghy behind. Maybe he wants you to go ashore."

He waves at me.

"Duty calls," he says.

I lean on the rail. Somewhere in the low fog banks where the ice floats out to sea is Tørk.

Far below there is a white wreath. Lukas's cigarette butts. They're not bobbing up and down; they're lying perfectly still. The water they're floating in is still black. But it's no longer shiny. It's covered with a dull membrane. The sea around the *Kronos* is about to freeze

386

over. The clouds overhead are being sucked up into the heavens. The air is completely still. The temperature has dropped at least ten degrees in the last half hour.

Nothing seems to have been touched in my cabin. I get out a pair of short rubber boots and put my *kamiks* in a plastic bag.

The mirror reveals that my nose isn't particularly swollen. But it's crooked, pressed over much too far to one side.

In a moment he's going to start diving. I remember the steam in the photo. The water is probably 10 or 12 °C. He's only human. It's not much. I know that from my own experience. Yet you always try to keep yourself alive.

I put on my thermal trousers, two thin woollen sweaters, and my down jacket. From my box I take out a wrist compass and a flat canteen. And a woollen blanket. Sometime long ago I must have been preparing for just this moment.

All three of them are sitting down; that's why I don't spot them until I'm actually up on deck. The air has been let out of the rubber dinghy; it's a grey blanket of rubber with yellow markings, lying flat against the aft superstructure.

The woman is squatting down. She shows me her knife.

"I let the air out with this," she says.

She hands it back to Hansen, who's leaning against the davits.

She stands up and comes towards me. I have my back to the ladder. Seidenfaden follows her hesitantly.

"Katja," he says.

None of them is wearing outdoor gear.

"He wanted you to go ashore," she says.

Seidenfaden puts his hand on her shoulder. She turns around and hits him. One corner of his mouth splits open. His face looks like a mask.

"I love him," she says.

Her remark isn't directed at anyone in particular. She comes closer.

"Hansen found Maurice," she says, as if in explanation. And then without transition she adds, "Do you want him?"

I've seen it before, the domain where jealousy and insanity run together, erasing reality.

387

"No," I say.

I move backwards and bump into something that won't budge. Urs is standing behind me. He still has his apron on. Over it he's wearing a fur coat. In his hand is a loaf of bread. It must have just come out of the oven; in the cold it's surrounded by a halo of dense steam. The woman ignores him. When she reaches for me, Urs places the bread against her throat. She falls on to the rubber dinghy and stays there. The burn appears on her throat like film being developed, with marks from the ridges on the bread.

"What should I do?" Urs asks me.

I hand him the mechanic's revolver.

"Can you buy me some time?" I ask.

He looks thoughtfully at Hansen.

"No problem," he says.

The pontoon bridge is still out. As soon as I see the ice, I realize that I've come too early. It's still too transparent to bear my weight. There is a chair. I sit down to wait. I prop my feet up on the cable box. This is where Jakkelsen once sat. And Hansen. On a ship you're continually crossing your own tracks. Just as in life.

It's snowing. Big flakes, *qanik*, like the snow over Isaiah's grave. The ice is still so warm that the flakes melt on it. If I stare at the snow long enough, the flakes don't seem to be falling but rather growing up from the sea, rising to the sky to settle on the top of the rock tower above me. At first the snow is six-sided, newly formed flakes. After forty-eight hours the flakes break down, their outlines blur. By the tenth day, the snow is a grainy crystal that becomes compacted after two months. After two years it enters the transitional stage between snow and firn. After three years it becomes *névé*. After four years, it's transformed into a large, blocky glacial crystal.

It wouldn't survive more than three years here on Gela Alta. By that time the glacier would push it out to sea. There it would break up and float outward to melt, disperse, and be absorbed by the sea. And then some day it would rise up as newly formed snow.

The ice is greyish now. I step down on to it. It's not good. Nothing is much good any more.

I stay in the shelter of the ship for as long as possible. At one point the ice is so thin that I have to make a detour. They probably wouldn't see me, anyway. It has started to grow dark. The light is drifting away, without having really been there. I have to crawl the last ten metres on my stomach. I put the blanket on the ice and squirm my way forward.

The motorboat is tied up at the edge of the ice. It's empty. The shore is still three hundred metres away. A kind of stairway has formed here where the submerged part of the glacier has thawed several times and then frozen up again.

What's overpowering me at the moment is the smell of earth. After so long at sea, the island smells like a garden. I scrape away the layer of snow that's about forty centimetres thick. Underneath are remnants of moss and withered Arctic willow.

There was a thin layer of snow when they arrived; their footprints are quite clear. They had two sleighs with them. The mechanic was pulling one of them, Tørk and Verlaine the other.

They've headed up the slope to avoid the steep portals where the ice runs out to sea. Here the loose snow is half a metre deep. They've been taking it in turns to stamp down a trail.

I put on my *kamiks*. I keep my eyes on the snow and simply concentrate on walking. It is as if I was a child again. We're going somewhere, I don't remember where, it's been a long journey, maybe many *sinik*; I start to stumble, I'm no longer one with my feet, they're walking by themselves, plodding, as if each step were a task to complete. Somewhere inside me I feel an urge to give up, to sit down and sleep.

Then my mother is behind me. She knows what's happening, she has known it for some time. She talks to me, she who is usually so taciturn. She gives me a box on the ear, part buffet, part caress, What kind of wind is it, Smilla? It's *kanangnaq*. That's wrong, Smilla, you're asleep. No, I'm not. The wind is faint and damp, the ice must have just started breaking up. Speak politely to your mother, Smilla. You've learned rudeness from *qallunaaq*.

We keep on going this way, and I wake up again. I know that we have to get there; long ago I grew too heavy for her to carry me.

I'm thirty-seven years old. Fifty years ago, that was a full lifetime in Thule. But I've never grown up. I've never grown used to walking alone. Somewhere deep inside I'm still hoping that someone will come up behind me and box my ear. My mother. Moritz. Some outside force.

I'm starting to stumble. I'm standing near the glacier. They paused here. They put crampons on their boots.

Close up, I understand how the glacier got its name. The wind has worn down its surface to a compact, slippery covering with no irregularities, like a white, fired ceramic glaze. Right in front of me it slides over a drop of about fifty metres. Here the surface of the ice is broken up into an ice fall. A network of grey, white, and greyish-blue steps. From a distance they seem quite regular; on closer inspection they form a labyrinth.

I can't tell which way they've headed. I can't see them either. So I start walking. The tracks are harder to follow. But not impossible. The snow has settled on the horizontal steps; there they've left their marks. At one point, when I lose my bearings and begin searching in semicircles, I spot a yellow trace of urine from far away.

I start hallucinating and fragments of conversations come back to me. I say something to Isaiah. He answers. The mechanic is there, too.

"Smilla."

I walked a metre past him without seeing him. It's Tørk. He has been waiting for me. He has spoken my name so gently. Like the time he called me on the telephone, on the last night in my apartment.

He's alone. He has no sleigh and no baggage. Sitting there, he looks so colourful. The yellow boots. His red jacket casting a rosy glow across the snow around him. The turquoise band around his pale hair.

"I knew you would come. But I didn't know how. I saw you walking across the water."

As if we've been friends all along but had to hide it from the rest of the world.

"There was a layer of ice."

"Before that you walked through locked doors."

"I had a key."

He shakes his head. "For people with resources, the right events *happen*. They may look like coincidences, but they arise out of necessity. Katja and Ralf wanted to put the brakes on you in Copenhagen. But I saw possibilities. You would point out things that we'd overlooked. That Ving and Loyen had overlooked. That people always overlook."

He hands me a climbing harness. I step into it and fasten it in front.

"But what about the *Northern Light*?" I ask. "And the fire?"

"Licht called Katja when he got the cassette. He tried to blackmail her. We had to do something. It was my fault you got involved in that. I turned things over to Maurice and Verlaine. Verlaine has this primitive hatred of women."

He gives me the end of the rope. I make a figure-of-eight hitch. He hands me a short ice axe.

He goes first. He has a long, thin stick. He uses it to test the ground for crevasses. When he's fifteen metres away, he speaks. The shiny walls around us create acoustics like those in a bathroom. Harsh and yet intimate, as if we were sitting in the bathtub together.

"Of course, I've read the things you've written. This passion for ice is certainly fascinating."

He jabs his ice axe into the snow, wraps the rope around it, and carefully pulls in the rope as I follow him. When I reach him, he speaks again.

"What does your expertise have to say about this glacier?"

We gaze around us in the growing darkness. The question is difficult to answer.

"It does not know what to say. If it were ten times bigger, one might classify it as a very small ice calotte. If it were lower one would say it was a botu glacier. If the current and wind conditions had been slightly different, the drifting and deflation would have reduced it so much within a month that one would say there wasn't any glacier here at all, just an island with a little snow on it. It defies classification."

I come up to him again, and he hands me the rope. I hack out a belay stance, and he continues on. His movements are agile and methodical, but the ice makes them slightly fumbling too, as with all Europeans. He resembles a blind man, practised in his blindness, perfectly adapted to his stick, but still blind.

"The limited ability of science to explain things has always interested me. My own field of biology is based on zoological and botanical systems of classification that have all collapsed. As a science, biology no longer has any foundation. What do you think about change?"

His question is as a *non sequitur*. I go up after him, and he winds in the woven double rope. We're connected by an umbilical cord, like mother and child.

"It's supposed to be the spice of life," I say.

He hands me his thermos. I take a sip. Hot tea with lemon. He bends down. On the snow there are some dark grains, crushed stone.

391

"Four point six times ten to the ninth; 4.6 billion years. That's when the solar system began to assume its present form. The difficulty with the earth's geological history is that it can't be studied. There are no traces. Because since that time, since the time of Creation, rocks like these have gone through a countless number of metamorphoses. The same is true of the ice around us, the air, and the water. Their origins can no longer be traced. There are no substances on the earth that have preserved their original form. That's why meteorites are so interesting. They come from outside, they've escaped the transformation processes that Lovelock described in his theory about Gaia. Their form goes back to the origin of the solar system. As a rule they consist of the first metals in the universe, iron, nickel, silicates. Do you read fiction?"

I shake my head.

"That's too bad. The writers see where we're headed before the scientists do. What we discover in nature is not really a matter of what exists; what we find is determined by our ability to understand. Like Jules Verne's *The Golden Globe*, about a meteorite that turns out to be the most valuable thing on earth. Or Wells's visions of other life forms. Or Piper's *Uller Uprising*, in which a special form of life is described. Bodies formed on the basis of inorganic substances, from silicates."

We've reached a flat, windswept plateau. A series of regular crevasses opens before us. We must have reached the ablation zone, that spot where the glacier's lower layers move up towards the surface. There's a knob of rock that has parted the flow of ice. I didn't notice it from below because it's some type of white stone. Now it gleams in the gathering gloom.

The snow has been stamped down where the base of the rock slopes towards a crevasse. They've stopped here for a while. This is where Tørk turned around to come and get me. I ask myself why he thought I would come. We sit down. The ice forms a big bowl-shaped hollow, like an open clam shell. He unscrews the lid of his thermos. He continues to talk as if the conversation hadn't been interrupted, and maybe it hasn't, maybe it has continued on inside him, maybe it never stops in there.

"It's a beautiful theory, the theory about Gaia. It's important for theories to be beautiful. But it's wrong, of course. Lovelock shows that the globe and its ecosystem are a complex machinery. But he doesn't show that it's more than a machine. Gaia is not fundamentally any different from a robot. Lovelock shares a flaw with other biologists. He fails to explain the beginning. The first forms of life, what came before cyanobacteria. Life based on inorganic matter would be a first step."

I move cautiously, to keep warm and to test his attentiveness.

"Loyen came here in the thirties. With a German expedition. They were going to do preliminary construction for an airport on a narrow strip of flat coastland on the north side. They brought Thule Eskimos with them. They couldn't get any West Greenlanders to come along because of the island's bad reputation. Loyen began his search the same way Knud Rasmussen did when he discovered his meteorites. By taking the Eskimo stories seriously. And he found it. In '66 he came back. He and Ving and Andreas Fine Licht. But they didn't know enough to solve the technical problems. They constructed a permanent passageway to the stone. Then the expedition was cut short. In 1991 they came back. That's when we came along, too. But we were forced to return home."

His face is almost invisible in the dark; the only solid thing is his voice. I'm trying to fathom why he's telling me all this. Why he's still lying, even under these circumstances, when he's totally in control.

"What about the pieces that were cut off?"

His hesitation solves the problem. Understanding is in a way a relief. It's still the question how much I know or whether I'm alone. Whether someone might be waiting for him, on the island, at sea, when he gets back home. For a short time, until I have told him what he wanted to know, he still has some need of me.

At the same time, another more important realization comes to me. The fact that he's waiting, that he *has* to wait, means that the mechanic hasn't told him everything; he hasn't told him that I'm alone.

"We examined the pieces. We didn't find anything unusual. They consisted of a mixture of iron, nickel, peridotite, magnesium, and silicates."

I'm sure he's telling the truth.

"So it's not alive?"

Through the darkness I can sense his smile.

"There's heat. It's definitely producing heat. Otherwise it would have been carried out along with the ice. It melts the walls surrounding it at a rate comparable to the movement of the glacier."

"Radioactivity?"

"We tested for it, but didn't find any."

"And the dead men?" I ask. "The X-rays? The light-coloured stripes inside their internal organs?"

He pauses for a moment.

"You wouldn't want to tell me how you know about that, would you?" he asks.

I don't answer.

"I knew it," he says. "You and I, we could have made a good team. When I called you that night, it was on an impulse; I trust my intuition. I knew you would pick up the phone. I had you all figured out. I could have said, 'Come over to our side.' Would you have come?"

"No."

The tunnel begins at the foot of the rock. It's a simple design. They dynamited their way down where the ice had a natural tendency to let go of the rock, and then they cemented large concrete sewer pipes to the wall of the tunnel. The pipes slant down at a steep angle; the steps inside are made of wood. This surprises me at first, until I remember how difficult it can be to pour cement on a permafrost foundation.

Ten metres down there's a fire.

The smoke is coming from a room next to the stairway, a cement shell reinforced with beams. Some sacks are spread on the floor. On top of the sacks there's an oil barrel filled with burning, chopped-up wooden crates.

Against the opposite wall on a wide table are instruments and equipment. Chromatographs, microscopes, large crystallization jars, an incubator, and an apparatus I've never seen before, built like a big plastic box with glass on the front. Underneath the table there's a generator and more wooden crates like the ones burning in the barrel. Everything is subject to fashion, even laboratory equipment, and these instruments remind me of the seventies. Everything is covered with a layer of grey ice. They must have been left behind in '66 or '91. What will we leave behind?

Tørk places his hand on the plastic box.

"Electrophoresis. To separate and analyse proteins. Loyen brought it along in '66. When they still thought they were dealing with some form of organic life."

He gives a nod. Everything he does is pervaded with the knowledge that these small signs and gestures are enough to make the

394

rest of the world snap into line. Verlaine is standing at a tall work-table with a dissecting microscope. He adjusts it for me, the ocular on 10 and the objective on 20. He moves a gas lamp closer.

"We're in the process of thawing out the generator."

At first I don't see a thing. Then I adjust the focus and see a coconut.

"*Cyclops marinus*," says Tørk. "Water flea. It or its relatives are found everywhere, in all the oceans of the globe. The threads are organs of equilibrium. We've given it a little hydrochloric acid; that's why it's so still. Try looking at the back of the body. What do you see?"

I don't see anything. He takes over the microscope, moving the petri dish under it and adjusting the focus again.

"The digestive system," I say. "The intestines."

"Those aren't intestines. That's a worm."

Now I see it. The intestines and stomach form a dark field along the underside of the animal. The long bright channel goes up along its back.

"The primary group is *Phylum nematoda*, roundworm, and it belongs to the subclass *Dracunculoidea*. Its name is *Dracunculus borealis*, the Arctic worm. Known and described since at least the Middle Ages. A large parasite. Found in whales, seals, and dolphins; it penetrates the musculature from the intestines. The males and females mate, the male dies, and the female moves to the subcutis, where it forms a nodule as big as a child's fist. When the mature worm senses that there are *Cyclops* in the surrounding water, it perforates the skin and releases millions of small living larvae into the sea, where they're eaten by the water fleas, who act as what is called a host, a place where the worms can go through a process of development lasting several weeks. When the flea, via seawater, gets into the mouth cavity or intestines of a larger mammal, it disintegrates and the larva gets out and bores into this new and larger host. There it matures, mates, makes its way to the subcutis, and completes the cycle. Apparently neither the water flea nor the mammal suffers any harm from it. One of the world's most well-adapted parasites. Have you ever wondered what prevents parasites from spreading?"

Verlaine puts on more wood and pulls the generator over to the fire. The radiant heat burns one side of my body; the other is cold. There's no proper ventilation. The smoke is suffocating. They must be in a hurry.

"Some kind of obstruction is what always stops the parasites. Take, for instance, the Guinea worm, which is the closest relative of the Arctic worm. It's dependent on heat and stagnant water. It's found wherever people are dependent on surface water."

"Such as on the border between Burma, Laos, and Cambodia," I say. "For instance, in Chiang Rai."

They both stiffen. In Tørk it's a barely visible pause.

"Yes," he says, "in Chiang Rai, for example, during the relatively rare periods of drought. As soon as it rained and the water began to flow, as soon as it cooled off, the conditions became more difficult for the worm. That's the way things have to be. Parasites have developed along with their hosts. The Guinea worm has developed along with human beings, perhaps over the past million years. They are mutually compatible. Every year 140 million people are exposed to the risk of being infected with the Guinea worm. There are ten million cases annually. Most of those who are infected endure a painful period of several months, but then the worm is expelled. Even in Chiang Rai only half a per cent of the adult population, at the most, suffer any permanent damage. This is one of the primary rules of nature's delicate balance: A good parasite does not kill its host."

He makes a small gesture, and involuntarily I step back. He looks in the microscope.

"Imagine their situation in '66 – Loyen, Ving, and Licht. Everything has been planned. There are problems, of course, but they're mere technicalities and solvable. They've pinpointed the stone, constructed the entryway and these rooms; they are lucky with the weather, and they have plenty of time, relatively. They realize that they can't bring the whole stone back, but they know they can take home a piece of it. There are photographs of their saws, a brilliant invention, a hardened steel band that ran across rollers. Loyen was opposed to cutting the stone with blowtorches. Then just as the Eskimos are putting the saw in position, they die. Forty-eight hours after their first dive. They die almost simultaneously, within an hour of each other. Everything changes. The project has failed and time all of a sudden is running out. They have to improvise an accident. Loyen is the one who does it, of course. He has enough presence of mind not to destroy the bodies. At that point he already has a feeling that something is wrong. As soon as they reach Nuuk he does an autopsy. And what does he find?"

"Time," Verlaine says.

Tørk ignores him. "He finds the Arctic worm. A widespread parasite. Big, thirty to forty centimetres long, but quite ordinary. A roundworm whose cycle is known and understood. There's only one thing wrong: it's not found in human beings. In whales, in seals, and dolphins, and occasionally in walruses. But not in human beings. Nearly every day infected meat is eaten, especially by Eskimos. But the moment the larva enters the human body, it's recognized by our immune system as a foreign object and is devoured by lymphocytes. It has never adapted to our immune system. It should always be limited to certain large sea mammals with which it must have developed simultaneously. It's part of the balance of nature. Imagine Loyen's astonishment when he finds it in the corpses. And quite by accident, too. Because at the last minute he was forced to take X-rays to identify the bodies."

I don't want to listen to him or talk to him, but I can't help it. And besides, it stretches out the time.

"Why did it happen?"

"That's the question Loyen couldn't answer. So he concentrated on a different question: *How* did it happen? He had brought samples home from the water around the stone. Aside from the meltwater, the lake is fed by another lake higher up, on the surface. There's some bird life up there. And quite a lot of trout. And several kinds of fleas. The water around the stone is full of them. All of the samples Loyen brought home were infested. So he decided to graft the larva on to living human tissue."

"That sounds lovely," I say. "How did he manage to do that?"

As I ask the question, the answer comes to me. He did it in Greenland. In Denmark the chance of being discovered would be too great.

Tørk sees that I have understood.

"It took him twenty-five years. But he found out that the larva had adapted to the human immune system. As soon as it's in the mouth it penetrates the open mucous membranes and forms a kind of skin, created from the person's own proteins. In this camouflage the parasite is mistaken for the human body itself and the defence system leaves it in peace. Then it starts to grow. Not slowly, over a period of months, the way it does in seals and whales, but rapidly, hour by hour and minute by minute. Even the mating and wandering through the body, which can take up to six months in a sea mammal, now take only a few days. But that's not the decisive factor."

Verlaine takes him by the arm. Tørk looks at him. Verlaine removes his hand.

"I want to ask her about something," says Tørk.

Maybe that's what he believes, but that's not why he's talking. He's talking in order to win attention and recognition. Beneath his self-confidence and apparent objectivity there is a wild pride and triumph at what he has discovered. Both Verlaine and I are sweating and have started to cough. But he is cool and at ease; in the flickering light of the fire his face is utterly calm. Maybe it's because we're standing in the middle of the ice, maybe it's because it's so obvious that we're nearing the end, that he suddenly becomes transparent to me. As always when an adult becomes transparent, the child inside him steps forth. I remember Victor Halkenhvad's letter, and suddenly, irresistibly, the words spew out of my mouth of their own accord.

"Like the bicycle you never had when you were a child."

The remark is so absurd that at first he doesn't understand it. Then the meaning sinks in, and for a moment he staggers as if I'd hit him. He almost drops everything on the floor, but then he pulls himself together.

"You might think we've discovered a new species. But that's not the case. It's the Arctic worm. But with a vital difference. It has adapted to the human immune system. But without adapting to our equilibrium. The pregnant female does not make its way to the subcutis after mating. It enters the internal organs, the heart and the liver. That's where it releases its larvae. The larvae that have been living inside the mother, that aren't familiar with the human body, that aren't covered with a protein skin. The body reacts to them with infection and inflammation. It goes into shock. There are ten million larvae in a single release. Inside the vital organs. The person dies on the spot. There's no way to save him. No matter what else has happened to the Arctic worm, it has upset the balance. It kills its host. It's a poor parasite, in terms of human beings. But an excellent killer."

Verlaine says something in a language that I don't understand. Tørk again ignores him.

"Verlaine grafted the larva on to all the fish we could get hold of: saltwater fish, freshwater fish, big ones and small ones, at varying temperatures. The parasite adapts to every single one. It can live anywhere. Do you know what that means?"

"That it's not fussy?"

"It means that one of the most important factors restricting its dispersal is lacking: the limitation of the hosts that are capable of transmitting it. It can live anywhere."

"Why hasn't it spread all over the world?"

He gathers up several coils of rope, picks up a bag, and dons a miner's lamp. His sense of time has returned.

"There are two answers to that question. The first is that its development in sea mammals is slow. Even if the parasite from this lake – and from other lakes on this island as well – is washed out to sea, it has to sit and wait for passing seals to carry it further, if it's still alive when the seals come by. One answer is that there still haven't been enough people here. The development process doesn't pick up speed until there are human beings involved."

He leads the way. I know I'm supposed to follow him. For a moment I hang back. As he leaves the room, I'm struck with a feeling of powerlessness. Verlaine looks at me.

"When we were working for Khum Na," he says, "twelve police officers arrived. The only one who escaped was a woman. Women are vermin."

"Ravn," I say. "Nathalie Ravn?"

He nods. "She came over as an English nurse. Spoke English and Thai without an accent. At that time we were at war with Laos, Cambodia, and, in the end, Burma too, with support from the US. There were many casualties."

He holds the petri dish between his thumb and forefinger and lifts it towards me. The body instinctively tries to shrink away from the worm. It must be sheer stubbornness that keeps me standing there.

"When it penetrates the skin, it pushes its womb out and emits a white fluid full of millions of larvae. I've seen it."

Disgust contorts his face.

"The females are much bigger than the males. They burrow into the flesh. We followed them with ultrasound scanners. Loyen had grafted them on to two Greenlanders who had AIDS. He had them flown to Denmark and admitted to one of the small private hospitals where they don't ask about anything except your bank account number. We could see everything – how it reached the heart and then emptied itself out. The womb and everything. All females are that way, even humans, especially humans."

He carefully puts down the petri dish.

"I can see that you're a fine connoisseur of women, Verlaine," I say. "What else were you doing in Chiang Rai?"

He's not unaffected by the compliment. That's why he answers the question. "I'm a lab technician. We were making heroin. At the time the woman arrived, they had sent the army after us, from all three countries. So Khum Na went on TV and said, 'Last year we put nine hundred tons on the market, this year we'll ship thirteen hundred, and next year two thousand tons, unless you call your soldiers home.' The day he made that announcement, the war was over."

I'm on my way out of the door when he speaks again. "Human beings are the parasites. The worm is an instrument of the gods. Like the poppy."

$$\begin{array}{c}\textcircled{3}\end{array}$$

TØRK IS WAITING FOR ME. When we reach the bottom, we've descended about twenty metres. The tunnel, which now runs horizontally, has a rough, rectangular concrete reinforcement. It ends in black emptiness. Tørk goes first. We stop in front of an abyss.

At our feet there's a drop of twenty-five metres to the floor of the cave. Stalagmites of ice stretch up towards us from the ground, glistening, rainbow-coloured.

He breaks off a piece of ice and tosses it into space. The abyss is transformed into a series of rings and then fog; then it ceases to exist. We've been looking at the ceiling of the cave reflected in a lake right at our feet; water so still that it could never exist above ground. Even now, as it's traversed by ripples, the eyes will not believe that it's water. Calm slowly returns, and the underground world is reestablished.

The growth patterns of stalactites and descriptions of their crystal formations were outlined by Hatakeyama and Nemoto in *The Geophysical Magazine*, no. 28, 1958. By Knight in the *Journal of Crystal Growth*, no. 49, 1980. And by Maeno and Takahashi in their article "Studies on Icicles", in *Low Temperature Science*, vol. A, no. 43, 1984. But the most viable configuration to date was proposed by myself and Lasse Makkonen at the Laboratory of Structural Engineering in Espoo, Finland. It demonstrates that a stalactite grows like a reed, a hollow tube of ice that closes around water in its liquid state. That the mass of the stalactite can be simply expressed as:

$$M = \frac{\pi D^2}{4} \rho_u L$$

where D is the diameter, L is the length, ρ_u is the density of the ice, and π in the numerator of the fraction is, of course, a result of the fact that we are calculating based on a hemispheric drop with a diameter set at 4.9 mm.

We proposed our formula out of fear of the ice. At a time when there had been a series of accidents in Japan with stalactites falling from the roofs of train tunnels and boring right through railway carriages. Here, above our heads, there are more stalactites and larger ones than I've ever seen in my life. Instinctively I want to move away, but I can sense Tørk next to me and give up the attempt.

The room is a cathedral. Overhead, the ceiling forms a vault at least fifteen metres high, reaching almost to the surface of the glacier. All around the dome there are fractured areas where pieces have broken off and fallen, and where the ice has covered the floor, filled the grotto, and then melted again.

During periods when Moritz was gone and we couldn't afford paraffin, or when supplies were short because the ship hadn't arrived, my mother would set paraffin candles on top of a mirror. Even with only a few candles, the effect of their reflections would be overwhelming. It's the same way with Tørk's miner's lamp. He holds it steady to give me time, and the light is seized by the ice, magnified, and thrown into the air like beams raining upwards.

The long spears of ice seem to be floating. Gleaming with prisms, they drip down from the ceiling, stretching towards the earth. Maybe there are ten thousand maybe there are more. Some of them are intertwined, like chains of cascading Gothic cathedrals; others are small and densely packed – pincushions of quartz.

Beneath them is the lake. Perhaps thirty metres across. In the middle lies the stone. Black and motionless. The water surrounding it is slightly milky with bubbles dissolving in the glacier ice. The room has no odour except for the light sting of ice in my throat. The only sounds are drops falling. At long intervals. The ceiling is such a distance from the stone that an equilibrium has been established. Very little freezes or melts in this room. Water circulation is minimal. The place is lifeless.

If it hadn't been for the heat, that is. It's exactly like the heat in the igloos of my childhood. The cold radiating from the walls makes the heat seem inviting. Even though the temperature is between zero and five degrees Celsius.

A pile of gear is lying near us. Air tanks, overalls, flippers, harpoons, and a crate containing plastic explosives. Ropes, torches, hand tools. No one is here except us. The ice creaks once, as if someone were moving a heavy piece of furniture in an adjoining room. But there are no adjoining rooms. There is only compact ice.

"How will you get it out?" I ask.

"We'll blast a tunnel," he says.

That's possible. It will have to be about a hundred metres long. But they won't have to reinforce it. And the stone will roll through the tunnel by itself, if it has the proper slant. Seidenfaden could take care of that. Katja Claussen will force him to do it. And Tørk will force her, and the mechanic. This is how I've experienced the world ever since I left Greenland. As a chain of coercion.

"Is it alive?" he asks quietly.

I shake my head. But that's because I don't want to believe it is. He cups his hands around the miner's lamp. Its beam is now directed at the snow beneath us. From there it's reflected upwards. In this way the individual stalactites are obscured but a cloud of hovering reflections is visible, like gemstones defying gravity.

"What happens if the worm gets out?" I ask.

"We'll keep the stone enclosed."

"You can't restrain it. It's microscopic."

He doesn't reply.

"You can't know," I say. "No one knows. You only know what you've learned from a few laboratory experiments. But there's a small chance that it's a real killer."

He doesn't reply.

"What was the other answer to my question about why the worm hasn't already spread?"

"As a child I spent a year in Greenland, on the west coast. There I collected fossils. Since then I've occasionally toyed with the idea that the extermination of various species in prehistoric times might have been caused by a parasite. Who knows, maybe it was the Arctic worm. It would have had the necessary characteristics. Maybe it was the worm that eradicated the dinosaurs."

His voice has a teasing undertone. Suddenly I understand him.

"But that's not important, is it?"

"No, it's not important." He looks at me. "The true reality of things is not important. What's important is what people *believe*. They will believe in this stone. Have you ever heard of Ilya Prigogine? A Belgian chemist who received the Nobel Prize in '77 for his description of dissipative structures. He and his students have been working nonstop on the idea that life originated from inorganic substances through which energy was flowing. These ideas have paved the way. People are *waiting* for this stone. Their belief and anticipation will make it real. They will make it *alive* regardless of the true nature of the stone."

"And the parasite?" I ask.

"I can already hear the first ranks of speculative journalists. They'll write that the Arctic worm represents a significant stage in the encounter between the stone, inorganic life, and higher organisms. They'll come to all sorts of conclusions, none of which is important. What's important are the forces of fear and hope that will be set free."

"Why, Tørk? What do you get out of it?"

"Money," he says. "Fame. More money. In reality it's unimportant whether the stone is alive or not. What counts is its size. Its heat. The worm around it. It's the biggest scientific discovery of the century. Not just numbers on a piece of paper. Or abstractions that take thirty years to get published in a form that can be sold to the public. A stone. That you can touch and feel. That you can cut up and sell. That you can photograph and film."

I'm reminded again of Victor Halkenhvad's letter. "The boy was ice," he wrote. That's not quite true. His coldness is superficial. Behind it there is passion. A sick, twisted desire for power. Suddenly whether the stone is alive or not is no longer important to me, either. Suddenly it has become a symbol. At this moment it becomes the crystallization of the attitude of Western science towards the world. Calculation, hatred, hope, fear, the attempt to measure everything. And above all else, stronger than any empathy for living things: the desire for money.

"You can't remove the worm and transport it to a densely populated part of the world," I say. "Not until you know what it is. You could set off a catastrophe. If it was once widespread around the globe, its numbers were not limited until it had exterminated its hosts."

He puts the lamp down on the snow. Without interruption it creates and maintains a conical tunnel of light, shining across the mirror of water and the stone. The rest of the world has been erased.

"Death is always a waste. But sometimes it's the only way to arouse people. Bohr participated in the construction of the atomic bomb and thought that it would promote peace."

I remember something Juliane once said during a moment of sobriety. She said that we shouldn't be afraid of a third world war; human beings need a new war in order to come to their senses.

My reaction is the same at this moment as it was then – I'm conscious of the insanity of the argument.

"You can't force people to feel love by degrading them as much as possible," I say.

I shift my weight to my other foot and grab hold of a coil of rope.

"You lack imagination, Smilla. That's unforgivable in a scientist."

If I can manage to swing the coil I might be able to knock him into the water. Then I could run.

"The boy?" I ask. "Isaiah. Why did Loyen examine him?"

I step further away to give my swing a bigger arc.

"He jumped into the water. We were forced to bring him along into the cave; he was afraid of heights. His father collapsed while he was still near the surface. The boy wanted to go to him. He was never afraid of cold water; he swam in the sea. Loyen was the one who came up with the idea of keeping him under observation. The worm was subcutaneous in him, not in his intestines. He never even felt it."

That explains the muscle biopsy. Loyen's desire to get one last, definitive sample. Information about the fate of the parasite when its carrier dies.

The water has a greenish tinge to it, a peaceful colour. It's the thought of death that is horrifying; the phenomenon itself always comes as naturally as a sunset. At Force Bay I once saw Major Guldbrandsen of the Sirius Patrol brandish an automatic weapon to force three Americans away from a bear liver infected with trichinosis. It was broad daylight, they knew the meat was infested, and all they had to do was wait forty-five minutes for it to be cooked. And yet they had cut small slices off the liver and had started to eat it when we reached them. It was all so ordinary. The blue highlights of the meat, the men's hunger, the major's rifle, and their astonishment.

He reaches behind me and takes the coil from my hand, the way you take sharp tools away from a child.

"Go up there and wait," he says.

He shines his lamp on the opposite wall, where the mouth of a tunnel opens. I walk towards it. Now I recognize the path. It doesn't lead upwards, it leads into the void. The entrance to the end has always been a tunnel. Like the entrance to life. He has led me up here. He has led me all the way from the ship.

For the first time I realize his brilliance as a strategist. He couldn't have done it on board. He still has to go back, and the *Kronos* still has to pull in to some port. He wouldn't be able to hide it. But this will be just one more desertion. A disappearance, like Jakkelsen's. No one saw me meet Tørk, no one will see me disappear.

The mechanic won't be going back either. He would figure things out, he would link me to Tørk as surely as if he had seen us together. Tørk will let him dive; they obviously have a need for him, at least in placing the first fuse. They'll let him dive, and then he will cease to exist. Tørk will return, and there will have been an accident. Maybe something went wrong with the oxygen gauge. Tørk will have planned it all out.

Now I understand the equipment near the lake. The mechanic has been unpacking it while Tørk was talking to me. That's why he took me into the laboratory.

The light from his lamp catches the stone, casting shadows on to the wall in front of me. When I enter the tunnel the light dims.

It's a rectangular horizontal shaft, two metres square. Several metres inside the entrance it gets wider and there's a table. On top of the table there are measuring devices, milk bottles, dried meat, oatmeal, everything is twenty-eight years old and covered with ice.

I let my eyes grow accustomed to the faint light from the ice and then continue on until everything is pitch dark, but I keep going, following the wall with my outstretched hand. The floor has a slight incline, but there's no draught that might indicate an exit up ahead; it's a dead end.

I come to a wall in front me, a wall of ice. This is where I wait.

There's no sound of footsteps, but there's a light in the distance, coming closer. He has fastened the lamp to his forehead. It locates me next to the wall, and the light stands still. Then he takes it off. It's Verlaine.

"I showed Lukas the refrigerator," I tell him. "When that's added on top of what you did to Jakkelsen, you'll get a life sentence without parole."

He stops halfway between me and the light.

"Even if they ripped off your arms and legs, you'd find some way to kick back," he says.

He bows his head and mutters to himself. It sounds like some kind of prayer. Then he steps towards me.

At first I think it's his shadow on the wall, but then I look back, anyway. A rose is growing on the ice, about three metres across, composed of little red dots spattered up on the wall. Then he lifts his feet off the ground, spreads his arms, rises half a metre in the air, and throws himself against the wall. He hangs there, impaled like a big insect, in the centre of the rose. That's when the sound comes. A brief whistle. A grey cloud drifts into the light from the lamp on the ground. Out of the cloud steps Lukas. He doesn't look at me. He looks at Verlaine. In his hand he's holding a compressed-air harpoon gun.

Verlaine moves. With one hand he fumbles at his back. Somewhere below his shoulder blade a thin black line sticks out. The metal must be a special alloy to have the strength to hold him off the ground. The point was no more than a metre and a half away when Lukas shot it at him. It entered his body in about the same place where Jakkelsen was stabbed.

I step out of the light and walk past Lukas.

I walk towards a rising white sun of light. When I emerge from the tunnel walls I see that a lamp is now burning, mounted high on a stanchion. They must have started the generator. Tørk is standing next to the lamp. The mechanic is standing in the water up to his knees. It takes a moment for me to recognize him. He's wearing a big yellow suit with boots and a helmet attached. I make it halfway over to them before Tørk catches sight of me. He bends down. From the gear he takes out a pipe about the size of a furled umbrella. The mechanic is looking down at the water. His helmet would prevent him from hearing me. I take off my compass and toss it in the water. He raises his head and sees me. Then he starts to slide back the glass on the front of his helmet. Tørk is struggling with the umbrella. Unfolds the stock of a weapon.

"S-Smilla," says the mechanic.

I keep walking forward. Behind me, in the resonating shaft of the tunnel, there are footsteps.

"I'm only going to m-make one d-dive. It's necessary for our work tomorrow."

"There won't be any tomorrow for you or me," I say. "Ask him where Verlaine is."

The mechanic turns towards Tørk. He looks at him and understands.

"The boy," I say. "Why?"

I ask the question for the mechanic's benefit and to stop time, not because I need any answer myself. I know what happened, as surely as if I had been on the roof myself.

I can feel Tørk as if he were a part of me. Through him I can feel the disastrous nature of the situation. All the balls he has in the air. The question of how well he can manage without the mechanic. His need to make a decision. And yet his voice is calm, almost sorrowful.

"He jumped."

I keep on walking as I talk. He snaps on a long magazine perpendicular to the weapon.

"He panicked," Tørk says.

"Why?" I ask.

"I wanted to ask him to give me the cassette tape back. But he ran away; he didn't recognize me. He thought I was a stranger. It was dark."

He releases the safety. The mechanic doesn't notice the weapon, he's looking at Tørk's face.

"We get up on to the roof. He doesn't see me."

"There were tracks," I lie. "I saw the tracks; he turned around."

"I shouted to him; he turned around, but he didn't see me."

He looks me in the eye.

"He was hard of hearing," I say. "He didn't turn around. He couldn't hear a thing."

There is ice under my feet. I'm on my way across the ice towards him, just as Isaiah was heading away from him. It's as if I am Isaiah. But on his way back now. To do something differently. To see whether there might be an alternative.

Lukas is five metres away when Tørk sees him. He has gone the other way around the stone. Tørk has been dividing his attention between me and the mechanic. You can't do everything. Even he can't do everything.

"Bernard is dead," says Lukas.

He's holding the harpoon gun in front of him. He must have loaded it again. It seems as long as a lance; for a moment his wasted and much too rigid figure makes him look like some kind of cartoon character. His trousers have frozen into an armour of ice. On his way ashore he must have fallen in.

"You will be held responsible," he says.

Tørk's umbrella shudders. A big invisible hand spins Lukas around on the spot. Then the dull blast follows, and Lukas has sketched a full pirouette. His face is once again turned towards us, but now his left arm is missing. He sits down on the ice and the bleeding starts.

408